THE ISLANDER

THE ISLANDER

Book Two of the White Woods Chronicles

A. C. Haeffner

5987-HAEF

ISBN #: Softcover 1-4010-0374-5

This is a work of fiction. Names, characters, places and incidents either are the product of the author's imagination or are used fictitiously, and any resemblance to any actual persons, living or dead, events, or locales is entirely coincidental.

This book was printed in the United States of America.

To order additional copies of this book, contact:
Xlibris Corporation
1-888-795-4274
www.Xlibris.com
Orders@Xlibris.com

CONTENTS

5987-HAEF

To my wife, Susan, who taught me about love;
and
to my parents, who taught me the strength of family.

PROLOGUE

The Legend of the Crystal

There is a saying that has long circulated in Europe, which on the face of it makes no sense. It goes like this:

"Death is life."

It was first attributed to gypsy bands that roamed the region. They used it when explaining the crystal–The Crystal of Death, Il Cristallo di Morte–to the uninitiated.

The story they would tell held that the crystal–actually several of identical shape and size, though nobody but gypsies has ever seen more than one at a time–had been given to an elder in a gypsy tribe many centuries before.

Just who gave the crystals is a matter of some debate. In one version of the myth, they came from an angel; in another, from an extraterrestrial visitor; in another, from a god or a celestial messenger who came to earth in the guise of a bear.

The reason for the gift, again, depended on the version. In the tale of the angel, it was given the elder for services rendered to mankind. In the alien version, it was because the elder had helped the visitor fix his spacecraft after the latter had crash-landed on Earth. In the one with the bear, it was because the elder was profoundly good, helping free the bear from a trap that had snared the beast while he was pursuing the old man through a forest glen.

The carpenter said he preferred the bear version, since he felt an affinity with the beasts of the forests, one reason for his choice of current living quarters. My old friend Jacques felt likewise.

That particular version, first related to me in a letter from

Jacques that reached me by mail just before I left on a trip to visit him on the Island–a kind of preamble to a much longer story that he planned to tell me–had the elder wandering out into the woods in search of firewood, and straying far from his tribe. Trying in vain to retrace his steps, the elder became disoriented and wandered even deeper into the forest, into a shaded portion where little light ever filtered through.

It was there that he heard the beast's roar, and saw the lumbering giant charge him–some say the derivation of the term "bearing down." The elder started running, although speed at his age, some four score years, did not come easily. The bear, therefore, was gaining rapidly when there was a sudden snapping sound and a shriek from the beast, who was no longer moving forward, but lying immobilized.

The elder, unclear what had happened but realizing the animal's pain, drew closer until he saw that the wooden spike of a trap had pierced the animal in the leg and side, drawing a bright viscous red. To compound matters, the trap had wound vines around the bear's neck and hindquarters, preventing all but the most minute of movements.

Debating whether to help or run, the elder chose to stay and, at great personal risk, pulled the spikes free of the animal and unwrapped the vines, freeing the beast. The animal, which the old man thought might thank him with a fatal swipe of his great paws, instead spoke in the old man's language.

"You have proven yourself a truly good man," the bear said, "and your reward shall be a gift of uncommon sight for you and your people."

Seemingly out of nowhere, the bear produced a small bag with a drawstring and handed it to the old man, who opened it. Inside he found a number of clear pyramid-shaped crystals of identical size, each giving off a soft light, an eerie glow in the darkness of the forest. Mixed among them were occasional blue oval gems.

"They are very nice," said the old man. "But how will they improve our sight?"

"The clear crystals," said the bear, "will give to those of unusual sensibilities the added ability to see beyond the earth and the stars, to that realm of mists and promise to which you all aspire."

"I don't understand," said the old man.

"A person who wears one of these and is worthy will be able to see that which is uncertain to his peers," the bear said, "to know that which the peers can only guess. It is a window to the outer reaches of the afterlife."

"The wearer can commune with the dead?" asked the old man.

"Not commune, but envision," the bear said. "By the simple cosmic law of the universe, it offers vision and knowledge of the hereafter to the worthy. And upon death, the wearer passes swiftly into the realm of good and plenty."

"And the unworthy?" asked the elder.

"It offers them nothing–they cannot see what the worthy can. And if, upon the advent of death, an unworthy person should be in contact with the crystal, it prevents that passage to the promised land that awaits the worthy in the same circumstance."

"How does it prevent it?"

"By imprisonment."

"Imprisonment? Where?"

"Within the stone itself . . . like a genie in a lamp. It is a solitary existence which can be broken only if the soul finds another host."

"How would the trapped soul accomplish that?" asked the old man.

"Where evil dwells, danger lurks," said the bear.

"Uh huh," said the elder, not really understanding. "And the blue crystals? What are they?"

"The blue crystals are much rarer, and must be dealt with cautiously. For they offer an ability to see what is yet to come."

"Why cautiously?" asked the elder.

"While knowledge of the future is a great power," said the bear, "it can carry dangerous consequences."

"Consequences?" the old man inquired.

"Only the strongest can carry the knowledge of what is to be without losing some soul . . . some humanity . . . some peace of mind. And such knowledge, in the hands of the wrong person, can be corrupted. There is, therefore, a built-in safeguard: Only a worthy person, or a person who has attained the crystal with the willing consent of its previous owner, can partake of its power."

"I don't understand," said the elder. "What kind of corruption?"

"If in the hands of a conscienceless individual, the future could be compromised; altered. And in that lies the potential for great destruction. Therefore, do not dispense the blue crystals lightly."

The old man and the bear stood silently for several moments, regarding each other. At last the old man spoke.

"Dispense?" he said. "Is that what I am supposed to do with them?"

"Yes," said the bear. "Distribute them to elders like yourself in tribes around the continent. They will give them as earned to persons who either exhibit good or do unselfish acts that benefit others."

"How many are here?" the old man asked, peering into the bag.

"Enough," the bear said. "And not too many. Now go . . . see to your task."

"Very well," said the old man as the bear turned and started away from him. "But wait . . . what do I say when someone asks the name of the crystal I am giving them?"

"Tell them it is the Crystal of Death," the bear called back over his shoulder.

The elder did not understand.

"Wait!" he called out. "If one stone offers a vision of everlasting life, and another a look at life ahead, how can either be called the Crystal of Death?"

"In death is eternal life," the bear said. "And in life is death."

And with that, he disappeared into the darkness.

ONE

The Call

The call came at 2 in the morning.

Nobody calls at that hour with good news. But this was uncommonly bad.

"Your father's been stricken," my mother's voice said across the lines from Florida. "You'd better come quickly."

She sounded strong–always sounded that way–but I knew she wasn't; not now. She was devoted to the man–more than fifty years' worth of devotion–and would not handle his passing well. So as shocked and saddened as I was at the news, I was more concerned for her. My father's God–if indeed there was one–would take care of him now; Mom would need earthly caretaking, at least for the short term. And so I moved quickly.

I rousted my wife and two youngest boys, and we packed, drove the six miles to pick up my eldest son at his apartment, and were airborne from Syracuse–a ninety-minute drive from home–as dawn broke. We were walking up the front walk to my parents' condo before lunch.

Mom met us at the door, looking as strong as ever . . . until we hugged. Then she started weeping, great heaving sobs into my chest. I patted her on the back and held her until she gathered her control and stood straight, smiled at Susan and the boys, and turned back to me, locking her blue eyes–hazel blue, now dimmed by cataracts–onto mine.

"He's in the bedroom," she said. "Asking for you."

"Where's Ben?" I asked. My oldest brother lived twenty miles

5987-HAEF

away. The middle brother, Jesse, was en route with his family from Michigan.

"Making arrangements," she said. "Making sure the minister is . . . you know . . . ready."

"Arrangements?" I said, the fear of imminence striking at me. "Soon, then?"

"Soon," she said, and reached out and ran her right hand up and down the fabric of my left sleeve.

"Any minute, really. Ben already said his goodbyes. Now . . . you'd best hurry."

I entered the condo while Mom tended to her grandchildren and daughter-in-law, made my way through the foyer, noticed the binoculars hanging in their familiar place, went through the living room with its view of the golf course my parents loved to play on, and entered the back corner bedroom. There, on their king-size bed, lay Dad, covered to his neck by a sheet, looking gaunt and pale. He no longer possessed a whisper of his younger self; was not even a shadow of the robust elderly gentleman I had last seen a few months before.

"Hey," I said softly after I pulled a cushioned chair from a corner of the room, placed it next to the bed and seated myself. Now that I was off my feet, I felt heavy, dull. Jet lag, I told myself, though I knew I was feeling the weight, too, of impending grief.

My father's eyelids fluttered, and he took several seconds before focusing on me. When he did, he smiled wanly.

"Hey," he said back, the word a whisper. "You made it."

"Yes," I said, thinking how eighty-four years can wear a man to nothing. "I made it, so don't you go leaving on me, now. You hear? It wouldn't be hospitable."

Dad laughed, a short bark that was more like a wheeze.

"Can't help it," he said. "Engraved invitation."

"Yeah, so I heard," I said. "Can't let those command performances go by."

His hand slid out from the side of the sheet and reached out to my hand; his finger tapped against one of my fingers. He was trying to say something more, but was having trouble finding the strength.

"What?" I said.

"The glasses," he whispered.

"Your glasses?" I said. "What? To read?"

He tapped my finger again.

"Binoculars," he managed to say. "You. The binoculars."

My father had brought back a pair of German binoculars from the war, his war, World War II–the binoculars I'd seen hanging from a hook in the foyer–and they had been a part of the family ever since. They'd been to ball games, on trips . . . wherever we had gone, they had gone. They were always kept near the front door, no matter where my parents had resided.

"What about them?" I said.

Dad had closed his eyes again, and I feared he might have passed away. But I saw a slight movement in his chest, and knew he was still present, if only barely.

"What about them?" I asked again.

He rallied, opened his eyes, stared at the ceiling and then–turning his head toward me–tapped my finger again.

"The binoculars," he said. "You take . . . carpenter . . . moose . . . bear . . . fill . . . terse . . . see . . . a . . . head . . .'"

His eyes suddenly lost focus, and then life. I could practically see it leave him. His chest, barely discernible in its rising and falling before, was definitely motionless now. The finger he had used to tap mine was no longer moving. His essence was . . . just no longer there.

I stared at his unseeing eyes for a full minute before reaching out and closing the lids over them. Then I stood, leaned down and kissed him on the cheek, turned and walked out of the bedroom, into the living room. There, everyone was seated–Mom in an armchair, Susan and our youngest boy, David, on the couch, his older brother Jonathan and grown brother Bill on a love seat.

They all looked at me, and knew. Susan hugged David; Bill and Jonathan leaned into each other, and Mom sat motionless, tears streaming down her face.

I walked over toward the front door and stopped in front of the binoculars. They were in their plain black case, hanging motionless by the case's black leather strap. I lifted them gently from the hook, unclasped the lid, slid the glasses out and replaced the case on the hook.

Then, gently and with a reverence clearly not intended for them, but for their previous owner, I wrapped the binoculars in my arms and drew them into my chest, and hugged them tightly.

And I wept.

TWO

Crossing the Straits Again

The binoculars were unremarkable in style or appearance: standard black, with markings that put their power at "7x50." I wasn't sure what that meant. I only knew that they were strong enough to pick out license-plate numbers at a hundred yards, to serve the needs of spectator or voyeur from three hundred yards, and to connect me in a spiritual way with my father.

They were maybe not what they used to be, but not bad considering their age was something approximating mine. They had a little nick here, a scratch there, a couple of eyepiece filters that were never used–tucked into small pockets near the mouth of the case–and a rawhide neck strap I'd recently had to substitute for the original leather one. But they were still sturdy, still functional, still a link to my past–a piece of family lore.

The stiff case–dull black with no distinguishing marks, and what appeared to be dark stains on either side–had kept the binoculars protected for all of their fifty-plus years, save for those few short bursts when they'd been removed for use at sporting events or to spy on the young blonde who lived three doors down from us when I was a teen-ager.

The rubber of the binocular eyepieces was still smooth, with no hint yet of the shredding that would seem inevitable after a half-century. But like I said, the case . . .

I had the binoculars out–the case at my feet, the rawhide around my neck and the glasses to my eyes, as the *Sylmar III* fought th surging waves on the crossing from Cheboygan on a chilli autumn day. Sunlight was sporadic as thick layers of cloud whisked by at the urging of insistent winds.

I had the glasses trained off to the left of the *Sylmar* bow, toward the Island's southwest corner. By necessity–spray-covered binoculars being of little practical use–I was in one of the *Sylmar*'s two protected passenger cabins. A sliding door was open several yards ahead, giving air flow to an otherwise stale interior. Windows along the port side gave me a clear view of the Island's southwestern shoreline.

Between the boat's rhythmic dips into the trough of the waves blanketing the Straits of Mackinac that day, I could make out the pump house on the Island's southwest point, a small cinder block structure that had once provided residents with extra water that could, if needed, be used to fight fires; it might yet. Beyond it, many years before, had sat an auto graveyard, an anomaly on an otherwise pristine shore; I couldn't see if it was still there. To the right of the pump house, on the southern shore to its east, were several cottages and a field–two fields, actually, traversed by a road that disappeared into the woods of birch and pine trees that dominated the Island.

"No hotel," I muttered, scanning the vacant lot on the road's left. Addie had told me years before that it was gone, the victim of lightning, but I had never seen the physical evidence. And to the right, across the road, was another vacancy.

"The mansion," I said softly, remembering. It, too, was gone, of course. I had seen its charred remains the night it burned. But in my mind, somehow, it still stood tall.

"What's that?" asked a voice at the doorway, and I looked there. t was the boat's skipper, making the rounds to check on his sengers. His first mate was manning the wheelhouse above us, ble by a ladder just outside the passenger area.

nothing," I said. "Just dredging up some old "

said, stepping inside and moving toward me. "Dad e a long time ago. When was that?"

teen-ager," I said, studying him. He was

middle-aged, four decades removed from the infant I remembered. He'd been too young back then, in 1956, to recall me now at all.

"Yeah? And never since?" he asked.

"Nope. No real reason to come back, at first, and then I moved away. You know . . . it's the old story: life kind of takes you over."

"Well, I don't really think the place has changed much," he said, leaning forward and peering through the port windows.

As he did so, I noticed the ease with which he bore the boat's undulating movement; I struggled to maintain balance, but he had no such problem. He was at ease with his craft and the Straits.

A sense of familiarity washed over me as I recalled my last visit, my last ferry journey to the Island. The familiarity wasn't in the craft I was riding, for the original *Sylmar* had been nothing much like this one; it had been smaller and homelier, but with more personality. This one was sleek, state-of-the art, built for speed, comfort and maximum effectiveness; it was wider, longer, and could carry a dozen or more cars compared to its forebear's one. No, the familiarity was in the crossing itself–the Island tree line growing from thin green ribbon to imposing, inviting forest as we approached–and in the skipper. This skipper was similar to the one I remembered from those years ago–not physically, but in his mannerisms. Look at this man directly, and it was difficult to see the connection. Look at him askance, with peripheral vision, and he could pass for his predecessor. Genetics can do that, play that little trick.

But this man, this skipper, Johnny Lafitte, was not his father. Johnny was too conventional, too thick in the middle, too tall: my height or a touch higher. His hair was too short. He wore glasses. And his eyes were neither as penetrating nor as knowing.

No, his father was unique. There was only one Jacques Lafitte, one Lightfoot Jack, captain of the original *Sylmar*.

That's who I was going to see now, across the straits from Cheboygan.

He was waiting for me on Bois Blanc Island.

****

"You staying out at the tavern? Nice cabins."

The question came from a woman, one of two people who had just entered the passenger cabin and seated themselves to my right. Most of the other passengers had opted to stay in their vehicles on the deck for the duration of the trip, a form of antisocialism that also provided the warmest crossing, for none would feel the knife of the Straits' cold northwest wind. Three or four hardy souls were standing outside, at the bow, braving the wind and spray. Johnny Lafitte was still at my side, though he seemed anxious to leave the cabin as soon as the woman entered.

I judged the woman to be a few years younger than me, but decided that she looked older. After 52 years, I still looked no more than 40 or 41. Again, genes; but in this case, they had little to do with mannerisms, for my father and I were dissimilar in that department. In truth, we had little in common physically other than height, and even that was of the unremarkable average variety. No, Dad and I were primarily similar in something a little less tangible–in the tardiness with which age made its visible appearance upon us.

At the same age that I now bore, my father had, thirty-some years before, earned the undying enmity of his former college classmates at a reunion that showcased his youthful mien in the reflection of their aged pallor. He was still young, and they were not. Thus, he was the embodiment of life's unfairness and worthy of their scorn. My, how he loved that.

Now, observing this woman on the *Sylmar III*, I felt a little of my father's pride . . . while recognizing it had nothing to do with personal achievement. But with prolonged youth comes vanity, and with it a measure of misguided ego. And so I chided myself while at the same time taking pleasure in the moment.

"No," I said to the woman. She was dressed in a parka that concealed what form she might possess; a knit cap, blue jeans and steel-toed boots completed the disguise. All I could tell for sure was that she was a good deal shorter than me, that her medium-cropped hair–peeking out from underneath the cap–had gone nearly white, and that her face was a map of long experience. The eyes, a light blue-gray, were surrounded by crows feet and bags; the nose was slightly crooked, as if broken and poorly repaired; the lips were downturned in a perpetual scowl, and a scar ran the length of her left cheek, from eye to jawbone.

"Haven't seen you around," she said in a raspy voice that fit with the rest of her. "Can't have rented a cottage, or I'd of heard. You're not packing camping gear. So . . . you're a guest. Who you staying with?"

"The old man," said Johnny.

"Lightfoot?" the woman asked.

I nodded.

"How you know that old buzzard?"

I shrugged.

"Don't, really. Well . . . that's not true. I knew him years ago. When I was a kid. A teen-ager, really. Thirteen."

"Yeah? When was that?" She was studying me now, trying to gauge my age. "Sixties, right? You knew him back about thirty . . . maybe twenty-six, twenty-seven years ago."

I smiled. It was over forty years, but I couldn't see the point of pricking her bubble.

"That's good," I said, smiling. "Twenty-seven it was."

She smiled, showing her best feature–white teeth, evenly placed. They looked like the real thing, anyway.

"Hey, you hear that, Claude? I guessed right on the money."

She had turned to the other passenger, a man roughly her age who had seated himself next to her on a bench along the right side of the cabin.

"I heard you, honey," he said. "You did good."

He gave me a disinterested once-over, and then looked straight ahead, toward the port windows, though I don't think he was paying attention to anything outside. He was either concentrating on warding off seasickness, I decided, or simply resting; it was impossible to tell which.

The woman turned back to me.

"My husband," she said. "Claude Smythe. I'm Wilda, but folks just call me Willi."

She held out her right hand, and I reached down and shook it. It was a firm grip, which I met with firmness.

"Avery Mann," I said. "Pleased." And we shook loose of each other.

"Where you from, Mr. Mann?" she asked.

"New York."

"Oooh," she said. "Hear that, Claude? He's from the city."

"No, actually," I said. "I'm from Upstate."

"Oh," she said, disappointed, and then looked to her right, through the cabin door, motioning toward the cars on the deck. "So which one's yours? That Rover out there?"

"None," I said. "I left it on the mainland. It's kind of old. If the Island's roads are still as I remember . . ."

She laughed.

"Oh, they're all of that," she said. "Bone-jarring. You'll be okay, though. Old Lightfoot has transportation. He'll get you around. What'd you say you're going over for?"

"Oh . . . a little unfinished business."

"Like what?"

Johnny interjected.

"He's writing a book. About my father."

Willi had cocked her head toward Johnny, but kept her eyes on me.

"That right?" she asked.

"Well . . . I don't know," I said. "That remains to be seen. I might do something on Jacques, but I might not. It's kind of up to him . . . how much he wants to tell me."

Willi snorted.

"Jacques?" she said. "You call him Jacques?"

"Well . . . yeah. I did when I was a kid," I said.

"Nobody calls him Jacques," she said. "Everybody calls him Lightfoot . . . or just crazy."

"Why's that?" I asked. "Why crazy?"

"He lives off by himself," she said. "Like a damn hermit. I'm surprised he's having you out there to that cabin. Never wants to see anybody. It's unnatural. He used to come see Claude and me regular. Now, months go by sometimes between visits. Isn't that right, Claude?"

He didn't even turn his head this time.

"That's right, honey."

"Well," I said, "some people, the older they get, the more they like their privacy."

"Privacy's one thing," she said. "Lightfoot's just plain antisocial. It ain't right."

She signaled an end to the conversation by making a dismissive sniffing noise, rearranging her rear end on the bench, straightening up and peering, as her husband was, at nothing in particular. I watched her, then glanced toward Johnny. He was smiling at me, and shaking his head.

I smiled back, and then–raising the binoculars to my eyes–took another look ahead at the Island. The boat was only about a half-mile out now, and closing fast.

"Well, later," I heard Johnny say, and I nodded without breaking contact with the binoculars.

"Right. See you," I said, as he strolled to the cabin door and onto the deck.

I scanned the shoreline to the west, near where the hotel and mansion had been, and could make out a dock, with a hint of cribs in the water on either side of it. Those cribs–laid bare by storms and waves–had once been the base of a portion of the former main dock. It had been years since I'd heard–in fact, it had been Addie who told me the last time I'd seen her–that the dock had been ripped up by waves, so I was a little surprised to see any part of it remaining. The section that still stood above water was directly perpendicular to the shore, and reached out a moderate distance; it had extended farther years before, not to mention to the sides. But though smaller now, its presence pleased me; it was a visible connection to my fond cache of Island memories.

I lowered the binoculars and–following Johnny's lead–strode from the cabin. Once on deck, I made my way past the parked vehicles, fighting the undulations created by the waves until I reached the bow. The boat was slowing now, and the mist and wind had diminished accordingly. Taking hold of the railing with my right hand, I raised the binoculars to my eyes with my left and studied the scene on the current main dock–a scene now just a hundred yards away.

There were several people who had braved the weather to meet the boat as it arrived, but one stood out as we approached–a short, slender, wiry old man with long gray hair blowing in the wind. I couldn't see the knowing eyes and confident, quiet smile at first, but as the distance between boat and dock diminished, there they were–though on a much older face than I had carried in my memory.

Lightfoot Jack–Jacques–had been true to his word.

If I came to the Island, he had told me, I'd have no trouble finding him.

"You get here, I'll be here," he had said. "And we'll talk."

And that's what I intended to get him to do. Only then could I hope to find the answer to a nagging question left dangling from that long-ago summer, that summer of Addie and Eliot and Grandpa and the storm.

What I didn't realize was that once Jacques opened up, I would learn far more than I bargained for–or perhaps had a right to know.

THREE

Memories

The main dock was much larger than its predecessor–a concrete and steel affair for the most part, bordered by a breakwater. As I stepped onto it from the *Sylmar III* and set my bag down, I noticed that it began as a dirt road, running out from the Island's primary road–also dirt–before yielding to the strong, inflexible surface upon which I now stood. The breakwater, built along the south and west perimeters, was composed of huge boulders that clearly–judging from the healthy condition of the dock–kept the elements at bay. The entire dock, which bent eastward to form an L, could probably take on the title of pier if the natives so desired.

The old dock, I recalled fleetingly, had been built with narrow boards that had given way under the slightest strain. Driving cars across them–necessary for ferried vehicles to reach or leave the *Sylmar*–had always seemed daring. But this newer dock . . . there was no give to it at all. It could handle a fleet of vehicles at once.

As soon as I completed this mental comparison, I looked for him among the faces moving to and fro. A couple of men were grabbing lines and securing the boat; another was helping Willi Smythe step off the boat and onto the dock; several more were just milling about. But I didn't see Jacques among them.

And then I felt a hand on my left elbow.

"We should go," he said. "We'll soon be losing light, and my night vision is not what it once was."

I turned at the touch, and stared speechless at the introductory remarks. I had somehow expected a welcome, perhaps a pat

5987-HAEF

on the back or a brief hug. But they would not be forthcoming, nor did they need to be. Old friends, if truly they are friends, can pick up where they left off after a separation of great distance or time.

In this case, it had been both. I had not lived in the state of Michigan for decades, and had rarely visited it in recent years; and on those visits I had come nowhere near the Island. And the matter of time . . . it was written in Jacques' face. A little weather-beaten and wild forty years before, it was still wild, but burnished and deeply etched now by the years of sun and wind along the Straits.

"What are you driving?" I asked him.

"Pickup," he said, pointing to an old red truck sitting amid a dozen vehicles parked in the dock's dirt lot.

"Let's go," I said. Lightfoot Jack nodded once and strode off. I picked up my bag and followed him.

****

The drive west and then north rekindled old memories–of childhood days bouncing along the rutted dirt roads in my parents' 1952 Ford station wagon on journeys to Snow Beach or to the dump or the airfield, and of a trip in a pickup driven by the state conservation officer, Al Jones, when he transported me and Grandpa and my friend Addie Winger to the lighthouse on the northern side of the Island.

On this present-day trip with Jacques, there was little said, for the pickup truck was very old and very loud, discouraging conversation. And so I enjoyed the time, jostling along, remembering, wrapping myself once more in the aura of Bois Blanc.

The first landmark I recognized was Al's old conservation office, off to the right, set well back from the road. The lawn in front was where Grandpa and Al and the Island's minister, the Reverend J.J. Stellingworth, had met periodically to discuss life's vagaries back in those halcyon summers of the mid-'50s. The last time was 1956.

That was when I had met Eliot Ness, at one of those sessions, telling tales about his crime-fighting days in Chicago.

We had never heard of Eliot before then, for he was not famous. The fame came later, after his death, with publication of his autobiography, "The Untouchables," and with a popular TV show of the same name that made him look like a super cop every week for several TV seasons. Which of course he wasn't–super, I mean, although I gather from my research that he was pretty good at his job. But like all of us, he was flawed, too: a defender of Prohibition who drank, sometimes to excess; a political creature who wasn't very good at politics, eventually leaving the limelight after losing election for the office of Cleveland mayor; a businessman who was constantly struggling in his last years to make ends meet. When he dropped dead, in 1957 at age 54, he had very few assets.

In that summer of '56, he had told his tales of Chicago and Prohibition and Al Capone as if clinging to his glory. I had believed his words, but the old men in the group were skeptical . . . at least until they'd been drawn into a web of intrigue created by an old gangster who had chosen to settle on Bois Blanc. Turk McGurk, a onetime fearsome hired gun of the Chicago mobs who'd been sent to prison largely through the efforts of Eliot, had anonymously drawn Eliot to the Island to even the score. It turned out, though, that the score had nothing to do with violent revenge. But that's a rather involved story that would lose something in the translation. For details, you can read this book's predecessor, *Island Nights.*

The point about Eliot here is that, in the end, he proved himself a hero in a nasty storm out near a tiny speck of land to Bois Blanc's southeast called Gull Island. Addie and I had been boating and took refuge there when the storm hit–and were at the point of exhaustion when Jacques and Eliot and Grandpa arrived on the original *Sylmar* to rescue us. In trying to grab a line they were tossing us, though, I lost my footing and my hold on Addie, and we both went tumbling into the churning surf. With the rain pouring down and lightning dancing about and waves crashing across Gull and into the side of the *Sylmar*, Eliot dove from the boat and pulled me out of the Straits as I was about to drown and then doubled the effort and found the seemingly lifeless body of Addie. He dragged her up from the dark, turbulent waters and back to the boat, handing that precious cargo up to me and my Grandpa and Jacques on the *Sylmar* deck.

It's perhaps churlish to suggest that if Eliot hadn't done that–risked his life to save ours–I might have known those many years ago if there was a power beyond this physical existence . . . might have known if there is a God. For without those heroics, I would surely have died. In the years that followed, I had given little conscious thought to that night or to God or eternity. But more recently, with images of that night imposing themselves upon me, I had been wondering . . . begun a mental quest, I suppose, for answers of a religious nature. The most prominent question was this: Is there a God? And a close second was this: Where do I look to find Him?

For inherent in Addie's rescue was a religious overtone. My grandfather–the victim of a stroke not many months before that had left him convinced that God required a selfless act of him–had pleaded on that storm-swept deck to be taken in Addie's place. While he had survived the storm–though physically and mentally spent by the effort–Addie had in fact come back to us. I had wondered at that . . . wondered if the old man had in fact effected a trade of sorts, but on a delayed basis. For it was not many more months before a second stroke took him from us.

The unresolved matter of Addie's experience that night–supported by those newly born religious questions–had helped bring me back now, decades later, to the Island. Despite my repression of the incident across the years, there was always–somewhere in my mind–a recognition that the subject must someday be faced. For it was in the saving of Addie that the greatest mystery of my life had always resided.

When fished from the waters, she had apparently been dead. Resuscitation efforts had failed. Grandpa's pleas to the heavens had had no seeming effect; she was simply not breathing. Jacques had proclaimed her passing with the words "God's will . . . God's will." And yet . . . and yet after all of that she had revived and had survived, seemingly after the fact of her death. Eliot pooh-poohed it as a trick of suspended animation, and neither Addie nor I knew what to make of it. But Jacques . . . he was sure she had died, a certainty that the Reverend said later was as ironclad as the next day's sunrise.

Jacques, he said, would recognize death, for–in addition to locally renowned empathic abilities–he had gained the capacity somewhere along the line to discern the moment when a soul crossed the fine line of transfer between life and whatever transpired afterward. Beyond that, the Reverend would say nothing.

After that summer I left the Island behind in both a physical and mental sense. I discarded the past in exchange for living the present of the '60s and '70s and '80s and '90s. But then, in the previous few months, I had suddenly felt compelled to delve into that summer–into that storm and that remarkable recovery by Addie, with the attendant religious questions–and did so in a kind of frenzied pursuit, with a need to grab hold of that which was tantalizingly beyond my grasp. I had examined the experience in my mind, and put it to paper in *Island Nights.* I had dreamed about it, analyzed it, talked about it, and–concerned that it was becoming an obsession–tried without success to forget about it. But whatever my approach to the subject, to that year, or to that evening at Gull, I was continually left with the unanswered questions that had remained dormant for decades, were always there and always nagging, and were now unleashed in all of their layers of ramifications.

How did Jacques know Addie had been dead?

And with an ironclad certainty?

How?

****

We rumbled along into Pointe aux Pins, the community in which I had stayed as a child, and turned at the corner that had once been the center of Bois Blanc social life. The remnant of the old main dock was on our left, and just before it was the boathouse that had once served as a candy shop; it was where Addie and I had met. North of there, on the road leading into the birch and pine woods, were the vacant sites of what had been the Vanderpool mansion on the right and the hotel on the left–buildings rife with memories but reduced to nothing by lightning. When we reached the woods and started negotiating the sharp turns of the narrow shaded road, I suddenly remembered the deer. They had been plentiful back in my childhood; I wondered how they had fared over the years.

Jacques tapped my shoulder and pointed to the right, into a clearing beyond a line of birch trees. There a family of deer, at their ease, stood watching us, but not with any evident alarm. It was as though they had expected us and were merely nodding acceptance at our passage. They peered our way until we were almost past, and then turned to forage for food along the forest floor.

I looked over at Jacques. He was intent on his driving, fighting the failing light of encroaching dusk, but there was a smile on his face, too.

"What?" I said, loud enough to be heard over the engine.

"They have always been important to you," he answered. It came out almost a shout.

"What have?"

"The deer. The way they roam the Island freely in all but hunting season. They are, for you, a treasure."

I smiled back at him.

"You think?" I said, knowing it to be the truth.

"I know," he said.

"I guess you probably do," I said.

I turned my attention to the road, thinking that my eyes might somehow help Jacques' in the dusk. And as I peered ahead, focused on the winding path ahead, my mind toyed with Jacques' keen insights, rolled them over as though caressing finely smoothed stones washed up at the water's edge, begging inspection.

Why wouldn't he know, after all? Jacques–a man of proven empathic powers, which had enabled him to locate Addie and me out there at Gull in the middle of that storm–had anticipated my recent phone call to him, my first overt contact with him since that summer. He had known I would be calling, he said on the phone, and for a simple reason: he had been empathically connected to me in a general way ever since Gull. Such connections were a minor albatross, he had told me, reserved for people who mattered to him.

I had thought briefly, between that phone conversation and my arrival on the Island, that perhaps I should feel a little violated by this psychic link; but I had discarded the notion. He had not been reading my mind; that was beyond his ability. And so my thoughts and secret pleasures and secret guilts remained mine. The link, he had indicated, was a non-specific one, keyed to my general welfare. I found the concept, after some study, to be comforting; it wasn't a bad thing, having somebody looking after me. Besides, the fact of the connection was seemingly beyond Jacques' control; had he been given a choice, I think he would not have borne the burden.

Along the way we passed a side road, hard to see in the deep shade cast by the trees; I might have missed it altogether if not for the man standing at its mouth, watching our approach. I spotted him several dozen yards away, for we were on one of the road's rare long straight-aways. He was an Island resident, I gathered, for it was after the summer-cottage-crowd season. Besides, he looked thoroughly at ease in what I imagined was standard garb among the natives: denims and a surplus military jacket over a flannel shirt. He had a neatly trimmed brown beard and appeared deeply tanned, his shoulder-length windblown hair a brown bronzed by the sun.

My eyes locked onto his figure as soon as I spotted it, for it was the only human form apart from Jacques' that I had seen since pulling away from the main dock in the pickup. As we neared, my eyes were drawn to the man's face, and I got the unnerving feeling that I should know him. As the pickup passed him, I could see that he was looking at me. He smiled gently and nodded; I returned the gesture, and could see as my face passed within mere feet of his that I did not, in fact, know him at all. But the look in his eyes seemed to say he knew me.

"Who was that?" I said to Jacques after we had passed by.

"Who was who?" he answered.

"The guy we just passed. In the military jacket and blue jeans." I pivoted in my seat and looked rearward; the man was growing small in the distance.

Jacques checked his rearview and side-view mirrors, then turned toward me.

"I didn't see anyone," he said. "What did he look like?"

"Didn't see him?" I said. "Jacques, he was right at the side of the road. Long hair, dark tan, flannel shirt. Tallish. Maybe six feet."

"Nope," said Jacques.

I studied my old friend, trying to see if he was having some fun at my expense. But he looked back at me and shook his head vigorously.

"Nope. Sorry. Didn't see him."

I nodded acquiescence, and turned my attention back to the road in front.

Odd, I decided. Jacques' eyesight was good enough to negotiate the curves and bumps of this narrow wooded road; and he had spotted the deer off to the side not long before. How could he not see that man?

I pondered it through a few more mild curves and sharp turns, and then gave it up, storing the matter away for future consideration, if the need arose.

****

We made the cabin in good time. After I took in the view across the Straits, where the Mackinac Bridge reigned majestically, and stood on the front stoop breathing deeply of the clean air–much cleaner, I realized, than the air back home–my eyes settled for a moment on a reed-filled field just west of the cabin. It had played a memorable role in my childhood adventure there.

"You remember when you snuck up on us in those reeds?" I asked as I entered the cabin. Jacques had gone inside ahead of me.

The reeds, though still flourishing, had yielded slightly over the years, permitting the widening of a path leading from the woods to the cabin. The path was now a full lane, indistinguishable in width or potholes from the track that it met at the tree line some fifty yards away–a track that cut through the woods from the wider road that had carried us north from Pointe aux Pins. The north-south road that crossed the Island had widened since my childhood, but was still primitive by most civilized standards: dirt, potholed, and barely wide enough for two vehicles.

Jacques, who was leaning against his kitchen counter, nodded, a slight crinkling around the eyes the only hint of his amusement.

"Sure," he said. "You came out here to see if Eliot was in trouble with Turk McGurk and maybe if your Grandpa and Al Jones had stuck their feet in it, too. But when you were sneaking through the field there, it sounded like wild boars chasing dinner. I had no idea reeds could make such a racket."

I laughed, looking around the cabin. I couldn't believe I was there again, after forty years. The place hadn't changed much since Turk had lived there with his two cousins–since he'd drawn Eliot north from his home in Pennsylvania. There was electricity now, though, and Jacques–who had purchased the place from Turk's estate in 1970–had installed running water and had an indoor toilet instead of the old outhouse. But that was about it as far as evolution had gone.

"Yeah, I know," I said. "Subtlety wasn't exactly my strong suit. But I couldn't believe how you suddenly appeared in the reeds next to us. I didn't hear you approaching at all."

He shrugged.

"You weren't supposed to."

"Yeah. Still . . . you remember what you told us?"

Jacques squinted in thought.

"That everyone was fine?" he asked. "That Eliot was in no real danger?"

"No. About the snakes."

He thought a moment, and then nodded.

"Sure," he said. "I'd forgotten. You thought that because of the drought, the rattlers would stay out of the dry reed bed; that they liked things wet."

"But you said I was wrong; that they liked it dry," I said. "Boy, did we ever get out of there in a hurry . . . at least when it sank in. I don't think it registered at first. But then Addie and Freddy kind of prodded me."

"Ah, Addie," said Jacques. "Yes. A gentle soul. Quite a lovely girl."

It was our first mention of her since our phone call. She would be a principal subject of our discussions, but for now . . . I didn't want to push too quickly. I wanted to get Jacques warmed to the idea of talking. If he was as much of a hermit or as crazy as Willi Smythe had said on the boat ride over, then he might not be inclined to speak too freely. I would have to work on him, develop a rapport. So I didn't dive right into the subject of Addie Winger and all the attendant questions.

"Yes, lovely," I agreed. "And Freddy . . ."

"Freddy Vanderpool," Jacques echoed. "I haven't thought of him in . . . I don't know how long. After the mansion burned, the Vanderpools left the Island, you know. Never came back. Freddy's mother pleaded ill health, said her constitution couldn't take any more. Fact is, I don't think she ever liked it much here. It was her husband and Freddy who liked it."

"They had a home near Detroit, right?"

"Yes, a huge place. The mansion here was just a summer place, a rich man's cottage. Better than any year-round homes on the Island back then, but that was the Vanderpools: bigger and better than everyone else. Anyway . . . they went back home to Grosse

Pointe. As far as I know, they spent the rest of their summers there, too."

"You ever hear anything about Freddy?" I asked.

"Oh, bits and pieces. Inherited the family fortune when his parents died. They went about a month apart; one had heart disease and the other cancer. I don't remember which had which. So Freddy got their millions, and as far as I know still lives in the family home. Married. Had a couple of kids; boys, I think. And he kept on racing boats. Lives near the Detroit River, so he used that."

"Right," I said. "He had the fastest boat on the Island. A two-cockpit job that really flew. Took it out every morning. In fact, that's what Addie and I rode in when Freddy brought us out here that day. She and I were kind of wedged into the rear cockpit. You think he takes those morning jaunts any more?"

"Oh . . . still his habit, I imagine," said Jacques.

FOUR

Nature's Light Show

I was admiring the clear northern night sky. It was cold sitting outside, but my wife had sent me on this journey prepared. In addition to sweaters and long johns, she had made sure I packed a winter coat, winter hat and winter gloves. I opted for all but the long johns after dinner, grabbed my binoculars from their case and wandered out Jacques' front door while he was cleaning up in the kitchen.

Once outside on the small front stoop, I breathed deeply of the fresh, crisp air, and stared skyward. The Big Dipper was easy to spot, along with the Pleiades and the Northern Star. The rest of the sky was filled with pinpoints of light, some bright, some barely discernible, a mix of intensities that seemed, in their inequality, to be dancing.

"Beautiful," I muttered, and stepped forward off the porch and down a hardened path to the dock that fronted the cabin. It was L-shaped, breaking off to the right at 90 degrees after three full steps out above the water. I couldn't tell in the darkness, and had not noticed in the light, what the age of the structure might be. But it was shaped exactly as I remembered the one there four decades before, the one Addie and I had sat on with Grandpa after discovering that Turk McGurk was not the malignancy I had imagined–that he was just an old man bent on regaining an edge on some level of his life, but peacefully.

It probably was the same dock, I surmised, but upgraded periodically, new boards replacing those rotted by the wind and the rain and the sun and the waves.

The moon, almost full, was high in the sky to the east, visible just over the woods bordering Jacques' cabin. I gave it a brief look through the binoculars, and marveled at the result. I could see craters clearly, the craterless Sea of Tranquility, and even some detail on the slivered portion that was still in shadow.

I was still looking when I heard the creak of the door to the right and behind me as Jacques came out, and his footsteps as he trod the path and the dock. He soon reached me at the end of the structure, and without a word we stood there together, looking eastward and then turning toward the northwest and the tourist mecca of Mackinac Island. The stores in the distant downtown section of Mackinac were brightly lit, a common sight in the late spring and throughout the summer, but not for long in the fall. They would be blackened before too many more nights passed. The shops that were the Island's primary draw–purveyors of fudge, leather goods, tourist trinkets, clothing and fine dining–would be closing with few exceptions for the winter season soon, as would the magnificent Grand Hotel.

Addie and I had visited the hotel, as had Eliot, during a daytrip there in 1956. According to brochures I'd seen in preparation for this journey more than four decades later, the hotel and its lush grounds were little changed; great care had been taken in its upkeep. It had in fact been used in the early 1980s for scenes in the movie *Somewhere in Time* with Christopher Reeve and Jane Seymour, which said something for its condition. Hollywood is, if nothing else, particular about its settings.

"You are remembering the last trip you took there," Jacques said. "The one with Addie and your grandfather and Al Jones."

"Yes," I said. "You ferried us over. Visited the cemetery up high in the Island's center, as I recall. Your ancestors."

"Indeed. I visit there regularly. I find it a fulfilling exercise, keeping touch with my roots."

We were silent again for a minute, each with our thoughts. I imagine he was contemplating those visits, or perhaps those ancestors. I was thinking back to the portion of that bygone day in which Addie and I, heated from riding a tandem bike around the Island perimeter, had shucked our clothes down to our underwear and jumped in the Straits to cool down. The proximity of her clearly defined flesh had, however, only served to heat me up again.

"She was in the water far too long to have survived," Jacques said, breaking into my thoughts.

I was momentarily confused, for Addie and I had stayed in the water off Mackinac's shore for but a few minutes, and nothing untoward–or at least dangerous–had occurred. Then I realized he was talking about the evening at Gull. I pondered how to respond, and opted for caution.

"I can't attest to that," I said slowly. "I was a little disoriented myself, almost drowning and all. And then the emotion of it, when I thought she was dead . . ."

"She was dead, my friend."

I was both surprised and not surprised by the declaration; I mean, I knew of his and the Reverend's belief in what had transpired out there, but the simplicity of the pronouncement was stunning. My answer, accordingly, was argumentative.

"But the line between life and death is not that easily defined, Jacques, not without medical equipment."

Jacques looked skyward, to the northwest, and picked out a star; I didn't know its name, but it was bright–easily outshining the others.

"See that?" he said, pointing. "The one that stands out most."

"Yes. Sure," I answered.

"Bright star, yes?"

"Obviously."

"Uh huh," said Jacques. "Obviously. But is it not true that by the time we see many of these stars, they have already burned out? That the light we are seeing is in fact a death throe that takes so long to reach us that it no longer exists at its point of origin?"

"Yes, as I understand it," I said. "We are, in essence, viewing the past."

"The past," said Jacques. "Yes. But more to the point, it is an example of things not being what they seem. The star seems to shine, but of course it no longer is."

"How does that relate to Addie?" I asked.

"How you perceive things and how they are can sometimes be radically different," he said. "For instance, there is your perception of Addie's drowning."

"If in fact she drowned . . ." I said.

"Do you know how long you were in the water . . . how long you were, in fact, underwater?" Jacques asked.

"I don't know," I answered. "As I was saying, it was confusing."

"Just so. Your perception was–and is–skewed by the shock of the event as it applied directly to you. It disoriented you. Do you remember that she went under first?"

I nodded.

"Yes," I said. "I fell into the water trying for the line, and by the time I got back up, she was gone. I desperately tried to find her, and was in the process of drowning when Eliot reached me."

"Yes, well, you struggled to find her for a good two minutes, and then another three passed while Eliot saved you, handed you the line and got you pointed toward the boat. Another couple went by as you thrashed about on the way to the boat, another one as you were hoisted aboard, three more as you regained your breath and your strength, and then at least six more until Eliot suddenly popped up with Addie."

"I thought that only took a couple of minutes, after I got my sea legs," I said.

"Okay, I'll compromise it to five," said Jacques. "No less than that. You were, as you say, confused. And that makes sixteen minutes from the time she went under to the time we fished her out."

I was shaking my head.

"But Eliot said it could happen. A suspended state, or maybe she wasn't underwater all that time."

"It was another seven minutes, easily, before she suddenly came alert," said Jacques. "That's twenty-three. But even without those last seven, I tell you she was dead."

I swiveled my head left to take in the old man at my side. But there was little to see in the darkness, for even with the moonlight his face was too burnished to reveal much.

"I'm afraid," I said, "that I can't be convinced of that on the basis of your time estimates. I just don't have enough facts. How long was she underwater? How long can a body survive without taking an apparent breath? Did the cold of the storm and the water somehow slow her heartbeat or breathing? Was there some sort of suspended animation?"

"There was no suspension," he said evenly.

"Perhaps not," I answered. "But Jacques, I need more. Look . . . In our phone conversation, you indicated a willingness to talk about your past–the past the Reverend said was the key to this thing. Are you still willing?"

Jacques took a deep breath.

"I suppose," he said. "Now that you are here, though, it is not as easy as I thought. But I said I would, and I shall. But not to-night, Avery. It is drawing close to my resting time, and I prefer to tackle this from a fresher perspective."

"And the tape recorder, Jacques? I brought it, with plenty of cassettes, as you suggested."

It was, in fact, at the bottom of my travel bag. I had harbored doubts as to whether he would accede to its use once I was here, but I had brought it nonetheless. Nothing ventured . . .

"As you wish," Jacques said. I could barely see his head nodding affirmation in the moonlight. "We will talk in the morning. But we must break in the afternoon. We have to go back across the Island for something."

"Okay," I said. "Business?"

"I have to pick up a package."

"Post office?"

"No," he said. "My son will be bringing it across on the boat. Now, let me say goodnight. I will be sleeping in the bedroom. You can take the couch."

"Okay, Jacques. If you don't mind, I think I'll stay out here a little while."

"That's fine," he said. "See you at first light."

He shuffled back along the dock and the path toward his front door, but stopped before going inside.

"Avery," he said.

"Yes?"

"Did you get the letter I sent you–about the Crystal of Death? About the bear myth?"

"Yes, just before I left from home," I answered. "I was wondering about that; you didn't explain why you sent it or what it meant."

"It is necessary preamble," he said. "You will understand. Good night."

"Good night."

He swung open his front door and stepped inside, closing it gently behind him.

Alone again, I scanned the shadow of land on the horizon, first to the west and the tip of Michigan's Lower Peninsula, and then to the north, where the Upper Peninsula sat in its quiet, wooded splendor. Then my eyes swung back toward Mackinac as, one by one, the lights of its shops shut down for the night, turning the Island from a bright beacon to . . . well, a barely discernible obstruction in the flow of the Straits.

With the glow muted, I couldn't understand at first why there was so much light above and to the right of Mackinac; it made no sense to me. It hadn't been there when all the lights were on, so why now?

It was their movement that identified them for me, a kind of wavering of different shades of white–with a few subtle pastels thrown in–that brought back the childhood image. For it was here, in the Straits of Mackinac, on some far-off night like this, that I had seen the Aurora Borealis for the first time–and one of the few times–in my life.

Now, the Northern Lights had just come out to play again. I don't know how common an occurrence it is there, to see them from Bois Blanc. But from a personal standpoint, a handful of sightings over half a century qualified the moment as unusual–and quite special.

And so I sat and gawked, marveling at nature's wonders, and wondering if they were the handiwork of some God . . . which of course would mean there was a God after all. Something so ethereal, so beautiful as those lights almost couldn't be a mere accident, I thought. Or could they? Just where could I find an answer?

Well, I had a sense of where I might look. Especially if Addie had really died . . . had been resurrected those many years before. If so, then wouldn't God have played a role?

Yes, I could look right there, on Bois Blanc. Right there, in the person of an old man thought crazy by his friends.

Maybe, just maybe, I could find some firm signpost in my visit that could point me in the direction of a deity . . . give my poor religiously muddled brain a shove away from its stubborn position in the middle, away from the morass that lies between faith and utter disbelief.

FIVE

A Predawn Visit

Sleep came fitfully, in part because of the nature of the bedding Jacques was providing me–a living room couch with vinyl covering that squeaked at every move–and in part, I suppose, because of a combination of fatigue from the long trip and anticipation of what I might learn from my old friend.

I think it took the better part of a half-hour for me to secure a stable sleeping pattern, to fall into a slumber that would guarantee me some vitality the next day. And somewhere along the line between dark of night and light of day, I slipped into the world of dreams. I suspect it was nearer dawn than not, for that is when most of my dreams occur, at least the ones I recall. And even those are usually vague.

This one was different, though, in that I remembered it vividly upon waking.

I suspect it was about five or six a.m. when the dream came, when–within the confines of its spectral framework–I felt the presence of someone besides myself.

"Jacques?" I mumbled as I struggled to wakefulness in the dream. "That you?"

I figured, from the sound of his footsteps, that he was passing from either the bathroom or his bedroom to the kitchen, maybe for an early-morning snack. The thought triggered an appetite of my own.

"If you're making a sandwich, how about one for me?" I said, my voice steadier now. "Or cookies or crackers. Whatever. Anything would be good."

The room was nearly pitch dark, so my visual senses weren't at their best. I was working with my hearing and with a sixth sense that told me almost immediately after uttering those words that this was not, in fact, my old friend at all.

I narrowed my eyes to try and see better, focusing in the direction of the last sound I had heard. Gradually, I discerned what I thought was a human figure, but it wasn't moving now, so I wasn't sure . . .

"Who are you?" I said; I had to know. I was becoming nervous . . . and maybe scared, though it's sometimes hard to tell in a dream.

The voice that responded was a gruff whisper.

"He's a little crazy, your old friend," it said.

I squinted harder, but it did no good. The features were obscured by the dark.

"So?" I answered. "I think everybody's a little squirrelly."

The gruff whisperer chuckled.

"Perhaps. But he seems a little more . . . unusual . . . than most."

I didn't know how to react; was a little afraid to say much at all, for fear of setting off an attack. An intruder visiting in the dark–even in a dream–is not something I accept very well. The voice sensed this, I guess.

"Don't be frightened," it said. "There is no harm here. I'm merely delivering a cautionary note. This man has done some very strange things in his life. Are you aware of them?"

"I hope to learn of them soon," I answered. My voice came out little more than a croak.

"He is . . . or was . . . a killer, you know," said the voice.

"So I gathered from something a minister once told me," I said. "But the minister said it was in wartime."

"Ah, yes, the Reverend J.J. Stellingworth."

"You knew him?" I asked.

"Knew him? I know him," said the voice. "But that is immaterial. Your friend talks to dead people, you know . . . up in that cemetery on Mackinac Island."

"Well, yes, I suppose," I said. "That's what people do when they go to the graves of loved ones and ancestors."

"No . . . he actually talks to them, or thinks he does. He thinks they are there, and holds counsel with them."

I was shaking my head.

"Wait a minute," I said. "If you know the Reverend, and he's dead, that would presumably make you dead, too. If you're not dead and are communing with the Reverend, then you're just as crazy as you say Jacques is. And if you're dead and I'm talking to you, that makes *me* just as crazy."

The voice chuckled again.

"You call him Jacques?" it asked. "Everybody calls him Lightfoot."

"Yeah, yeah," I said curtly, gaining courage by the moment. "Who cares? Or more to the point, what do I call you?"

"Hmmm," said the voice. "An interesting question. Why not call me . . . the owner of this cabin?"

My eyes were adjusting–barely, but enough to make out the shape of the figure. It was a man, no doubt, but a very large man. With a very round head, as though . . . bald. Cue-ball bald. The image of Eliot's nemesis flashed clearly in my mind.

"Turk?" I gasped. "Turk McGurk?"

"Do not be so surprised, Mr. Mann. This was my home for years, and so it shall always be. It suits me."

The ludicrous nature of this encounter–for I could identify it in the dream as a dream–set me on the edge of laughter. A titter escaped my lips.

Turk did not respond for a few seconds, until he was sure I had regained control.

"You do not believe in me," he said. "I understand. But to show my validity, let me provide a piece of information you are currently without."

There was a silence that I took to be a dramatic pause. Old Turk had become quite the thespian.

"Okay," I said, finally biting. "I'm listening."

"The package arriving on the boat tomorrow afternoon . . ."

Another silence.

"Yes. Go on. Jacques mentioned it."

"But he did not say what it was, did he?"

"No," I answered. "And you are going to tell me?"

"I shall. But to call it a package is inaccurate. It is, in fact, a person."

"A person? Who?"

"Someone from your past, of course, summoned here by your crazy friend."

"Who?" I asked again, growing impatient. "I'm not in the mood for twenty questions."

"I think you know who," Turk said.

The revelation hit me hard. After all these years . . .

"Not Addie," I said.

"Who else?" said the Turk.

"But why?"

"You'll have to figure that one out yourself," Turk said. "I'm just giving you fair warning. Your friend is crazy."

"So you said," I mumbled . . .

*****

"So you said," I mumbled again. And again: "So you said."

I shook myself to wakefulness, and sat upright on the couch. A slight hint of dawn was playing through the windows, barely illuminating the room. I looked around, but found myself alone.

There was no Turk McGurk. There was only me and the furniture. I slapped myself lightly on both cheeks, driving out the cobwebs, and swung my feet around to the floor.

"What a dream!" I said softly. "The Turk, indeed."

Standing slowly, working out the creaks and kinks that seemed to be accumulating with the years, I stretched, wandered over to the kitchen, turned on a light over the sink, fetched a glass from a cupboard and filled it from a half-gallon container of orange juice I found in the refrigerator.

As I sipped, I swung the refrigerator door shut and smiled at the metallic yellow glint of the appliance.

"Electric," I said with some satisfaction. There had been no such thing on the Island four decades before; iceboxes had been in vogue. It had been practically a primitive existence back then, appealing to a youngster not yet at puberty; even appealing in memory years later. But now that I was on the Island again, I was glad for the modern conveniences; roughing it held no particular attraction in the here and now.

Electricity had, in fact, created a number of changes in basic Island living habits. With it, furnaces instead of fireplaces were the norm; light bulbs had replaced kerosene lanterns; and electric pumps had replaced hand pumps, permitting indoor plumbing. Accordingly, chemical toilets and, where practical, toilets connected to septic fields had replaced outhouses.

The odd thing was, little else had changed in the Island's physical appearance. The roads were still dirt; the cottages still rustic, the population still limited, the bulk of the land still occupied by birch and pines and assorted other trees. What was lacking, Jacques had said, was a sustained sense of social interaction, a recreational mentality among the Bois Blanc residents beyond that exhibited by evening cocktail get-togethers, memorial services or wakes for the recently deceased, an annual one-day festival at the airport, and an annual "primitive" weekend featuring Native American crafts and artifacts at a remote–and difficult to reach–point on the western shore.

"Part of the problem," Jacques had told me during dinner the night before, "was the loss of the hotel and the mansion. They were our real centers of activity. With them gone, there were no more big parties such as the Vanderpools offered, and no dances such as provided by the hotel."

"Then why doesn't somebody rebuild?" I asked. "If not a hotel, then a recreation center?"

Jacques shrugged.

"There is one now, near the church. But it is not large, and not the same as its predecessors. It offers an occasional square dance, but has barely enough room for that. The population is spread out across the Island now, too, and with the main dock farther east, the community of Pointe aux Pins is no longer the center–as it were–of the Island universe. People no longer congregate there. But there is more to it than that, of course. There is TV."

"Television?" I said. "What has that got to do with it?"

"We had none here until electricity. Now sets are commonplace . . . they're in every Island home."

I looked about me. There was no sign of a TV in the cabin. Jacques noticed the look.

"Almost every home," he amended. "Not in mine. I want nothing to do with it. It is a contaminant; kills initiative and imagination; keeps too many people from doing other, more worthwhile things."

Now, standing in the kitchen sipping my orange juice, I nodded a delayed agreement; knew it would do me good to be away from that infernal machine for a while–knew it was one modern convenience I could do without during this trip.

I looked through the window and out across the Straits to the northwest. Round Island, a private preserve, sat a few hundred yards away. Past that and to the right was Mackinac, visible again in the morning light, its old British fort standing sentry atop a high bluff. And to the left, connecting the Lower and Upper Peninsulas, was the Mackinac Bridge. I had noticed it upon my arrival; before that, I had last seen it when it was still under construction, in 1956. Fresh then, old and a little decrepit now.

Which only reminded me of me.

Well, I thought, Jacques might be crazy, but if he was–if staying by himself was, as Willi Smythe had thought, grounds for a judgment of insanity–then the case could be made that almost everybody else, by choosing to stay inside and stare at a picture screen instead of socializing or pursuing a more productive course, had gone slightly daft, too.

There had been no startling geographical or visual change to the Island over the years. In that sense, Johnny Lafitte had been right. But the advent of electricity–while enhancing the quality of Island life in many ways–had undermined it in the same way that it had undermined the civilized world at large: by providing hypnotic visual and intellectual mush for humankind through the device known as TV.

From my perspective–as someone who had experienced the Island decades before–I could understand that in a spiritual sense, in the matter of its heart, Bois Blanc might indeed have been tarnished by civilization without civilization even going to the trouble of physically crossing the Straits.

SIX

An Ocular Connection

I tapped the microphone and held it to my mouth.

"Testing, one two three four. Testing, one two. Testing, testing."

I hit the stop, rewind and play buttons, and my words came back at me clearly. Satisfied, I set the microphone on the card table between us. The black-vinyl-topped table was much like one I remembered Turk owning, but instead of occupying a spot in the southwest corner as Turk's had, Jacques' table had just now been pulled from a closet and set up in the center of the room, near the couch.

"Okay, Jacques," I said. He was seated directly across from me, his back to the kitchen, and looking uncomfortable. "How do you want to do this?"

"I'm not sure where you want me to begin," he said.

"Well, I'm not, either. So let's go back a minute to the Reverend, and what he told me."

"Okay," he said. "Tell me what he told you, and I'll try to respond."

"Right. Okay. What he said. Right." For some reason, I was nervous, too. "Let me think . . . okay. He said that you knew–*knew*–that Addie had died because you knew death, because you had had–let me see if I can remember exactly–'extensive experience in situations involving lifeless bodies.' He said you had seen much of the world, and that you were a great warrior. But he would go no further, other than to say that we should trust him on this, and believe what you said."

"Is there a question in there, then?" asked Jacques.

I looked at him across the table. He looked well-rested, clear-headed, anything but crazy. I didn't really think he was, anyway. What did Willi Smythe and a ghost in a dream know, anyway?

"Yes. The question is simple: How did you know–ironclad know–that she was dead? And I don't mean the sixteen minutes in the water and the seven minutes on board. I mean . . . what was the Reverend talking about?"

Jacques studied his fingernails, cut short and scrubbed clean and really nothing remarkable to look at. They were, I reasoned, a point at which he could stare without really seeing while he formulated an answer. Although . . . it seemed he must have been formulating it since our phone call, before my visit; he must have known this was where I was heading with my questions.

"Well, he was talking about a great many things, I suppose," said Jacques in his gravelly voice, but softly, with his volume turned down. I pointed at the microphone and raised my hand slowly, signaling louder on his part. He nodded.

"I said he was talking about a lot of things."

He stopped, looking past me to the couch.

"Yes, but what kinds of things?" I prompted.

Jacques suddenly rose from his seat and strode past me.

"Jacques?" I said, suddenly alarmed. Was this going to end before it even began? I swiveled as he passed by, and watched in confusion as he stopped at the couch, looked down at it for several seconds, and then reached to pick something up. His body was blocking my view, so I couldn't immediately see what had drawn him there.

"Jacques?" I asked again. "What is it?"

He turned around slowly, and in his hands was the case that holds my binoculars. He was opening it, and sliding the glasses out. After examining them silently, he slid them back in and carried the case with him to the table, setting it next to the recorder.

"I didn't notice these yesterday," he said. "Did you have them out?"

I couldn't imagine why he would want to know, but went along with him.

"I had them out on the boat," I said, "but stored them in my bag just before we reached the Island. But you could have noticed them last night. I had them around my neck out on your dock."

He shook his head.

"It was too dark. Like I told you, my night vision is not good."

"Right," I said, remembering; they were his first words upon my arrival. But I still couldn't fathom where he was going with this.

"These were your father's," he said. It came out a statement, not a question.

I looked at him, then the case, and back again.

"Yes," I said, amazed. There was no marking on the case or on the glasses to identify their owner. "How could you know that? Don't tell me you remember them from forty years ago. Even I don't remember that."

But even as I said it, I concluded that that had to be it. My parents had taken those binoculars everywhere, so they had no doubt brought them to the Island those many years ago, when we visited annually, though I couldn't specifically recall them in conjunction with Bois Blanc. So how did Jacques remember what I couldn't?

"No," he said. "I don't remember them here, though they might have been; I never noticed. But I think I would have, for they were significant in the matter you are pursuing."

I was completely lost.

"What are you talking about?" I said. "Significant in what matter? The death thing?"

Jacques nodded, still looking at the case.

"How?" I asked. "How could my father's binoculars be significant?"

Jacques raised his eyes to mine.

"Because I saw these long before your parents ever set foot on this Island."

I shook my head, trying to make sense of this. My parents had gone to the Island first in 1952 at the urging of some old friends who had summered there for several years and had passed along the news of its charm. Or so I had been told.

"I don't follow," I said. "My Dad said he got these in World War Two. That's right, isn't it?"

Jacques was nodding his head slowly.

"Yes," he said. "They were your father's ever since he . . . took possession of them in the war. Do you know how he came by them?"

"Yeah, sure," I said. "They were Nazi glasses, left behind by a German officer after the surrender. In Bremerhaven."

Jacques was smiling.

"In a manner of speaking, that is true. But only after a fashion."

He reached out and caressed the case.

"You are sure you want to hear this?" he said. "It could be more than you are prepared to know."

I returned his look.

"This story is going to involve my father, I take it."

Jacques stroked the case a couple more times.

"Indeed," he said. "He plays a pivotal role."

I rubbed my chin whiskers, unshaven since the previous morning and fast attaining the consistency of sandpaper. I couldn't imagine what my father's role could have been. A peaceful man who downplayed any personal importance in his wartime experience–who, in fact, had said the highlight of his war was winning the Navy tennis doubles crown during a furlough at Wimbledon–and who quietly raised a family and carved out a successful career as a traveling shoe salesman, he hardly seemed the type to have been significant in anything related to Jacques' acquired knowledge of death.

But now, the binoculars–longer a part of my family history than I was; an item so familiar to me that I had seldom given them more thought than breathing; an item that my father had passed to me upon his death; an item that had, with the brief exception of a strap-replacement interlude, sat on a shelf since then until I had snatched them on my way out the door as I departed on this Island journey–were suddenly a key to what gave hint of being an unsettling account.

Or . . . perhaps I was reading more into Jacques' mysterious approach to the story than was really there . . .

"Avery," Jacques was saying. "Do you want me to tell you, or not?"

I held up my hand, searching for the right words. Before Jacques was to proceed, I needed an answer to something that, from what had been said, already seemed evident.

"First tell me this," I said. "Did you know my father in the war?"

Jacques let out a harsh snort.

"Know him? Well, I'm not sure anybody can ever truly know another person. But were we acquainted? Yes. You wish to know how?"

I was wary now. It seemed that the underpinning of my immediate ancestry–my family's history–was about to undergo a radical revision. Family being of utmost importance to me, I naturally feared unwanted blemishes. But I had come here to learn, and learn I must. And so I nodded, a motion that Jacques returned in kind.

"Just so," he said. "Well, to put it bluntly, your father saved my life. That's how we met . . ."

My jaw quite literally dropped at the mention of this heretofore-unknown deed, but I said nothing, at least for a while. I let Jacques go on, spinning out a tale that stands by itself as an intriguing story. My feelings were mixed as he rambled on, for I was discovering a side of my father I never suspected–a history hidden for unknown reasons. But I saw no reason to abort Jacques' effort.

What follows I later transcribed from the recorder as closely to verbatim as I could. Occasionally I smoothed a grammatical point or two, or broke a run-on sentence into two or three, or filled in a word or two that Jacques mumbled. But whatever the editing, it was judicious and designed solely to help the reader.

This is how his account went:

SEVEN

The Elite Killer

"I grew up here, you know, on this Island. Wasn't born here, though; that took place on the mainland, over in Mackinaw City.

"My mother was a full-blooded Cherokee; my father's ancestry traces back to the French and English and probably a pinch of a few others.

"I went to school here in the two-room schoolhouse we still use for the handful of full-timers that are left. Like you, Avery, I found magic in the summers of childhood, especially at night. The rest of the year wasn't as good, of course, although spring and autumn were bearable. But winter . . .

"There was little to do in the winter. We didn't have snowmobiles to travel across the ice to Cheboygan back then; we used sleds, with dogs. We had no TV, of course, and very little radio, there being no electricity and no transistors. A few short-wave radios ran off generators, but none in my immediate circle. So we had knowledge of the outside only through occasional visitors and newspapers, and even that limited knowledge was often days or weeks old.

"There was only sporadic ferry service back then. Someone always held the mail contract, and so that crossing–with letters and packages–was regular in all but winter. But generally, someone else would do the honors for other necessities–go over to Cheboygan in a private boat and bring back food and papers and such every few days. But with cold weather's uncertainties–storms, thin ice, whatever–winter trips and deliveries were infrequent.

"My early years were in what was known as the Roaring Twenties, but there was no roaring around here; that was reserved for the

metropolitan areas. Then I hit my primary maturation years in the 1930s, in the Great Depression. But again, there was no depression to speak of here, since that was pretty much how we already lived.

"This Island looks primitive now, perhaps, and in its way it is, but nothing like it was then. Without any of the conveniences we know today, there was one overbearing feature: the winter cold. We had wood-burning stoves, and homes that served well as shelters despite their thin walls, but the lifestyle dictated that we–well, my father and I–spend a great deal of time out in the frigid weather, out in the woods and on the ice. The cold was a great teacher, in its way. I actually learned to ignore it, I was subjected to it so often. I guess I didn't really think of it in a particularly negative light. I merely figured that this was how people lived in the winter: cold.

"There are always ways to keep from freezing when exposed to the elements, of course. There are windbreaks, multiple layers of clothing, newspapers stuffed in boots or moccasins . . . we never discarded the papers, you know. They were too useful in the winter as footwear or wall insulation.

"And really, the act of hunting itself kept me warm, or within range of it. Sometimes a hunt kept me moving, but even those times when I'd be lying motionless, in wait, I was so focused and my blood coursed so quickly that I thought little of the temperature.

"And that is where I first took a life, an animal life–came face-to-face with violent death, with a ravaged body and a spent will, and came to recognize when the spirit had indeed departed the body; not witness it leave, but recognize its leaving. I see your look; yes, animals have souls, too, despite what some religions think. And why not? What makes us think we would be the only ones with such a blessing? For we are animals, too–even more so, sometimes, than the beasts of the forests.

"I had but two siblings, both sisters, and they were not hunters, so it was up to my father and me to gather the meat for the table. Meat and fish. We spent many hours every week hunting–in warm weather, cold weather, dry weather, wet weather, year-round. The vegetables were left to the sisters and my mother. They had a large garden and did well supplementing what the men–well, what the father and the boy–would

bring home. And we brought it home with regularity. We were quite good at it; and on those occasions when fortune might be working against us, we would just persevere. Skill, when mixed with patience, can sway luck from bad to good.

"We hunted with rifles, but ammunition was scarce and quite expensive, so we used bows and arrows, too, just like my forebears. Perhaps I had a genetic propensity for the bow; I don't know. My father, a trapper by trade since a young man, taught me the particulars; but it was my own abilities that made me as good as he was early on. Beyond that, my empathic powers had begun to develop, enabling me to locate prey simply by tuning into their fear or alarm and tracking that signal. Consequently, I could match my father's skills and kills by the time I was 15.

"When I reached 21, the war broke out, and the federal government–rarely felt in our little niche of the world–imposed itself upon us with conscription. I was drafted out of my wilderness and sent to a basic training facility where I was taught how to kill–but men this time. There were drills, and competency tests, and an effort early on to cull from the ranks of recruits those few of us with an unusual inclination toward firearms or other means of destruction, as well as a capacity for acquiring foreign tongues–for learning the basics of other languages. In my case, as far as weapons went, I was exceptional primarily with the gun and the bow, although I was handy with knives as well, and for that matter with spears. My father and I had pierced the scales of many a fish with homemade spears in the waters of the Straits or on our inland lakes.

"We select few–with a need for haste in the face of the conflict thrust upon us–were moved away from the main units of trainees and given intensified, specialized training in the many ways of killing: garroting, disembowelment, vertebrae snaps, shooting, stabbing, hanging, dismemberment, whatever. And we learned how to handle explosives, although back then they were rather primitive compared to what's on the market today. And each day there was an intense session in foreign languages–German, Italian, Polish, French, Spanish and Scandinavian tongues for some of us; Japanese, Chinese and the like for others.

Some struggled with that aspect of the work, but I was pleased that I picked up what I needed rather easily.

"In the other areas I excelled, quite frankly, because of my upbringing: I had little experience with social intercourse, and therefore had learned to depend upon myself, which would prove useful in the assignments planned for me; I had experience with weapons, although rudimentary ones; I knew how to kill living things, which was important in the development of a man-killer; and I had an uncommon stamina for uncomfortable weather or environmental conditions. On top of that, I had great patience and the ability to move quickly and quietly–some of that inbred, I suppose, and some acquired.

"When training was completed, my unit was shipped overseas. Well, we weren't really a unit in the sense of physical unity after our training, because we operated individually and far apart from one another geographically. But we were a unit in the sense of mission and purpose. Anyway, some of my "classmates" were sent to the Pacific Theater, while I–along with a few others–was placed in Europe. The brass figured I would excel in the weather conditions in France, Belgium, Poland and so on; they would be similar to conditions we experience here. It was a good call on their part.

"What I did was top secret, of course. Very few people knew of the existence of our unit, because what we were doing was contrary to the articles of war: we were assassins–weapons, really, in the Allied arsenal, designed to take out strategically offensive people of both military and quasi-military standing. This practice, if discovered by the international community, would have unleashed an unpleasant set of circumstances: accusations, recriminations, possibly retributions in-kind. But aside from that, it was just good business not to let on we existed, for in that way our targets would be totally unsuspecting and thereby much easier to terminate.

"Of course, the down side from the standpoint of personal safety was that if captured, I would be disavowed by my superiors. I didn't exist, in effect. I was a bit of a ghost, floating from assignment to assignment throughout Europe without a permanent identity, living mostly in the wild, occasionally changing name and appearance.

"That's how the unit got its name–because we were like ghosts. The name was a little dramatic maybe, but its alliteration gave it a kind of appealing lilt. I liked it, anyway.

"We were known as The Specter Squad."

EIGHT

"About Your Dad . . ."

"Excuse me," I said, breaking into Jacques' account.

He nodded, and held up his hand, stopping me.

"Yes, Avery, I understand," he said. "You wish to know if your father was part of the unit. Would the fact of his membership greatly disturb you?"

Good question, I thought. We were, after all, talking about my kindly, paternal, very-family-oriented Dad. Amory Mann, son of Augustus Mann, father of Avery. Devoted father, successful shoe salesman, good neighbor to his neighbors, good friend to his friends. A pacifist, on the face of it: he banned guns in the home, never introduced his sons to weapons, and thus never took his boys hunting.

The only hunting I *ever* knew him to do was preserved in an old family movie, taken down South after the war–in Mississippi, where my parents lived for a time, and where I was conceived. The film shows Dad nattily attired in hunting gear, heading out toward the woods with his good friend Otie Thompson, shotgun in his hands.

I always thought, watching that film, that Dad looked uneasy with the weapon–that it was probably a gun borrowed from Otie, and that Dad would have been lucky to know which end to point where, let alone hit anything with it. But now, sitting there with Jacques, my mind flashed back to the start of that footage, before Dad noticed the camera and started carrying the shotgun awkwardly. Now, my memory was telling me, he was carrying it at the outset of the film with an unmistakable familiarity, an ease born of experience. In my mind's eye, he was, in that unguarded moment, a person very sure of himself and of what he was about to do with the armament cradled in his arms.

I looked at Jacques, who was waiting placidly for my answer. Would I be upset if Dad had been part of the Specter Squad?

"You bet," I said. "I don't think I'd be pleased at all."

"Oh? And why not?" said Jacques. "The men in the squad performed a valuable and, I think, necessary service."

"Perhaps," I said, "but . . . it would be difficult to accept him in that role. It took me a great many years to come to a meeting of the minds with my father, Jacques, but in his last decade or so I felt like we built a bridge based on trust. And him being a . . . anything other than a peace-loving man would seem to me a violation of that trust."

"I see. Well, first, Avery, let me say that what a person does in wartime is quite often not what that person is truly about. Circumstance can impose deviation from his normal tendencies. Duty can demand it. If your father was a man of violence during the war, he was only doing what he was supposed to do. I don't see how you could blame him for that. And second . . . your father was not part of my unit."

He delivered the news just that quickly, at the end of his sermonette, as though it were a minor addendum.

I'd really expected the opposite answer, and found my reaction to be one of gratitude.

"Thank God!" I sputtered. "Thank God."

But the relief was fleeting.

"What your father was," Jacques went on, "was part of a war machine that was trying to prevent the takeover of the world by a very nasty Axis made up of Germany, Italy and Japan."

"I'm aware of the history," I answered, wary again.

"Good. Then you should understand my point. While your father was not part of my unit, not a Specter, that did not leave him free of the war's underbelly. He was, in fact, very much a part of that, and very important in the effort to turn back the Axis."

"What are you saying?" I whispered.

"I am saying that your father was an Allied spy, Avery . . . and a damn good one."

NINE

Operation Mussolini

"I can feel your shock, Avery, but it does not show on your face. That is good. It is a trait that served your father well. A poker face, I believe they call it. He was a man who, even in a life-and-death struggle, hardly broke a sweat–certainly gave no hint of fear.

"Hmmmm . . . Now your face is showing a touch of surprise. Well . . . not to get too specific yet . . . your father was very good at what he did in the war, although he would have disclaimed any credit for his exploits. He was never comfortable with the violence of that period; but, as I said, in wartime, violence was often the only way.

"But I'm getting ahead of myself . . . ahead of the story. Let me try to stay chronological. We were where? The start of the war? Well, the start of my European service. Let's back it up to there, and I'll get back around to your father. Okay? Okay.

"I was dropped in to occupied Poland first, after dark, on a particularly stormy night in which visual sighting of anything–even a chute–was virtually impossible. This was not by chance, for my superiors took great care in protecting the secret of my existence and that of the Specter Squad from the outset. But out of necessity, once inside I was on my own; I was not even to count on the help of locals–or help them if it meant endangering the mission–for fear of compromising that secret. Only twice did I break the rule, but I'll get back to that shortly.

"Let me just say that my assignments were plentiful and, for the most part, quite risky. My targets were rarely of the sort I could eliminate in, say, an isolated farmhouse. No, more often than not they were

political figures or particularly noxious military officers who lived in either cities or fortified villages. I had to use creativity and the elements.

"For instance, for one officer–a Nazi who had ordered the execution of dozens of Polish villagers on a whim–I had to venture through two lines of defense: a perimeter of explosives strung around his village compound, and a cadre of marksmen on the compound walls. Since it was early winter and Poland is notorious for its storms, I simply waited for a good snowfall. It didn't take long, either; the snow started coming down late one afternoon at the rate of about three or four inches an hour. As soon as it was dark, I simply strolled up to the village; nobody could see me through the snow and the gloom. You are no doubt wondering how I approached so blithely if I knew the area was rigged with land mines. Well, my reconnaissance told me, for one thing, but common sense would have led me to the same conclusion.

"The Nazis, you see, made a big show of having villagers set the mines out in the fields and minor roads daily to discourage partisan attacks. While the villagers were going about this chore, the Nazi marksmen in the compound would shoot near them to keep them moving . . . and of course, petrified. And on occasion, such as on the morning of the day the storm hit, they went too far, in this case setting off a mine while an old man was near it. He was ripped to shreds. I watched this from my perch in the nearby forest with great dismay.

"But I knew I would avenge that old man and all the other villagers who had been massacred if I were patient, for I knew the main road to the village was mine-free. That was where supplies came in, and where the military entered and exited the immediate vicinity. Even if I hadn't seen that activity, though, I would have known. While the Nazis routinely mapped out the locations of all of their mines, and thus could negotiate any booby-trapped road–albeit slowly and carefully–no commander in his right mind would leave himself and his men without rapid transit in and out.

"That night it was snowing so hard that visibility wasn't more than a dozen feet, and I was able to pad right up to the compound–a high-walled affair in the heart of the village that was built centuries before, I suspect, as defense in another warring time. Scaling the wall

and taking out the marksmen was a small matter, and after that I exacted a measure of justice on the Nazi officer. He was sleeping, so I woke him up before I disemboweled him. That seemed to be a favorite of that particular regime, that and hanging people with piano wire, so I deliberately chose a like retribution. It sent a message of sorts, but without a signature. Again, what I did had to remain covert at all costs.

"Anyway . . . I mentioned the two instances when I circumvented my own rules. The first was when I encountered a small German unit marching some townfolk–this was in Belgium–into the woods toward a freshly dug gravesite. It was obvious what was about to happen, and I instinctively reacted. Unloaded my semi-automatic into the Germans, killing all five rather quickly. I nicked one of the locals, but that certainly was a far cry better than the alternative. Anyway, the group couldn't just be left there for the next Nazi unit that came along, so I stepped forward and hustled them away a safe distance–into the foothills a couple of miles off–before leaving them.

"That was, in the strictest sense of my mission, unprofessional, for I was supposed to remain invisible. But it did not, to my knowledge, end up working against me, and I have never regretted it.

"The second instance came in 1945 in northern Italy, near the war's end. The Allies were all over the countryside, along with pockets of Italian partisans–some of them true patriots, others Communist dupes–and more than a few retreating German units. The north was where the Nazis had set up a puppet government headed by Benito Mussolini, the former fascist dictator of Italy, after he'd been toppled from power in the Allied invasion a couple of years earlier. But now the Germans, along with their puppets, were beating a hasty retreat, trying to cross into Germany before the border was slammed shut by the Allies or, worse, by the vengeful partisans.

"I had been sent into Italy a couple of months earlier for some other jobs, but now this one took precedence: my new target was Mussolini himself, just recently put under house arrest and the subject of intense debate among the various factions. It was a real mess up there in the north; nobody was in power, and everybody had conflicting orders. Some

of the partisans wanted a public trial of all the fascists, and some wanted immediate executions. However it was sliced, Mussolini was looking at a short life span.

In my particular line of work, I knew the identity of only one of my superiors–a gentleman I hesitate even now to identify, and so will simply call by the fictitious name of Colonel Henshaw. He was the only officer with whom I had any official contact, and that was done at a distance. My orders were received from him by coded message–never in person. I never saw him; he never saw me. And that was how it was when word came that I should impose myself into the middle of the Mussolini situation.

My directive from Colonel Henshaw was simple: get Mussolini.

TEN

An Interruption

"Whoa," I interjected, cutting him off. "You're not gonna tell me you killed Mussolini, are you? As I recall, the history books don't have it anywhere near that way."

"Just what do you recall?" asked Jacques.

"Well, let's see . . . I think he was hanged, and left dangling in a town square so a bloodthirsty crowd could stone his body."

Jacques was nodding.

"I can understand your confusion. There was a hanging, in Milan. But the historical reports clearly state he was hung upside down *after* his death, and then stoned, as you say, by his fellow countrymen. Those same reports will tell you that before the hanging, he was shot at a roadside orchard by a partisan faction that had spirited him out of a farmhouse in which he'd been imprisoned."

"Oh. Then you didn't kill him," I said. "One of the factions did."

Jacques was shaking his head slowly.

"That's not what I said. I said that's what was reported. Although, in truth, he *was* shot after the faction got him free of the farmhouse."

"I don't follow," I said. "Just who *did* kill him?"

"Well," said Jacques, "I don't think a simple answer will suffice. This whole matter was . . . a little complex."

I was shaking my head, completely befuddled now.

"Okay," I said. "I'll bite. How was it complex?"

"Well," said Jacques, "there's the obvious magnitude of the subject. I mean . . . Mussolini was important, even then, after he'd been ousted from power. He'd been a major influence in the area for a good many years. There were a lot of people who wanted a piece of him. And remember that I was officially a nonentity, and supposed to stay that way. This assignment, considering the person involved, could have blown up in my face and made the maintenance of my secrecy a bit difficult."

He smiled.

"But not," he added, "as difficult as these interruptions are making the telling of this story."

I was taken aback by the words, but then saw the smile. He wasn't really upset . . . at least not yet. But if I wanted all the facts, maybe I'd do well to shut up. I held up my hand in a sign of surrender.

"Okay," I said. "I'll be quiet. Go ahead. Tell me what happened."

"You sure?"

"Honest," I said.

Jacques studied his fingernails for a few moments, gathering himself.

"All right," he said. "The assignment was succinct, which belied its difficulty. I received the directive from Colonel Henshaw: Get Mussolini . . ."

ELEVEN

The Demise of Il Duce

"I received the directive from Colonel Henshaw: Get Mussolini.

"I moved as quickly as I could, but like I said, the countryside was in chaos, and I had to be careful. There was no telling for sure who was on whose side at that point; while the Germans were easy enough to identify, there were rogue bands by the score–many of them marauders out only for themselves. Most of the units were Italian–and some of them probably friendly to our cause—but there were also Russians and Czechs and other nationalities who had descended on Italy's carcass to tear off a piece of meat while it was vulnerable. It was prudent to avoid all of them.

"Il Duce. That's what they called Mussolini, you know: The Leader. The guy who had run that country for a lot of years, but then screwed it up when he teamed up with Hitler. That put him in over his head. Mussolini was a bully, and like most bullies didn't have a clue on how to follow through on boasts that were beyond him. When he put his country into war, he had to produce military victory or be held accountable. And of course he failed. That's why he was in this pickle. He'd already been captured two years before, but had been rescued by the Nazis and set up again in the north. But now it was every man for himself, and the Nazis had left Mussolini and his henchmen to scramble for safety. There was no such thing for him in Italy, though, so he tried crossing at the Swiss border. Unfortunately for him, he was recognized by partisans on guard there and put under arrest.

"So there he was, confined to this farmhouse outside Milan by various quarreling partisan factions. Some wanted a show trial; some wanted

a summary execution. It was up to me to get there fast. I started about a hundred kilometers away, but managed to commandeer a jeep that took me most of the way through terrain that was uninhabitable and mostly ignored by the military. Then I went my preferred route–by foot and under cover of the woods that heavily dotted the Milan area. It was the element in which I was most at ease.

"Of course, being at ease didn't mean it was easy. The closer I got to Milan, the more soldiers and pseudo soldiers I had to avoid. The hills and valleys were dotted with them–armed zealots all following their own particular agendas. The end of a war is a dangerous time.

"So with the dual obstacles of difficult terrain–including snow in the higher elevations, it being April–and a military in flux, I didn't move as quickly as I would have liked. Consequently, I lost valuable time.

"And so I arrived at the farmhouse too late to do this thing cleanly. It was maddening timing, for I saw Mussolini and his mistress, Claretta Petacci, hustled out to a van-like vehicle as I crested the nearest hill and paused to gain my bearings. It was that close. Despite the recent nightfall, the moon shone brightly, and I could tell even from that distance–by the body language of the men taking them away–that the prisoners were being led to their slaughter. Mussolini and the woman didn't seem to know that; appeared eager to go, as though they thought they were being rescued by friendly elements, just like two years before. But this time they were being deceived. I can only assume that fatigue and fear clouded their instincts.

"I did the only thing I reasonably could, which was watch the van to see which direction, which turn it took in the distance, and then to angle across the hills as quickly as I could in that direction. I didn't know if I could find them again–in fact thought probably not–but had to try something. There were my orders, you see . . .

"Well, I traveled an hour, staying under wooded cover, alternating between high and low ground, when I came over a rise that looked down on a roadside orchard. It was a peaceful spot, a pull-off at the side of a dirt track, with a stone wall and–I could see it in the moonlight–a view of the valley and hills beyond. And there, lying near the wall, were two dark bundles.

"I knew instantly what they were–bodies–and went down for a closer look. There was no sign of the van, no indication of anyone else present. As I neared the bodies, staying in the shadows as much as possible, I could see it was Mussolini and his mistress. She was lying on top of him, on her back and across his torso, her arms splayed outward, her chest a dark cavity: blood was everywhere. It looked like a pose of protection, as though she had tried to take the bullets for him. But he was there too, supine, motionless, covered in blood.

"It was at that moment that I detected a fear–a palpable human reaction that told me somebody was nearby. I retreated a few yards to the safety of some thick brush, and then slowly maneuvered around the wall, checking its far side and the orchard itself. But there was no one there.

"'What the hell?' I said to myself, and then suddenly realized where the fear was coming from. It was near the wall, underneath the corpse of the woman.

"Mussolini was still alive.

"I approached the two of them. The mistress, Claretta, was an awful mess, her intestines hanging out and the sharp ends of a couple of ribs pointing skyward through her tattered dress. But I heard it almost immediately upon entering the garden: a grunting sound. It was Mussolini, I think only recently returned to consciousness, struggling to move under the dead weight of the woman who had shielded him.

"I moved quickly then, grabbing the woman's corpse and twisting it off of Mussolini and reaching down for his left arm and hoisting him off the ground–not an easy feat. He was a thick, rather heavy man–better looking than his pictures, I decided in the moonlight, but mean-looking–who had a bald dome that made him look taller, I think, than he was. In any event, he was taller than me. When I lifted him, he winced and moaned, for he had been shot in the arm I grabbed. But it was only a flesh wound, hardly more than an inconvenience.

"He staggered up, still dazed, caught his balance, and peered around. When he realized where he was, he looked for Claretta, saw the corpse and turned pale. Then, finally realizing that I was standing practically next to him, he straightened up, pulled his suit jacket down

tight–a little incongruous, considering it was dripping blood–and looked me in the eye without apparent fear; although I could sense clearly that he was petrified.

"'I am ready,' he said, his voice shakier than he wanted, I'm sure. 'Go ahead and shoot. You do not frighten me. I will not be frightened any more.'"

987-HAEF

TWELVE

Another Interruption

"Okay," I said, interrupting again. I couldn't help it. History has always been sacred script to me, and here it was being rewritten. "So you did kill him. How come the history books have it all wrong?"

Jacques rolled his eyes and held up his hand.

"Please," he said. "Who's telling this?"

"You are," I said. "But this could be pretty big news, you know, if you actually pulled the trigger. I mean, it's historic."

He was shaking his head.

"Avery, Avery," he said. "You get ahead of things so easily, are so emotional. You didn't get that from your father, that's for sure."

"Well . . . no, I suppose not," I said. "He was always pretty low-keyed."

Jacques was laughing gently.

"What's so funny?" I said.

"Low-keyed," he said. "That is so true, and yet so untrue. He was far beyond that, my boy. Your father, when faced with danger, was the calmest person–and yet the most focused, the most intense–that I ever met."

I was shaking my head.

"I still can't see it," I said. "Not Dad. Besides, who could be calmer than you? You went around Europe on dangerous assignment after dangerous assignment, infiltrating and taking out presumably lethal people. And yet you didn't panic."

"I was in my element, Avery," he said. "I lived outdoors, in the woods, almost exclusively. It was what I was raised to do. And I was not being hunted, for I did not exist. I was the hunter. There is a world of difference. But your father . . . the spy game is an open book between intelligence agencies. Always was, always will be. He was definitely on the list of existing agents, and constantly sought by military, political and police arms of the enemy. That, compared to my work, was true stress. But I doubt that he ever showed it, and in my experience performed with precision. Definitely the man to have in your corner in a pinch."

I shook my head again, trying to mesh the image of the father I had known with the image of the spy that Jacques had known.

"Well," I said, giving up the effort, "you still haven't said how you and Dad hooked up, or what you did together, or how he saved your bacon."

Jacques was nodding.

"I was going to get to that," he said. "But you saw fit to interject again."

"Sorry," I said, properly chastised. "Oh . . . that's right! You were about to kill Mussolini. Oh, man. I don't think I want to know the details . . . No, I take that back. How did you do it? What did you use? A pistol?"

"Like I said," Jacques answered, "you are always getting ahead of things. No, I did not use a pistol. Nor a knife, nor a club, nor a garrote wire, nor a rope, nor anything."

"I don't follow," I said.

"I did not kill him," said Jacques.

"Say what? You didn't kill him?"

"No. I didn't kill him."

"Why not?"

"Orders."

"Orders?" I said. "I thought your orders said to 'get Mussolini.'"

"Right, they did," he said. "But they didn't say to kill him. Just to get him. Get him and take him out of immediate harm's way. Out of the partisans' grasp. So that's what I did."

I was surprised, and suppose I looked it.

"But, Jacques, you yourself said it. History shows that Mussolini and his mistress were hung upside down in a Milan plaza after their death and stoned by an angry, vengeful crowd of former subjects."

"Wasn't him in the square, obviously," said Jacques. "I'm betting it was one of those hooligans who tried to kill him, who killed Claretta. I got a pretty good look–a general look in the moonlight–at two of them when they were taking Mussolini from the farmhouse. One, the most nervous of the pair, was similar in appearance to Mussolini, at least from a distance. Bald, stocky, a square jaw. In death, bullet-riddled and upside down, with the crowd in a frenzy and punishing the body even more with their rocks, who could or would tell the difference?"

"My God," I said, softly now. "This is even bigger than you killing him would've been. You saved him."

"I did not save him," said Jacques. "It was our government, the men I worked for. I was merely an extension of their will. Besides, they were not saving him to live a long life."

"They weren't? For what, then?"

"I don't know precisely what the thinking was. I thought at the time that my superiors had feared the partisan factions might debate his fate just long enough to allow him to wriggle free of the guard at the farmhouse. As I said, that had happened once before, in 1943, when German paratroopers grabbed him from a partisan mountaintop retreat. I figured my superiors didn't want anything of the kind to happen again.

"In retrospect, though, I believe that was not their line of thinking at all. I think they simply wanted to get their hands on him for a war crimes trial run by an independent commission, a show trial that would dispense a justice satisfactory to all the Allies. A cathartic exercise, as it were. But whatever the thinking, I was sent in to get him."

"Get him out, you mean," I said. "Okay, so you arrive and rescue him. Then what? How does my father fit in?"

"I'm getting to that," said Jacques. "Now . . . may I?"

I held my right hand out, palm up, signaling a resumption.

"You're sure?" he said.

"Right. No problem. Go on," I said. "Please . . ."

"Okay," he said, and took a moment to gather his thoughts. "So . . . we were by the orchard . . ."

THIRTEEN

Cross Country

"So we were by the orchard, and Mussolini was mildly wounded and in a daze but acting rather boldly–especially considering the fear I sensed within him. Perhaps it was because of that daze. Anyway, he told me to go ahead and shoot, which I wasn't about to do; my pistol was holstered and my rifle was slung across my shoulder, so I wasn't even in a threatening position.

"He was, naturally, speaking Italian. He knew a smattering of German, too, but no English. No matter. Since I had training in the European tongues, conversation was easy on a basic level.

"I assured him I posed no threat, as long as he did what I said. He wanted to know who I was, whom I represented; he could tell right away I was not European, but had no clue beyond that as to my background. The man had apparently had little or no direct contact with Americans, and so wouldn't readily identify one on sight. Besides, I resembled something closer to a creature of the forest than a particular nationality: camouflage clothing and mud covering was my normal apparel. I could disappear into the overgrowth in moments, a human chameleon.

"And that's what we would do this time. I motioned to the woods, up the hill from the garden, in the direction from which I had just come. I wanted high ground, and quickly. There was no telling when Mussolini's would-be killers might return.

"But he was stubborn; wanted to know our destination.

"'I must know where you are taking me,' he said.

"I didn't want to stand and debate, and so told him the general truth.

"'Some Allied folks would like to speak to you,' I said. 'Now . . . let's move out.'

"He considered but a moment, and nodded twice in affirmation. But as I turned to go, he moved in the opposite direction, kneeling over the body of his mistress one last time. I was surprised, because everything I'd heard had told me he was a cold-hearted bastard with feelings for nobody but himself.

"He knelt with some difficulty–encroaching age and the vicissitudes of the day having taken their toll, I reasoned–but said nothing. No prayer, no words of farewell. Instead, he lifted the dead woman's left hand and removed two rings from her fingers, and then plucked a silver pendant from around her neck.

"Struggling to his feet, he looked me squarely in the eye and said, 'They are mine.'

"I was speechless at first, for I had misread his intention completely. But then I understood in a flash his essence, and knew he would be no great difficulty as long as power was withheld from his grasp. He was indeed the bully of the playground, a forlorn and slightly ridiculous figure with his artificial trappings stripped away. But always, in such people, I've found a core of evil. Do not stoke the core, do not feed its flame, and it will languish. But always be mindful of its presence.

"'You're a true slice of worm pie,' I said to him in English. He did not understand, and simply smiled. I suspect, had he understood, the reaction would have been the same.

"'Come on,' I said in Italian. 'Up the hill.'

"Away we went, and none too soon, I think, for I heard the sound of an engine approaching. Not wishing to risk losing my gains–I did not trust Mussolini to do the right thing, to be silent if I were to watch the scene below–I instead prodded him over the hill and out of sight, on toward the next rise, and the next, always under the cover of the forest.

"Eventually, as we walked, Mussolini told me what had happened–the 'outrage,' as he called it, perpetrated by his would-be killers.

"The partisans–four men–had talked Mussolini out of the farmhouse with promises of protection from execution, and he'd gone for it. And why not? He was a man born to luck. He was Il Duce, one-time

ruler of Italy, a world force in his own mind. He had escaped two years before in the face of almost certain death, and had ruled again–at least after a fashion, as figurehead of a puppet regime of the Nazis. So he went along with these men, wishfully thinking–no, convinced–that everything would work out one more time. The mistress was not so trusting–I had misread that part of it–and had tried to convey her concern to Mussolini. But he wouldn't listen.

"And so they had gone with the men, traveling out into the country, to the north, toward presumed safety. And then there was an excuse–there was supposed to be somebody else to meet–and the van had stopped at the orchard. One of the partisans said he heard something, went to look, came back and urged Mussolini and Claretta to be quiet and go over to the wall. When they reached it, they heard the click of the machine gun lever being pulled; turning in sudden terror, they saw the same man pointing his weapon at them and squeezing the trigger. Claretta moved fast, stepping in front of her lover and taking the brunt of the blast. Mussolini was nicked, and fell with her, and passed out.

"And the next thing he knew, I had shown up."

****

"We kept moving, stopped to eat some dried food and berries and a raw rabbit I snared, and continued on in the darkness, heading toward a pre-arranged rendezvous set up by Colonel Henshaw. It was several hours away by foot.

"I could have traveled the distance quickly alone, but with Mussolini along, the pace dragged considerably. He suffered mightily in my company, though it was nothing I did that created the suffering. For a military man, he was soft, and being soft he had little stamina. We would go a mile, rest, go another mile, rest, and so on. And he was not equipped for the journey, wearing only the clothes he had worn to the garden, plus whatever extras I provided–a poncho and a cap. Fortunately, the cold–once we had reached the mountains and neared the snow line, it was bitter–did not seem to affect him greatly, for he was a thick man, laden with layers of fatty insulation. The only problems

were his feet, for he was wearing shoes instead of boots; his hands, for he had no gloves; and his head, which was a source of great heat loss before I provided the cap. We tended to the hands and feet by wrapping them in strips of canvas torn from a flap on my knapsack.

"It took most of the night to make our way to the transfer point–a clearing in a woods west of Milan. There, I was to turn Mussolini over to a special agent of the OSS–the Office of Strategic Services, our spy operation. The agent would in turn transfer Il Duce to his OSS superiors for disposition.

"When we reached the spot, just before sunup, we sat along the edge of the clearing, in the dark, waiting. Little was said.

"Mussolini had just taken his shoes off and was massaging his toes–trying to warm them–when a series of shots rang out and bullets started dancing all around us. Several sent sparks flying from some rocks behind and beside us, but the majority just lodged quietly in the soft earth.

"'What the hell?' Mussolini shouted.

"I reached over and grabbed him and pulled him up and started yanking him away from the clearing, away from the assault, toward some sort of cover. But he started swearing, and then tried pulling away from me, back toward the clearing.

"'Damn it, my shoes! I need my shoes, you crazy bastard!' he was yelling. But I wasn't too concerned with the loss of footwear, and managed to reverse his motion and drag him, literally, toward a sheltering clump of boulders some twenty yards distant.

"I couldn't understand how our attackers–whoever they were–had managed to sneak up on us. I thought at the time that it was an inattention to detail on my part, an unforgivable abrogation of my responsibilities. I mean, I should have heard or smelled them coming, or at the very least picked up on their feelings, for that ability was a long-standing part of my arsenal. But I hadn't felt anyone, and figured it was because of the distasteful distraction of sharing time and space with an evil slug like Mussolini.

"That, as it turned out, was not quite the problem, although I was on something of the right track. The actual problem . . . but no, I'm

getting ahead of myself again. The explanation will have to wait for its proper introduction.

"Anyway, we were headed for cover, somehow avoiding a collision with any flying lead, and dove–well, I dove, and he followed me, because by that time I had an arm around the bastard's neck–behind the boulders, which were backed by thickets. We were protected well by the rocks, somewhat by the thickets, but not at all if the attackers went up high enough into the trees and fired down on us. I had not set down either my weapons or my knapsack at the clearing, so I was as prepared for battle as I had a right to expect. Mussolini was wearing just stockings on his feet and had no weapon, and so was basically dead weight. I could have passed my pistol to him, but considered him as trustworthy as one of those massasauga rattlers we have on Bois Blanc. He would just have to fend without.

"It occurred to me that I could make my escape alone, and that I probably wouldn't escape if I dragged him along. But orders were orders, and mine said I had to stay with him until the transfer. So I stayed to fight. It was not a situation I savored, but sometimes life-and-death situations offer no options.

"I could hear the enemy now, but still couldn't feel them. So I would have to depend on traditional human reflexes. Reaction is always a poor cousin to action, but the former was all I had left for strategy. I listened closely for any sounds that might help pinpoint the opposition.

"'Do something!' Mussolini hissed at me, and I ignored him. I had to home in on the movements around me. Where were they setting up?

"'Give me a gun, you prick!' he blustered, and I ignored him again. I heard one attacker shinnying up a tree somewhere ahead, low still but gaining height and therefore advantage.

"'You will get us killed . . .'

"I slid my pistol out of its holster and swung it fast in Mussolini's direction, barrel up, so the butt met his cranium before he even knew it was en route. Mussolini crumpled, silent now, no longer a voluble distraction.

"I could listen completely now, focus on the scene unfolding before and above us. I couldn't see anything because of the dense foliage and

boulders and pre-dawn darkness, but I could tell there were four men, and that one was still climbing the tree. I now figured the tree was a little right of center from the direction I faced, perhaps forty yards out, maybe less; it was hard to gauge exactly, but I was trying mightily. I needed to zero in on it. If the climber got up high, and his friends then instituted a crossfire, it would be all over for us. I felt my ammunition pouch: full. And my weapons: fully loaded. I had two grenades on my belt, but they would do little good here: there was not enough clearance to throw them; they'd likely hit a branch or a tree and bounce right back in my lap. So it would have to be bullets. But I had serious doubts whether I'd get the chance to use all of those I was carrying before one of the attackers got me. It was, all in all, a tight spot.

"But just when I thought our time was down to seconds, three explosions sounded–grenades, to my right, left, and left of center, well away from me and Mussolini, out where the enemy lay poised, apparently hurled in their direction from the far edge of the clearing. Two of the blasts were followed by screams, and one by no sound at all . . . by a deathly void.

"'Alfonso! Vito! Tomasso! What's happening?'" The voice–full of the chill of fear that recognizes death at the door–came in Italian from above, in the tree ahead; the question drew no response, at least from Alfonso, Vito and Tomasso. But it was like a signpost to me, a specific mapping where before I had lacked proper coordinates. In the moment that followed, I took quick aim at the spot where the voice had emanated, and squeezed off a couple of rounds. I heard them hit, heard a branch crack and some leaves sing as the body hurtled through space and met the ground with finality.

"And then there was silence. The assault was over; only the forest remained–that and an unknown entity.

"I peered through the foliage and the dark, but could see nothing. Something–someone–was out there, though. It could be a friend, of course, and in a sense already was. But in a country torn apart by factionalism and an invading army, it could also be someone who was out to kill everybody just for the sake of clearing out the neighborhood.

"And so I waited . . . and listened. And tried to feel something, gain some telltale hint about my benefactor."

FOURTEEN

Lunch Break

"So, Avery, you want a bite to eat?"

I looked across the card table at my host with some disbelief. Now it was him interrupting the narrative–and at a crucial juncture.

"What? Jacques! You can't stop there. You're right at the good part! What happened?"

Jacques patted the binocular case and stood up from the card table.

"All in good time, my boy," he said, and moved past me into the kitchen. "Let's see what we might scrounge up for lunch. You hungry or not?"

I couldn't believe this. How could he think of food at a time like this? Time . . . what time was it, anyway? I checked my watch and was surprised to see it was late morning. We had been at the table longer than I had thought.

But not long enough . . .

"No," I said. "I'm not hungry. Come on, Jacques. I'd like to hear what happened."

"After a little food," he said. "I've found that the older I get, the better I perform on a full stomach."

I shook my head in disgust, and leaned forward, head down, elbows on the table. Jacques was evidently watching, because he spoke again, but softer this time.

"It's no big mystery, Avery," he said. "In the end, I survived. Just give me a few minutes, and I'll explain."

I reached out and, as he had, touched the binocular case.

"Jacques," I said.

"In a minute," he said again. "Be patient."

"It was my father out there, wasn't it? That's how you survived."

I turned toward Jacques and watched as he buttered a piece of bread. He reached for a head of lettuce he'd pulled from the refrigerator and was tearing a piece off when he answered.

"Patience," he said again. "I told you I would get to him in due time. It will be soon."

"Kind of a roundabout soon," I said.

"It needs preamble," Jacques said. "Besides, I've always thought the Mussolini matter of some interest. Top secret, of course . . ."

"Then why are you telling me?"

Jacques reopened the refrigerator, replaced the lettuce, pulled out a packet with some meat and extracted a slab of turkey and another of ham. After adding the two slabs to the lettuce, he closed his sandwich and sliced it in two, corner to corner, with one smooth move of a large knife. It looked more like a Bowie knife than a kitchen blade. He held it up and wiped it with a towel.

"Hunting knife," he said. "Had it for years. I use it for everything."

"Jacques . . ." I said.

"Right, right," he said impatiently. "Why am I telling you? Because I don't think it's top secret any more, or at least shouldn't be. I mean, it was but a small part of the war and impacted on almost nobody. So what's the difference? Besides, I get a little tired of these history books that don't tell the truth. Mussolini dead at the hands of partisans . . . please!"

"Then he was okay . . . after you hit him, I mean."

"What? Oh, sure. I just gave him a love tap. Knocked him out for a few minutes. Why? Did you think I killed him?"

"I didn't know. You didn't say."

Jacques' mouth was full with his first bite of sandwich, and it took him nearly fifteen seconds to chew and swallow.

"Sorry. But like I said, a full stomach . . ."

He poured a glass of milk, strolled back to the table and set down the glass and a plate holding the rest of the sandwich; I hadn't noticed where he got the plate. Then he reseated himself.

"Plenty of food," he said, nodding in the direction of the kitchen. He took another bite, and a sip of milk, and I debated whether to go get some, too. But then, evidently sated despite the uneaten presence of most of the sandwich, he suddenly pushed the plate away, lifted the glass and took two big gulps that drained half of it. He set the container down on the table and issued a light burp.

"Sorry," he said again, covering his mouth too late. "Now . . . where were we?"

"Somebody–my father, I hope–had just saved your ass."

It came out slightly petulant, and a little on the raw side, but Jacques seemed not to notice. Instead, he pursed his lips, thinking, and gave one short nod of his head.

"Right," he said. "I think this is the part you will like."

And he resumed.

FIFTEEN

The Spy

"So I was keeping quiet, not to mention low, and listening for some sign that might tell me who or what I was dealing with. It was so still, the only sound I could hear for several moments was the raspy breathing of Mussolini at my feet.

"But then the darndest thing . . . I heard laughter. Very soft at first, then a bit stronger, and finally a heartfelt belly buster. And it was so bizarre, out on that killing field, to hear this sound, this perception of humor, that I felt it wash over me as well . . . and I soon joined in, and the quiet of the forest was supplanted by two fools guffawing.

"It was when we were winding down that he managed to formulate any words, throwing them to me from the other side of the clearing.

"'Oh, lord,' his voice said, 'I haven't had such a time since . . . well, I don't know when. How about you?'

"The language was English, and the voice apparently American. I brought my laughter under control before answering.

"'No, me neither,' I yelled out. 'I take it you are perhaps a friend?'

"'If not,' the voice called back, the mirth leaving it, 'you would be quite as dead now as the others. All I need to know is this: Are you the Mussolini courier?'

"'The fat one is with me,' I answered, 'although not speaking at the moment. Who are you?'

"'I'm your contact. Look . . . why don't we stop yelling? I have some news that's of particular interest to you. I'll meet you in the clearing.'

"I thought on this a moment, debating whether I was walking into an ambush, but decided I wasn't. This guy was right, whoever he was;

I'd have been as dead as my attackers if he had desired it. And so I rose, leaving Mussolini to his nap, and strode from behind the boulders, through some bushes, around a couple of trees and into the clearing. He was already there waiting for me.

"We stood several paces apart, studying each other despite the dark–not for physical characteristics so much as a sense of each other's mettle. I could tell he was not tall–but neither am I–nor particularly memorable in structure. But he had a sense about him of utmost calm and confidence. Whoever he was, he was in total control of himself and, I suspected, of any situation he might encounter. He'd certainly just demonstrated as much.

"'You're with Specter,' he said. It wasn't a question.

"I nodded, but realized he might not see the motion. 'Yes,' I answered. 'OSS?'

"'Right,' he said. 'Colonel Henshaw sent me. I understand you're familiar with him.'

"'I am,' I said.

"'So where's the gentleman you've been escorting?' the man asked.

"I motioned behind me.

"'Back there. He was a little too mouthy for the situation, so I helped him shut it.'

"'How long you figure before he comes to?' the man asked.

"'Not long,' I said. 'Anybody else in the immediate area?'

"He shook his head.

"'No,' he said. 'But if you don't mind my asking, how did you let those four get so close? I'd been told to expect someone a little more efficient than that. Someone . . . pardon me if I'm a little skeptical . . . someone empathic.'

"'Good question,' I said. 'I do in fact depend on my senses, and they're usually reliable, but this time they failed me. It was almost like my normal input channels were jammed.'

"The man chuckled.

"'You sound a bit like a radio.'

"'Well, I am, after a fashion,' I told him. 'But like I said, the frequencies were jammed up. Some sort of interference. What I'm really concerned about, though, is the possibility that they might have been

following for some time–maybe since I snatched Il Duce. If that's so, I've really lost my edge.'

"The man gave a quick shake of his head.

"'No,' he said. 'No worry there. These were locals. I've seen them in the area before, but had no call to confront them till now.'

"'Good,' I said, nodding. 'That makes it a little less of a burden. And means, I hope, that nobody has tumbled to our whereabouts. I imagine the partisans are in a tizzy, along with everybody else, wondering what happened to Il Duce.'

"'I don't think you have a worry there,' the man said.

"'How's that?' I said. 'I didn't exactly snatch a low-level flunky. There must have been waves.'

"The man stared at me a few moments, mouth open.

"'You don't know,' he said. 'I gather you don't carry any communications equipment.'

"'None,' I said. 'No need. Why?'

"'If you did, you might have heard.'

"'Heard what? What don't I know?'

"'There was a switch,' he said.

"'Switch?' I said. 'What are you talking about?'

"'Well,' the man said, 'after you absconded with the goods, they put on a sham show. Strung up some poor guy who looked like Mussolini; hung him with the mistress in a public square in Milan.'

"I nodded. 'I think I know who,' I said. 'Any idea how many partisans delivered the body to Milan?'

"He shrugged. 'No. Just that after they tried to kill Mussolini–killed his mistress–they continued up the road a few miles, executed some more fascists, and then went back to pick up the bodies at the orchard en route to Milan. They had decided to put on a show for the populace by hanging all of the corpses upside down. They obviously came up one short at the orchard, though, and found a substitute. I don't have any specifics beyond that. Why?'

"'I think,' I said, 'that the four partisans I saw at the farmhouse might be down to three; they may have elected one of their own to play Mussolini's corpse. There was one who resembled him.'

"'Oh, brother,' the man said. 'They kill their own guy, mutilate him beyond recognition, and pass him off as the real deal. And then they choose silence rather than incur the wrath of the other partisans–not to mention a populace that smells fascist blood. Of course . . . they couldn't very well say, oh yeah, Mussolini really got away. Hell, they'd hardly dare think it, I imagine. No . . . they're not a problem.'

"Something nagging at the back of my mind suddenly sprang forward.

"'Weapons,' I said. 'Maybe we better round up the bandits' weapons. Don't want Il Duce to get any ideas when he comes to.'

"'Good idea. You get those two guys,' the man said, pointing to the shadowed figures of two corpses off to our left, 'and I'll get the one on the right and the one from the tree.'

"It took us but a minute to finish and return to the center of the clearing, where we both placed the newly acquired weapons–rifles and handguns and hand grenades–and our backpacks, and sat down. We were only a yard apart now, and I could see that the man was not particularly young, probably ten years older than me, with dark hair worn fairly long–at least long for those days. It was hanging down his forehead nearly to his eyes, and had curled over his ears. He had narrow lips and a slightly aquiline nose. The eyes, though I couldn't tell for sure, struck me as dark–brown or black.

"'The plan has changed a little,' he said. 'I was going to come out here and simply take this guy off your hands, but now that he's supposed to be dead–now that everybody believes he is–my superiors don't want him delivered.'

"'What?'

"'They don't want him. At least not right now. Not here, anyway.'"

"'Why not?'

"'They're a little concerned about backlash. The guy's supposed to be dead, and from the reception his substitute corpse got in Milan, the Italians are celebrating that fact. If he turns up alive right away, they're afraid the passions might be a little on the, say, vengeful side. They're thinking retaliation against our forces might not be out of the question.'

"'Christ,' I said, 'why didn't they think of this before? For that matter, why'd they want him in the first place?'

"'Well, they wanted him so they could control the situation, I guess. Who can say for sure? Maybe even they don't know. But they didn't plan on everybody thinking he was dead and getting all frenzied about it. They figured there'd just be a few pissed-off partisans, and that would be that. But now . . .'

"'Just what are we supposed to do with him?'

"'Ah, there's the tricky part. We're supposed to spirit him out of the country without anyone seeing him.'

"'Oh? And how do we manage that?'

"'Well,' he said, 'it shouldn't be too hard.'

"'Yeah? Maybe you better spell it out,' I said.

"The man hesitated while reaching down and retying a boot.

"'Came loose in the excitement,' he said, knotting it. 'There! Okay, here's what was suggested: We head south, toward the coast near Genoa, steal a small boat and cross the Ligurian Sea to France. Then go overland to the channel and across to England. Someone from OSS will meet us there–and then take our cargo off our hands.'

"'England,' I said.

"'England,' he repeated.

"'Why not just head northwest or west into France? No, don't tell me. The partisans are watching the border.'

"'That's right. Besides, I'm not too keen on tackling the Alps this time of year. Are you?'

"'I could manage,' I said, 'but I doubt Il Duce could.'

"'No, I don't suppose,' the man said.

"'England,' I said again. 'Might be nice to take a vacation from the Continent.'

"'We haven't much choice,' the man said.

"A moan came from over in the bushes. Mussolini was regaining consciousness.

"'Well,' I said, 'if we're going to be traveling together, perhaps we should introduce ourselves. Did your superiors happen to mention my name?'

"'No,' the man said. 'I asked, and they declined to inform me. Said it was because you are a Specter.'

"'Yeah. I'm not supposed to even exist.'

"'So I gather. Well . . . we can keep going without names. By the rules of security, that would be the proper course.'

"'No,' I said. 'That would be a bit silly if we're going all the way to England. I suspect we'll need to trust each other completely before this is over. I think names are an excellent step in that direction.'

"I thrust my right hand out toward him, and he momentarily flinched. But then seeing it empty, he leaned in with his hand and, after a momentary hesitation, grasped mine and shook it.

"'My name,' I told him, 'is Lafitte. Jacques Lafitte.'

"'Pleased to meet you, Jacques. My name is Mann. Amory Mann. My friends call me Amo.'"

SIXTEEN

The Package

Jacques stopped and looked at me. He was smiling.

"Satisfied?" he asked.

"So it *was* my father," I said. "And he really did save you."

"Oh, yes," said Jacques. "That time, and again later. But we must dispense with that for now, for it is time to go meet the boat on its afternoon run."

"What? Now? Your story was just getting interesting."

"Really?" he said. "I thought it interesting from the start. But come . . . we must depart. I must pick up that package I mentioned."

He stood, and headed toward the front door, grabbing his coat from a hook on the way out. He had moved so suddenly, I was still seated when the door was swinging shut behind him.

"Wait!" I said, pushing myself up. My bones were creaking from the effort, and I swore at the aging process. But then I recalled how quickly Jacques had just moved, and wondered at it. Staggering after him, I took my coat down from the hook next to his and hurried out the door. I caught up to him only after he had started the engine and was turning his pickup south, in the direction of the forest track. I jumped in, and was no sooner seated than he accelerated rapidly, throwing me back against the seat.

"What's the hurry?" I said.

"I want to be there on time," he said. "Sometimes Johnny gets in a little early."

"Oh," I said, and then thought of the strange dream I'd had, the one with the visit from Turk McGurk. I wasn't about to mention the dream itself, but it had prompted a curiosity about the mysterious package we were going to get.

"Jacques," I said, "if you don't mind my being a little nosy, just what is it we're in such a hurry to pick up? What's this package all about? Does it have anything to do with me?"

Jacques glanced over at me.

"Does everything have to do with you?" he asked. "Maybe this has only to do with me. Maybe it's none of your business."

"Oh. Sorry," I said, chastised. Well, I thought, that clears up the matter of the dream. It was no prophecy. But then I realized Jacques hadn't given me a definitive answer; had, in fact, sidestepped my questions with a question and a couple of maybes.

I ventured a look over in his direction, and thought I detected a small smile playing at his lips. Then I caught the glint in his eye, and was sure. He was toying with me.

"Jacques," I said again. "It does have to do with me, doesn't it?"

He didn't answer for a while, and I thought perhaps he wouldn't. But after the truck went through a couple of deep and chassis-rattling potholes, the words seemed to shake right out of him.

"The package," he said, "is an old friend of yours."

"Addie," I said.

"Addie," he echoed.

****

I let that sink in while we traveled the narrow track, and pondered it some more as we reached the wider road, passed the airfield and–at a speed I considered injudicious–made our way toward Pointe aux Pins.

Addie Winger.

I hadn't seen her since . . . well, since she had paid an awkward visit to my college one day years after our adventurous summer of 1956. The meeting, having gone badly, seemed a perfect harbinger of a lifetime apart. We'd had our time, and that was that.

But now, more than thirty years out of college and forty years removed from our Island adventure, I was in a pickup truck racing along a twisting forest road on the way to see her once again. And I was suddenly very nervous at the prospect.

Don't be silly, I told myself. You're not a kid any more; you're happily married, a family man. And she, remember, is no spring chicken either. Funny, I thought. She had always remained young in my mind–as though it wasn't possible for her to age despite the fact that I, and everyone else, had. But she had gone on to her own adult life, and was probably not anywhere near the person I remembered–neither the bubbly, engaging, totally mesmerizing youngster I had first known, nor the sullen, secretive, gum-chewing teen I had last seen.

And then it struck me.

"What in heaven's name is she doing here, Jacques?" I asked.

"I wondered when you'd get around to that question," he said.

"Well?"

"She is coming at my request," he said. "In light of your visit, I wanted her present."

"What, you called her after I got here?" I said. "No . . . that can't be. We've been together since I arrived yesterday. You must have called her after my phone call to you from New York . . ."

Jacques was shaking his head.

"No, Avery, I didn't call her. She called me. The same day you did."

"The same day?"

I had called Jacques out of the blue–what was it, just the previous week?–upon the urging of my wife, after I'd written *Island Nights*. I had called because, after writing the book, I–along with my wife–had been bothered by those unanswered questions surrounding Addie's Gull Island experience.

I had called, really, out of random chance, at the end of a

sequence of events triggered by a thought uttered by a friend–my minister's wife–longing for the magic of the summer nights of her youth. From that phrase–*summer nights*–had come the memories of my own Island summers, and the book, and the questions (both religious and practical), and my call to Jacques, and his invitation to visit the Island.

How could Addie have called on the same day?

"That's too much to buy," I said to Jacques. "Come on, you can't expect me to believe a coincidence like that."

"Oh," he said, "it was no coincidence."

"No coincidence. What was it, then?"

"Addie and I . . . have been in touch from time to time," he said. "She feels she owes me a favor, and so prompting her to come here was a simple matter of . . . suggestion. She understood, and called to confirm her arrival. Not that she needed to; I would have met her at the dock regardless."

"Suggestion," I said. "No need to call. What the hell are you talking about, Jacques?"

And then I understood, to a point.

"You mean that you . . . I thought you could only pick up signals, not send them," I said.

Jacques shrugged in response.

"Do you mean to tell me," I said, "that you sent a mental suggestion to Addie?"

"Well . . . yes," he said.

"Right after I called."

"Well . . . no."

"I don't follow," I said.

"Actually, it was before you called."

"Before?" I said. "But how . . ."

And then I understood completely. Jacques, when I had first called him, had said he'd been expecting me; and that he had long been tuned in to me empathically, able to pick up stress and distress signals from me for years. But now I realized it went beyond that.

"Jacques," I said. "Have you been messing with my mind?"

We were coming out of the shade of the forested road, onto the stretch that had once run past the hotel and mansion and down to the old main dock–ghosts of summers past. In the sudden light, I could see a touch of embarrassment on Jacques' face.

"The truth, Jacques," I urged.

"The truth," he said. "The truth is, I beckoned you here, too, in a fashion. Although it took quite a different form from my contact with Addie. You, after all, had divorced yourself years ago from the Island and all that it meant to you. Drawing you here required something . . . a little more time-consuming, a little more persuasive."

"How's that?" I said. "Give."

"Well . . . I sent you some images of that summer, of when you knew Addie, in the hopes that it might rekindle your interest in the Island. It actually worked better than I thought. The images prompted a headlong rush of memories that you turned into that book of yours. Of course, it took a while. What was your writing time? Twelve weeks? No, thirteen."

"What?" I said, incredulous. "You mean to tell me that you were responsible for my writing the book? Don't tell me you made the minister's wife wax poetic about her childhood summers."

"No, no," he said. "I had nothing to do with any minister's wife. If you were prompted to write by anything anybody said, it was only because the images were there, waiting for your conscious mind to settle on them. That's all. And so you wrote, and when you were done with your book, I could sense your consternation, your need for answers, and your intent to come here . . . knew you would come here."

"You read my mind?" The words came out raspy, barely audible over the engine.

"No," said Jacques. "That I cannot do. But I know you well enough to know your inclinations under duress. This was a logical progression."

"Good God," I said. "Why me?"

"You are your father's son," he said. "I needed somebody I could trust, and you are the person most approximating him now that he is gone. And . . . I needed your ability to observe objectively; your journalistic training."

It was quite a stunning pronouncement, and one I would have to think about. At the least, the matter of my professional standing–I'd had a long career as a newspaperman–struck a sympathetic chord . . .

"Okay," I said. "Well, not okay . . . but I'll live with your answer for now. But what about Addie? Why beckon her? And don't tell me she wrote a book, too."

"A book? No. I . . . signaled her only after I was certain you were coming."

"Before I called you," I said, double-checking that fact.

"Yes," he said. "Before. Your path was clear before you consciously settled on the date of this journey. It was of small consequence to have her arrival occur near yours."

"And on the basis of a signal from you, she decided to up and come," I said. "Just like that."

"Like I said, she feels she owes me something."

I gave him a questioning look.

"It has to do with . . . religion," he said obliquely. "I guess you could say she has been spending a great deal of time lately in prayer, conversing with her God."

"Her God?" I said.

"Yes, it's her way of dealing with things, just as yours is in writing. You write, she prays."

"Funny," I said. "I never envisioned her as religious–especially after our last visit. Of course, it was a long time ago, back when we were teens. But she seemed very dour about . . . well . . . about almost everything."

"She was going through a difficult time back then," said Jacques. "It was a difficult age for her, those teen years, compounded by the conflicting feelings she had regarding Gull Island. It affected her deeply, and still does."

"Wow," I said. "So she turned to religion. Well, it serves as solace for a lot of people. Why not her?"

"Indeed," said Jacques. "But it goes beyond that with her."

"Beyond? How?"

"Addie is a woman of the cloth, Avery."

"Cloth?"

"She is an Episcopalian minister, my friend. A woman of God."

SEVENTEEN

Addie Redux

We reached the shoreline parking area just as the *Sylmar III* was pulling into the dock, swinging its tail end around to offload its cargo. Jacques certainly knew his son's proclivities, for Johnny was early by a full ten minutes.

As Jacques and I strode across the concrete surface of the dock toward the boat, I turned my coat collar up against the breeze coming in from the west and thought how cold even a moderate day seemed to me lately. Jacques, however, had his coat open and seemed impervious to the chill; he was more intent, I noticed, on watching the passengers disembark. Following his gaze, I saw an elderly man get off first, then a young man, and then two middle-aged women. They were both stout, and gray-haired, and I looked closely to see if there was any resemblance at all to the Addie I remembered. But there wasn't, and we passed by them; and as we neared to within a dozen paces of the craft, there appeared to be no more passengers.

I felt a twinge of disappointment, but with it some relief. I wasn't really sure about this meeting. It seemed like it might be equally as awkward as our last one.

As Jacques halted and I followed suit beside him, Johnny appeared from the area of the boat's portside passenger cabin, and strode across the deck toward the dock. He waved to Jacques and me as he stepped off the boat, but didn't wait for return acknowledgement. Instead, he veered off to the side, toward a group of men who had watched the *Sylmar III* come in, and engaged them in conversation.

Watching this, I missed seeing the woman in the navy blue pea jacket come out of the passenger area, missed seeing her approach across the deck until she was almost to the stern. But Jacques saw her, and sprang to her side, and offered his arm as she stepped from the sway of the boat to the firmness of the dock.

I stood still, quite stunned, as she gained her footing, and watched her as she thanked Jacques, gave him a hug and looked around at the Island before her. She was nothing like I imagined she would be–which is to say aged. Not at all. She was instead almost as slight as she had been that summer long ago, and her hair was only marginally longer than the short cut she had once worn. Her face was practically the same–a touch of crow's feet around the eyes and a slight etching at the edge of the mouth the only signs of forty years' passage–and her carriage was as straight as ever, almost military-stiff with chin held high, as if daring the world to take its best shot. This was not at all the image she had portrayed in her visit to my college; it was instead a throwback to the girl I had known in 1956 and to whom I had grown enticingly close.

Now, here, four decades later, she was back. Back on the Island.

Addie Winger had arrived at Bois Blanc.

****

After surveying the shoreline, she turned back to Jacques and smiled broadly; she had not noticed me. She and Jacques exchanged a few words I couldn't hear, and he hurried on board, returning moments later with a suitcase. Then he nodded in my general direction, and the two of them approached me.

But as they did, Johnny called out to her; he wanted a moment, perhaps to confirm her return date. While they talked, Jacques continued on to my side.

"She didn't even see me," I said when he reached me; and then it occurred to me: "She doesn't even know I'm here, does she?"

"No," Jacques said. "I didn't wish to complicate matters. I needed you both."

I shook my head.

"Well, you succeeded," I said, feeling a bit used and more than mildly perturbed by it. "I'd like to discuss this later . . ."

"It's done, Avery," he responded, and fixed me with an earnest gaze. "Now let's make the most of it."

Addie finished with Johnny and walked over to us. Her eyes were fastened on those of Jacques, and a smile brightened her face. I noticed, in that moment, that her pea jacket was unbuttoned near the top, and I checked for a ministerial white collar. None was there, though and–as it turned out–wouldn't be until near the end of my stay. Since she wasn't on official duty, I decided, she probably wasn't required to wear one.

"Jacques," she said, "the place still looks wonderful."

She reached out, touched his shoulder, examined his face and added: "And so do you."

Despite my discomfort at what might soon transpire, I found myself smiling.

Addie let go of Jacques and backed away from him, studying him from top to bottom.

"Yes, you look well, Jacques," she said. "I see the Island still agrees with you."

"Always has, Addie," he said. "Listen, I hope you don't mind, but I've got somebody here I want you to say hello to. He's staying with me out at the cabin."

Addie swiveled slowly toward me, her eyes still on Jacques, as if awaiting further introduction. But he didn't provide it, and she was soon looking directly at me for the first time in more than thirty years.

"How do you do?" she said at last. There was no recognition.

"How do *you* do?" I said back. "It's been a very long time, Addie."

Her face registered surprise, and a touch of confusion. She glanced back toward Jacques, saw his smile, and returned her gaze to mine. She studied my features, and locked finally on my eyes, peering inside, seeking something to grab onto.

And slowly, ever so slowly, her eyes widened in disbelief.

"My God," she said. "Avery . . . Avery Mann."

I laughed, pleased at the effect of my presence.

"I didn't think I'd changed so much," I said. "You certainly haven't."

"Avery," she said again, and her smile was back. "Oh my, but this is grand."

She moved in toward me, reached up, grabbed my neck and pulled me down toward her for a hug. This was quite a bit different from our last hug–the one she gave me on the day she had departed the Island, the day that had left me licking the wounds of first lost love.

Now . . . now, in addition to being forty years older and much less emotional than I had been back then, there was a physical difference: I was nine inches taller, while she had gained but two or three inches, barely topping five feet. The disparity made the hug a bit awkward.

But awkward or not, we stayed like that for fully ten seconds, stopping only when I noticed her body vibrating, a motion that I took to be sobbing. I gently disengaged, pushing her back so I could dry her tears. But she wasn't crying; she was laughing.

"Oh, my lord," she said, the laughter still coming, "I cannot believe this." She reached toward Jacques and stroked his cheek gently, and then turned and did the same to mine. Then she stepped back and looked at the two of us, and brought her laughter under control.

"Imagine," she said. "Two of my favorite men in the whole world, and we're all here together. This is a good day."

EIGHTEEN

The Twin Lakes

The journey back to Jacques' cabin was anything but direct.

First came a detour–at my request--to the southwest shore, beyond the turnoff Jacques would normally have taken north.

"Why?" said Jacques. "Not much there."

"Humor me," I said. "I just want to see it."

What I hoped–rather expected–to see was the auto graveyard that had played a role in my summer with Addie so many years before.

The graveyard–a junkyard of the Island residents' old, dead vehicles–had been perched alongside a privately owned pump house those many years ago, reaching down almost to the lapping waves. It was a most unlikely setting for rusting hulks, chosen for a reason I never knew, though I suspected it had to do with erosion prevention.

But that was years before environmentalists and state mandates dealing with such things. Now–in an age of excessive state and federal regulations–what greeted us should not have surprised me. Instead of finding the auto graveyard intact, we encountered the old pump house, a stony beach . . . and little else.

The cars that I remembered from childhood, canted at crazy angles–'30s and '40s roadsters, '50s sedans–were no longer there. The multi-colored gathering had been dismantled and moved–probably inland somewhere.

"Where'd they go?" I asked Jacques.

"What? You mean the cars? I'm not sure," he said. "I seem to remember a row about them some years ago. But I didn't pay much attention."

I got out of the pickup and walked along the shore, looking for some telltale sign of what had been. Addie was not far behind me. Jacques stayed in the truck.

"We last talked to Eliot Ness here," I said after a minute. We had stopped moving and were standing, facing west, hair tousled by the incoming wind. "You remember that?"

"Sure," she said. "He was scavenging for parts for his car. Left the next day, as I recall. Kind of a sad old guy."

"Not so old," I said. "He was only 54 when he died. I'm 52 now, and you're . . . what . . . 50?"

She nodded.

"Yes," she said, "and feeling all of it. But in truth he was old when we knew him, at least in terms of how old he would live to be. He was in the last small percentage of a rather fruitful life."

"Hmmmm," I said. "Interesting perspective. But fruitful? I don't think he thought so."

"Sometimes," Addie said, "the individual is the last person to know his own true worth."

"Shall we go?" Jacques called.

"Yeah, sure," I answered, and Addie and I moved toward the pickup. But within a couple of steps, something in a bush to my left caught my eye, and I bent down for a closer look. There, left over from the environmental cleanup, was a piece of metal perhaps eighteen inches long. It was concealed from sight, but obviously not from the elements: it was rusted red.

"What is it?" asked Addie.

"Part of an old bumper, looks like," I said. "I guess they didn't get everything."

I reached out, touched it lightly, and decided to leave it there. It belonged.

****

Jacques doubled back toward the north turnoff, but stopped again at Addie's urging.

"Oooh, pull over there," she said, pointing to a small structure off to the right, almost directly across from the north road–the boathouse that had once been a candy shop and a social center for kids, the place where Addie and I had first met. As soon as the vehicle stopped, she climbed out to look closer.

I followed her as she circled the building, studying it from different angles, and then as she approached it and peered in through one of its windows; I chose one in the same west wall. But the effort to see inside was a failure: the windows were grime-covered and the interior was dark. Any thought that we might glimpse a fragment of our past was blocked by the present.

Addie and I stepped back from the windows and turned to each other and shrugged. We returned to the pickup without a word, and rode northward in relative quiet.

****

We'd gone maybe two miles inland when Jacques slowed the pickup and pulled to the side of the road.

"What are we stopping for?" I asked.

Jacques failed to speak for several seconds, peering into his steering wheel as if for an answer.

"There is a turnoff ahead," he said. "I would appreciate it if you both consented to take it."

"Why? Where does it go?" asked Addie, clearly as mystified as I was at Jacques' tenuous approach.

"It leads back to the Twin Lakes," he said.

"The Twin Lakes!" I exclaimed. "I remember those. I went there once when I was a kid, with my brother Ben and a friend of his. We went boating."

Addie silenced me with a glance that signaled annoyance.

"Jacques," she said, "what's back there that you want us to see?"

"Not what . . . who," he said. "I want you to join me in a visit to my father's cabin."

"Your father!" I said. "Good lord, Jacques. I had no idea he was still alive. You didn't say." And then, trying to figure his approximate age based on how old I thought Jacques was, I asked: "How old is he, anyway? Ninety-five?"

"Ninety-seven in a couple of days," he said.

"Well, of course, Jacques," said Addie, placing a hand on his forearm. "But why would you be so hesitant to ask? We'd love to see him. In fact, I don't recall ever meeting him before. Did you, Avery?"

"Not that I remember," I said.

Jacques was shaking his head.

"Not likely," he said. "Papa was always a private person. More so after Mama died. He's lived out in the woods ever since. Moved to a spot on the Twin Lakes about twenty years ago, and says that's where he'll stay. Hardly ever gets out any more, so Johnny and I take out supplies, and visit and such . . ."

"Well, by all means, let's go," said Addie.

Jacques hesitated again, this time staring through the windshield. Then he nodded, restarted the engine and moved forward toward the turnoff.

It was a road easily missed–both narrow and heavily shaded. I would not have been able to find it myself, in fact, so protected was the entrance and so foggy my memory of the last time I had traveled out there–if in fact it was this track I had taken.

Jacques slowed the truck considerably after turning onto the road, a one-lane path that passed perilously close to a good many of the trees lining it. Speed here would very likely translate into dented fenders and smashed quarter-panels. This section of Island was nearly as it had been centuries before; it had, in the interim, yielded only grudgingly to the advance of modern technology. It would let a vehicle pass, but only barely.

About a mile down the track, I picked up an unsavory scent. It was kind of a cross between week-old garbage and a bed of festering maggots. Considering the cool weather–it was only about forty-five degrees and hadn't cleared fifty-five for days–the presence of a rancid smell normally reserved for heat waves struck me as odd.

"What the hell is that?" I asked.

"Oh . . . yes," said Addie, her nose twitching. "I just picked it up."

"Yes," said Jacques, "it's become rather strong of late. Unpleasant . . . but on the plus side, any strangers who wander in tend not to stay too long. Last deer season, the woods around here were crawling with hunters. I doubt very much whether there will be more than a handful of the hardiest souls with the strongest stomachs this time around."

"But what is it?" I said again.

Jacques gave a little headshake.

"Maybe you can tell me before you leave the Island," he said.

"Well, it just smells like rot," I said.

"It is," said Jacques. "The flora and fauna in a line around the cabin, but well out from it, are dying. But more than that: they are putrefying. That's the smell."

"Then I don't need to tell you," I said. "You already know."

"I know the basic what," said Jacques. "I want you to figure out the why."

He stopped the truck another couple hundred yards up the track, in a small clearing at the side of the road.

"Why here?" I asked. "I don't see the lakes."

"We haven't reached them," said Jacques. "They're just ahead and to the right. But this track goes no closer, and the only one in to the lakes is too rutted and potholed for any machine that wishes to keep running for long. I've long intended to fix it, but my father prefers that I don't; says it keeps his visitors at a minimum this way. He prizes his privacy. So . . . this is the last best place to park in case any other vehicle comes along."

"Vehicles? I thought you said the smell kept people away."

"Well, like I said, Johnny comes out sometimes. And there are a few other cabins farther up the track, toward the Island's center, beyond the stench. So . . . we walk from here. Ready?"

"Let's go," said Addie.

And we did.

****

For the first two hundred yards, there was ample evidence of the spoilage that was creating the smell. Carcasses of small animals and birds littered the forest floor, and hardy perennial plants were drooping as if stricken ill. The bases of many of the birch and pine trees were black and pus-laden.

But as we neared the first lake, a circular body of several acres, the smell abated, to the point that I almost thought I'd imagined it. Along the shore of the lake the plant life was burgeoning, and several squirrels and birds were scampering about.

The water itself, once we cleared the trees, was a brighter blue than I would have expected under the grayish skies, with lily pads in heavy residence near the shoreline. Frogs, unseen, were croaking to each other, probably about our approach.

"I didn't think they'd be out in such force this late in the year," I said, pointing to the pads.

"Yes. Odd," Jacques said. "But notice it's warmer here? That helps preserve the summer foliage."

I hadn't noticed, the change had been so gradual. But now I did. The temperature here, as compared to that back at Pointe aux Pins or, for that matter, at the turnoff to the lakes, was significantly higher–perhaps fifteen degrees. It felt like about sixty degrees now.

"Why is that?" said Addie. "Is there some sort of geothermal pool or pocket around here?"

Jacques shook his head.

"No," he said. "And it's not because it's protected from the wind. It comes howling through here pretty good sometimes. The change in temperature has only been recent, in fact; noticeable in just the past few weeks, with the demise of summer.

I unzipped the jacket I was wearing. It was almost warm enough to remove it.

"Weird," I said. "But there must be some simple scientific explanation."

"Perhaps," said Jacques. "Come, we'll stay near the shoreline. His cabin is not far. It's on the north shore of the second lake."

NINETEEN

Jacques' Father

The home of Jacques' father was a rust-stained cabin made of logs hewn from the nearby forest. It sat, as advertised, on the northern shore of the eastern of the Twin Lakes–two inland bodies of water connected by a wide channel. The cabin was surrounded on three sides by woods and on the fourth by water. A small rowboat and canoe were pulled up on shore and tethered to nearby trees that had either fallen or been cut and dragged from the woods for that very purpose.

Our approach–at first along the northern shore of the first lake, and then through a forest copse–ended with passage across a clearing separating the surrounding woods from the cabin. When we cleared the woods, we were but twenty yards from the side of the structure. A couple of dozen paces later, Jacques was rapping lightly on the front door and then opening it without awaiting a response.

"Papa!" he called out gently. "I've brought some friends with me I'd like you to meet. Papa?"

Addie and I entered the cabin's living room behind Jacques. A floor lamp was on over in the far left corner, next to a cushioned rocking chair. A book was open, face down, on a small table adjacent to the chair's left arm.

The room probably accounted for half of the cabin space. An open doorway to the rear led to the kitchen, and one to our right led into a bedroom; I could see a bed and dresser in there. One other door, closed, was to the right of the kitchen. It was from there that we heard the first sign of Jacques' father's presence: the flush of a chemical toilet. I found the sound jarring on an Island that for me had always meant sand, surf, kerosene lamps, hand pumps . . . and outhouses.

A moment later, the bathroom door opened, and out shuffled a man who clearly wore a great many years; they had bent him over at the waist, slowing his step and reducing his muscle and fat to mere memories. But when he spotted us, I could see in his eyes a defiance that had not been quelled.

He stopped when he saw us, and studied Addie and me in great detail–first her, then me.

"Who are they?" he asked gruffly of Jacques.

"Friends," said Jacques. "Sorry to startle you. I'd expected to find you reading."

"Yeah, well, I'm not dead yet," said the old man. "So I gotta use the crapper just like everybody else."

He resumed his shuffle, returning to his chair and his lamp. He lowered himself carefully into the rocker, and then looked up at us again.

"Well?" he said. "What do you want?"

Jacques looked at us as if to say, "Sorry," but there was no need. My arrival at middle age had brought with it enough creaking pains to alert me to the struggles ahead as time and gravity had their way. What I saw now, in this cabin in the woods, was simply an elderly gentleman who was trying to get through another day with all the physical and mental aches that life leaves as its calling cards.

"Like I said, Papa," said Jacques, "these are friends. This is Avery Mann and Addie Winger. They used to come to the Island years ago, when they were children."

"Don't remember them," the old man said.

"No, I don't expect so," said Jacques. "I don't think they ever met you. That's why I wanted to introduce you now: to correct that oversight."

The old man's eyes locked on to his son's.

"I don't consider not wanting to see people to be an oversight," he said. Then he addressed Addie. "Young woman, my apologies, but I'm not quite up to company today. I hope you'll forgive my son's rashness in bringing you here, but I must ask you all to please go back to wherever it is you came from."

Addie didn't hesitate. She walked right up to the old man and held out her right hand. He considered it, but made no move to accept it. She didn't withdraw it, though, as she spoke.

"I understand, Mr. Lafitte. Avery and I just wish to let you know that we think the world of your son, and that he is a credit to you. I know such a fine man must come from a fine father."

The old man did not take his eyes from Addie during–or for the several seconds of silence after–that little speech. Finally, a smile curled his lips, revealing two strong lines of white teeth. I idly wondered if they were his own.

Slowly, as if pulled by an unseen force, his hand rose toward Addie's; finally, they met and clasped. An odd silence dominated the scene, one that I was not about to break, not after Addie's little show. Anything I said would sound trite or, worse, flippant. Jacques too remained silent, observing this ceremony with what looked like intense interest.

At last, the two unclasped the hands and Addie, still peering into the old man's eyes, backed away until she was standing next to me. I thought about offering my hand, but the old man froze me with a look.

"Well," said Jacques.

"Well," said his father.

"We'll be going now," said Jacques. "Perhaps we can call again, before Avery and Addie leave."

The old man dismissed me with another look, but pointed a bony finger toward Addie.

"She can," he said. "Nobody else."

Addie nodded at him, and he back at her. Then, without further words, we three turned and exited, leaving the old man to his rocker and his lamp and–I could see him reaching for it before I had cleared the doorway–his book.

We returned almost without conversation to the pickup truck. The lone exception came just as the truck came into sight.

"So what did you make of that?" I asked Addie. "He took a shine to you, huh?"

Addie looked at me as though I were daft, and shook her head without answering.

****

We had reached and reentered the pickup, retraced the forest path to the northern road, passed the airport and entered the narrow track to Jacques' cabin before I spoke again.

"You visit him often?" I asked over the engine noise.

Jacques glanced over at me, across Addie.

"Used to," he said. "Less now."

"Is he always . . ." I hesitated, trying to find a diplomatic way to finish the question.

"Ornery?" said Jacques.

"Well," I said, "that's not the word I would have used. But . . . yes."

"Didn't used to be," said Jacques tightly. He turned his attention back to the narrow roadway, downshifting suddenly, frowning at the effort.

I took the hint, and embraced silence.

****

Back in Jacques' home, the other two seemed preoccupied, walking from point to point in the living room, touching things without really looking at them, leaving a verbal void that finally drove me to speak.

"Well, Addie," I said, "you look very well."

She was behind the couch, still wandering aimlessly, and it took a moment for my words to sink in. Then, gradually, she brought her attention back to the room, and to me.

"Oh," she said, advancing toward the card table, where I was seated. "Thank you, Avery. I take it you mean considering my advanced years and all . . ."

"Not at all," I said. "I'm older than you, remember."

"Yes, so you are," she said, and lowered herself to the chair on my right. In front of us lay the binocular case. "I'd forgotten. I seem to have trouble imagining you beyond your teen-aged years."

"It's my youthful good looks," I said.

She smiled.

"Well, no," she said, "though you don't look more than 40 or so. No, I was thinking that you still have a rather youthful . . . attitude, I guess . . ."

"She means," said Jacques from a spot behind me, in the kitchen, "that you seem to have never quite grown up."

I twisted around, expecting to see a good-natured grin on Jacques' face, but his look was instead impassive. I turned back to Addie, hoping she was wearing a smile, but instead saw a touch of red spreading across her cheeks.

"Geez," I said, a bit stunned. It struck me as a quick judgment–and not altogether fair.

Addie reached out and lightly touched my hand.

"It's okay, Avery," she said. "It's not a big deal . . . just a first impression, really. It's just that you don't seem very . . . grounded."

I thought about that as she slowly retracted her hand.

"Okay," I said. "You want grounded?"

She acknowledged as much with a barely perceptible shrug.

"Okay," I said, adopting my best interview voice. "So, Addie. It's been awhile. I take it you've learned volumes in the past forty years. What exactly is your philosophy of life, and for that matter, what are your thoughts on the disintegration of the family unit in the face of modern society's workplace demands?"

A laugh escaped her, a sudden throaty reaction that came from down deep. It was a genuine release, reminiscent of her childhood laugh but a couple of decibels lower.

"Wow!" she said when she'd regained her composure. "You don't really want to know all that, do you?"

I smiled, but still felt at a disadvantage; still felt defensive. I looked to Jacques for help, but he was on the move, digging out some cold cuts with which to fortify us. I caught his eye, but only got an amused smile in return.

"Well, uh, no," I said, flustered. "It's just . . . you know . . . fill me in on yourself. Jacques says you're a minister now. How'd that happen?"

She laughed again, but softer now, and her expression was kindly. She reached out and this time patted my hand.

"Ah, Avery," she said. "I didn't mean to make you ill at ease. I'm just a person like you, making her way through life, trying to understand its whys and wherefores."

She pulled her hand back again, and set it on the table near the binocular case. For the first time, it caught her attention, and she lightly touched its leather surface with her fingers. Then she placed her palm, fingers splayed, upon the smooth case siding. A look of curiosity swept across her face. She inquired silently of me and–seeing no answer there–called to Jacques over my shoulder.

"What is this?" she asked.

I knew by the sound of scraping that Jacques was at the sink, facing away from us, peeling carrots. He had been at it for the past few seconds, and answered so quickly that he couldn't possibly have had time to turn and see what she was referring to. And his voice, slightly muffled, indicated he wasn't looking our way when he answered.

"Binoculars," he said almost instantly. "They belonged to Avery's father. Avery brought them along."

Addie kept touching the case, as if gauging its temperature.

"Whose were they before?" she asked. "Where did his father get them?"

Jacques kept working at the sink.

"The Nazis," he said. "World War Two."

Addie nodded, as if satisfied the answer was correct.

"Does this have to do with why you summoned me here?" she asked.

Jacques cut the carrot into sticks, placed them on a plate with some celery sticks neatly arranged in a circle along the plate's perimeter, and moved in from the kitchen.

"Why, Addie," he said, "you're the one who called me, remember?"

She narrowed her eyes, measuring him.

"Right," she said. "Like I'd call you out of the blue and just happen to arrive at the same time that Avery decides to visit for the first time in God-knows-how-many years."

"Well, forty, actually," I said.

They both looked at me with a modicum of disapproval.

"Sorry," I said. "Shutting up."

Addie resumed her conversation with Jacques.

"Why summon me?" she said.

"Because of who you are and what you are," said Jacques, seating himself to my left, across from Addie. "You are the one person I know who is truly committed to God. You are a good woman, Addie, and I say 'good' in the purest sense of the word. And in that goodness, I think you sensed something of my concern today. I'm fairly certain in my diagnosis, but require you–and Avery, too–to confirm it and hopefully help me reach a solution."

I didn't have a clue what Jacques was talking about, but Addie did.

"Yes," she said. "Apart from the smell near the lakes, I sensed something in the atmosphere, and thought it emanated from within him. I felt a . . . dichotomy . . . when I touched his hand. Care to explain?"

Jacques chewed on a carrot stick, thinking.

"I'll have to do so in greater detail than you're looking for," he said.

"That's okay," said Addie. "I'd like to know what's bothering you . . . what you think is happening out there. Has it been going on long?"

"For a while," said Jacques. "I might have let it run its course, but . . . there is my age. I didn't want to leave a problem like this untended. I felt I could wait no longer; the number of my days is diminishing. If the remaining number is low, then my action in beckoning you–you and Avery–is not precipitate. Had I not done so, I didn't know what consequences might result."

"Excuse me," I said, "but you've thoroughly lost me."

"What do you need to know?" asked Jacques.

"Well, for starters," I said, "what are you two talking about? What dichotomy?"

"In my father," said Jacques. "But it is rather involved. It will take a continuation of the tale I was telling you earlier."

"Why?" I said. "You mean World War Two has something to do with this dichotomy?"

"Oh, assuredly," he said.

"Then I take it . . . my father's involved in all of this," I said.

"In an indirect way, yes," said Jacques. "What has transpired clearly could not have done so without his contributions."

"You mean saving your life."

"That, yes . . . and Mussolini's."

"Mussolini has something to do with this?"

Jacques took his time formulating an answer.

"Let's just say . . . it would be best if you allowed me to continue."

I looked at Addie, who was passively waiting.

"What about her?" I said. "She hasn't heard the first part of your story."

"Correct," said Jacques. "So I trust you will bear with me if I recap briefly what I have told you. Then we can proceed."

I looked at Addie again, and she nodded approval.

"Okay, sure," I said. "Go ahead."

"Good," said Jacques. "Avery, turn on the recorder."

I did as he asked, and he began.

"All right, Addie. As I was telling Avery earlier, I was a special assignment soldier working as part of a unit called the Specter Squad . . ."

Jacques spoke for about 10 minutes, filling in the story as quickly and as sparingly as he thought he could before reaching the point where we had left off: the introductions between my father and Jacques after Dad had rescued him in the woods between Milan and Genoa, northern Italy. In the bushes nearby, Benito Mussolini was stirring, recovering from a knock to the head Jacques had given him to shut him up.

"We were still sitting there, Avery's Dad and I," said Jacques, "when Mussolini decided to join the party . . ."

TWENTY

Where To?

"We were still sitting there, Avery's Dad and I, when Mussolini decided to join the party. He came staggering out of the bushes like a bull elephant, bellowing.

"'What did you do that for?' he was yelling in that brusque Italian of his. 'Why did you hit me, you son of a bitch?'

"When he spotted Avery's dad–well, we'll simply call him Amo–Mussolini stopped suddenly, shoulders bunched up, head retracted.

"'Who are you?' he demanded.

"Amo simply looked at him, seemingly disinterested, although I suspect he was examining him rather closely.

"'I asked a question,' Mussolini said. He was clearly accustomed to getting answers when he asked.

"'Cool off, Duce,' I said to him. 'He's a friend. Saved our behinds after I cold-cocked you.'

"Mussolini spent but two more seconds gauging Amo, and then turned on me again.

"'Why did you do that?' he said again. 'I could have you shot for such behavior.'

"Amo snorted, and I smiled.

"'You better get used to a new order of things, my large companion,' I said, 'for you no longer have the clout. In fact, I think you should start thinking of us as the guys who are keeping you alive. Without us, you are literally nothing.'"

"'Nothing!'

"I motioned to our surroundings.

"'Nothing,' I said. 'If we choose to leave you here, I dare say you won't survive long. The best you might hope for is a quick death at the hands of some hungry predator. You sure don't want the partisans getting hold of you again.'

"I said this in a friendly enough fashion, but the words seemed to chill Mussolini. His eyes flickered around, checking the dark for possible attack.

"'Predators?' he asked. 'What predators?'

"'Well, wolves, bears, maybe big cats,' I said, getting up from my seat next to Amo. 'Or maybe the human variety. You might be interested in these fellows.'

"I took him by the elbow and led him to the areas where our attackers had been killed by Amo's grenades and my bullet. Seeing the corpses was easier now, for dawn was at hand and the first strands of daylight were filtering down through the trees. Next to each body was a pool of blood, easily identified by a reflective glint.

"'I think,' I said, 'that we might be able to use some of these clothes.'

"I eyeballed Mussolini and then the corpse of the largest of the bandits.

"'What are you suggesting?' Mussolini said. 'That I wear the clothing of a dead man? I shall never.'

"'Haven't you been a little cold?' I asked. 'These things look warmer than what you've got on.' He was still wearing the basics with which he had left the farmhouse–shirt, pants, suit jacket–and the poncho and cap I had provided him. His shoes were out somewhere in the clearing, where he had left them when we'd been attacked. The corpses had cold-weather gear, a must for a chilly April like that one.

"'I shall not wear the clothing of the dead,' he insisted, and turned back toward the clearing. 'And where are my shoes? You made me leave my shoes.' He added something else, but I couldn't make it out; he might have just been mumbling.

"'Suit yourself, you fat bastard,' I said softly, and rose to follow him. Then, thinking he might change his mind, I removed the boots and jacket from the largest corpse.

"When I got back to the clearing, Mussolini–his volume turned

down–was addressing Amo while scanning the area around them, presumably still looking for his footwear.

"'I thank you,' he was saying. 'You did well.'

"Amo looked up and raised his left eyebrow.

"'Yeah, I did,' he said, in Italian that was superior to mine. 'But it wasn't for you. I did it for my compadre here. I'd just as soon it was you they strung up in Milan.'

"Mussolini looked to me for an explanation.

"'What is he talking about?'

"'Everybody thinks you're dead, Duce,' I said. 'Somebody else—somebody who resembled you–took the fall for you and got stoned by your adoring masses. You are, for now, in the clear.'

"Mussolini waved toward the bodies in the bushes.

"'But if they knew . . .'

"'They didn't,' said Amo. 'Local bandits, is all. So stop flattering yourself. The universe no longer revolves around you.' Amo pushed himself up from the ground, grabbed his knapsack and shouldered his rifle and the weaponry he'd claimed from the bandits. 'What say we start moving?' he asked me. 'I didn't see any other roving gangs, but that doesn't mean we won't run into one.'

"'Where are we going?' Mussolini asked.

"'Well,' Amo said, 'right now, we're gonna head south. Eventually, we're gonna take a little pleasure cruise away from these friendly shores.'

"'Pleasure cruise?' Mussolini said.

"'Boat . . . water . . . away,' Amo answered.

"'Do not treat me like an imbecile,' Mussolini retorted. 'I meant, where are we going? I thought we were heading to Allied lines here in Italy.' He turned toward me. 'Isn't that what you told me?'

"I shrugged, and let Amo explain.

"'Yeah, well, seems like you're persona non grata all over the place, Duce,' said Amo. 'So we're taking a little side trip . . . to England.'

"'All the way by boat? It is a long trip.'

"'No. Part water, part land. Let's move out.'

"'Let's,' I said, and reached down to gather my equipment. After tightening my knapsack and securing my rifle–as well as the two I'd

taken from the bandits along with their handguns and grenades–I motioned to Mussolini to follow us.

"'I can't,' he said. 'I've lost my shoes.'

"I turned to Amo, a smile playing on my face; Duce's discomfort pleased me. 'He had his shoes off when the attack came,' I said. 'Dumped them around here somewhere.'

"I reached back down to the ground and picked up the boots I'd taken from the corpse.

"'Here,' I said. I tossed them to Mussolini, and then turned to follow Amo, who had already started walking.

"'Where did you get these?' Mussolini called after me.

"'Wear 'em or don't wear 'em,' I called back. 'I don't care.'

"Mussolini decided quickly. He tried to simultaneously walk and put on the boots, but fell with the effort, hitting the ground hard.

"'Wait, damn it,' he said. 'I am not ready.'

"We continued walking.

"'Wait!' he called again. 'Please.'

"It was the first polite word I'd heard from the man, and it had its desired effect. We stopped at the edge of the clearing, waited until he had donned and laced his new boots, and then–Mussolini bringing up the rear–started moving south, toward Genoa.

****

"Having Amo along was good in more ways than one. It not only gave me some companionship for once–I hardly considered Il Duce to be in that category–but also reduced the chance I'd be caught off guard again by any bandits or other roving units.

"I still couldn't understand how that had happened–how four guys could have approached without my knowing. They might have been exceedingly quiet–professional stealths, as it were–but I still should have detected them empathically. The power had never failed me so completely before.

"As we headed in the direction of Genoa, I had ample time to consider the matter, but could gain no insight whatsoever.

"'Ah, well,' I muttered to myself, deciding that perhaps I'd do best to stop worrying about what might have been a simple anomaly, and pay closer attention to my current surroundings. This was likely to be a perilous journey, and no time to be caught napping mentally again."

TWENTY-ONE

The Signal-Jammer

"Since full daylight was soon upon us, we stayed deep in the woods, which reduced our pace. But the speed of our journey didn't really matter, since we were under no deadline. My impression was that the American officials who had conceived the plan to grab Mussolini now rather regretted it, and were in no hurry to have to deal with him.

"Anyway, they'd given Amo no particular target date to reach England, which was a good thing considering the absence of any scheduled transportation on our itinerary. This would be an improvisational trip, and as such could take more than a little while.

"Well into that first day, about fifteen or sixteen hard miles after we'd left the clearing, we heard some metallic banging off to our left, beyond the tree line.

"'What's that?' Amo asked.

"'Beats me,' I said. 'You want to go look?'

"Amo thought a moment, then nodded.

"'Yeah, we better,' he said. 'It won't hurt to know what's going on around us.'

"'Okay,' I said, and turned and spoke to Mussolini. 'We're gonna go check out that noise. Just stay close, and don't let anyone see you. Remember . . . we're trying to help. You expose us and get caught by somebody else, then you'll likely get yourself strung up for real. Understand?'

"'Of course, I do,' he said. 'I am no fool.'

"'Yeah, well, that remains to be seen,' I said in English.

"We moved east then, to the edge of the tree line, and from there

discovered brush cover running most of the way across a field to a rise beyond. Again, we heard the metallic clanging; it was apparently coming from over that rise.

"'Maybe I better go check this out alone,' I said, thinking that if it was a trap set by more bandits or by partisans, we'd do well to split up. 'You see any trouble from here, whistle.'

"'Gotcha,' said Amo. 'Go to it.'

"Without further preamble, I entered the nearby brush–low-lying scrub–and, staying low, used it as much as possible to cover my approach up the hill. When I reached the rise, I lay flat and peered over it, down a gentle slope that flattened out about a hundred yards from me and stretched another hundred yards to a small building in the distance: a hangar. I was looking at a rural airfield.

"There were no aircraft in sight, but another metallic clang from the direction of the hangar suggested, at least, that there might be one inside being worked on. It didn't take a large leap of imagination to entertain the possibility of procuring the craft and using that to get us out of Italy and pointed toward England. My own flying skills were negligible, but I thought maybe Amo or Mussolini might manage. Anyway, it was worth a closer look; then I could report back with something substantive.

"Off to my left, just over the rise, was the beginning of a stand of trees that could take me around the northern end of the field, to within reconnoitering range of the building. The only open spaces were the thirty yards before the stand, and a gap of what looked like ten yards midway along it. If I was quick and stayed low, I figured no one would see me.

"Rising and sprinting to the tree stand, I paused to check on any possible trouble, saw none, and moved forward in the cover of the trees. At the next gap I waited a minute, decided it was safe, sprinted across to the trees on the far side, and resumed my approach.

"In that fashion, I reached a spot a mere twenty yards from the rear of the hangar. It was mostly open ground from there to the building; three large trees set in a line at five-yard intervals were the only offer of cover.

"I was debating whether to step out into that area of vulnerability, to get a closer look at the hangar, when my internal sensors suddenly snapped on. It was almost an overload, I was picking up so many signals.

"'What the hell?' I said. The signals were coming from inside the hangar. It was almost as if a platoon-sized contingent was sitting in there, and more than a little edgy. I knew it as surely as if it were being announced over a loudspeaker. With my survival instincts suddenly taking over–I was obviously not equipped to engage a sizable force of the enemy–I backed into the woods and turned to retrace my steps.

"But I hadn't gone a half-dozen paces when I heard the metallic clang again, and stopped. The internal signals were still strong, but something else was coming through now that I hadn't picked up at first: fear. And a sense of helplessness. Not exactly qualities to expect from a military unit. No . . . something was wrong in there. I had to check it out.

"Taking a deep breath, I raced out of the woods and up behind the first of the three trees in the clearing, and then around that one to the second tree. A moment later I reached the third, and all that stood between me and the building was ten feet.

"Straight ahead was nothing but wall, but down to the right about fifteen feet was a small window. I would have to chance a peek through that if I wanted an answer. Another clang convinced me. I covered the final distance and, without hesitation, leaned forward so that my right eye could see through the bottom left corner of the pane and into the building. It was dark in there compared to the daylight, though, and it took a few moments for my vision to adjust to the difference. It occurred to me rather vividly in those seconds that I couldn't stay in the window like that for long without inviting disaster.

"Finally, though, my eyesight adjusted, and I could see inside. And I knew instantly why the people inside were exuding fear.

"Instead of a plane in there, it was a group of gypsies, securely bound by ropes, lying on their sides on the ground. Several were tied together, back to back. All of them were gagged. I could see at least two looking at me, and could feel their pain. But even without my suddenly

operational power of empathy, the desperation these people were experiencing would have been unmistakable. These folks were not just being held prisoner, they were clearly fearful of a more frightening and final treatment.

"Considering the state of affairs in Italy–the roving partisans and bandits, the summary executions, the spasms of a country in upheaval–it was easy to conclude that these people were very possibly awaiting termination.

"I glanced about me to make sure of my safety, and then ventured a better view of the interior by placing my head squarely against the pane and peering through with both eyes. There were probably two dozen gypsies tied up in there, but no sign of anybody else. Whoever had trussed them was clearly gone for the moment, but expected back.

"And then another clang–nearly deafening from my spot at the window–startled me so much that I dove to the dirt. Fully expecting enemy footsteps to follow, I shouldered my rifle and swung it into position before realizing there was no sound now except for those I was making. I waited a few seconds, stood up again, and peeked back through the window, trying to locate the source of the sound; it was clear to me now that it was being generated by one of the prisoners within.

"I didn't see its source at first, but when I leaned far to the right and turned so my right cheek was against the glass, I secured a visual angle to the left that gave me my answer: one of the gypsies, tied up but not roped to anyone else, had gripped a metal pipe between his feet and was, with considerable difficulty, swinging it to his left and into the metallic wall. As I watched, he dropped the pipe, struggled to retrieve it, gripped it again between his boots, and swung.

"This time I was prepared. As the sound reverberated along the hangar's siding, it seemed to me more pathetic than alarming: the last gasp of a doomed man.

"But I quickly amended my judgment to acknowledge the courage in such an act–for certainly if the sound had attracted me, it might bring his captors back early to complete their grisly task

"I thought the problem out quickly–there was possibly no time to lose–and opted to take immediate action. Going back to get Amo would

take too long, and expose me again without good reason. No, I would have to help these people now.

"The large hangar doors were on the opposite side of the building, so I headed to my left, intending to open them. But as I rounded the first corner, I found a standard-sized hinged door and, trying it, found it unlocked. I entered the building and without pausing extracted my knife and started slicing at the ropes binding the gypsies–stopping first at the man with the pipe. As they were freed, the gypsies untied their own gags, nodded their appreciation and hurried out the door.

"Within a couple of minutes, almost all of them had exited the building. Three remained, an old man whose mobility was limited by a painful limp, and two men who were helping him walk. They stopped next to me near the door, and the old man spoke in an Italian dialect.

"'You have saved us,' he said.

"'Who was it?' I asked.

"'The Nazis,' he said. 'They promised to come back and kill us. But first they wished to gather a few more of their own–the rest of their unit, I suppose. One of them said he would not want to deprive them of their sport.'

"'Nazis still wandering around here?' I said. 'I thought they were making a beeline for the border.'

"'I know,' said the old man. 'But this is a renegade unit, and a very brutal one. If you see them, try to avoid them. They are easy to spot; they wear red armbands.'

"I had not heard of such an accouterment on any German uniform.

"'What does that signify?' I asked.

"'The blood of innocents, I should think,' said the old man. 'Now we must go. We are indebted. If ever we can repay the debt, we shall not hesitate to do so.'

"He started to move off, slowly, his weight supported by the men on either side of him. But then he held his right hand up, motioning another stop, and turned back toward me.

"'Here,' he said, and reached for a jeweled object at the end of a chain around his neck. He moved the object up past his face and then lifted the chain over his head, until it was free of him. Then he held the

chain out in his right hand, exhibiting the jewel. It was a clear pyramid-shaped crystal; even in the dim light of the building's interior, it was emanating a soft multi-colored hue.

"'What is this?' I asked.

"'I sense,' said the old man, 'that you are a person of unusual sensibilities. This will enhance those qualities, make you stronger in those areas of good that dominate your existence. It is called Il Cristallo di Morte.'

"Now, I had heard of such a crystal in my European travels–heard the myths–but I had never had occasion to see one.

"'The Crystal of Death,' I said in my own tongue, and then I added in Italian: 'I know of the myth. It is supposed to connect its wearer in a visual sense with the spirit world.'

"The old man was nodding.

"'Yes,' he said. 'This has that power for those who are worthy–and provides swift passage to the other side upon the advent of the wearer's death. For you, for your kindness, you deserve both considerations.'

"He then reached up and slid the crystal's chain over my head, and patted the jewel lightly as it came to rest on my breastbone.

"'Thank you,' I said, feeling a sudden earnestness. 'I shall treat it with the reverence it deserves.'

"The old man touched my cheek gently.

"'Be cautious, though,' he said. 'Guard it well. Do not let the unworthy touch it, especially at their death.'

I was not sure what he meant–was not familiar enough with the myth at that point–and so merely nodded my agreement. The old man then motioned to his two companions, and they led him through the door and across a clearing to the relative safety of the woods.

"I didn't want to wait for the red-banded Nazis myself, so I followed the gypsies out the door, rounded the corner of the hangar, hurried into the forest from which I'd emerged minutes earlier, and started retracing my steps.

"I could no longer hear the sounds of the gypsies making their getaway, for they were doing so in near-silence. But I could still sense their alarm, though muted from what it had been. As quickly as a

single step, though, I lost that connection, as though a wall had been thrown between us. I stopped, momentarily confused, and thought of the bandits who had descended upon me, and of my inability–even during their attack–to sense them empathically. A theory formed rapidly, and I acted upon it, stepping backward one pace, and then a second.

"As suddenly as I had lost the connection with the gypsies, it was there again. Another step forward, and I'd lost it again. A step backward once more, and it was reconnected.

"I shook my head in disbelief. This wasn't right. The signals were never governed by distance–not short distances, anyway. They could be good for miles, and never faulty within a few hundred yards. Here, there was a distance of perhaps two hundred feet separating me and the last of the gypsies.

"And then it struck me. How could I have not picked up on this before? If I was within a certain range of Mussolini, then my abilities were impaired. That had to be it.

"'Damn,' I muttered. 'I'm getting jammed by that bastard.'

"It was the best explanation I had, the one thing that made sense to me, for he was the only unsettling addition to my world that was present both while the bandits closed upon me and now, when the gypsies' signals were abruptly fading in and out. I guess I could have suspected Amo, as well; he had, after all, been in the general area before the bandits attacked, and was with Mussolini now. But I never even considered that a possibility; the moment I pinpointed the problem, I knew in my heart that the jamming had been taking place ever since Il Duce had regained his senses back at the orchard.

"I gauged the distance from the hangar to my companions. It must be an eighth of a mile. Well, there was one surefire solution to the problem, short of killing Mussolini. If I wanted to be at maximum defensive effectiveness, I was going to have to keep my distance from him.

****

"I hurried back to Amo, taking care to keep cover at all possible moments, and reported the news–the good about the gypsies, the bad about the Nazi redbands and about Mussolini's effect on my powers.

"'Jamming you?' said Amo. 'Wait a minute. The empathy thing, right?'

"'Right.'

"'Okay . . . let's assume for a minute that you really do have this . . . ability. How can it be jammed?'

"'I don't know,' I said. 'It's gotta be like he gives off a frequency that interferes with my reception.'

"'A frequency.'

"'Well, yeah, in layman's terms. I don't know what it is, really, because there's no scientific explanation for what it is I can do. I mean, empathy is a gift, you know? A God-given gift.'

"'God-given,' Amo repeated, and chuckled. 'Maybe that's the problem. Our friend here'–Mussolini was seated nearby, eyes closed and apparently napping–'is anything but God's product. Maybe his gift for mayhem is a gift from the devil.'

"I was stunned at the revelation. Amo meant it half in jest, of course, but it made perfect sense to me. I had, despite the violent nature of my war duties, become something of a believer in God. And as such, I had come to believe in the equal possibility of the devil. Clearly, people like Hitler and Mussolini were in league with the latter and not the former. So why shouldn't my incoming signals–a God-given gift–be working at cross-purposes with any that Mussolini might give out?

"'By golly,' I said, 'I think you're right.'

"'Oh, come on,' said Amo. 'I was just joking.'

"'No, I don't think you were,' I said. 'I mean, it's no joke to me. I happen to think you're onto something.'

"'So let me get this straight,' he said. 'As long as Mussolini is anywhere nearby, you're in more danger than normal?'

"'Oh, yeah, a lot more. If I don't get away from this bastard soon, he might quite literally be the death of me . . . of us.'

"Amo took a deep breath and let it out slowly.

"'I don't normally subscribe to this kind of theory,' he said. 'Religious, I

mean. But if you believe it, then . . . well . . . maybe we should split up, keep a distance. It probably can't hurt. How far away were you when you cleared the interference?'

"'An eighth of a mile.'

"'Okay,' said Amo, 'then I suggest we stay at least that far apart. Take parallel routes, and in that way watch each other's tail. What do you think?'

"'Yeah, I'd feel better doing that.'

"'Right. But let's leave now,' said Amo. 'I'd prefer a little distance between us and those Nazis. You go west of us. Okay?'

"'Yeah, okay. Give me about fifteen minutes to get set up on a parallel course. Then let's travel until dusk. I'll whistle once when I want to stop. You return it.'

"'Right,' said Amo. 'Just be careful.'

"'You too,' I said. 'Ciao.'"

TWENTY-TWO

The Crystal

Jacques paused. He was looking at Addie.

"I still have it, you know," he said.

"Of course," she said. "May I see it again?"

Jacques gently touched a chain around his neck; I hadn't noticed it before. Then, dipping the fingers of his right hand inside his open collar, he pulled on the chain until a jewel appeared at the end of it from beneath his shirt. He lifted chain and jewel–pendant–over his head and handed it across the table to Addie.

"It's just as beautiful as I remembered," she said, dangling it in front of her.

We all were staring at it: a clear pyramid-shaped crystal hanging from a golden chain. The crystal seemed to issue a soft light, pastel blue, then red, then green–but so subtle that I decided my eyes were playing tricks. It had to be the room light dancing through it.

"Yes," said Jacques. "But I wish now you hadn't returned it."

"Oh? Why?" said Addie.

"I am getting to that," said Jacques. "In due time."

"Okay," I said, "what's going on? You're saying this is the Crystal of Death, right?"

"Quite so," said Jacques.

"Uh huh," I said. "Okay, fine. But what do you mean it's as beautiful as ever, Addie? And what do you mean she returned it, Jacques? When did she have it?"

Addie answered without taking her eyes from the crystal.

"I had it for a long time," she said, "starting shortly after Gull Island."

"Gull?" I said. "In '56?"

Jacques cleared his throat.

"I gave it to her the day she left the Island that summer," he said.

"I don't recall that," I said.

"You wouldn't," said Jacques. "It was over in Cheboygan, after Addie and her family had left Bois Blanc. We had just docked, everybody was offloading, and I took her aside and gave her the necklace."

"It was sweet," Addie said, smiling at Jacques. Then she turned her eyes toward me.

"We had just docked," she said, "and I was about to step off with my parents and sister, when Jacques reached out and stopped me with a touch to my shoulder. I remember it so clearly . . ."

She paused, thinking.

"Addie," I prodded.

"Oh. Sorry," she said. "Well, he motioned me back into the passenger area, under the *Sylmar*'s canopy–out of sight of the rest of my family–and took my hand and placed the necklace in it. And he said: 'The truth is within this.' And I said, 'Truth about what?' And he said, 'About life . . . and death . . . and what is between. Wear it always, and you shall come to learn what has happened to you.'"

She paused, seemingly mesmerized by the jewel's refracted, dancing colors.

"And?" I asked.

"And," she said, and looked at me, "he was right. I put it on then and there, and for the next twenty years took it off only for sleep–its points are sharp, and hell to roll onto. But even then, while sleeping, I kept it within reach, under my pillow."

"Then you were wearing it . . . when you visited me at college," I said.

"Yes," she answered.

"But it didn't seem to be bringing you any peace. You seemed . . . unhappy," I said.

"I didn't say it made me happy," Addie said. "I said it taught me. And the learning process took time . . . years."

"Years," I echoed.

"Years," she repeated.

"And what did it teach?"

"Everything," she said. "It showed me . . . things . . . and in the showing pointed me on my life's path."

"Things," I said. "What kinds of things?"

Addie exchanged a look with Jacques, and he shrugged.

""It showed me . . . spirits," she said.

I studied her, trying to understand, and then looked to Jacques for assistance. None was forthcoming.

"Spirits," I repeated. "You mean like . . . what . . . ghosts?"

"Well," she said. "I wouldn't say ghosts. But . . . the afterlife."

"Uh huh," I said, trying not to judge, but finding myself fighting back a smile at the absurdity of it. I had been introduced to the basic concept in the letter Jacques had sent me about the bear and the gypsy. But that was, after all, just a myth–and a pretty far-fetched one, at that.

"And then what?" I asked. "You gave it back?"

"Yes."

"How? You mailed it?"

"No," Jacques interjected. "I'm afraid I appeared at her doorstep and requested its return."

Addie grimaced.

"I guess I should've returned it sooner," she said, "but . . ."

"No, no," said Jacques. "It was a gift without strings. It's just that . . . well, Avery, my wife was dying and I required the crystal for personal reasons. I'm afraid I imposed my friendship upon Addie. But she relinquished the pendant without complaint."

"Complaint?" she said. "How could I complain, considering your need? And after all it taught me?"

"But do you remember what I told you, Addie?" said Jacques. "That if ever we met again, I would return it to you?"

"Well, yes," said Addie, "but I didn't really expect . . ."

Jacques raised himself from his chair and rounded the table to Addie, took the necklace carefully from her grasp and placed it over her head.

"Are you sure, Jacques?" she said.

"I am," he said. "It belongs to no one, but should be worn by the worthy. You have always been that, Addie Winger."

"God bless," she said softly.

"I hope so," answered Jacques, returning to his chair.

I watched this exchange with some confusion, my predominant state during much of the Island visit. Jacques noticed my look.

"You seem perplexed," he said. "What don't you understand?"

"Well," I said, trying to distill my jumbled thoughts down to a few words, "if Addie has seen spirits, and you believe her, then I've got to assume that you've seen them, too."

"Yes," he answered. "I was going to get to that."

"And the logical extension," I added, "is that you're saying you know she died the night of Gull because you saw her spirit."

Jacques smiled.

"Always trying to leap ahead," he said. "So impatient. I could give you the fast answer, Avery, but I prefer to stay on course here."

"On course," I said. "Meaning?"

"Meaning it all goes back to what I was saying about Italy," he answered. "About your father, and Mussolini, and especially about the red-banded Nazis."

"More story," I said. "I should have guessed. Will we soon be getting to the point of all of this?"

"Absolutely. It shall not take much longer."

"Fine," I said. "Be my guest."

And he resumed his tale.

TWENTY-THREE

A Revelation

"As I said earlier, there were two instances in which I broke my own rule by helping locals. One was at the mass grave, when I gunned down the German executioners. And the second was, of course, when I freed the gypsies. Neither instance I regret; in fact, by saving the gypsies I may well have saved both Amo and myself. Let me explain by picking up the account at the point where I had split away from Amo and Mussolini . . . where I was out in the woods alone.

"Being on my own like that, separated from the two of them, brought me great relief. I felt I was once more in control of my destiny. I started picking up little woodland signals that I'd known for years but had, I now realized, been missing of late–first because of assignments that had put me in inhabited territories with woods nowhere in sight, and now, on this assignment, because of the effect Mussolini had been having on my sensory system.

"But now I could detect the fear of animals who either ran or, in some cases, dug in for a fight upon my approach; the serenity of birds high enough and camouflaged enough to know I could do them no harm; the soft hum of plants awakening to the spring.

"All of these signals, all of these living things, were like salve to my psyche. They relaxed me, put me in a comfort zone.

"And so I moved south, away from Milan, toward the coast, staying well into the woods, in the shadows. I was once again non-existent, or as close to it as possible. Of course, Mussolini knew of me, and so did Amo and his superiors. But that all seemed of little importance out in the wild.

"We were perhaps two days of leisurely travel away from the coast,

so the journey promised to be of great therapeutic benefit. By the time we reached water and located a boat, I would be well-primed for the next phase of my altered assignment: the sea and then land travel north across France to the English Channel. It would actually be good to get up there to England, cold and dreary as it might be compared to Italy, for the compensation would be in the form of little danger and no violence. Italy's social structure was like a great spinning top, careening about and crashing into all sorts of objects, be they human or otherwise. It was an unstable and unsafe environment. England would be a welcome contrast.

"Alas, the spinning top touched us once again before we had finished out that day. It was late afternoon, with the sun setting and the chill of evening already starting to descend. I had stayed within a reasonable distance of Amo and Mussolini, sometimes barely within sight but more often merely detecting them empathically, that ability having been restored with the distance between us.

"We had just traversed a sparse stand of firs and entered a thick and heavily shaded section of maples, oaks and pines when I picked up more than just the life forms of those two men. Someone–some group–was out there too. It was a blip on my internal radar at first, but then it was on my screen like a gang of angry insects–a gang that was buzzing in from the north and east on an unsuspecting Amo and Mussolini. I couldn't be sure of the identity of this group, but I was of the definite opinion that it might be the redbands.

"I immediately let out a whistle, but my mouth was dry and it came out feebly. Wetting my lips with my tongue, I tried again and failed again, but on a third effort cut loose with an ear-splitting alarm. An answering whistle came back a few moments later, and then nothing. I waited, trying to feel what was going on, and detected nothing different. Amo and Mussolini were still unperturbed, and the angry swarm of trouble had nearly reached them.

"'Damn!' I said, realizing the mistake. The whistle had been our signal for stopping. If either Amo or I whistled, both of us would stop for the night; that way, we'd stay within range of one another. We hadn't made provision for a trouble signal.

"This time, I cut loose with two whistles, and followed that with an owl cry. I didn't know what else to do, short of firing off my weapon, which I was afraid might stir up trouble more quickly and, worse, bring it toward me. I couldn't send any sort of telepathic suggestion, either, since I hadn't developed that particular ability yet.

"I received an identical whistle/cry combination in return, and then a sense of determination–no doubt Amo–and fear (Mussolini), and was satisfied that the alert had worked. Now it was up to me to help them. I could not very well do it from an eighth of a mile away, so I headed in their direction–sensory jamming or not. I moved cautiously at first, keeping under cover as much as possible and gliding as silently as my hunting skills allowed.

"I was about halfway there when I heard the first gunshots, and then some louder sounds that I took to be grenades, though there was no way to tell who was heaving them at whom. I picked up the pace a little, daring to expose myself in small clearings, deciding that the attackers were focused now on the quarry at hand and paying scant or no attention to the area outside their attack perimeter.

"With the element of surprise adding weight to my resume, I decided I had the advantage going in, or as much of an edge as one man can have against what could be a small platoon.

"I was carrying a few grenades hung from my belt, and had two of them in my hands as I swept in on the enemy. I could see, as I came charging up behind a couple of them, that they were wearing red armbands, and decided that they had probably picked up our trail back near the hangar. No doubt they were agitated by the loss of their gypsy playthings, and were taking it out on us.

"I was on the first two before they knew it, pulling the pin from one grenade and dropping it at their feet as I raced by on my way to the next target–a trio some twenty-five yards beyond, concealed by foliage but whose firearm sparks were clearly visible. I dodged behind some trees just as the grenade went off and the two Nazis let out short-lived screams. I didn't hesitate to check their condition, battlefield concerns taking precedence, and pulled the pin on the second grenade just after the first exploded. The trio ahead of me was pivoting in my direction–drawn

there by the blast–as I burst through the foliage and repeated the procedure I had used on the first two men. Before they could react, I was gone and the grenade shards were ripping into their flesh. This time I paused, leaning against a shielding tree, getting my bearings, trying to hear where the remaining Nazis were. I couldn't sense them–the Mussolini jamming had taken effect long since–but could hear their weapons; or more precisely all of the remaining weapons concentrated in a small area. Judging from the reports–and assuming Amo had not given Mussolini a weapon–there were perhaps five rifles firing: four against one. No . . . I adjusted that to three against one when I heard a scream and sensed a slight reduction in the shooting. Amo had gotten one of them, I was sure. It wasn't his scream, because the fight was still going on.

Before moving ahead, I peered back around the tree at the carnage I had just created on its other side. Three bodies were there, all right, but something else I hadn't counted on; something I'd sensed in animals I had killed but now, for the first time, could see as clearly as if the bodies themselves were rising.

Misty renditions of the newly departed–whole versions of the decimated meat at their feet–were rising from the bodies, horizontal at first, but then straightening as they would if climbing to their feet. Only they had no feet; instead, a vague shapelessness formed their base, a mist-like V-shape that was nearly transparent.

Mesmerized at first, I forced myself to turn my attention back to the living; if I didn't, my body might end up like those on the ground. I ventured one last look–the mists were moving away, into the gathering darkness of the forest–and then shifted my focus to the three remaining problems, the three remaining redbanded Nazis. They were up ahead still; I could tell from the gunfire that they hadn't moved.

I couldn't tell what condition my comrades might be in, but knew they were both alive: Amo was still firing a weapon, and I now heard a steady stream of Italian swear words. It had to be Mussolini, since he was the only Italian present; and it sounded like he was both angry and in pain. He had evidently sustained a wound, but whether by bullet or from one of the grenades I had heard at the outset, I couldn't determine.

I considered employing grenades in my assault, for I had two remaining, but could see that the dense nature of the brush and trees ahead precluded their effective use. And I considered using my gun. But I opted to tackle the first of the three Nazis silently. I had the feeling that the other two might, if given a sound bearing caused by gunshots, turn their weapons in my direction with some effect.

Crouching low, I slid through an opening in some nearby bushes and came upon my prey almost instantly; he was but a few feet away and didn't see me, my entrance coming from behind his left shoulder. Pulling a garroting cord from a pouch at my belt, I pounced on him, bringing the cord over his head and around his neck before he knew I was there. A sudden yank back took him off his feet, and his rifle, aimed a moment before at my allies, was hurtling several feet away, a useless piece of metal now. Holding him down from behind with a scissors leg-lock, I increased pressure with the cord until he stopped squirming, and then grabbing hold of his neck, snapped it to the left, making sure of the kill.

"And that was my first experience at close range with that strange mist rising from the dead. I was still holding the corpse, unclenching my legs and rolling it off of me, when the fog-like shape rose from the body and passed right around my head on the way up to a vertical position. I didn't feel anything, or smell anything, but had a sense of being enveloped very briefly as if by a cloud. And then the figure, like the others, wafted off into the woods, into the darkness.

"I watched it go while still sitting on the ground, and thus lost my edge. Before I could regain my bearings, one of the last two redbands had found me and was leaping through the air, knife unsheathed and extended. I caught the movement just as I turned away from the disappearing spirit, and managed to barely twist out of range of the blade, which struck the dirt next to my ribcage.

"We were both on the ground, him on top and still in control of the knife, and me grabbing his knife arm and trying to hold it at bay until I could regain the advantage. But he was strong, and the blade was inexorably moving downward, on a track toward my upper stomach. And it was a big blade, akin in size to the famed Bowie knife, but with

serrations along its top edge. If it went in, I would be incapacitated; if it came back out at an angle, I would be gutted.

"There was little going through my mind–certainly no life-meaning revelations–as the knife descended, except for a frantic assessment of a way out. I tried a knee to the man's groin, but was positioned wrong and struck his thigh; I tried rolling, but was too tightly pinned; I considered biting, but couldn't reach any portion of his body with my mouth. It was, I decided, going to be a very bad day.

"But no sooner had I thought it then the tide turned, the knife moving slowly away from my belly and the weight of the man's body gradually diminishing. I couldn't tell at first–his body obscured what was beyond him–but we had been joined by a third party who had grabbed the man's hair and knife arm and was pulling backward, twisting the attacker away from me. Amo had arrived again in the nick of time.

"As the Nazi was lifted away, I rolled free and–trying to regain my breath–watched as Amo shifted weight and applied a wrestling hold, curling his arms beneath the man's armpits and upward until his hands locked behind the man's head. The right arm of my former attacker was now immobilized, the knife extending aimlessly outward.

"'Christ, Amo,' I said, 'why didn't you just stab him?'

"'Couldn't,' he answered, struggling. 'Dropped my knife in the bushes.'

"'Well, you could have shot him, then,' I said, climbing to my feet.

"'Out of bullets,' he answered.

"'Well, I'm not,' I said, pulling my weapon and putting the barrel to the man's temple.

"'No!' hissed Amo. 'It might hit bone and ricochet into me. Besides, the other guy . . .'

"'Right,' I said. The remaining Nazi was still out there, in what I now realized was a silent forest. A single gunshot would certainly attract him; he might even be on his way toward us, looking for a sound to guide him.

"Re-holstering the weapon, I grabbed the man's extended arm, and dug my fingernails into his wrist until the pain forced him to drop the

knife into my hand. I caught it by the blade and was about to flip it over with the intention of thrusting it forward into his neck, when I spotted a dark figure with a red band pushing aside the branches of brush straight ahead, maybe twenty feet away. Drawing the knife back quickly, I unleashed it with an abrupt wrist flip, and sent it hurtling across the distance between us. It was not a well-aimed throw, but the man was just shifting his weight to draw a bead on us with his rifle, and twisted his head slightly left and into the knife's path.

"His death was nearly instantaneous. The blade buried itself halfway to its hilt in his left eye socket; a deeper penetration was prevented only by the thickness of his socket bone as the blade bit into it. With the handle end of the knife protruding from his eye, the man's body did a slow upward dance and poised, half-standing and half-crouched, and slowly fell forward.

"Without waiting any longer, I brought my knee up into the groin of the Nazi immobilized by the wrestling hold, and he sagged with the pain, dropping free of Amo's grip and sliding toward the ground. He had no sooner collapsed than I launched myself upward and came down on his neck with my knee, bent at the joint, the full force of my weight behind it. It crushed his larynx and probably a few bones, and left him writhing. Drawing my pistol again, I leaned over and pressed the barrel into his mouth and fired.

"Amo and I looked at each other in the silence that followed. We were both spent, and simply shook our heads at the lunacy of what had just happened.

"As my breath gradually returned to me, my attention was diverted by the mists rising from the two new corpses, and I watched them as they gained a vertical attitude and, like their predecessors, drifted off into the darkness.

"Amo was watching me watch them, but he couldn't see what I saw.

"'What is it?' he said softly. 'More Nazis?'

"'No,' I answered. 'They're all gone.'

****

"Mussolini, as it turned out, had caught a piece of shrapnel in the same arm that had been winged by the partisans in the execution attempt at the roadside orchard. The piece was easily removed, though, and we disinfected the wound and wrapped it tight to keep the dirt out.

"Then we settled in for a rest.

"'Sure you don't want to keep a distance?' Amo asked. 'Or isn't he jamming you any more?'

"'Oh, he's jamming me,' I said. 'But look what trouble you found when he wasn't. Just do me a favor; keep your own senses on the alert, and let me get a little shuteye. We can split up again tomorrow.'

"I sat there a moment, thinking of sleep and of the day and of the misty remains of the Nazis–wondering if my mind or the light had been playing tricks–and absentmindedly toyed with the pendant given me by the old gypsy. Mussolini, seated nearby, saw my motion and moved in for a closer look.

"'That looks like Il Cristallo di Morte,' he said. 'Where did you get this?'

"'An old gypsy, back at that hangar. And yes, that's what it's supposed to be.'

"In truth, I hadn't connected the pendant with what I had seen on the battlefield until that moment; the heat of battle obscured the obvious, I guess. But if those mists were spirits and not just my imagination, then the old gypsy had been right: The crystal had given me the ability to see an aspect of the spirit world, the departure of souls from bodies. And its power outweighed any negative influence Mussolini had; he might jam my senses, but not the images generated by the crystal.

"Mussolini reached out and touched the crystal, and it started shining and vibrating–was hot, in fact, and thus uncomfortable on my breastbone. So I swatted his hand aside.

"'Mitts off, Duce,' I said.

"'It is the first one I have seen, except in pictures,' he said. 'You are aware of the stories surrounding it? Of its origin? The myths of the aliens and the bear?'

"'Yeah,' I said, holding it out in front of me to study it closer. Its light had disappeared, but it was still warm to the touch. 'I've heard of them.'

"'You realize,' said Mussolini, 'the myth says if a person who possesses the crystal is in tune with the natural order of things, he can see what others may not. Into the spirit world.'

"Well, I thought, he had that much right.

"'So you believe that stuff?' I asked.

"'Not really,' he said. 'But there are many who do, who would probably give their firstborn for the right to own it. You are very fortunate. Very few exist.'

"'Just how many are there?' I asked.

"'They are nearly as rare as the hair on my head,' he answered. 'It is said the elders of the camps give them only as measures of extreme gratitude. I tell you what. I will give you great fortune for that crystal, my friend. Great power.'

"I scoffed.

"'Right, Duce, like I'd entrust this to the hands of a dog like you, even if you could afford it.'

"I glanced over at Amo, who had been watching with an amused expression. He rolled his eyes at me, and I smiled.

"'Well, you think about it,' Mussolini was saying. 'I have hidden riches. I can truly pay you well for it.'

"'Forget it, Duce,' I said. I turned away and lay down, leaving Mussolini no doubt miffed, and me wondering if I'd have to watch my backside. If he really wanted the crystal badly enough, he might try something–even though Amo and I were his only protection against dangers natural and man-made out there. But sometimes greed outweighs common sense . . .

"Well, I told myself, I would be careful. At the very least–especially in light of the cautionary note from the old gypsy–I would make sure Mussolini didn't so much as touch the stone again.

"Or so I thought.

****

"In that heightened state of alert, I couldn't sleep. The adrenalin was pumping entirely too quickly.

"Images of departing spirits danced in my mind, visions that offered an altered perspective of the meaning of my life and life in general.

"'What are you thinking?' Amo asked. 'You're not sleeping.'

"'No,' I said. 'I'm too revved up.'

"'Yeah, a lot of excitement,' he said.

"'You could say that,' I answered. I sat up and looked over toward Mussolini. He was dozing.

"'Kind of hard to defend a prick like that,' Amo said.

"'Yes, it is,' I agreed. 'But it wasn't too tough against those redbands. Nasty people . . .'

"In the quiet that followed, we listened to the chirping of some crickets that had regained ownership of the battleground.

"'Where you from, anyway?' Amo asked. 'What state?'

"We had exchanged names, but no background . . . no history . . . no geography. I pondered this new question, weighing the wisdom of an answer versus the need for secrecy, and reached the same conclusion I had reached in telling him my name.

"'I'm from Michigan,' I said. 'You?'

"'New York State. A little town called Auburn. My father was born there, and so was I. Before that, the family came from Germany, of all places.' He looked out to the woods behind me, to the killing field laden with bodies of dead Germans. 'What's your hometown?'

"'Not a town,' I said. 'It's an Island up in the northern part of the state. Kind of primitive. No electricity, no running water, no indoor bathrooms. It's called Bois Blanc.'

"'White Woods?'

"'Yeah,' I said. 'A lot of birch trees. Some pine, too. They call the main community Pointe aux Pins. Point of Pines.'

"'Sounds like a nice place to get away from things,' Amo said. 'A lot of people?'

"'No, not at all, most seasons,' I said. 'More in the summer. There are quite a few cottages now–some built by rich folks. But they all have a rustic charm.'

"'Sounds nice,' said Amo. 'Maybe I'll get there some day. Hard to reach?'

"'Nah,' I said. 'It's in the Straits of Mackinac, across from a port called Cheboygan. There's no major road to Cheboygan, but it's on the map and easy to find. Then just catch a boat across. There's been sporadic ferry service, but before I left I heard talk of more daily runs. So that shouldn't be much of a problem. Really, after the war, you oughta come out. I'll be there, show you around. It's great hunting and fishing.'

"'Well, tell you the truth,' Amo said, 'if I get out of this war, I don't think I'm ever gonna want to look at another gun again, let alone fire one. You know? But I must say, the fishing sounds nice.'

"'Consider it an invitation,' I said."

TWENTY-FOUR

Flawed Memories

"That doesn't mesh at all with what I was told," I said to Jacques. He was still seated on my left at the card table. Addie was to my right. The tape recorder, still running, was nearer Jacques than me.

"Mesh?" he said. "I don't understand. I thought this was all new to you."

"It is. It's just . . . my folks said they first came here in 1952 at the urging of some friends from back East–the Ballards. We had just moved to Michigan–a new job for Dad–and the Ballards stopped by on their drive out here from New York. Talked my folks into visiting the Island, and then . . . well, we started coming each year, for several years. But my folks didn't say anything about an invitation from you."

Jacques shook his head.

"Let me get this straight," he said. "I have told you a great many unsettling things about your father that you did not know, and you are concerned about the genesis of your summers here?"

I smiled, amused at the truth of the insight.

"Yeah. Sounds stupid, huh?"

"No," Addie interjected softly. "It's not stupid. You're probably a bit overwhelmed with what you've learned, and are just grasping for something familiar. Family history can be like a life preserver."

I considered her, and–relieved that she was siding with me on this point–decided she was half right. Family history unsullied is the expected norm; a dependable constant; the life preserver she mentioned. But family history upended can provoke disorientation of the first order, and was beginning to feel like a cement albatross.

"Well," said Jacques, "in point of fact, your memory–or the information that provided that memory–is not truly flawed, Avery. Your family's first vacation here was indeed in 1952. It's just that your father was here long before that. He encountered the Ballards while on one such visit; they had not, to my knowledge, known each other before that. I suspect that the Ballards–in stopping by, as you say, at your home–were merely responding to an invitation from your Dad, and in the process touting the benefits of an Island summer to your mother. Arno, after all, really liked it up here."

"Whoa, back up. You mean my father was here before '52? When?"

"Oh, several times."

"Now, see, I didn't know that. Why wouldn't I know that?"

"Avery," Jacques said kindly. "I don't think this particular matter should be of great concern–I mean, it could just be that you misunderstood as a child, and have carried that misconception since. His coming here was not exactly a secret."

I nodded. He was right. Maybe it was my own mistake. But it bothered me, nonetheless. There seemed to be so much of my father that I had not known. And now he was gone.

"What did he do up here?" I asked. "Did you guys do that fishing you were talking about?"

"No," said Jacques. "It turns out he didn't like that any more than hunting. Anything that smacked of outdoor living was anathema. He'd had too much of that in Europe."

"He didn't like doing things that reminded him of the war, then," I ventured.

"Oh, I wouldn't say that," Jacques answered. "Actually, every time he came up here, he was reminded of the war."

"Because of you," I offered.

"That, yes, but more," Jacques said.

"Such as?"

"Well, I'm getting to that with my account of Italy. If you'll be patient . . ."

I held my hands up in surrender.

"Of course," I said. "More Italy. Why not? Go on."

"Thank you. Where was I?"

"You'd just invited Amo to the Island," said Addie.

"Right. We were resting after dispatching the redbands, and the matter of hometowns had come up. Okay, then. I got a little sleep after that . . ."

TWENTY-FIVE

To The Coast . . . And Beyond

"I got a little sleep after that, and was awakened at first light when Amo nudged me.

"'We should go,' he said. 'We still have more than a day to the coast, and then must try to find transport.'

"'Yeah, I've been thinking about that,' I said. 'Why didn't your superiors line up some passage for us? Fly us out or have a boat waiting?'

"'Secrecy,' he said. 'They decided they wanted literally no one to see this guy alive. If we took him in to catch a flight, someone would see him–pilot, airmen, somebody. And if they lined up a boat, there would still be that problem, plus it might be too open–too easily compromised by other craft in the area, or by some possible witness on shore. Either way, too risky. No . . . they want us to try and do it without garnering any attention–on our own schedule, in our own good time. Secrecy is, after all, what we're good at–that and thinking on our feet. Anyway, we just have to keep things quiet until we get him to England.'

"'And then?'

"Amo shrugged.

"'Then it's none of our concern. But I'm guessing that now, with him supposedly dead, they might keep him on ice for a while, hidden away until things settle a little. Well . . . shall we move out?'

"'Might as well,' I said, rising. I looked over toward Mussolini. He was still sleeping. 'Hey, Duce,' I said, striding over to his bedding and giving him a kick in the rear. 'Time to go.'

"Mussolini tried to raise himself, but put his weight on his bandaged arm and winced.

"'Son of a bitch,' he muttered in Italian. 'Son of a bitch.'

"'Yeah, yeah,' I said, sliding into his language. 'Suck it up, tough guy, and let's get moving.'

"He gave me what I took to be a threatening look, but without the weight of office or an army behind him, it came out merely petulant.

"'Kind of pathetic,' I said in English to Amo.

"'What is?'

"'This guy was supposed to be one mean mother. Now . . .'

"'Doesn't seem like much, does he?' Amo asked.

"'No, he doesn't,' I said.

"'Yeah, well, don't let looks fool you, my friend. This is not a nice person. I have a feeling that were circumstances as they used to be for him, he'd have your gonads for supper.'

"'Bully of the playground,' I said.

"'Yes,' said Amo. 'But not all bullies confine themselves to the playground. Some are just pure mean wherever they go.'

****

"We traveled nearly all day and well into the night, staying as usual in the woods wherever possible, sliding quickly across a couple of open meadows when we had to, resting for scant minutes at two-hour intervals. We were making good time–and were within hours of our destination when we stopped to camp for the night.

"But no sooner had we spread our bedding and settled in than Amo decided it would be better to push on.

"'Let's not sleep,' he said. 'We leave now, we can actually get to the coast before daylight. It would be easier and safer to commandeer a craft under moonlight than sunlight.'

"'Why not stay the night, finish the trek tomorrow and then wait for nightfall?' I asked. 'That way, we'll be rested. Keep pushing, and we'll be exhausted before we even hit open water, and that's not likely to be any picnic.'

"Amo was shaking his head vigorously.

"'No,' he said. 'I'd feel better if we got this done sooner.'

"'Why?' I asked. 'What's the rush? We're not operating on any timetable.'

"Amo was looking around nervously. Mussolini, though not understanding the words, had been put on edge by Amo's attitude, and was sitting upright, head pivoting, taking in the surroundings. For my part, I heard and saw nothing, but then . . . I didn't expect to with Mussolini so close.

"'I don't know what it is,' Amo said. 'It's a feeling. Like . . . if we don't get through this next part quickly, it could go sour.'

"'Sour,' I repeated. 'Sour, how? Like another renegade Nazi unit? I doubt we'll find one this far down-country. And the Italian partisans are concentrating on the border region.'

"'I don't know how,' he said. 'But there's something . . .'

"Mussolini and I exchanged a look, and I motioned toward the south. Without prodding, he bounced to his feet and gathered what little he was carrying and was ready to move.

"'I don't think he likes Italy much anymore,' I said. 'Seems awful anxious to leave it.'

"'Yeah, well, he's not alone,' said Amo. 'Now would be none too soon, and I don't have the world hating me like he does.'

"'The world doesn't hate him,' I said. 'He's dead, remember?'

"'Dead or not,' said Amo, 'the world's gonna hate this guy forever. Poison, unlike wine, does not improve with age.'

"I looked over toward Mussolini, who was waiting at the edge of the clearing. He was shifting from left foot to right and back again, impatient to start.

"'Okay,' I said to Amo. 'Let's go. Old hemlock over there is getting antsy.'

"And with that, we were on our way in the dark without another word.

****

"We reached the coast of the Ligurian Sea–or more specifically the tree line a hundred rocky feet above it–about an hour before daybreak. To

the south a mile or so lay the outskirts of Genoa, placid in the moonlight; between Genoa and our position stood the docks. We could get to the shore directly by descending the steep rocky face before us, or stick to the high ground–and the woods–and approach it in a roundabout, gently sloped fashion that would take us along the town's northern border.

"'Let's keep cover,' I said. 'It's a much easier route.'

"'It'll take longer that way,' said Amo. 'Besides, we lose cover near the city's edge, and could be spotted before we reach the docks.'

"'This place was falling to the Allies two weeks ago,' I said. 'I'm sure our people control it.'

"'Doesn't matter,' said Amo. 'We can't let our cargo be seen by anyone. He's dead. Remember our orders? If we climb down here and make our approach along the beach, we can steer clear of town and grab a boat before sunup.'

"'How about we keep cover for half the distance, and then descend?' I suggested.

"Amo shook his head.

"'Good idea, except the cliff looks even steeper–and I think higher–for the next half-mile. Besides, the closer we get to town, the more chance of discovery. Let's just go here.'

"Amo was right; the daunting descent had momentarily wrested common sense from me. I didn't relish the thought of what amounted in some spots–sixty-degree and greater angles–to mountain climbing. But if we could avoid discovery, we could avoid unnecessary trouble. So I didn't argue further.

"Before starting, I scanned the scene below us. In the moonlight, I could see several small craft moored out in the Ligurian waters. Those we would bypass, since we'd first need to grab a dinghy to reach them, leaving ourselves vulnerable should anybody be sleeping aboard one and, waking, see our approach.

"Down the coast, nearer Genoa but a fairly safe distance from any dwellings, lay the first of the docks, with dozens of fishing boats moored at them. Grabbing one of those boats would be infinitely easier. And so, with that basic plan in mind, we set foot out onto the hardscrabble path that led to the first sharp decline.

****

"The descent went off without a hitch or a scratch, much to my relief. When we reached the beach, everything looked good. There was no evidence of any activity anywhere ahead, though I rather expected that some of the local fishermen would be arising soon to start their workday. Of course, war being war, there would likely be no young men in their ranks; the youngest adults had long since been conscripted and were either dead or still out in the hills. No, this group would be women and old men, which was not exactly a serious impediment.

"The walk to the docks went quickly–we double-paced, although Mussolini had some trouble keeping up–and we slowed only when we reached the first of them, one that served as mooring for three boats. Two of the boats were similar in size and shape–about twenty-five feet long with nets and poles and other equipment hanging from hooks alongside their raised pilot housings. Both boats were powered by inboard engines. The third was a sailboat, exactly what we needed in the still of the wee hours: something as quiet as the morning.

"'Think there's anyone on board?' Amo asked in a whisper.

"'Doubt it,' I said. 'If they bothered to dock, they've probably got a warm home to go to up in the hills or in the city. But one way to find out.'

"The three of us strode out onto the wooden planking casually, as though belonging–though in retrospect I don't think any resident of the area who might've stumbled upon us would have accepted us as such.

"Somehow, despite my words to Amo, I expected trouble of one sort or another in this part of the operation. At the top of my list of possibilities was the obvious: a disagreeable boat owner who might, in fact, have stayed aboard or who might show up momentarily . . . although renegade soldiers or local gendarmes also came to mind. But none of that happened. We simply boarded the boat, made sure nobody was aboard, hoisted the jib and floated away from the dock, lifting the mainsail out on the dark waters.

"As we sailed away, there was no interference, no difficulty, nothing. We soon traveled far enough to be out of sight of anybody on land, and the first rays of the new day peeked above the shoreline we were

leaving behind. It looked like the journey to the south of France would be a simpler matter than we had a right to hope for.

"That–as seems to be the way when things are going too smoothly–was when all hell broke loose.

****

"The clear azure sky of morning lent no hint of atmospheric difficulties, and so the storm–a vicious little localized maelstrom–hit us almost before we saw it.

"'Hold on!' Amo yelled from the helm, the first hint I had that anything was wrong. I was below deck with Mussolini, dressing his wound. Forgoing that task, I quickly climbed topside, and was met with a nasty blast of wind and spray, the precursor to a dark cloud that enveloped us and started heaving the boat about, pitching it sideways one way and then another. Then the waves seemed to grow in an instant, from peaceful swells to raging walls, and the boat's sideway lurches began alternating with deep forward dives and equally frightening ascensions. It was like a carnival ride gone amok.

"'It came out of nowhere!' Amo shouted, as I sprang to lower the mainsail. The jib, being smaller, would be no trouble, I reasoned, and might help Amo turn the boat into the wind, if the wind would only stop its violent shifts and give him a point to aim for. But the mainsail, if filled with the power of these winds, could push us right over. It had to be lowered quickly. I freed the line securing it and let the canvas drop, and almost instantly regretted it. It slid down the mast quickly, whipping in the wind, and a portion of it smacked me in the head, momentarily stunning me. In the few moments it took me to regain my senses, the sound of the wind and the sea reached a deafening level, and the amount of water we were taking on from sky and sea made footing treacherously slick. Conversation was useless, but Amo was shouting, anyway, venting his frustration as he worked the rudder, as he tried to maneuver the boat into the wind. 'I can't control the damn boat! It's like it came right for us! Out of goddamn nowhere! It's coming from every direction!' he yelled.

"I felt something bump my elbow, and turned to see Mussolini there. He had just staggered up from below, was instantly drenched, and looked ghost-white as the rain cascaded down his bald pate.

"'Turn it into the wind!' he yelled into my ear in Italian. 'Tell him to turn it into the wind. That will help stabilize it.'

"'Can't!' I shouted back. 'The wind is swirling. It has no single direction!'

"'Do something, damn it!' he yelled in return.

"But there was nothing to do except hold on tight to the nearest railing or permanent fixture. And even that was of little use in another minute, for a huge swell lifted us high and leaning to starboard, and a hurricane-like blast sent us the rest of the way over. Lowering the sail had not prevented what I feared most: capsizing.

"I can attest that there is no time for introspection or conscious analysis when your body is hurtling through space and then being consumed by massive amounts of churning water. For that is what happened to all three of us; we all let go of our tenuous holds rather than be trapped underneath a boat that was being rolled and tossed about like so much tumbleweed.

"Once in the water, that is when you start to think–start trying to figure out which way is up, and how to get there before your air supply is depleted. It really is, in those circumstances, a matter of scant seconds before a wrong decision becomes a fatal one. Or, in the case of Mussolini, scant seconds before he tried to take me down with him.

"He was a very poor swimmer–not to mention overweight and out of shape and probably older than his years. The last couple of weeks alone had probably taken a toll, what with his being run out of his puppet throne, arrested, shot and generally maligned–all the while knowing he'd picked the wrong ally for the wrong war at the wrong time. He was, in the modern vernacular, going down one way or another.

"He had landed in the water near me, and we had both managed to thrash our way to the surface within a dozen feet of each other. I couldn't see where Amo was, but was more concerned with keeping myself afloat at that point than with the welfare of anyone else. Accordingly, I had stripped off my jacket and was trying to remove my boots;

those items of clothing made it very difficult to float and impossible to tread water.

"Amid that struggle, with one boot jettisoned and the other unlaced, I suddenly had an extra burden climb aboard: Mussolini, panicking, had managed to reach me and throw his arms around my neck, trying to get a piggy-back ride. That was the last thing I needed, for it instantly put me back underwater. Twisting to my right, I thrust an elbow into his midsection, which loosened his grip. Then–facing him now–I placed both hands on his chest and pushed his body away.

"But as I did that, he grabbed out in desperation, grabbed for something to hold fast to, and got his fingers twined in the necklace the gypsy had given me, twined in that portion of the chain that ended with the pyramid-shaped crystal. He held fast, fighting my efforts to extricate myself–something I had to do, since he was sinking and taking me down with him. I tried to move back up with him in tow, but the combination of his weight, his gyrations and the swirling currents were too much. We were both about to drown.

"I don't know where I got the breath, but I think it came from acquiescence. Unable to escape Mussolini, I simply relaxed, sinking downward with him, and thus retained oxygen at the same time that he was expending his. And so it was that he gasped for breath and took in water instead, the salt water of the Ligurian Sea, and went into a seizure, and stopped moving, and ever-so-slowly loosed his grip on the necklace and the crystal, and sank slowly into the dark regions below. Free of his weight, I removed my one remaining boot, and kicking with all of my strength, knifed upward.

"I broke the surface scant yards from the upturned boat, which had settled into a gentle rotating motion as the seas, whipped into such a sudden frenzy, were just as suddenly calming. Taking in massive gulps of air, I wheeled around looking for Amo, turning away from the boat and out toward the open sea. But then I heard his voice behind me.

"'Over here!' he was yelling, and I directed my gaze back to the boat, only this time to its rear, where I spotted him holding fast to the exposed rudder. He was waving me over, and so I dog-paddled–had no energy left for full strokes–until I too could get a handhold.

"'Mussolini?' he said as I reached him. He did not have to yell now, for the howling of the wind had subsided to a whisper.

"I shook my head. 'Gone,' I said.

"'Damn,' Amo answered softly. 'I guess it was his time, after all.'

"'I guess so,' I said.

TWENTY-SIX

Through the Crystal, Darkly

Jacques paused in his narrative. He reached out to the tape recorder to shut it off, paused, then changed his mind.

"Ah, well," he said. "I guess it doesn't matter if it's on tape. Look, Avery, this may sound a little crazy, but . . . recent events have led me to believe that I may have been quite wrong."

I had trouble digesting what he was saying . . . did not, in fact, understand this pronouncement at all.

"Say what?" I answered.

"I think I was wrong," he repeated.

"What do you mean, you were wrong?" I said. "About what?"

"About Mussolini's death."

"You said he drowned. How can you be wrong about that?"

Jacques studied me, then glanced nervously at Addie.

"About that, no," Jacques said. "He did."

"Christ," I said. "You're not making any sense. If he drowned, then what are you talking about?"

"Well," said Jacques, "you remember how I said that your father had been really anxious to move on to the coast–to Genoa–rather than camp for the night? That he kept looking behind us?"

"Yes," I said. "He spooked both you and Mussolini, and so you hustled out of there. Why? Were there more Nazis?"

"No."

"Partisans?"

"No."

"Bandits?"

"No."

"Okay. You're not going to say that Colonel Henshaw sent some of our own boys to terminate Mussolini, are you?"

"No," said Jacques, "although the thought did cross my mind a couple of times. I bet the possibility was discussed, at any rate. Mussolini's permanent disappearance would not have been met–was not met, as it turned out–with any great sorrow on the part of the officials involved in his rescue. But no, that didn't happen."

I shook my head, wide-eyed by the riddle.

"I give up," I said. "What–or who–was behind you?"

Jacques hesitated, stood, started pacing and then answered.

"The devil," he said.

The room was silent while the answer reverberated.

"The devil," I echoed.

"Yes," said Jacques.

"Uh huh," I said noncommittally. This sounded as misguided to me as the previous pronouncements of spirit sightings. "And how did you arrive at that?"

"I think," said Jacques, standing behind his seat, "that we were–at least from that point at which Amo was first unnerved–being driven toward a demonic rendezvous. That was no ordinary storm we encountered. I have found no earthly reason for it to this day. It was, in my opinion, of supernatural origin."

I shook my head. Discussion of anything beyond the known physical world had not, until this meeting, been part of my experience. And now, having been introduced to it, I found myself balancing on that fine line where incredulity gives way to scorn. But I steered clear of any disrespect. This was, after all, a man I not only revered–but also one who had, after all, certain powers that went beyond conventional explanation. And so I answered in kind.

"Okay," I said, "let's assume it was supernatural. Why couldn't it have been God-created? Mussolini died, after all. Maybe that was God's punishment."

Jacques frowned.

"No," he said. "You have not been listening. I was wrong about

Mussolini's death. His life–or more accurately, his time on Earth–did not end in the Ligurian Sea."

"We're back to that," I said.

"We're back to that," said Jacques. "I believe Mussolini found a way to cheat death . . . although I confess I didn't realize it until recently."

"Cheat death," I said. I turned to Addie. "Is any of this making sense to you?"

She considered me, then Jacques, then me again.

"I think so," she said.

"You do," I said.

"Yes."

"Okay," I said. "Maybe somebody would like to explain it to me."

"It has to do with this," Addie said, holding the crystal pendant out from her neck. "Right?" That last was directed to Jacques.

"Yes," he said. "It has everything to do with that."

"With the necklace . . ." I said.

"The crystal," said Addie, sounding impatient. "Don't you listen? The old gypsy who gave Jacques the crystal said it would enhance his sensibilities; but he also warned about letting a dying person touch it."

"One portion of the legend," Jacques reminded me, "says the crystal can imprison the unworthy in such a circumstance–prevent him or her from passing through to an afterlife."

"And it was exactly that situation," Addie said. "It was in Mussolini's hands when he drowned. Jacques is saying that the soul of Mussolini passed into the crystal. Right, Jacques?"

Jacques eased himself back around his chair and sat down again. He took a deep breath and let it out slowly–a sign of relief, I thought, at finding an ally.

"Absolutely," he said. "Very astute, Addie."

"I've had some experience with this," she said, giving the crystal a little shake in her hand. "It has . . . unusual qualities."

"Whoa," I said. "Are you telling me Mussolini's in there?"

Addie laughed.

"No, silly."

"Good," I said.

"He used to be in here," she added.

I looked at Jacques, and he was nodding. He looked tired, but pleased.

"I believe it's true," he said. "That his soul was in there."

I was silent, thinking. I had two people in front of me–two friends–who ascribed to this theory, so I was outvoted. I wasn't in the least swayed by their conviction, but neither was I about to start calling them lunatics. Good form dictated it.

"Okay," I said, "let's assume for the sake of argument that this is true. How is it, Jacques, that you didn't see a misty substance leave Mussolini's body when it entered the crystal?"

"Easy," he said. "We were underwater, and it was dark, and the light was already refracted, doing all sorts of visual calisthenics. Besides, I was concentrating on surviving, not on observing any unusual phenomena. Plus, it's possible that it takes a different, and perhaps invisible, shape when it enters the crystal."

"Avery," said Addie. "Why don't we let him finish his story? Then you can ask more questions. There is more to the story, isn't there, Jacques?'

"Oh, yes," he said. "Assuredly."

"Avery?" said Addie.

"Fine," I said. "No problem." I suddenly felt fatigued, and in that moment discussion seemed pointless. At least with Jacques continuing his account, I could add to my growing store of information on my father, tinged however the tale might be by supernatural mumbo-jumbo.

"Go ahead, Jacques," said Addie.

He nodded.

"Okay," he said. "Let's see . . . Amo and I were in the Ligurian Sea, holding onto the exposed rudder . . .

TWENTY-SEVEN

The Binoculars

"The boat, though turned upside down, managed to stay afloat, which certainly made our survival easier. We hung on like that for a while, and then managed to get up on the boat's hull, and were resting there when another fishing boat–a motorized one–came by from a village south of Genoa and took us aboard.

"To say the fishermen were curious at our plight would perhaps be an understatement, but war being war, they weren't really surprised. They took us to their village, dragging the capsized craft in behind us. Amo and I then caught a ride north into Genoa, which was, like most of northern Italy, in turmoil. American troops had swept into the city, as I'd heard, chasing out the Germans who had taken control two years earlier. But there was very little discernible organization in the city. I mean, the whole country was a mess; so why not Genoa, too? But food and lodging–and new boots–were easy to find, so we ate a hot meal, bathed, shaved, and contacted Henshaw by wireless code–told him in effect that we'd lost our cargo at the bottom of the sea and needed payment for damages to the boat. I imagine he might have danced a jig over Mussolini, and then cursed us in the next breath for the expense.

"In any event, my orders were almost instantaneous: I was to proceed to the northern part of Germany, to a port city that had a potential for trouble. As it turned out–though we didn't know it until we met there later–Amo was given the same destination.

"I don't think Henshaw actually gave any thought to the parallel nature of our orders; he was just filling in the blanks at that point, keeping everybody busy. There was no thought to teaming us up again;

it was just easier to sign off on nearly identical paperwork. And so Amo and I headed in the same direction, but by different routes, following procedure for our respective units. Amo first went back to OSS headquarters; I linked up with an airborne unit leaving Genoa.

"I don't know what course Amo followed after that; but I landed in Kassel, Germany, and then traveled solo, wreaking what havoc I could on pockets of resistance being thrown up by the German troops and high command. Everybody was targeting Berlin by then, and the race was on to see who might swing into it first.

*****

"It was quite a time in Germany in those final days of the war. Exciting, life-affirming–and very deadly.

"I would have liked to go into Berlin and seek out Hitler and do that madman myself, but I missed my chance. He'd already put a bullet in his brain on April 30, just a couple of days after the partisans had tried to kill Mussolini–and the day before Mussolini went down in the Ligurian Sea. We didn't get word of Hitler's death right away, so I was well into Germany before I heard about it. Of course, there were rumors for years afterward that he had escaped Berlin and taken up residence with some other Nazis in Argentina after the war, but I think they were just that–rumors.

"Anyway, I spent a few days hop-scotching my way through Germany, avoiding most of the major conflicts, concentrating on taking out particular German officers who were considered difficult enough to prolong matters and increase the Allied body count. Eventually, on May 8, I reached my destination: Bremerhaven, a port city on the North Sea.

"By that point, the conflict had, with the exception of small and inconsequential firefights, come to a halt. An unconditional surrender was imminent; Germany was supposed to be giving up at midnight that night, although the final paperwork wouldn't be in place until the next day.

"The U.S. Navy had landed in the port at Bremerhaven, and its sailors were all over the streets, securing the place preparatory to

implementation of the official Allied terms. The town being German, these sailors were not exactly welcomed, but the populace tolerated them well enough. Of more concern was a unit of German soldiers–a platoon that had been trapped in the city and told by our people to stay in place right where they had taken up temporary residence–at the local Bremerhaven Industrial School, a place that had housed transient military personnel and little else since the Normandy invasion. It was a case of admirable restraint on the part of our Navy, considering the bloodshed running rampant across much of the rest of the country.

"This particular German unit had been surrounded overnight, and had nowhere to go, so it was either fight or sit. With the coming armistice, their commander decided to sit. He was probably a family man who just wanted to get home. If he and his men did as they were told–didn't cause any undue trouble–then safe passage from the school and Bremerhaven was but a day away.

"Not that the situation didn't have its moments. The most perilous came after the Navy found out the Germans were housed in just one half of the school–a large, ramshackle brick building just a block off the main street. The order came down for our boys to move into that portion still open–for the convenience of the lodging, of course; but also, I think, to emphasize our authority by getting in the Germans' collective face. It was, from all reports, a tense few minutes as the sailors approached the building and entered. They made a point to go slowly, so as not to trigger a conflict. But even so, there was significant concern that the Germans, still armed, might open fire.

"When I arrived it was dusk, and the school situation was the talk of the town. Germans occupied the north wing; the Americans were in the south wing. Townspeople kept an eye on the complex from street corners, sidewalks, windows, nearby cafes. Others did the prudent thing and sought cover. Conventional wisdom said it wouldn't take much to set off a bloodbath.

"I didn't dare approach the school myself, because I wasn't exactly dressed for the part, which would be militarily; I was instead in my woodland garb, and looked and smelled like I'd been without a bath for many days, which was in fact the case. But there were enough strangely

dressed civilians by this point to make my presence on the street acceptable, and observation of the school a simple matter.

"It was there, at my stakeout on a side street overlooking the school, where he found me. I didn't see him approach since he came from the rear, and I had no reason to sense him since he gave off no fear and was, in any event, one of many people whose signals were mixing on the street. He was at my elbow before I noticed him.

"'I'm betting some fool German fires off a round and gets the whole damn mess of krauts killed,' he said, and I turned at the voice and smiled.

"'My God,' I said, 'there's no getting away from you for long, is there, Amo?'

"My erstwhile Italy companion was dressed in the uniform of a sailor, which I guess spies did with some regularity: took on different identities, different roles.

"'Join the Navy, did we?' I asked puckishly.

"'For the next day or so,' he said. 'I would have preferred Berlin, myself, though I hear it's been pretty well blasted by the bombers. Why are you here?'

"'Who knows?' I said. 'I don't think anybody's got a grip on what's been going on the past few weeks. Germany's crumbling, and all that our generals can seem to do is keep everybody moving. I can't see a specific pattern to it.'

"'Well, that about sums it up,' said Amo. 'But hey . . . this is the first chance I've had to wear Navy. Nifty outfit, huh?'

"I examined his starchy whites with some distaste.

"'Looks uncomfortable,' I said. 'I never could stand uniforms. Say, you have access to the school in that outfit?'

"'Of course,' he said. 'It's my ticket in. Why?'

"'I'd like to go in, get the feel of things . . . to see if there are any Germans in there giving off specific signals that might indicate trouble. See if I should perhaps be expecting to do anything extracurricular, so to speak.'

"'Well, you're welcome to accompany me. I've got orders that give me pretty much carte blanche. But Jacques, don't go starting anything unless it's really necessary, okay?'

"'No problem,' I said. 'Lead on.'
"And we headed toward the school.

****

"It started out as one of my more relaxing nights of the war: a warm interior instead of the cold woods; and a friend to watch my back, and vice versa. The place was tense, of course, but that was old hat to me. It didn't disturb my slumber at all.

"The Navy boys didn't sleep, I guess, they were so worked up about the Germans in the same complex. The tension was heightened, I suspect, when the naval officer in charge, a commander by the name of Jensen, made it clear to the German in charge that if any harm came to even one American in that building, he–Jensen–would personally see that the entire German platoon was annihilated . . . armistice or not.

"Of course, issuing such a threat and getting satisfactory, unilateral results from it can often be two completely different things. So Amo and I decided to set up our own little camp in a supply room away from the main contingent of sailors, off an unoccupied hallway that would give us easy access to either wing should we need to move quickly.

"The warmth of the place made me drowsy, and Amo told me to catch some shuteye; we would alternate sleeping. I took him up on it. I'm not sure how long I was napping, but I snapped awake at a gurgling sound coming from the hallway just outside our door. I was on my feet and moving in a crouch toward the sound before I was fully awake, and was upon it about the time my conscious senses were kicking in.

"There, in the hallway, a German soldier had Amo from behind, with something around Amo's neck. It looked like a strap of some kind. Alarmed, I started to move in to break the Nazi's grip when Amo suddenly elbowed him sharply, whipped the strap free, reversed position so that he was behind the German, flipped the strap over the soldier's head, pressed a raised knee into the soldier's back, and tightened the strap around the neck–all within about a second. He then held on tightly as the soldier went through the violent vibrations of his death throes. It was all done almost silently, and was over before Amo eased

the forward pressure he was exerting on the man's back and the tension of the strap. I know, because I saw a fine mist flow outward from the soldier's body and waft away down the hall while Amo still had the man upright.

"'He's dead,' I hissed to Amo.

"'How can you tell?' he said.

"'Trust me on this,' I whispered. 'He's long gone.'

"Amo let the soldier's body down gently to the floor, and disengaged the strap from the neck. Then, holding the strap aloft, I could see what was connected to its end: a binocular case.

"Amo stared at the case for a few moments before opening it and extracting its contents. Sure enough, a large pair of binoculars was inside. He examined the item briefly and then slid it back into the case and hung the case by its strap from his shoulder. Then he motioned me over, and together we hauled the body into the supply room and over to a closet at the rear. We stuffed the body in there, and shut the door on it. Then we sat down.

"'I think he was looking for a place to take a leak,' Amo said softly. 'Might have gotten turned around. No weapons, so I'm guessing they all are under orders not to carry them around in here. Don't know why he'd be carrying binoculars at night, though. Well, maybe I do; they're officer's glasses. He probably lifted them from someone and didn't want anyone else taking them from him. It would've been something concrete for after the war; a memento, or maybe to pawn. Well, he won't pawn them now. Crazy.'

"'Yeah,' I agreed.

"'I was just coming out of the can, into the hallway, and thought at first it was one of our guys. I couldn't believe any of theirs would wander out here–and when I realized it was *one of them I told him to get his ass back to his own side.'*

"'Which he obviously didn't,' I said.

"'Jumped me,' said Amo. 'I still can't believe it. I turned and he jumped me. The end of the war, and it's all lost for him, and the fool jumps me. With binoculars, no less. Young guy, too; pretty strong . . . Weird, though.'

"'What is?' I asked.

"'I didn't try to kill him, but it was like the binoculars took over. Of course, that's not possible. Must be the adrenalin flow. I didn't know my own strength, or something.'

"I looked at my watch. It said ten minutes past midnight.

"'The surrender went into effect ten minutes ago,' I said.

"'Well, then that's that,' said Amo.

****

"The German unit moved out at daybreak, and without further incident. I'm not even sure they missed the dead soldier; probably not. In those last few weeks alone, there were an unbelievable number of casualties on both sides: tens of thousands dead, wounded, missing. Another one wouldn't matter.

"My war was effectively over. There was still a need for spies, I guess, but someone decided, in the aftermath of the armistice, that my peculiar talents were no longer required on the Continent. I was airlifted over to England within days, cooled my heels for a few weeks waiting for further orders–so I spent some time there, after all–and then much to my surprise was shipped home. It was like someone decided it would be best, in the new developing order of things, not to let on that such a cold-blooded operation as the Specter Squad had ever existed–and that the best way to do that was to disband the unit and hide its elements in the huge population of the United States; to send its members home. Before I knew it, I was back here on the Island, back here where the only killing was in the hunt for food, where the only secrecy was in matters of personal privacy.

"Amo stayed on in Europe for some more assignments, but they were brief ones and of little significance. It wasn't too long–a couple of months, perhaps–before he was stateside and selling shoes–his pre-war profession.

"And life went on. The war seemed like just a bad dream, and faded into history . . . succeeded by Korea, and later Vietnam, and eventually those little firefights like Grenada and Iraq that our leaders like to adopt to keep the troops sharp.

"And in that time the crystal passed to Addie, and ultimately back to me at a time of great personal stress. And it wasn't until recently that the first signs of trouble began, so subtly that I did not recognize them for what I now believe them to be.

"And then they worsened, these signs . . .

TWENTY-EIGHT

Papa's Death Watch

"But let me go back a bit.

"After Mussolini drowned, I regained the ability to empathize without interruption–without being jammed. It wasn't a sensation constantly inundating me, though; I could tune it in and out at will, as the need arose.

"I really didn't give a thought at first to the possibility that I was carrying around my neck an object that would do anything except provide me with a glimpse of the hereafter–if in fact it really did that; if in fact I had really seen souls leaving the bodies of those Nazis; if in fact I hadn't been hallucinating under the stress of battle. Being a man who had always relied on sight as well as sound and feelings, I was, nonetheless, still in considerable doubt about just what I'd seen in the woods and in that hallway after the Nazis had died. Had it all been real, or illusion?

"Of course, once I resumed my Island hunting and notched my first kills, I started seeing something I never had before on hunting trips. A very light mist issued from each animal corpse, although neither as definitive nor as large as those of the Nazis. Even then, though, I told myself it might just be a phenomenon that had always been present . . . that I just hadn't noticed.

"Beyond that, I had no evidence, no inkling, of anything else untoward involving the crystal–no inkling, to be specific, that Mussolini's desperate grab had been anything more than that: a desperate grab.

"And so I resumed my life, making plans to improve the Lafitte family's lot with a new business. I had saved much of my military pay,

and decided to purchase a boat with which I could ferry Island residents and visitors back and forth between Bois Blanc and the mainland. There had been such a service periodically and sporadically, and talk of it being instituted with some regularity and permanence. But nobody before me had seriously committed to it–even though improved transportation like that could not but help improve life for all the Islanders. Extra visitors, attracted by the ease of ferry travel, would add cash flow and tax dollars to the Island coffers.

"With the start of that service, I felt secure enough to start my own family as well, and accordingly married a young woman of the Island whom I had known since childhood. It is not my purpose here to relate my romantic or private family matters, so let me just say that with marriage came a sense of purpose unlike any I had felt before. I was focused on the task at hand–the building of the business–and as such put completely from my mind the events of the war, and the myth of the crystal.

"A year went by, and then two, and we had our first child, Sylvia, and a year later our second, Mary, and re-christened the boat–which until then had been the Gypsy *(okay, maybe I did not forget* everything *about the war). We now called it the* Sylmar *after the two girls.*

"And in the midst of that period, your father came to visit, Avery, and we did as we had intended: went fishing and swapped war stories, though he demurred from the fishing after our first couple of outings. He preferred, in warm weather, to spend time on the beach or playing tennis; in cold weather, he limited his outdoors experience to brisk walks. He had to keep moving, he said, or his blood would coagulate. And he liked to spend time with my father, who–despite a disdain for outsiders in general–grew to appreciate Amo. There was, of course, a bit of gratitude there, for Amo had saved me from those Italian bandits and, later, from that redbanded Nazi with the big knife.

"They talked, the two of them, though it was predominantly Amo. My father always seemed to want to hear about the war–about Italy, and Bremerhaven, and some of Amo's other exploits. And yes, your father and I related our experience with Mussolini, too, and told about the legend of the crystal, and my father was much entertained.

"He was, in fact, the only person I ever confided in regarding that chapter for years . . . for as I've said before, the Mussolini rescue was a matter deemed top secret and would have only roiled waters best left calm. My father has always been, among other admirable qualities, extremely close-mouthed. And so it was after I told him of Il Duce, and so it has been for the decades since.

"Your father visited here each year by himself until the early '50s, when he started bringing the entire family. I've explained how that came to be. And so your mother and you boys sampled the Island's charms until about five years passed, and then you came no more. Other pursuits beckoned in Bois Blanc's stead.

****

"During the years of your visits, I finally came to know–to truly comprehend–some of the power of the crystal, for it was in this period that a couple of longtime Island residents died in my presence. One was old Ferris Tompkins, who lived in a shack on the eastern end. My mother, who served locally as a nurse though never trained as one, asked my assistance in his care, and I complied. Old Tompkins had gone sour, and lost all control of his bodily functions, and mother needed someone to help clean while she tended. It was on one of those visits that the old man died, and I saw his misty form, as surely as I see you two, rise from his deathbed and look us over, and then move on through the cracks in the shack's walls.

"I was a bit stunned at first, but then not. I had, after all, seen much the same thing–a mist of human form–in the heat of battle. This was simply confirmation of a possibility I had tended to repress.

"And then it happened again under similar circumstances a couple of months later, only this time at an elderly woman's house–an old friend of my mother. This time my mother, being close to the deceased, was crestfallen at the death. But witnessing the departing soul as I did, I tried comforting mother, and finally told her what I had seen–both this time and the others–through the power of the crystal. I told her in general terms how I had come to possess it, and of the myth. She

naturally thought me a little crazy, and suggested I visit Reverend Stellingworth for counseling.

"I didn't particularly see the need, but agreed nonetheless in order to make her happy.

"The odd thing was, of course, that he believed my story–was in fact excited by it, and asked if he might not try the crystal at his next deathwatch or, failing that, funeral. I agreed with some reluctance, but with the knowledge that if he saw what I had seen, then he could allay my mother's fears over my sanity. I did not, in truth, even think to lend the crystal to my mother; and even if I had, I doubt there was much chance that she would have seen what I had seen, as skeptical as she was at my words. I doubted that the Reverend might see a spirit, for that matter–but I thought that being religious, and thus closer to God than most, he stood at least a chance.

"It was mere weeks later that another Islander passed on, and while the Reverend was not present at the passing, he did officiate at the funeral. I made a point to attend, too–the first religious service I had been at since the war–and lent him the crystal before the service. I was curious whether anything could be seen beyond the period immediately following death–if the soul of the deceased might show up later for its own funeral.

"It didn't take me long to find out. The service, at the Island's Church of the Transfiguration, was attended by only a handful of people, the deceased having been something of a hermit. It was barely under way when the Reverend, normally flawless in his delivery, started hesitating, going over the same phrases twice, stuttering a little as he looked over from the pulpit toward the casket set in front of the sanctuary. And I knew–by the mix of confusion, fear and excitement in his eyes–that he could see the old hermit there in spirit, hovering about his burial box.

"The Reverend and I gathered in a study at the side of the church entrance afterward.

"'My God,' he said, handing the crystal back to me, 'it really does work. He was there, my son–as bold as can be, smiling, enjoying the eulogy. I imagine it was the most attention he had had in many a year,

and he was savoring it. Incredible. Well . . . if you wish, I will speak to your mother.'

"And he did, and she accepted what he said, and was at ease over my mental health. With her belief in me reinstated, I thought finally to offer her a chance to try the crystal, thinking it might give her comfort. But she declined, saying it was not her desire to mingle with the departed until it became necessary to do so.

"Eventually, your final summer came along, Avery, and with it came Addie . . . and the storm . . . and Gull. You remember the particulars–how you two got caught out there in that little boat of yours, how you made for Gull because it was the only land within reach, how the lightning shattered your boat, how you tied yourselves to the Island's lone tree and sat through the storm until I arrived with Eliot and your Grandpa, how you and Addie fell in and went under when you tried to grab the line we tossed you, how you were saved by Eliot and how he found Addie and handed her up to us on the Sylmar *. . . and how we couldn't revive her.*

"It was then that I saw her essence rise from her body–come right out of her and around my hands as they worked to restore her breathing, and hover, and then disappear over the side. She had died as surely as those Nazis and old man Tompkins and the hermit. And so it was that I stood with you and your Grandpa and told you, 'God's will.'

"I was as shocked as you to find that she was breathing and talking and laughing a short time later. Having turned away–having quieted your Grandpa from his keening, from his selfless offer to God to take him instead of the girl–I did not see the mist return, did not see it re-enter the body, as it must have. And so I was surprised with you.

"But after the fact, after consideration, I concluded that your Grandpa's offer had indeed been accepted, and that it was but a matter of time before he would be called in her place. And so it came to pass.

"The years rolled by, and now Addie had the crystal, and I no longer had the ability to see the spirits of the departed, though my empathic abilities, not dependent upon that particular item, grew keener with age.

"Along in the mid-'60s, my wife became ill with cancer and started

fading away. It was at this time that I ventured away from the Island, to Ohio, to find Addie and ask for the crystal back. She complied willingly, without question–I think understanding without the need of explanation. And so I was able, in my wife's final days, to know that I would be able to see her off after she had risen from her body.

"And when it happened, when she passed on, it was a great relief to me to know that she still existed, that I could see her both in the room after death and at her funeral. I think anyone who has lost a loved one has looked around, wondering if the loved one is still present, but has been frustrated by the limitations of our earthly vision. I tell you, the grief is greatly minimized with the knowledge of an afterlife.

"In the years after your summer visits stopped, Avery, your father continued to make annual visits here in the late fall–in the midst of business trips to shoe stores not far off on the mainland. And he and my father continued their camaraderie, sharing anecdotes about their lives, and observations about the crooks running Washington, and whatever else entertained them. And each year my father wanted to hear again about the Crystal of Death and about Mussolini, though he had heard it time and again; it was as if a touch of senility had crept in, and he was reverting to a childhood need to hear a favorite story over and over. Your father thought it amusing for several seasons, but eventually grew a little irritated at the request. Nonetheless, he never upbraided my father about it, though he called on me more and more to provide the bulk of the narrative.

"Eventually, within this past decade, after he had passed his 90th year, my father became ill and started to worsen, to lose his will to live. The entire family–a sister, my daughters, and Johnny; my mother had long since died–pitched in to help him in his time of need, taking regular turns at his bedside. I probably spent more hours with him in those weeks than at any other time since my childhood, and we talked more than we ever had, period.

"And this is when things started to go strange. I noticed an increasing warmth and, on occasion, a brighter-than-normal glow in the crystal, which–yes–I had worn religiously in my waking hours since retrieving it. At night when it was under my pillow–Addie is right, the

points are painful and disruptive of rest unless removed–I sensed in my sleep that it was vibrating, but even more than that: it was trembling, building up to a shake. Of course, you can imagine a lot of things in your sleep, and this could easily have passed for just that sort of trifle. Except . . .

"I was with my father, within what looked like about a week of his death, when the crystal warmed, lit and trembled all at once. And it was not just something I noticed; my father did too, through my shirt, and asked me to lift the crystal free of the fabric so he could see what in heaven's name was going on.

"'So odd,' he said, and reached out and touched the stone, and recoiled quickly. 'It's hot,' he said. 'Red-hot. How can you stand it?'

"I felt of it, and it was warm, but not in the extreme.

"'What are you talking about?' I said, and reached out to feel his forehead, to see if perhaps he was overtaken by a fever that had rendered hot anything that was warm. But he felt only slightly feverish.

"'It burns!' he said, and I shook my head.

"'Not at all,' I said. 'It is but warm to the touch.'

"My father reached out again and touched the crystal, and again drew his hand back sharply, and blew on his fingers. Then, fear in his eyes, he looked up at me.

"'It's possessed,' he said.

"'Nonsense,' I replied. 'It is not possessed.'

"'Something's wrong!' he said, the words a hiss, his eyes wide with fright. 'It would not burn so . . . if everything was as it should be.'

I was shaking my head.

"'It's probably just one of its odd qualities, papa. Perhaps it's reacting to your illness, empathizing by adopting a fever of its own. It has strange qualities, no?'

"'Has it ever shimmied and shone and burned?' he asked.

"'Shone, yes,' I answered. 'Shimmied . . . I'm not sure. Recently, perhaps. But it never has burned, no.'

"'Tell me again about Mussolini,' he said.

"'Mussolini?' I said. 'What? You mean about his dictatorship? Or about . . .'

"'His death,' my father said. 'Tell me about his death. The one in the sea. Specifically what happened when you were underwater.'

"Now . . . in all those years that had gone by, I had not even considered the possibility of Mussolini's spirit passing into the crystal. I remembered well the old gypsy's warning about keeping the crystal from the hands of the dying, and the portion of the myth about the solitary imprisonment within the stone. But I had truly seen no sign that anything unusual had transpired immediately following Il Duce's Ligurian death, nor in the decades since. So I rejected the idea now.

"'I can see where you're headed, Papa,' I said, 'but I think it's a bit farfetched.'

"'Is it?' he said. 'Doesn't the myth say that imprisonment in the crystal awaits the unworthy who have contact with it upon their passing?'

"'Yes, papa, but good lord, Mussolini's death came years ago. Don't you think his spirit would have announced its presence before now?'

My father was shaking his head, a look of disapproval on his face.

"'I thought you were more open to possibilities than that,' he said. 'Didn't I teach you to commune with nature, to listen to the heart of things? Do you not have an ability to hear and feel what others cannot?'

"'Yes, Papa, but . . .'

"'Then why do you assume that a trapped spirit–an evil spirit–would overtly let you know its intentions? Why have you not instead listened for telltale signs? Wasn't this Mussolini devious and untrustworthy in life?'

"'Yes, Papa, I guess he was that.'

"'Then why are you blind to the possibility of his presence?'

"'Well, for one thing, my signals have not been jammed since his demise. If he were here, with me, would I not have that same difficulty I had in the woods of northern Italy?'

"'Why do you suppose,' said my father, 'that the effect of the qualities of a soul in our world would be the same from within the crystal? Why do you reject that portion of the myth?'

"'But Papa, I do not reject the myth. It's just . . .'

"'You have closed your mind, Jacques, to possibilities. Open it, my son, and perhaps we can learn a truth here beyond what we can see.

Let's concentrate on the crystal, and perhaps witness that which the old gypsy told you. Maybe we will see within it the soul of Mussolini himself, or hear his cry to get out.'

"'Papa,' I said, trying to interrupt.

"'And if truly fortunate,' he went on, ignoring me, 'perhaps we'll witness his escape, and his overdue passage from this world to the other side. Maybe that's all that's required to trigger it: the knowledge that he's there, and a witness to the passage. I cannot but think the man has some answering to do to the Almighty.'

"Now, while he was talking, I was getting very nervous. That's why I had tried to interrupt. While I realized the general wisdom of his words, they made me uneasy. Call it a fear of the unknown; of the possibility of what might transpire if what he said was true–if Mussolini was within the crystal. And so it was only with reluctance–a bowing, as it were, to the authority of my mentor–that I took the pendant from around my neck and hung it from the arm of a crucifix that stood like a guardian in a base on my father's bedside stand. There, me sitting and him prone, we could both study the crystal's pulsating light and visually probe the possibility of its spiritual message without thought of being burned as my father's hand had been–though again I found the surface of the stone to be but warm.

"For the remainder of my stay that afternoon, we passed the time talking aimlessly, somehow mesmerized by the crystal, comforted by it, but not really seeing anything beyond the smooth surface and soft glow pulsing from within.

"I left–with the crystal–when relieved by Johnny for the evening shift, and returned for the late-night vigil around midnight. My father was sleeping, and soon I was nodding off. As my last act before joining him in slumber, I again hung the necklace from the crucifix, and my final conscious thought before falling asleep in a nearby easy chair pertained to the simple beauty of the crystal.

"When I awakened a short time later, I found my father watching me while sitting up in bed, a position he had not attained in some days. The ravages of disease seemed temporarily to have faded, and he was carrying on his face the kind of smile that comes with knowledge.

"'What is it, Papa?' I asked.

"'Nothing,' he said. 'It is just that I feel better. Almost well enough to rise.'

"I reached out and patted his hand, and thought it a little clammy to the touch.

"'It is good to hear, Papa, but do not push. You must conserve what strength you have left.'

"'For what?' he said. 'To lie here some more, waiting for death? I tell you, I wish to rise, if only for a few minutes, and to step outside and breathe the night air.'

"'Up?' I said. 'You wish to go outside? But Papa . . .'

"'Come, Jacques,' he said, 'help me up.' And with that he tossed aside his covers and held out his hands for my help. I was so stunned by this sudden surge of energy that I complied, and helped him as he wobbled to the door of his bedroom, and then across the living room to the front door.

"Once outside, he leaned into me, and together we looked skyward. It was pitch black on the ground; the moon, a mere sliver, was failing to light the night. But above us, in the clearing over the Twin Lakes, the stars were thick, the visible portion of the Milky Way crossing in an east-west trajectory. The Big Dipper sat bold and clear on the northwestern horizon, and bright points of shooting light–shooting stars–were visible every few seconds.

"'It's wonderful, the night sky,' he said.

"'Yes, Papa,' I said. 'It has always inspired me. And apparently, tonight, it has inspired you.'

"He turned his head up to me, and smiled.

"'You have no idea,' he said.

TWENTY-NINE

"My Father, Il Duce"

"That night, before we'd gone outside, something had happened in my father's bedroom. And I had slept through it. Consequently, I did not know nor could I know that instead of dealing with a short-term terminal illness, we of the Lafitte clan would still have our patriarch for years.

"At first, and until recently, it seemed like my father was simply the recipient of a remarkable recovery. He slowly regained his health, and then his vitality, and eventually returned to his old ways: a little trapping, a little hunting, a little fishing, though mostly he would stay at his cabin, reading. There is, after all, only so much physical ability in a man of nine decades. Beyond that, he expressed a desire for more privacy, and we obliged. His cabin is so far removed that it was actually a relief not to have to go there too often. Still . . . the request was colored by something else. There had been a new facet to his personality–an altered trait, if you will–since that night by his deathbed. I had taken little notice, though, rejoicing instead in the fact of his renewed vigor.

"But eventually, that new facet started gaining more and more of the total personality, and my father became less of a quiet, assured presence who governed his family with love and wisdom, and more of a bully who directed us with bluster.

"This was gradual, though, not easily discerned–as though a devious creeping malignancy were edging in under cover of fog or night. But being exposed to the man as long as I have been, I finally did notice–though not, as I said, until recently.

"This realization did not come suddenly, but built, as I recognized

more and more the same personality expressing itself that I had seen in Mussolini in the Italian woods. And as the realization dawned, a dread grew inside of me–and then a certainty.

"One day, while nearing his cabin to visit him, I noticed the start of the rotting in the woods circling his home, and a slight temperature deviation the closer I came to my destination. Being summer, though, hot and hotter are more difficult to delineate than variations in other seasons. The telltale sign, though, came when I stumbled upon a wounded and obviously dying squirrel that had been evidently mauled by another animal. I wouldn't have noticed him except for a sudden spasmodic movement on his part as I passed nearby. And that was the problem: I wouldn't have noticed.

"Here was an animal in obvious distress, and no doubt sending out accompanying signals, but I wasn't picking them up–wasn't empathizing, as though my signal was being jammed . . . as it had been in the woods of Italy.

"And that was, for me, the giveaway–the announcement that Mussolini could well be at hand. It set me to analyzing, and I began to see what might well have happened, and to believe that the myth of the crystal may indeed be one hundred percent accurate.

"It was a perception that was hard to dispute, no matter how much I might want to. And subsequent events only tended to support it. Here is an example:

"I had gone to his place one day for dinner, arriving early to help him prepare the meal. When I entered the kitchen, though, he started screaming at me to stay out. This had never happened before. The kitchen had long been a room in which we shared talk and chores; where we prepared meals from the animals we had trapped or shot in the wild. But now . . .

"'Stay the hell out,' he yelled at me as I stepped through the kitchen door.

"'Why?' I asked. 'Are you brewing up state secrets?'

"'Lasagna!' he yelled. 'Now out!'

"I stepped back into the living room, but with him still in my line of sight. He was moving feverishly, grabbing condiments and oils and

diced vegetables and mixing them furiously in a large bowl, then layering them into a large pan . . . one I had not seen before.

"'Where did you get the pan?' I asked.

"'Mail order,' he said. 'How can I be expected to bake lasagna without an appropriate pan?'

"'I didn't even know you liked lasagna,' I said.

"Without further preamble, he launched into a tirade laced with obscenities, directed at me and the cabin and the Island and his cookware . . . all in Italian; or more precisely, all in the tongue of an accomplished Italian. It literally set me backward a couple more steps, for I had never heard my father use such language–either foul or Italian. The only foreign language he knew, had ever spoken, was the French handed down by his forebears. He knew no Italian; had never, to my knowledge, had contact with any Italians.

"I didn't know what to say, at first, but then decided. I could answer in the same language . . . maybe catch him in a verbal error that would truly identify him for who I thought he was.

"'So you didn't perish completely in the Ligurian Sea,' I said in Italian.

"He didn't respond at first, other than to continue his work on the lasagna. But the pace of that slowed noticeably.

"'You took refuge in the crystal,' I said next, again with no response.

"'Give me back my Papa, you bastard,' I said next, my anger boiling. My father–or the person occupying his body–straightened at that, stopping his food preparations, and slowly turned. On his face was a smile, a ghastly, toothy smile, and his eyes were wide, alight with pleasure.

"'Jacques,' he said in English. 'I don't know what you're saying, my boy, but it sounds quite wonderful. Italian, correct?'

"And with that he turned back to the lasagna and continued his preparations, though at a measured pace.

"I stood in the doorway, silently puzzling, convinced . . . but knowing there was nothing I could do to convince anyone else. And even if I did, what could be done? How does one rid oneself of an unwelcome neighbor, especially when the neighborhood is the body of an old man? I must have stood there, watching, for three or four minutes. Finally I turned

and walked away without another word, out the front door, along the lake, through the now putrefying forest rim, and home.

"In the days that followed, I stayed away, doing some small-game hunting, and noticing something I hadn't noticed before. After each kill, as the mist of the creatures I dispatched were wafting upward above their corpses, I could see them looking at me. Some of the looks were, I sensed, baleful, but most struck me as accepting, as though the movement out of the body was a fully expected and not unpleasant sensation.

"And each time I observed these looks, I was reminded of the crystal, and of my father's inability to depart his body as these creatures were departing theirs. And any doubts I entertained as to the need for action just melted away with the days.

"We had not lost Mussolini in the depths of the Ligurian Sea; his body, yes, but not his spirit. It should, by all rights, have gone someplace hot, but by happenstance had entered the crystal around my neck. And ultimately, when death was near in my father, in a body that had lost its will, this evil spirit found a host. And like a renter bent on owning, it was staking its claim to more and more of the property. And at some point in this process of moving in, the Mussolini spirit had become dominant, and had begun jamming me.

"My father would have passed on to another plane without this intrusion. He would have been lost to us, and we would have mourned; but he would have been free to follow his own path, to join his wife in whatever comes after. But now . . . now he was trapped in his body, held there in a tightly wedged symbiosis with a man rightfully despised throughout the world, a man everybody thought had died at the hand of partisans, a man I saved and who, in saving, I inflicted upon my own flesh and blood, upon my own father.

"This is why I have brought you here, Addie, and you, Avery.

"First, I need confirmation of what I believe with all my heart to be true. I believe–despite your doubts, Avery–that you will see the truth after more exposure to my father. You are a journalist, trained in the techniques of the interview, in eliciting information that a subject might be loathe to divulge. I know he was difficult today, that he said he will talk only to Addie . . . but I'm sure it was because he dismissed you

without consideration; that he did not know–did not sense in you–that you are a writer, a preserver of words. My guess is, when he does know, he will speak to you. He might not open up–too much truth could unearth more than he wishes, starting with retribution–but I think he will drop tantalizing hints toward the truth. Mussolini had a large ego, and I seriously doubt it was reduced by his time in the crystal. A chance to go on the record at this late date–to be heard once again, even cryptically–may well prove attractive.

"My father–or rather Mussolini–has never said, "Yes, I am here, the man you saved from the partisan bullets." He has been too shrewd for that, but the signs are all there. Beyond the lasagna incident, he has on occasion let slip an Italian phrase or accent. I have heard him in sleep mutter barely discernible but nonetheless identifiable words–names, really, of people and places in Mussolini's life. His mistress, Claretta, for instance. A brother-in-law he had executed. Hitler, once.

"And then–I hate to subject anyone to this, but it is another signpost–there is an unspeakable stench that utters forth from his mouth at times of great agitation, as if from a great foul place; the same kind of smell we encountered in the ringed area around the Twin Lakes. It is simply not of human derivation.

"'So I need you to speak to him, Avery, and determine the probability, at least, that what I say is legitimate. Or better yet, to subscribe to it. For coming from you–a person of limited religious belief steeped in the laws and ways of mankind on earth–such subscription would equate to validation of what I say.

"And once Avery has confirmed my belief, Addie, then I want you–for it is apparent that you already understand the situation for what it is–to help me get rid of Mussolini once and for all. Once we are all of a mind that this . . . possession . . . has happened, that my father has not simply adopted in senility the ways of a man whose story he was told time and again, then I want to send the intruder packing.

"I will want you, Addie, to perform an exorcism."

THIRTY

Jacques' Goal

"An exorcism!" I said. "Good God, Jacques, that's positively medieval. I think you've been reading a little too much popular fiction lately. That kind of thing just isn't done any more–is it, Addie?"

That last I asked a bit tentatively, for it occurred to me that I might not know what I was talking about, exorcisms being an area of religion and, hence, of some mystery to me.

Both Jacques and I looked to Addie, but she didn't respond immediately. When she did, the words came out slowly, carefully.

"My church," she said, "has historically avoided the practice, though there is provision in some of the older canons for its application in extreme cases. As I indicated, Avery, I . . . tend to believe what Jacques believes about his father, for I sensed a dichotomy when I shook the man's hand. Don't ask me how. It's an acquired sense."

"Whoa," I said. "Do you mean to tell me you've had experience with things like this before?"

"Like this, no," she said. "Not possessions by wandering spirits, but . . . let's say there have been questions of demonic possession."

"Demonic," I said.

"Well, that was what the victims believed, and when their minds are fixed upon such a thing–even when it isn't so–it can have the same effect. There is, in those cases, a dichotomy, too. So yes, I've had experience in these things; but no, nothing quite like this."

"And what makes this so different?" I asked. "What makes you think this dichotomy isn't like those others: self-delusional?"

She motioned to Jacques.

"For one thing, he's jammed," she said. "For another, the Italian language. It's highly unlikely the old man would be spouting that without a possession; I haven't seen anything like that before. And there's the stench . . . and the warm temperature around the lakes and the cabin. Those are really weird, and I think tied to the invading spirit. And there's my knowledge of the crystal, and my experiences with seeing spirits. And . . . shall I go on?"

I shook my head, not so much in disagreement as resignation. I didn't believe this stuff–thought there must be alternative logic that would apply–but could see where we were headed. Jacques knew I wouldn't buy into it right away, and so I didn't have to explain myself; he knew I was grounded in earthly pursuits. But having come this far–having traveled to the Island in search of answers–I felt obliged to go farther, to do Jacques' bidding and at least get an accurate reading on his father. Call it friendship; call it loyalty; call it journalistic curiosity. All three were at work here, guiding me toward the inevitable.

"I'll do what I can, Jacques," I said, "but I make no promises. If I think your father's just being delusional or senile, I'll call it that way."

"Understood," said Jacques. "And if you decide otherwise?"

"Well . . . in that unlikely case," I said, "I guess I'd have to know this from Addie: If push comes to shove, are you equipped or empowered to perform an exorcism?"

Addie rubbed a finger over her lip before answering. Her words came out softly, as though a gentle musing.

"It depends," she said, "on what we would be driving from the body. If it were a literal demon instead of a delusion, no; I'd have to go to a higher authority. If it is Mussolini himself, I don't think anybody in my church would be qualified to address it. I don't know of any such documented case. Gypsy mythology and Episcopalian canon are not exactly bedfellows. In fact, I'm not even sure an exorcism would do any good. We'd be dealing with the embodiment of evil, as it were, instead of evil itself. So . . ."

"So you're in the dark," I offered.

"So I'm in the dark," she agreed.

We all sat silently, each with his or her own thoughts. I broke the mood.

"There is this, too," I said. "An exorcism, from the little I know of it, is a strenuous exercise. The strain would be intense on everyone, and could conceivably be too much for your father, Jacques. And even if it were successful, if Mussolini is in there and were driven out, then wouldn't that rob the body of the will that has kept it alive?"

"My father's time should have ended already," said Jacques. "He deserves his freedom, even if that means physical death."

"Okay; I understand," I said. "But let's chew on this for a moment. If Mussolini feared our efforts, wouldn't he do something to stop us? You know, use his evil somehow."

"Maybe," said Jacques. "But he's smart. I don't think he'd do anything to hurt anyone; bring the law into it. I'm sure he doesn't want that kind of complication. Oh, he'll try to make things unpleasant–bombard the physical senses with unsavory elements, for instance. But that only offends the nose. Beyond that . . . he may try to win you over with his sweetness, Avery; he can be all of that, despite what you saw at his cabin. But beware: any sweetness would be the slender remnants of my father, being used by the bully."

"Which brings us back to something I still don't understand," I said. "Just how do you explain Mussolini getting in there in the first place?"

Jacques shrugged.

"I was sleeping the night that it happened," he said. "I tried to pump my father for that information later, after I suspected what had happened, but by then Mussolini was asserting himself and wouldn't say. But I can only guess that Papa–stubborn as he was on occasion–steeled himself to touch and hold the crystal despite its heat, and in whatever moment or moments he succeeded in the challenge, Mussolini went barging through. I do not believe that my father would have permitted the intrusion had he possessed the strength to fight it. But there you are."

I was shaking my head, unhappy with the entire scenario. A crystal that provided a window of sorts into the spirit world; a transfer of a tyrant into a dying man's body; evil spreading its talons into an old man and his surrounding land; talk of an exorcism . . . it was far too much for a professional skeptic to accept. But something else was nagging . . .

"Pardon me for saying so, Jacques," I said, "but wouldn't it make sense to just wait for him to die of natural causes? He is, after all, 97 years old."

Jacques grimaced.

"He was, by all rights, supposed to be dead years ago," he said. "Now, the evil is so entrenched that I fear it might have the effect on the body of, if not immortality, then an extension of significant duration."

"And that is not acceptable?" I said.

"Most assuredly not," said Jacques.

I sighed. Well . . . in for a penny, in for a pound.

"When can we see him again?" I asked.

"Tomorrow," said Jacques. "But now . . . I think we are all probably hungry." He jumped up from the table and headed for the kitchen. "Sit tight and I'll round up some cold cuts and vegetables."

****

I looked at Addie in the quiet that followed, and marveled again at how little she seemed to have changed physically in the four decades since our Island summer. But there was a great deal there behind those big eyes of hers: a history far removed from mine and, I suspected, a great deal more interesting. She was a person with heartfelt beliefs, ones to which she was committed; I didn't know what I believed, other than that life was a confusing mess. She had a sense upon meeting Jacques' father that something might be amiss, and knew right away upon seeing me that Jacques had manipulated her to Bois Blanc; I had no inkling of evil within the old man, and couldn't see Jacques' manipulation until it was practically explained to me. In sum, she was a participant, a doer in life's struggles; while I was a spectator, a reporter and editor who cheered and jeered from the sidelines.

"Jacques," she was saying now, "if we end up doing an exorcism, if it's indeed the path we choose, will you help?"

"No," said Jacques from his spot at the kitchen counter; he was placing food on a tray. "I think I am too close to the situation. I might be too easily manipulated by the intruder; he could use my emotions against me, and thus impede the process. Besides, you do not need me with Avery present. He will be your strength, should you require more than you alone possess."

I looked up, a bit surprised. I had not quite envisioned direct involvement in the ritual, should it come to pass. And I was on the verge of mild protest.

But Addie responded before I could form the words.

"I don't know," she said. "I don't think he will do it. I might accept what you say, Jacques, but Avery seems to be beyond convincing–beyond the belief that comes with faith."

"Oh, he will believe," said Jacques. "It merely requires hands-on knowledge. That shall come tomorrow."

"Maybe," said Addie. "But he was always so literal. If he can't see a creature with horns and a pitchfork, then I fear he may not accept what you've said."

"I think he will accept it," said Jacques. "He may be cautious, but he always struck me as level-headed, too."

"Excuse me," I said, "but do you mind not talking as though I'm elsewhere?"

Addie broke into a mischievous grin.

"You're so easy," she said. "Always were, always will be."

I shook my head and smiled back–pleased despite myself at being toyed with; pleased, I think, at being once again within Addie's sphere of attention.

"Chow," said Jacques, carrying plates, silverware, a tray of cold cuts and a bowl of cold corn to the table. Then he got three glasses of milk and brought them back, and we dug in, clearing the contents of the tray and bowl in short order.

"Got some pie, too" he said. "Apple."

He brought it in, and we did nearly the same to that, leaving but a quarter of it within two or three minutes. Then we sat back, sated.

"Well," said Jacques. "It's getting on toward eight, so I think we should turn in and get an early start tomorrow."

I hadn't even thought of where Addie was staying. There was no longer a hotel on the Island, but there were a couple of places with accommodations: a small motel out past the main dock, and cabins near the Island's eastern end, I had been given to understand. Maybe Jacques was going to drive her to one of those establishments.

"Addie, you take the couch," Jacques was saying. "Avery and I get the bedroom. Bunk beds. But I get the bottom, Avery. And if you want more privacy changing, Addie, use the bathroom."

"Thanks, Jacques," she said.

"Whoa. She's staying here?" I asked.

"Of course," said Jacques. "What did you think? We're all adults here. I think we can handle cohabitation."

"Well . . . yeah, I guess so," I said.

Addie laughed.

"Don't worry, Avery," she said. "I don't bite."

"Well, I . . . it's just . . ."

"What?" said Jacques. "What is your problem?"

"Oh, Christ," I said. "No problem; it's fine. Just . . ."

"Just what?" said Jacques.

Visions of intimate moments I shared with Addie four decades earlier flashed through my mind, quickly followed by a vision of the woman waiting for me back home in New York.

"Just don't tell my wife," I said. "I'm not sure she'd approve."

Jacques let loose a guttural sound that I assumed was some sort of laughter; humor at my expense.

"What?" I said, turning to him and then to Addie. In so doing, I saw them exchange a look of mutual satisfaction. They were enjoying my discomfort.

"Nothing," said Jacques. "Nothing at all. You just shouldn't worry so much. I'm going to bed, and so are you. Come on, Avery. Say goodnight."

I shook my head–he was right; I always worried too much–and grinned sheepishly at Addie.

"'Night," I said.

"Good night, Avery," said Addie. "Good night, Jacques. Sweet dreams."

The words struck a chord . . . resonated from something earlier in the day. For the first time in hours, I thought of my pre-dawn dream.

As I entered the bunkroom behind Jacques and swung the door closed, I wondered if–and I think I hoped that–Turk McGurk would visit me again before morning.

THIRTY-ONE

Turk's Return

The bunkroom was black save for one small stream of moonlight making its way through a crack in the curtains on the window facing the Straits.

The door was closed, giving Addie a sense of privacy out in the other room, and in the process closing off any light source from that direction. I was just hoping I wouldn't have to go to the bathroom in the night; it was tucked into the back corner of the cabin, accessible only through the living room. I'd feel a little strange–yes, maybe even guilty–wandering out into what essentially had become Addie's bedroom.

Somewhere between trying to see through the dark and worrying about a call of nature, I slipped into sleep. It was, as far as I can tell, a dreamless sleep for the most part; at least I don't recall any images of Mussolini or Nazis or spirits or a pendant. But near morning, I think, a dream did take hold; and as on the previous morning, it was vivid and included a discussion with the late Mr. McGurk.

I don't recall any sound, but sensed his presence again nonetheless. Looking down from the upper bunk, I squinted through the poor light toward the floor. There he was, his large heft barely visible, leaning against the wall next to the door; he was examining his fingernails, but looked up after I had observed him for several seconds. This time I wasn't frightened, for I knew him to be but part of a dream.

"I told you old Lightfoot was crazy," he said to open the

conversation–a conversation which, being in a dream, did not disturb Jacques as he slumbered nearby.

"Oh?" I said. "And why is that? You don't think he was a great soldier?"

"Well, he was a great soldier, all right," said Turk. "A very effective little terminator, from what I hear. I've met some of the people he dispatched, you know. They are not exactly enamored of him. They, too, think he's crazy."

"Why?" I asked. "Is it so crazy to serve your country well in time of war?"

"No, not that," said Turk. "It's just that he put a little too much zeal into his performance. Pretty ruthless."

"Oh, and like you weren't," I said. "From what I hear, you terminated quite a few men with a certain gusto yourself."

"Yes," said Turk, "but I never said I wasn't crazy."

"But if you're crazy," I asked, "why should I believe what you say? It might just be an extension of your mental condition."

"Judge for yourself, Mr. Mann," said Turk. "I'm not really concerned with his war record, anyway. I am concerned, and so should you be, with his talk about the crystal, and the spirit mists, and his father. I mean, doesn't that sound like just about the biggest load of crap you've heard in awhile?"

I smiled. Jacques' story had indeed strained credulity. But I had promised to keep an open mind until our visit the next day at his father's place.

"Perhaps it is, and perhaps it isn't," I said. "But it also strikes me that if I can have a lucid discussion on the merits of Jacques' tale with a ghost, then maybe it is I who am crazy. Maybe everybody's crazy. Well . . . not Addie."

"I beg to differ," said Turk. "She may be the craziest of all. Come on. She thinks the crystal gives her special insights, that she too sees spirits. And this from a woman of the cloth. And now . . . now she's thinking of taking on the mantle of exorcist? I think maybe she's had one sacramental wine too many."

"Or," I said, feeling contentious, "she might truly have been touched by the hand of God out there at Gull Island."

Turk snorted.

"The Gull Island thing," he said. "I notice she hasn't commented specifically yet on her so-called 'death' out there."

"No," I said. "She doesn't remember. But I think with everything else she says she's experienced, that she trusts Jacques on that one. If he said he saw her die, saw her mist leave her body, then that's probably good enough for her."

"The mist thing again," said Turk, shaking his head. "So sad. Well, if they want to believe fairy tales, they're entitled. But if I were you, I'd get away from that crazy Lightfoot as fast as I could. He's dangerous. I don't think you're safe here."

I studied Turk, gauging. There was something so determined, almost desperate, in the tack he was taking . . . he was clearly trying hard to discredit Jacques. And in my experience, the word itself implied that credit existed where the discredit was aimed.

"Why are you so determined to undermine this man?" I asked.

"Determined? What do you mean? I am merely trying to do you a favor . . . save you some grief."

"Turk McGurk? A protector?" I asked. "What's wrong with this picture?"

"Look, Mr. Mann, I don't have to stand here and be insulted. I have plenty of fellow ghosts who can fill that need."

"He sent you, didn't he?" I asked.

"Who? What are you talking about?"

"Mussolini," I said. "He sent you to try and discourage me . . . scare me off."

"I don't know what you're talking about. And I think I'm through here. Good night, Mr. Mann."

"Good night, Turk. Don't let the door hit you on the way out."

"I don't use doors."

And with that he was gone, had disappeared almost as though he was never present. I lay there, staring into the blackness above me, pondering the visit, noticing the first indication of approaching daylight, and wondering when I would wake up.

Which in due time I did.

****

"Morning, Miss Addie," I said with a faux Southern accent as she, Jacques and I gathered at the card table for breakfast.

In return, Addie shot me a withering look.

"Whoa," I said, leaning back away from her. "Somebody got up on the wrong side this morning."

"You were talking in your sleep," she said, "and rather loudly. I don't appreciate my sleep being disrupted by . . . noise."

"Oh?" I said, recalling my "chat" with Turk McGurk. "And what was I saying?"

"I don't know," she said. "It sounded like a bunch of loud mumbling and moaning. It really pissed me off."

"Right," I said. "Spoken like a true minister."

"What would you know of ministers, Avery?" she snapped. "You ever go to church?"

She had me there. I rarely attended.

"Uh huh," she said after I failed to answer for several seconds. "I thought not. Great choice for an exorcism, Jacques."

I looked at Jacques, my eyebrows up, inquiring silently. He gave me an almost imperceptible nod, warning me off.

"Addie," he said softly. "I realize I've put you both in a situation that for various reasons–stress, contrasting beliefs, whatever–might put you at odds. But please . . . I gave this great thought, and need you two to work in tandem. Do not let anything destroy the bond between you and Avery. I am depending upon its strength."

Addie was inhaling in short, sharp breaths, as though fighting to keep her emotion in check. Finally, she steadied her intakes and spoke calmly.

"I'm sorry," she said. "My apologies to both of you. I don't know what came over me. You're right. It's just . . . I feel the presence of evil nearby. It's perhaps affecting me."

"Very well," said Jacques. "Then we haven't time to lose. Let's finish up here and get on the road. Whatever can be done must be done soon. Or I fear we will lose our way. Come, come, eat up. You will need your strength. Oh . . . and Avery . . ."

"Yes?"

"Make sure to take the binoculars."

"Yeah, okay," I said. "Is that important?"

"Could be," he said. "They were of an evil regime, and still possess a measure of that evil. They very nearly killed your father, and were used by him in turn to kill. So they are both of evil and its very antithesis. They might, for that reason, be of help to you."

I wasn't sure how.

"You're not suggesting I strangle the old man with the binocular strap, I hope."

"Not at all," said Jacques. "But I cannot help but feel that the binoculars' presence might, in some way, mitigate the effect he has over you. Perhaps they will distract him; he is certain to detect their presence and their aura. Addie noticed that aura, and I suspect he is even more likely to. I would not let him so much as touch them, though, for whatever good they might possess could be eradicated by the powerful nature of his evil. Do you understand?"

I frankly didn't, for despite the bizarre way in which Jacques said the binoculars had been acquired, I thought of them not in philosophical terms, but as an heirloom. They had been in my family as far back as I could remember, had served their visual purpose well, and were a direct link back to my father. But I nodded.

"Yes," I said. "I'll guard them closely. I owe that to Dad."

"Good," said Jacques. "Good. Keep that thought."

THIRTY-TWO

Back to the Lakes

"You really think he'll see me?" I asked.

We had just cleared the narrow track and emerged on the main road next to the airport. I was in the passenger side of Jacques' truck, and Addie was seated between us. As usual, I had to shout to be heard over the roar of the truck's engine.

"Yes, I think so," said Jacques. "Like I said, as soon as he finds out you're a journalist, I'm betting he won't be able to resist. He'll at least want to drop some hints. You have your tape recorder, right?"

It was in a backpack I'd placed at my side, between Addie and me.

"Yes," I said, patting it. "In here."

"Good," said Jacques. "But don't use it at first. Set it up too quickly, and he's likely to clam up. That's how those things affect me, anyway."

"That's how they affect most people," I said. "Don't worry; I'll make sure he's talking–that he wants to talk–before I pull it out. But he might balk anyway."

"I know," Jacques said. "But I'd love to get something on tape–something Italian, something . . . you know, Mussolini-ish. Something to maybe hold over him."

I understood. Jacques felt helpless in the face of what he believed had happened to his father; was seeking some sort of beacon in a sea of uncertainty. For my part, I doubted that a recorder would do any good, for I thought the entire Mussolini-spirit thing was farfetched.

Still . . . despite my skepticism, I found myself toying with its possible ramifications from a professional standpoint. As a news story, it would seem to have tremendous value if true. But there was the obvious underlying problem: even if I were convinced that Mussolini was living on an island in northern Michigan, disseminating it as acceptable newspaper fact was an entirely different thing–and probably impossible, except perhaps in tabloids like *The Examiner* or *The Star*. Those papers, however, I considered beneath my journalistic integrity.

There had from the outset been another option, though: a second book–a sequel to *Island Nights*. Even if, as seemed likely, the old man turned out to be just an old man with delusions or senility, I could still write it. Books play by different rules than newspapers or magazines. They can cater to the fantastic or the lunatic and still retain a certain dignity. By using the old man's taped words, and Jacques' taped words, and whatever else I might unearth, I could conceivably turn it into compelling reading.

Jacques took the next two curves a little faster than seemed prudent, the body of the truck leaning hard right and then left, throwing Addie against me and then against Jacques.

"Hey, slow down, old man," I said. "We're not going to get anything accomplished unless we get there in one piece."

Jacques let up on the accelerator.

"Sorry," he said. "Keyed up. I'm a little anxious. You might miss the truth and decide not to help."

"We'll help you," said Addie, "in whatever way we can."

"We'll see," I answered.

Addie shot me a look.

"What?" I said. "I'm not going to commit to something until I have all the facts."

"He told you the facts," she hissed near my left ear.

"I know, I know," I said, leaning in toward her. "And if half of what he said is true, then there's a problem here. And if I can, I'll be glad to help. But let's just wait and see, okay?"

Addie turned to Jacques.

"He'll help, too," she said to him.

****

Anyway, that was the plan. We were going to go to the old man's cabin and try to weasel our way into his good graces and get him to spill his guts and then somehow, if warranted, effect a makeshift exorcism to drive out the soul of Mussolini–assuming he was indeed in the old man's body.

I admit it sounds feeble, and no doubt was. But we never found out for sure, for the plan as it stood was never implemented.

My stay on the Island, in fact, took quite a different turn–a right turn onto the waters of the first of the Twin Lakes, as it happened.

Jacques and Addie and I had traveled the road back toward the lakes, walked through the smelly perimeter surrounding them and reached the northern shore of the first lake. We had turned east and headed up along its shoreline toward the second lake when, about seventy yards from the channel connecting the two bodies of water, a motion ninety degrees to my right caught my attention. An old man and a young boy were out in the middle of the lake, in a rowboat, and the boy had just cast his fishing line out in my general direction, although well shy of the shore. I can't explain it exactly, but as the line touched down on the water, I stopped walking, mesmerized, immobile really.

I remember Addie saying something like "Avery, keep up," but I didn't bother answering. Everything–time, in particular–seemed to slow and then freeze. I remember glancing toward Addie and Jacques for a moment, and thinking how they seemed to have stopped too, though they weren't looking out onto the water; they were in mid-stride, facing away from me and toward the channel. And then, slowly, I turned back toward the old man and the boy just as the boy, in what seemed normal speed, recast the line, again in my direction. Only this time, it flew higher and farther, and started snaking its way closer and closer toward me, and as it approached I could see a shiny silver shape on its tip, but not a hook. It looked instead very much like a silver cross, and I wondered if this was death on the way, if this was how death looked when it came for you–if being struck by the end of the boy's fishing line was, in some cruel-joke sort of way, indeed the end of the line.

THIRTY-THREE

The Bear and the Carpenter

The line kept floating closer and closer to me, an impossibly long cast that I knew should not be able to reach that far, but still it came, seemingly drawn to me as if with a homing device.

I threw my right arm up at the last moment to ward off the incoming missile, but instead of striking me dead, the line wound around my forearm three times, maybe four, before coming momentarily to rest. In that moment, I glanced at it and saw two things: the small metal crucifix up close, on my forearm, facing me, and an eerie light emanating from the line, as though it were glowing in the dark. Only it was daylight, and quite bright out.

Following that momentary hesitation, the boy started reeling in the line, and it wasn't more than a few seconds before it grew taut and I felt the tug on my arm. Then, despite my resistance, my arm was yanked outward and I momentarily lost my balance. Struggling to right myself, the binocular case I had taken along at Jacques' request was dislodged from my left shoulder and slid down and off my arm, bouncing on the ground and coming to rest a yard shy of the waterline. The pull of the fishing line was insistent, and my body started moving forward, step by gradual step. I fought as the water's edge came close and then–setting my right foot forward to try to maintain my body's balance–I took a step out onto the lake. But I did not get wet.

My foot came to rest on top of the liquid, which gave way only slightly. Another tug of the line by the boy, and I took another forced step out onto the water. Then, teetering to keep my equilibrium on the solid but sponge-like surface, I called out.

"Wait a minute! Just wait a minute! I gotta get my footing!"

The boy waited a few seconds, time enough for me to accomplish the task. In that moment, I glanced at the boat and its occupants. The boy, small and about twelve years of age, was wearing a bright red short-sleeved shirt. The old man, pale white and bald, was in a bright white jacket and white slacks. The hull of the boat was painted a two-toned red and white.

The boy gave the line another gentle tug, and reeled me in, out toward the boat, the water under foot holding its consistency, leaving me literally high and dry. It took but a couple of minutes to reach the boat, where the old man held out his right hand and took my left, helping me over the edge and onto a seat. Then he and the boy put down their lines, and the boat–without a motor and, I noticed now, without any oars–started moving southerly, toward the reeds on the far shore. As we started moving, the boy disengaged the fishing line from my arm and rewound his reel.

From this perspective I could see he was unusual in only a couple of regards, but they were telling. A lad of some five feet, two inches with short-cropped brown hair, he had what I think were the bluest eyes I had ever seen–blue not in the sense of color so much as depth, as though I were peering into the deepest blue of the highest reaches of the atmosphere itself, on the edge of the cosmos. They were mesmerizing, but not–as I said–his only significant trait; and so I did not focus on them for long. No, my attention was also drawn to a point lower on his face. The boy had a very small mouth, or what I assumed to be a mouth. It was in the right place, but it was no more than a quarter-inch long. In fact, I never saw it open, never heard him speak; cannot be sure that he even had the ability to communicate verbally. I cannot, in truth, be certain exactly what kind of being I was dealing with.

Nor, for that matter, can I attest to the nature of the old man. I must confess I paid him little attention. He seemed, again, normal enough–circumstances excepted. White hair, tousled in the wind, the aforementioned white jacket, a white stubble on his cheeks and chin, white chino pants, and white sneakers over white socks.

When we were within a dozen feet of the shore, the boat slowed to a stop and the boy pointed at me and then at the land. I nodded, and climbed out onto the water. From there, it was but four or five paces–once again dry–to solid earth. As soon as I reached it, I turned back toward the boat for further instructions, but it was out of sight. Where it had gone, I had no idea; but considering what had been transpiring, I was not surprised by its sudden disappearance.

Sighing, I turned my attention back to land, looking for a path that might cut through the overgrowth.

But before I could spot one, a frightening roar came from one of the thickets to my left a few yards away, and I backed into the water–this time soaking my shoes as the surface gave way to the law of physics.

"Damn!" I muttered, and stepped back onto the shore, but edging toward the right. I hadn't gone three steps when the brush on my left seemingly parted of its own accord, and a huge brown bear came lumbering through.

"Stop!" it said, or so I thought, and I did–as much from the novelty of the situation as from fear.

"Turn!" it said next, and I pivoted on the spot where my intended escape had ended, pivoted until I was facing the beast.

There, in front of me, barely two-dozen feet distant, the bear was standing on its hind legs, its forepaws crossed in front of it, its claws resting on its powerful chest. We stood staring at each other, me in fascination and him in–well, I'm not sure what he was feeling. But the meaning of his words were clear.

"You will follow me, Mr. Mann," the bear intoned in a rumble, and I in turn nodded meekly.

"Of course," I said. "Lead on."

The bear got down on all four legs, turned, and ambled back toward the woods. As he neared it, the heavy growth of bushes at the perimeter leaned to either side, clearing the way for his passage. And the same phenomenon continued as he made his way through the forest. I was several feet behind, and fully expecting a branch to come swinging back and slap me in the face, so I proceeded with my hands up to ward off the blow. But it did not come; the plants–the bushes and branches that bent at his approach–remained parted until I had passed. Looking back over my shoulder, I could see them close gently behind me.

We walked on soundlessly for what seemed like a quarter of an hour, though it was so surreal–being led through magically parted bushes by an English-spouting bear–that I did not seem to have a firm grasp of time. It felt, beyond that, as though we were moving in a timelessness; but that was an unfounded feeling, for I had nothing physical to base it upon.

Moving through bushes, across clearings, around clumps of birch trees and pine and oak, and through more bushes, we advanced steadily, deeper into the woods, where there was no wind, where the sunlight was only suggested, where silence reigned. I saw no deer, no squirrels, no wildlife save the bear, and heard no sound of birds–and so deduced that we had passed beyond the realm of normal Island geography. But where exactly we were eluded me.

At last, we reached a clearing of significant proportion, barren of all plant life. In its center, thirty yards from where we came through a large bush, sat a partially built home. This exceeded the cabin occupied by Jacques' father in both size and ambition. The structure was made of wood, stone and brick, with fireplaces at either end and a huge picture window facing us, wrapped around two sides where they met in a V. The window did not yet have its finished framing–appeared to be set in place tenuously–and portions of the brick wall were not yet complete, piles of bricks to complete the task lying nearby.

The roof was clearly a recent addition: Tar paper gave way to bare boards halfway up, and stacks of shingles still packaged were arranged in three locations in front of the structure. At one end–the left, from my vantage point–the sleek, even line of the roof rose to a second, rectangular level, topped by a tapered peak. I was studying the second story, thinking its lines awkward when compared to the rest of the building, when the bear spoke for the first time since the start of our journey.

"It's a loft," he said of the upper floor. He was still on all four legs by my side at the clearing's edge. "He uses it for meditation. It puts him closer, at least metaphorically, to heaven."

I looked at the bear, not too much shorter than me though down on his paws; as I did, he slowly swung his head left, toward me, until our eyes met.

"Go," he said.

"Where?" I asked.

"Inside," he answered. "He awaits you."

"Who?"

"Your host," said the bear. He then turned and shuffled off into the surrounding woods, past a clump of trees and then between a pair of bushes that parted for him.

I watched him go, took a deep breath, turned to the cabin and stepped toward it, wondering what I could possibly encounter next.

****

"So . . . what do you think?"

The voice came from the right. I had just swung the door inward and stepped through the entrance, and was scanning the interior to my left. I whirled around, seeking the source of the sound, and found it in the far right corner. He was kneeling there, turned away from me, measuring something near the fireplace set into the wall to his left; I couldn't quite make out his features.

"What?" I responded.

"What do you think of the place?" he said, and swiveled in my direction. I could see now, despite the poor illumination–oil lamps were burning along the back walls in either wing, casting soft flickering light–that he was a bearded man with wavy blondish hair combed neatly in the center but falling loosely down the sides and back to his shoulders. As I squinted to see him better, he rose and faced me, which told me his approximate height: he was taller than me by at least three inches, putting him a little over six feet. A long-sleeved flannel work shirt hung from his wide shoulders, and rolled-up sleeves showed powerful forearms. He was wearing blue denim trousers, narrow at the waist.

It was the man I had spotted at the side of the road shortly after I had arrived on the Island; the man Jacques had driven past without seeing. I looked around for the surplus military jacket he had worn that day, and saw it draped over a sawhorse not far from the front door.

"Nice," I conceded. "Your home?"

"Will be; yeah. Well, already is. Has been since I got the roof on. Now it's a matter of shingling, bricking and interior work. So yeah, I spend my free time here; sleep here." He swept his arm back and pointed to my left, toward the building's V, the point where the two wings joined. A doorway led to the right from there, into a darkened room.

"Eat here, too," he said. "The kitchen's functional."

"Right," I said. "So . . . I didn't imagine you on the road."

"Not at all."

"I didn't think so. But Jacques didn't see you."

The man shrugged.

"Does he know you?" I asked.

"Oh, yes. Indeed he does," the man said.

"Then why didn't he see you? Or recognize you from my description?"

"Oh, that," the man said. "We've never actually met."

"I thought you just said . . ." But then I dropped the matter, struck silent by a revelation–a sudden glimmering of the heart of this situation. Whether hallucination or reality, I knew who I was talking to.

The garb, the tools . . . the message was clear. He was a carpenter.

The carpenter, my father had said in his last moments.

This man, whoever or whatever he was, was part of the riddle of my father's final message. Of that much I was sure. Beyond that, I knew little, and clearly needed more information.

"Why was I led here?" I asked.

"Ah, of course," he said. "You have the curious mind of a journalist. Ask the question, get an answer. Not always a cogent or correct response, but a response nonetheless. That satisfies you, does it not?"

"Sometimes," I said. "So am I gonna get one from you?"

The man smiled, nodded, and moved off toward the kitchen. "Want something to drink?" he said. "Milk? Water? Pop?"'

"Ummm . . . water," I said.

He entered the kitchen, and suddenly there was bright light in there. It didn't look like he had reached out toward a switch; the light just flicked on as he crossed the threshold. Curious, I took three or four steps in that direction. But the man suddenly reappeared, a glass in each hand, the light going off as he stepped through the doorway. I was still staring at the darkened entrance when the glass of water was thrust into my right hand.

"How'd you do that?" I asked. "With the light."

The man quickly looked back over his shoulder.

"Oh, that. That's automatic."

"You have electricity out here, then," I said. "But why not in this portion of the house?"

"Oh, long story," he said, waving his hand in dismissal. "Well, to change the subject, you wished to know why you were brought here."

I took one last look at the kitchen door.

"Yes. Of course," I said. "Why was I? And what's with the bear? How is it he can talk? And move bushes? And for that matter . . . exactly who are *you*? I mean . . . I see you're a carpenter . . ."

The man drank from his glass–water, it looked like–and smiled.

"You wish to know if I am *the* carpenter; if I am Jesus?" he said. "Is that your question?"

I hadn't actually thought that; not overtly, anyway, since it seemed so . . . religious. But now that he had actually said the name, I realized the idea might have subconsciously crossed my mind.

And so I shrugged, my way of giving grudging assent.

He took another sip before answering.

"If I say no," he said, "I might not be truthful. But if I say yes, then it is in your nature to disbelieve."

I waited for more, but it was not forthcoming.

"Then you're saying you are," I finally said.

"That is for you to judge," he responded. "It is for you to judge, as well, whether what you are experiencing is real or a dream. I'm sure that, being the skeptic, you will no doubt find ample reason to disbelieve the reality of this."

I thought of the boy and the old man on the lake, and of the bear, and of the bushes that parted; and I thought of the story of Mussolini and the necklace, and of the possible presence of that selfsame Italian bastard in the body of Jacques' father, and of the fact that this all seemed un-dreamlike . . . and couldn't make a snap judgment as to its reality. And the man smiled again.

"Ah," he said. "I see you are starting to doubt your entrenched observational system. What seemed incomprehensible–fable-like–before now gives you pause. Well . . . it is a start."

"Why am I here?" I asked again.

"Ah, that," he said. "You truly wish to know?"

"Yes," I said. "That's why I'm asking."

"Very well," he said. "I shall tell you. But only if you agree to withhold judgment–and debate–until I have finished."

"Finished with what?" I asked.

"With a story," he said.

I moaned. Another story. First Jacques' war account, and now . . .

"Is there a problem?" the carpenter asked.

I took a deep breath. A problem? How could there be a problem, I thought. I had been pulled from the safety of the shoreline out to a boat manned by a couple of strange male figures, and then escorted by a beast of the forest to God-knows-where. And now I was talking to a carpenter who had hinted that he may be Jesus . . . and I had absolutely no control over the situation.

"No, no problem," I said.

"Good," he said. "Then you agree to my terms?"

I nodded.

"Agreed," I said.

"Good," he answered.

And he began.

****

"There once was a young man–well, a boy actually–who witnessed a miracle amid the violence of a deadly storm. It happened, in fact, not far from here, out in the Straits of Mackinac."

I cut him off.

"This wouldn't have been, say, about forty years ago, would it?" I asked.

"I thought you agreed not to interrupt," said the carpenter.

"I agreed not to debate," I corrected him.

"Well, don't interrupt, either," said the carpenter, "for you will just break my concentration and make this much longer than need be. Are we agreed on this?"

I waved him on.

"Whatever," I said.

"Very good," he responded. "Now then, this boy, he witnessed a resurrection, a true miracle, that was brought on by the selflessness of an old man who offered himself in exchange for a victim of the storm–a young girl of roughly the young boy's age, as it were.

"But the young boy couldn't countenance what his eyes had seen, and opted to believe it was a secular, physically explicable occurrence–this despite the assurances of a wise old churchman and a wizened mariner. And so the boy entered into adulthood, and into a career well-suited to a skeptic: journalism. And he went from decade to decade, and from a first wife to a second, and from youth to middle age with a stoicism bought not through faith and a belief in the Almighty, but through a resignation that all he was able to see was all there was to see–and through a resignation that with the end of life came the end.

"He gave up, in other words, and in so doing lost sight of some of the truly good things in life: the birds, the flowers, the stars, his memories and an abiding faith. And he would have proceeded farther down that same path had he not been . . . prompted . . . to recall that summer of the storm and the resurrection and the girl and the old man and the mariner, and to start questioning what he had seen and what he had now become.

"And he came to this rock–this island–to seek some answers, and in the seeking learned much more than he had bargained for, and was asked to stretch his perceptions beyond the immediate and into the spiritual, to accept the presence within the mariner's father of an unwelcomed visitor, a visitor believed to be steeped in evil. But through his reasoning powers, the journalist deduced that his friends–the wizened mariner and the young resurrected girl turned woman–had most probably erred in their assumption of the presence of the evil.

"And of this he was quite proud. For in rejecting their belief and faith and observational abilities, he had reverted to the cocoon of his training. And in that cocoon he was warm and snug . . . and quite smug. For in close-mindedness is arrogance."

The carpenter stopped, and stood staring at me–somewhat sadly, I thought.

"Arrogance?" I asked, stung by the accusation. "You think me arrogant?"

"And the man," the carpenter said, "was satisfied with himself, and in his satisfaction exhibited a vanity both unbecoming and . . . misdirecting."

"Misdirecting? How?" I asked.

"Misdirecting in that he led himself away from a very important learning experience," said the carpenter. "But all is not yet lost. He needs but apply logic and intellect while discharging his preconceived notions. Then he can see the truth. Well . . . would you like more water? I see your glass is empty."

"What? Oh. Yes. I guess so," I said, handing him the glass. I hadn't even realized I'd been drinking from it. "But what is it I–this man–should be seeing?"

The carpenter turned and walked back toward the kitchen, speaking over his shoulder.

"Meditate on it while I am gone," he said, entering the kitchen and the sudden bright light.

In his absence, I tried to work my way past the sting of criticism to the truth he professed was out there, but to no avail. And inasmuch as his return was as swift as his first one had been, there was not much time to pursue it.

He handed me my glass, now nearly full.

"Well?" he said. "Have you thought on it?"

"Mmmmm," I said, taking a sip and swallowing. "Yes. But I'm afraid I don't know where you're headed."

"No idea?"

"None," I confessed.

"Not an inkling?"

"Not even that," I said.

"I see," said the carpenter, and he took a large swallow of his water. "Well, okay . . . I guess I had best direct you, then."

"I'd appreciate it," I said.

"It has to do with an item that belonged to your father," he said.

"My father?" I said. "The only thing of my father's that I brought to the Island would be the binoculars."

"Yes," he said. "It is those of which I speak."

"What about them?"

"You know of their history?" asked the carpenter.

"Yes," I said. "Nazi officer derivation. Procured by a soldier, who then assaulted my father. Dad used them to strangle the fellow. They apparently still retain some semblance of Nazi evil. Both Jacques and Addie seemed to pick up on it almost immediately."

"Ah . . . I see," said the carpenter. "Then you have no knowledge of their history before your father . . . came to possess them?"

I must have been wearing a blank expression, for the carpenter merely nodded before continuing.

"Very well," he said. "It is instructive. So pay close attention."

And I did.

THIRTY-FOUR

The Binoculars' Origin

"There was an ocular craftsman of considerable repute in a small shop-filled neighborhood of Berlin in the early third of the twentieth century," the carpenter began. "It was a craft which back then was very time-consuming, very laborious, and thus not nearly as prosperous as it is today. Eyeglasses were not as easy to come by as they are now; in fact, the poor and middle-income residents of practically any civilized area did without. Twenty-twenty vision was not considered a birthright.

"Accordingly, this craftsman–himself of no higher than the middle class–did most of his work for the wealthy, the upper class. He started with standard eyewear, eventually graduated to bifocal construction, and ultimately into the areas of binoculars and microscopes and telescopes.

"He built up quite a reputation, this fellow did–quite a following among the German aristocracy, and among the aristocracy's various cousins across the German borders. His fame, though limited to his particular narrow talent, grew to European proportion.

"Alas, his fate was not one of upward mobility, for even as the craftsman started to make small strides in an economic ascent, Adolf Hitler and his band of cutthroats started taking control of the country, gradually stifling the economy, creativity, ambition, freedom and, ultimately, the very existence of men like the craftsman. For the craftsman was, in the eyes of Hitler's Nazis, of the worst possible persuasion.

"He was a Jew."

The carpenter paused, took a sip from his water glass, and considered me. It appeared he was waiting for me to say something, so I did.

"And did this craftsman have a name?" I asked.

The carpenter shook his head.

"That is not what I expected you to say," he replied.

"Oh?" I answered. "What did you expect?"

"Perhaps something along the line of the horrible plight of the Jews under Hitler, at which point I was going to explain patiently that the Jews have been persecuted for centuries."

"Sorry to disappoint you," I said, "but I knew that."

"Uh huh," the carpenter said absently. "What was your question again?"

"The name of the craftsman," I prompted.

"Oh, right," he said. "Why? Does it matter?"

"I don't know," I said. "You tell me. Was he somebody I would have heard of?"

"Perhaps. Perhaps not," said the carpenter.

"Nonetheless," I said. "It would help bring your story closer to home. Personalize it."

"Oh, it gets personal enough," he said.

"Yes, I somehow expected that," I said. "Nonetheless . . ."

"The name . . ." said the carpenter.

"The name," I answered.

He shrugged.

"Abraham," he said.

"Abraham," I echoed. "Did he have a last name?"

"Of course."

"Well? What was it?"

"I preferred to tell you this later," he said.

"Tell me what?" I asked.

"The name," the carpenter said. "The last name. But, I guess it won't hurt. So, since you ask, it was . . . Mann."

I started to smile at the coincidence, and then even wider at the thought that the carpenter was having a little fun. But the look on his face brought me back from any thoughts of levity. He was looking at me both seriously and kindly–a look I recalled having seen on the face of old J.J. Stellingworth years before. It was one of ministerial kindness, exhibited for those poor earthly souls who are in need of spiritual counseling.

"Okay . . . you're not kidding," I said softly. "So . . . it was a coincidence, right? His name? Mine?"

The carpenter's look varied not at all as he slowly shook his head. The meaning was clear enough.

"A relative?" I said. "But I don't recall any mention of another branch of Manns in our family history . . . and certainly not a . . . oh, Good Lord. Are you saying my family is Jewish?"

The carpenter smiled gently, and shrugged.

"The past is so murky," he said. "Are we not all God's children? Derived from one gene pool? Would it really matter?"

"I don't know," I said, trying to grasp the concept of a Jewish ancestor–and perhaps mildly stunned by it. "You tell me."

"Very well," he said. "As to whether it would matter . . . that is for you to decide. But as to whether your family–you and your immediate forebears–is Jewish . . . no. Your branch, the one with which you are familiar, is not. But somewhere in the past, one of your people married into the Jewish faith, and it led down through the generations to Abraham Mann. Now . . . do you wish me to go on?"

I didn't know what else to say, still focused as I was on the sudden, albeit aborted, concept of a personal Jewishness being thrust upon me. I had always viewed the Jewish persecution from a distance, with the "tsk tsk" utilized so often by gentiles who are, after all, just glad to be clear of the persecution themselves. But now, with a few short moments of the ancient faith in my frame of personal reference, and a newfound Jewish relative the centerpiece of this tale, I had been drawn instantly closer to the people and their religion and the unfairness that life had visited upon them time and again.

And so I nodded my acquiescence. I wanted to know more; know it all. And in response, the carpenter resumed his tale.

"The Nazis took Abraham during an early-morning sweep, one of many going on in the late 1930s. They rounded him and his neighbors up and put them in a controlled, walled-in ghetto, and from there, months later, sent them packing on a train to one of the Third Reich's concentration camps: Buchenwald.

"Of course, well before that particular inevitability, before he and his fellow Jews had been gathered up and sent away, before the camps, they had been stripped of most of their rights and all but the most basic of their economic options. They were a people deprived of the comfort of tomorrow, waiting for the other shoe–or in this case military boot–to drop. And it did. Hard.

"Until the night he was seized, Abraham's ocular business had been allowed to continue, but Abraham had seen none of the proceeds, or had seen them but briefly, before they had been transferred into the hands of the state. Accordingly, he had slowed his production pace to a crawl–his way of rebelling–and ignored some of the ocular orders coming in. This did not set well with the Nazis, but it was of small moment in their overall scheme. They knew they would become wealthy beyond imagination by ultimately taking possession of the property of the Jewish people–an immense array of art and jewels and currency–and so the small rebellion of one of their victims did not register very loudly. Besides, they were still getting some work out of him, and hence some income.

"In fact, though, Abraham was not just working a slowdown; he was busy in secret, mostly late at night behind drawn curtains and locked doors, fashioning what he hoped would be the crowning achievement of his career. His project, to the casual observer, would not seem like much–just another product, one of many over the years from the talented hands of the master craftsman. In fact, compared to the stunningly ornate work he had done in telescopes and microscopes, and to the exquisite level of artistry he had achieved in fashioning chic eyewear for the aristocracy, this was a rather plebeian-looking effort.

"His project was a pair of binoculars: basic black, mid-sized binoculars with black rubber eyepieces and a dull black case. These were clearly–to the uninitiated–a product of less than the first order. In fact, so common looking were they that Abraham did not, when away from his shop, bother to hide them. He felt that by leaving them out on a table or shelf, in clear view, he would have a better chance of keeping them and finishing them should the Nazis raid his small business or should one of his Nazi customers get it in his head to abscond with any goods that looked promising enough to fetch a sizable price.

"And so he hid them in plain sight, and kept them through two raids and one such customer visit, and worked on them always late at night, perfecting them, turning them from a basic visual unit into something special, something that would be a testament to the evil that was gathering force in Berlin and elsewhere in his country, something that would enable the holder of the binoculars to see, through the eyepieces, a basic truth afoot in the Europe of the 1930s and, indeed, in decades yet to come, in totalitarian regimes yet unimagined."

"I'm afraid I don't quite understand," I said to the carpenter. "These particular binoculars are no doubt the ones handed down to me by my father . . ."

"I thought that was clear," answered the carpenter.

"But aside from a sense that Jacques and Addie had about their Nazi influence, I've seen nothing unusual about them," I said. "And I've had them–my family has had them–for years. Had them and used them. Looked through them a thousand times. They're well crafted, to be sure, to have lasted in such fine condition for so many years. And they're fairly powerful. But possessed of a special quality beyond the normal, measurable ones? I don't think so."

"No?" said the carpenter. "Well, you are wrong . . . very wrong. I think, accordingly, that you will find the rest of my story to be most educational. Are you ready?"

I pursed my lips and nodded. Where in heaven's name was he heading?

"Okay," I said. "Go on."

****

"Abraham," the carpenter continued, "finished the binoculars just two short nights before he was taken by the Nazis and sent on to the ghetto and Buchenwald and, alas, his doom. His departure to the ghetto was a hasty one, and among the possessions he failed to take–whether by choice or not is unclear–were the binoculars. Perhaps he left them deliberately to prey on the psyche of his malefactors. It is difficult to say.

"In any event, he was a man who, while not uncommonly old, was possessed of a physical frailty diametrically opposed to the strength of his spirit. He did not last long in the camp. He avoided the fate of many of his fellow prisoners–gas, a bullet, a hangman's noose–dying instead of a sudden and massive stroke after a particularly grueling day of manual labor. He was, by comparison, one of the fortunate ones.

"After they had sent Abraham to the ghetto, the Nazis had cleaned out his shop, throwing anything of value into sacks and tossing the sacks onto trucks bearing the goods of other Jews in other shops, as well. The trucks were driven to a warehouse and unloaded, and their cargoes divided into categories–jewelry, art, metals to be melted, and so on. And it was here that the binoculars passed into the hands of their first non-Jewish owner, a low-level Nazi officer who decided they were plain enough not to draw suspicion if he were to walk out of the warehouse with them. Which is what he did. He put them under his chair until the end of his shift, and then placed them around his neck and strode out with them in plain sight–the same method, basically, that Abraham had used in keeping them for so long.

"The soldier's name was Rammelkamp, a feckless little man who had been drafted into the military and was truly amazed at his own audacity in stealing the binoculars. With the temptations laid before him every day in that warehouse, he had not even entertained the concept of theft, realizing the consequences of discovery far outweighed any potential gain. But there was something about the binoculars that made him set them aside and then boldly walk out of work with them dangling from his neck.

"He took them to his barracks and stowed them in his knapsack, and there they stayed for all but short periods of each night. In the cover of darkness, Rammelkamp would pull them out and caress them, feeling their metal contours and smooth glass lenses, run his hands over the exterior of the carrying case, and hold the case's strap up close to his nose and smell it. It was leather, and being fairly new it had the strong pleasing aroma that only fresh leather can give. He would take several deep inhalations and, sated, tuck the binoculars back into the knapsack until his next surreptitious examination.

"Eventually, Rammelkamp was transferred out of Berlin. The rape of the Jewish wealth was nearly complete, and able-bodied soldiers were required in many of the far-flung areas into which Germany was expanding. Rammelkamp's unit was sent to Poland, then over to France, then eventually east to the Russian front.

"Alas, it was there, in the frigid Russian winter, that Rammelkamp and the binoculars parted company. His unit was drawn into a firefight with Russian partisans who had set up a crossfire, and Rammelkamp was one of the first ones hit. He fell, mortally wounded, and as his final act worked his knapsack off his back and pulled free the binoculars tucked within. Freeing the glasses from their case, he held them close as one might a security blanket, shuddered his last breath and died, blood pouring out of his nose and over the binoculars and onto the exterior of the case that lay at his side. There, inside, secure in small pockets near the lip of the case, were two eyepiece filters that Abraham Mann had worked long and hard to perfect. They, however, were untouched by the blood of Rammelkamp.

"The binoculars fell into the hands of one of the Russian partisans who stripped the bodies of the fallen Germans. This was a man named Grinkov, and while his personal history is interesting, for our purposes it need only be said that he held the glasses for but a short time before he fell in much the same way that

Rammelkamp had, and likewise spilled his life's blood on the binoculars and on the case.

"It went on like this for some months. The binoculars, never damaged, survived battle after battle that claimed a half-dozen owners before they finally ended up near war's end in Bremerhaven, northern Germany, at an industrial school occupied by German soldiers. There, in the final tense hours before the end of the war, the soldiers were confronted with the presence of American naval personnel who, on the final night of the conflict, moved into an empty portion of the school to await the peace.

"And in that uneasy truce, the binoculars' latest owner was the first to relinquish them in a non-violent way–in a way that did not end in his death. A lieutenant in the German army, he was in charge of one of the units housed at the school. In the tension created by the arrival of the Americans and the concurrent orders to stand fast for the armistice, he had been making the rounds of his troops, urging them not to fail their responsibility–urging them not to engage the Americans. No good could come of such a confrontation; indeed, it would be like suicide given the promise of the American commander at the school to exact frightening revenge for any American casualties.

During the lieutenant's rounds, a subordinate who disdained rank decided to separate the officer from one of his possessions–and chose the binoculars. It was easy, for the lieutenant had left them lying unattended in his duffel bag in a private room he had been using.

"When the soldier was convinced the lieutenant was safely out of sight, he entered the darkened room and grabbed the binocular case. Lifting it in the dim light cast from the hallway, he smiled. This would show the lieutenant, he thought; the bastard had worn them around his neck in two recent skirmishes, brandishing them as though they were a special privilege of lieutenancy. Besides, there had always been something about the binoculars that had drawn the soldier to them . . .

"He draped the binocular case around his neck and made his

way to the door, peered carefully into the hall and, seeing it clear, scurried out and in the opposite direction from which he had seen his lieutenant go. His immediate thoughts were of finding a safe place to hide his prize. He was not familiar with the portion of the building into which he was heading, though, since he'd had no call in the past to learn its labyrinthine corridors and lounges and alcoves, and so inadvertently wandered closer than he imagined to the American side. While moving about he came upon a bathroom, and feeling a sudden and powerful need to urinate, was about to enter when the door swung open and a man dressed in the uniform of a United States naval officer came out and, seeing him, told him in German to get back to his unit.

****

"I see by the look on your face," said the carpenter, "that you realize the German soldier had entered that section of the building in which Jacques Lafitte and your father had set up camp, and had just encountered your father himself."

"Yes," I said. "I'm familiar with the scene."

"Perhaps, but I think this will lend new perspective."

"Why am I not surprised?" I said. "Please . . . go on."

"Just so," said the carpenter.

****

"The German, frozen in place upon seeing the American and then intimidated by his directive, turned back in the direction from which he had come; as he did, your father–I must refer to him as 'Mann' from here on out, for it is simpler–turned and took a couple of steps toward the supply room he was sharing with Lafitte.

In that moment, the German, quite free of his own wishes–under the influence of some power that directed his motions–lifted the binocular case from his neck, wheeled back around and, covering the distance to Mann in one leap, swung the case strap over

Mann's head. The German's suddenly independent hands quickly yanked backward on the strap and twisted hard, bringing the leather tightly around Mann's neck. The American, though surprised and at first gasping for air in the struggle, reacted with equal violence–reaching back to grab hold of the strap and then pulling it forward, creating a slack in it. His strength surprised the German, and since the attacker's body had not worked in tandem with the hands and thus was not positioned properly–he was, in fact, shocked at his own actions and wishing to be any place but where he was–it was but a moment before Mann had reversed positions and was tightening the strap around the German's neck.

"This last was witnessed by Lafitte, who had heard the commotion and appeared around a corner looking for the cause of the noise–and now saw his friend strangle the life out of the German soldier. Only it wasn't quite that simple, things sometimes not being what they seem.

"For in gaining the advantage, Mann was not exerting superior strength or superior fighting technique. Having been surprised and very nearly strangled himself, he wanted merely to keep the German off of him until help could arrive or he could neutralize his opponent. He did not want to stir up any unnecessary trouble by killing anyone in the school on the last night before the armistice. But it was almost as if the German were helping him. Not only was there little resistance after he had pulled the soldier in front of him, but it almost seemed as if the German was trying to get the strap around his own throat and, once it was there, helping Mann pull it tighter and tighter.

"The German soldier, for his part, was not trying to do that, but his hands were still operating on their own, as if possessed, and once the American was behind him and pulling on the strap, the German's hands reached back and grabbed hold of the strap too and pulled in an almost spasmodic, superhuman fashion that took the soldier to the edge of consciousness and then beyond. But even there, in his darkness, the German continued to tug, exerting more force by far than Mann, who at that point was just trying to extricate himself from a puzzling situation.

"But he couldn't, and the soldier slumped, and the pressure continued until death arrived and blood poured forth from the soldier's nose and mouth, running down his chin and underneath to the binocular strap.

"'He's dead,' Lafitte then told Mann in a whisper.

"'How can you tell?' Mann answered.

"'Trust me on this,' said Lafitte. 'He's long gone.'

"Only then did the pressure abate; only then did Mann manage to loosen the grip of the strap, allowing the soldier to slide to the ground.

"And there was total silence. In truth, there had been little noise in the course of the struggle, but it had been cacophonous next to the quiet that succeeded it.

"Mann, his breathing barely pushed beyond normal levels by the struggle, stood above the body, binocular case in hand, agape in confusion.

"Lafitte remained to one side, marveling at the savagery of his friend, oblivious to the truth of what he had seen."

THIRTY-FIVE

Abraham and the Filters

We stood silently there, in the carpenter's house, each of us with a glass in his hand. Mine was empty, and my mouth dry. He raised his to his lips and took a sip, and then tossed the small remaining portion of liquid down his throat in one quick move.

I cleared my throat, trying to find my voice.

"What are you saying?" I finally managed, but he didn't answer right away. Instead, he took the glass from my hand and retreated once more to the kitchen and the automatic lighting, returning quickly with refills. He handed me a full glass, which I promptly half-drained.

"Better?" he asked.

I nodded.

"Yeah," I said. "Thanks."

"No problem," he said. "Now where were we? Oh, yes. You wanted to know what I was 'saying.' Which I assume means you want me to explain what happened there in that school with your father and the binoculars."

"For starters," I said.

"Oh?" said the carpenter. "What else is puzzling you?"

"What isn't?" I answered. "I mean, these binoculars made by a relative of mine just happen to travel across Europe a couple or more times, passing through the doomed hands of several owners until they're delivered into those of my father–who obtains them when some poor German thief gets his neck tangled in the strap and helps my father tighten the leather noose. A bit too much coincidence, I'm afraid. From Mann to Mann, as it were, by way of war."

The carpenter chuckled.

"Something funny?" I asked, a little annoyed.

"As a matter of fact, yes," he said. "You are quite right, but the way you put it amused me. But okay . . . I will explain it all."

"That would be nice," I said. "But just how long will it take? My friends will be expecting me back. Hell, they're probably already wondering where I am."

I looked at my watch, but in the dim light could not read the digitized numbers.

"I don't think they are," said the carpenter. "If you could see your watch, you would discover that there has been no passage of time as you know it since you set foot on that lake back there."

I started to look at my watch face again, but decided not to bother. Even if I could somehow get a reading, I knew in my heart he was right. Jacques and Addie, I recalled, had seemingly stopped in mid-stride back at the Twin Lakes. Besides, there was something in the carpenter's manner that was . . . believable.

"Oddly, I trust you on that," I said. "Hell, why not? I've walked on water, been given a guided tour by a bear, and heard a fairly incredible story. So why not timelessness? Okay . . . explain away, will you?"

The carpenter took another swallow of water, wiped his mouth with the back of his free hand, licked his lips and nodded.

****

"Right," he said. "Where was I? Oh, yes. The binoculars and that soldier. Well . . . I'd better go back a ways, back to your relative, old Abraham Mann.

"I told you he was a master craftsman, and that he spent a lot of time working on those binoculars, but what I didn't explain was what was so special about the binoculars . . . or rather the lenses and filters. You have, of course, heard from your friend Jacques about the special powers of the gem given him by an old gypsy in the Second World War."

"Yes," I said, though I failed to see the relevance.

"Well," said the carpenter, "the gem of the pendant he has so long possessed has its own particular powers. But there is another gem–with different attributes–that stems from the same source, a source described by myth. Are you aware of that? Of the Legend of the Crystal? Perhaps the one with the bear?"

I couldn't help but look behind me, through a window to the woods.

"No, not that bear," said the carpenter.

"Well . . . yes, as a matter of fact," I said, turning back. "Jacques wrote me an account of the legend before I came up here to the Straits. He was preparing me for his Mussolini theory."

The carpenter smiled gently.

"Theory," he repeated. "Interesting. And his version of the legend was the one with the bear? Not the ones with the alien or the angel?"

"The bear, right," I said.

"Good," he said. "Being a forest-dweller, that is my preferred story as well. But the version doesn't matter, really; however it happened, the gypsies came into possession of a number of these crystals, and dispensed them sparingly. They did not have a bottomless supply, and so were careful in their distribution. Among the crystals was an extremely limited supply of blue ovals–one of which ultimately reached your relative, Abraham Mann, through a circuitous route that would probably fill a book by itself . . ."

"Excuse me," I interrupted. "If you know so much about it, is it reasonable to assume that you had something to do with the route the crystal followed? Or with the fact that it just happened to reach Abraham? Or, for that matter, with the fact a relative of his–me–just happens to be acquainted with the possessor of yet another crystal from the same legend?"

The carpenter was shaking his head and smiling ruefully.

"Think what you may, Mr. Mann. If you have that much faith in me, all the better. Now . . . may I continue?"

"Sorry," I said.

"Very well," said the carpenter. "The blue crystal made its way to Abraham Mann, but through–as I said–a circuitous route, one that left him unaware of its purported powers. He was quite taken by the crystal, though, to the extent that he fashioned a finger ring in which to hold it–a ring that, when completed, he immediately started wearing on his right hand. He did not know–could not–that in so doing he was about to receive from the crystal not the certitude of an afterlife, but rather a vision of what was to be on this orb, in this life.

"For through his crystal, he would attain the wherewithal to see the future–a power as told in the legend. He would find that he could discover, in moments of introspection or great concentration, events that had not yet occurred.

"This ability came unexpectedly, as he sat resting in a rocking chair early one evening, and he thought it a dream. He saw in his mind a neighbor of his, a kindly old woman named Frau Burkoff, walking the street on a bright day and then suddenly crumpling, falling to the pavement at the base of a gaslight, one foot over the curbing, a black leather shoe on her left foot dangling on her toes, suspended between foot and pavement. The shoe balanced precariously until her lifeless body was moved by someone–maybe a friend–who cradled her; then it dropped to the street.

"The dream unnerved him, but there was little to be done about it. He could not very well tell old Mrs. Burkoff, for it would serve no purpose other than to perhaps really frighten her to death. And being a bachelor, he had no wife to whom he could confide this odd vision. He had friends, to be sure, but did not tell them for fear they would mock him or think him mad, or perhaps suspect he was harboring secret feelings for the old woman, which he was not.

"And so perhaps a week passed, until one sunny day he left his shop early to take advantage of the clear sky and warm temperatures.

A walk, he thought, would help shake a slight depression he had been carrying since the vision. And so he wandered the streets in his section of Berlin, looking at the goods in the various shop windows, greeting the other Berliners out for a walk or merely sunning themselves on the sidewalks and front stoops, until he rounded a corner heading toward his apartment. Almost immediately, he saw Frau Burkoff across the street, striding purposefully toward her own apartment a half-block distant. It did not register at first, the similarity to his dream–she was wearing the same clothing and it was a bright day–until she passed a gaslight. Only then, as she approached another one, did Abraham's fear rise in his throat, and he took a deep breath with which to yell across to her . . . but could not utter a sound before the old woman suddenly collapsed, buckling at the knees, hitting the sidewalk hard, her head bouncing and her legs kicking out, one of them coming to rest over the curbing, her black shoe hanging from her toes, suspended between foot and pavement.

"Abraham raced across the street and knelt at the woman's side, saw her lifeless eyes looking ahead, and knew she was gone. But he reached out anyway and cradled her, and felt futilely for a pulse in her neck, and as he did her shoe fell to the street, a sudden light thud in the silence of the moment, a silence that had settled despite the gathering of a growing number of people, a silence at odds with the screaming fear that was raging in Abraham at the thought that he had seen it coming . . . had foreseen it . . . had glimpsed the future.

*****

"To say this was a significant event in Abraham's life would be something of an understatement, for he was terribly unnerved by it, so much so that he retired for a week to his lodgings to ruminate upon it and perhaps bring some sense to it. And it was there, in the darkness of his apartment, that he had another vision, this one of jackbooted troops rousting the residents of a nearby neighborhood in the still of the night, smashing store windows, bloodying innocents, ransacking businesses and setting fire to several shops. Abraham recognized the exact locale–a diamond district some six blocks from his own shop–but again doubted the validity of what he was seeing. It wasn't that he disbelieved it–or thought it only a dream, as he had in the case of poor Frau Burkoff–but that he didn't want to believe it. If it did not happen, then he would be free of the curse of visions, and life would be easier to live. Besides, while certain rights had been gradually stripped from the Jewish population by the Nazi regime under Hitler, nothing quite like the violence in his vision had yet occurred. If the events foreseen by Abraham were to prove true, then it would bode terribly ill for him and his people.

"This time, a fortnight passed before the vision came true, and this time he did not actually witness it. It was described to him in detail by diamond-district merchants and in secondhand accounts the next day, but the descriptions ran perilously close to what he had pictured. He went with a group to the district to view the damage in the afternoon, and it only confirmed for him what had become quite obvious. He knew which windows would be broken before he saw the shattered glass; knew which stores would be burned-out shells before he saw the smoldering remains. There was no doubt in his mind now. He could see ahead. But he did not know why.

"The next time a vision struck, though, he understood its genesis. The knowledge came to him as stunningly as lightning brightens the sky–a flash of intuition. For in the grip of the next vision, he realized that his ring finger was warm, and that it had been warm on both of the previous occasions; accordingly, he placed a finger from his opposite hand–his left–onto the blue crystal in the ring, and felt more than warmth. It was actually hot to the touch, and he recoiled, and in the shock of the moment lost the vision. But he had seen enough. An elder of his synagogue would be gunned down in broad daylight by a brown-shirted young man, a member of one of Hitler's youth groups–outside of the synagogue.

"This time, Abraham knew two things. First, he must warn the elder; and second, he must not wear this ring if he wanted to keep control of his existence. These visions were frightening and, to the degree that they had driven him to seclusion, debilitating. And so he immediately removed the ring and put it in a drawer, and within the hour had visited the elder to warn him of the danger awaiting him.

"Two resultant things happened. First, the elder, though kindly, considered Abraham's warning to be that of a man who had lost touch with reality; he had no intention of giving the story any credence. Alas, he was gunned down within a matter of days, his last moments no doubt a mixture of shock, confusion and wonder at the vision Abraham had shared with him.

"The second thing was less predictable. Abraham, despite his fear of the crystal, pulled it out of the drawer the day after the elder was murdered, to examine and perhaps understand it. He did not stop to mourn the elder, nor–after extended meditation and prayer over a period of days–did he let his fear stop him from taking what he had somehow grown to consider the next logical step. He had decided, in the confusion of his odd circumstance, that a rare opportunity was at hand for a man of his talents–that he could take unique advantage of the insight he had gained into the nature of the crystal.

"He was now imbued with a drive to create something from this power that might be better controlled–that he could utilize only when he wished, if he wished. Or which he could leave alone, but in the full knowledge that he had the power to use it, to command it, instead of the other way around. And that was where his optical training came in.

"His idea–no more than a theory, and thus suspect–was to create a future-vision of a physical rather than internal, abstract nature: to shape the crystal into something that could be altered in its intensity with a turn of a knob, brought into focus at a touch of the fingertips; to use the crystal to see the future of whatever or whomever he wished by merely pointing it in a specific direction or at a specific object or person. In other words, he wanted–hoped, wished–to view the future through an optical device that had control knobs: a telescope or binoculars.

"This was obviously a matter of faith, though not in a deity: a faith in the field in which he excelled, the only area of his life over which he held mastery. He chose the binoculars for their portable and, by comparison with the telescope, inconspicuous nature. And he decided that with the small mass of crystal with which he was working, the only effective means at his disposal would be to segment the crystal into a couple of circular, flat filters that could fit into binocular eyepieces.

"A jeweler friend split the crystal for him, and Abraham proceeded to polish the pieces until they had acquired the consistency he needed. He then placed them in the eyepieces of several different pairs of binoculars he had in his shop, but could not acquire the desired results. He was getting refracted images that were more abstract art than reality, prisms instead of pictures. It was obvious to him that the crystal was incompatible with the traditional mode of optics in binoculars. And so he began an arduous testing sequence, grinding glass and checking its compatibility with the crystal pieces, setting up distances and different powers of magnification, altering the heat used to shape the glass, changing from one kind of grinding compound to another–trying every variation of construction and component that he could think of. And failing for months.

"But a deep obsession had taken root, and Abraham pressed on, and one day–quite by accident–he succeeded in attaining his goal. It came about when he left a kiln on too long and overheated a silicone compound with which he was working. He was going to discard it, but decided at the last moment to use it anyway. Heating by kiln was just one small step in a lengthy process, but it proved–in that instance–to be the key. When he had completed the lenses using the overheated compound, and for the hundredth-plus time put crystal to glass and peered through it, he knew instantly that he had succeeded.

"He always ran a visual test using the scene immediately outside his shop. He would place the new oculars in vices placed a proper distance apart, with the crystal filters, now in metal borders he had constructed for them, held in front of the smaller of the oculars by a makeshift device that resembled a tiny crane. The entire experiment was placed on a table by his front window. By merely leaning his chin on the innermost edge of the table, he could peer through the filters held in place from above by the "arms" of his crane-like device, and through the two pieces of ground glass set in line beyond the filters, and thus through his window and out onto the street.

"Up to this particular attempt, the scene outside his window had been of the aforementioned abstract variety–with but two exceptions in which proper magnification and focus had been attained, but there had been no hint of the future. But now his heart started racing, for what he was seeing outside was not what was happening there at that moment. In actuality, it was a cloudy and blustery day, with very few people braving the streets. Shop owners were nowhere to be seen as they would be on a pleasanter day, when they would stand by their doorways and chat with the passing populace. No, they were inside, out of the wind and the chill. And the residents of the neighborhood were likewise scarce that day, justifiably disinclined to be out walking for the sake of the constitutional; the weather was just unpleasant enough to discourage casual exercise.

"But the scene Abraham was seeing through his filters and newly ground pieces of glass was very different from a scene of cold desolation. It was bright outside in the view through the lenses, and the people were plentiful. He was, in fact, seeing a traditional street festival held in various of the neighborhoods annually. The next one for his street was still a month distant; but here it was in front of him now, and he could not help but smile at it. The people at the festival–many of them familiar faces and old friends–were enjoying a glorious day, celebrating life despite the hardships that had been imposed and the fear invoked by the Nazi regime. Ah, he thought, the indomitable spirit of the Jewish people.

"He watched like that, mesmerized by the festivities in front of him but still yet to come, for fully an hour. Here, at last, was a glimpse ahead that was not fraught with peril and death. It was a harbinger instead of a better time. It showed his people at play, happy, engaging each other in a celebration of spirit as well as of the street.

"He pulled himself away only when hunger started to intrude, and left his shop briefly to secure food at a local delicatessen. But he was back in short order, eating a sandwich as he settled in to look once again through the filters and the glass. He had just taken a large bite of his food, chewed it and was in the process of swallowing it when his eyes focused once again on the scene in front of him . . . a scene of such horror that he sat abruptly upright, his heart racing–and inhaled so violently that the food lodged in his windpipe and he started to choke.

"His immediate concern–his own existence–sent him reeling toward a bottle of flavored water he had brought home with the sandwich and set on a table near the door. Grabbing the bottle, he pulled the cardboard cap from its opening and poured some of the liquid into his mouth, trying to dislodge the food; at the same time, he started to cough, sending most of the water and some of the food in his mouth two yards out and onto the floor in front of him. Another dose of water freed the remainder of the food, and a third brought him out of his spasms and back to a regular–though labored–breathing pattern. He stood quietly, reflecting on the tenuous hold we have on life, took another swallow of the liquid, and looked out across the table that held the binocular pieces, out onto the street. It was nearing sundown, even colder now, and still very quiet.

"Shaking his head, Abraham edged slowly toward the table, tossed the remainder of his sandwich into a waste can near the wall to his right, and reseated himself. Taking a deep breath, he leaned forward and peered through the filters and glass to the street scene that had so appalled him, and forced himself not to recoil this time.

"It was still bright out there, in his optical view of the street, but the festival was long since shed of its gaiety. Brown-shirted youths and jackbooted Nazis were storming the roadway and sidewalks, clubbing the people who had been so happy so short a time before; the intruders were smashing store windows, dragging the people who could still walk onto the flatbeds of trucks and hauling them away, and piling the crumpled and, Abraham feared, lifeless forms of dozens of his neighbors onto other trucks. The Nazis then looted stores and set fire to piles of debris they were hauling from the shops and apartments along the street, until the brightness of the day was obscured by the black of smoke hanging in the air between the street's buildings.

"And Abraham watched all of this–forced himself to–until the Nazi soldiers and brown shirts had left, and the street was deserted, and all that remained was smoke and an eerie light cast by the flames. Only then did he rise from his table. Stumbling to his shop door, he opened it and walked down the short hallway to the building's entrance and out onto the street–the cold deserted street of a Jewish neighborhood in downtown Berlin–and knelt at the curbside and cried out to the dreariness in front of him, cried out to the desolation that was to come.

"'Why?' he yelled in the gathering darkness. 'Why?'

"And was greeted only with silence."

****

"But he finished the binoculars," I said after the carpenter had stopped speaking for several seconds. "Despite the horror of what he had foreseen."

"Oh, yes," the carpenter said, brought out of his brief reverie. "Indeed. He had come so far, and succeeded so well, that he didn't wish to stop. In truth, it is hard to imagine anyone wanting to proceed when all that the glasses had done was foreshadow evil.

But Abraham did not see it that way. The glasses foretold the future, and in the particular case of Nazi Germany and the fate of the Jews, the coming evil was inevitable. And so he proceeded, thinking he might leave something of substance behind–truly the wish of much of humankind–and hoping that with further experimentation he could learn to gain some control of the events he was foreseeing. That seems naive and foolish to the average observer, I am sure, but to Abraham it was a point of faith. He had no control over the events unfolding in his own life, and so was hoping to gain some control in some other way. I believe the accurate term would be 'grasping at straws.'

"In any event, he proceeded to construct the glasses–really just a matter of encasing the elements properly. But in so doing he did not want to risk the theft of his invention, and so he made the binoculars far short of fancy or flashy. The tubular housings were all black and quite dull, and there was no ornamental trim. And the leather case was black as well, with a dull sheen. He even went so far as to chip out small dents from the metal surface of the binoculars, to carve small strips of leather from the exterior of the case, and to run the surface of each through a mud puddle outside his shop late one night. Thus the glasses were old looking when new; unobtrusive and lacking allure. Abraham felt it was the only way to ensure–if such a thing were possible–that they would not be stolen. And as I have said, he was successful in that regard.

"And so they remained in his possession until the day the Nazis came–in another sweep weeks after the day of the festival. He had sidestepped the festival assault by visiting relatives on the outskirts of the city, but had not foreseen the one in which he was rounded up. Or perhaps he knew of it and had resigned himself to his fate. He had surely engaged the power of the glasses again; maybe they had told him his fate, and maybe they hadn't. He was a tired man, though, entering what would have been his twilight years, and disinclined to run. Whatever his thinking, he was snatched from his sleep and taken away to a ghetto, and sent to Buchenwald, and there died. And the glasses passed into the hands of the soldier at the warehouse, and began their journey to your father, and ultimately to you."

THIRTY-SIX

The Gospel According to the Carpenter

I handed the carpenter my empty water glass and shook my head; three drinks had been enough. He wordlessly took it and placed it on a roughhewn crate set endwise nearby.

"Why didn't . . ." I said, and then stopped. I was going to finish with " . . . he tell me," but decided that sounded like finger pointing. I wasn't really upset with my father for withholding all of this information about the binoculars–figured he had his reasons for not telling me. I was, however, upset with myself for not knowing. It's a badge of honor among journalists: It's best if we ferret out the facts, not have them delivered gift-wrapped.

The carpenter considered me carefully, and responded as though reading my mind.

"There was no way for you to know about them, unless you happened to use the filters at some point. But I doubt he ever loaned the glasses out–to you or anybody–with the filters still in the case. They are in there now, though, I believe."

"Yes, they are," I said; I had noticed them, just as I had noticed them many times in the case since inheriting them. It's just that I had never utilized them; had never seen the need; considered them, in fact, to be an odd supplement–a mere means of reducing or altering the available light reaching the eyes. But to what end? I never pursued the matter beyond that. I couldn't recall, though, whether they had been in there whenever I had used the glasses before my father's death. Maybe; maybe not. Perhaps the carpenter was right; Dad might have removed the filters when the glasses were about to go outside his sphere of control; or even replaced them with look-alikes.

"Wait," I said suddenly, shaking off the image. It was also possible that neither maneuver had occurred. "Maybe my father didn't know about the binoculars' powers."

"How could he not?" said the carpenter. "They basically strangled the German soldier in that school hallway by themselves. It is not likely he would let that pass without a careful study of the properties of such a thing. Your father was, by his wartime training and, I think, by his nature, a meticulous man."

I thought back to the many times I had seen Dad working rows of figures related to his business, and to the times he had carefully planned out business and vacation trips–each stop and each point of lodging mapped out and arranged before the trips began.

So yes, I could believe he would know–if indeed such a thing were true. I was still not ready to embrace all of this supernaturally charged information, though. But it occurred to me that even if the legend were true, and even if my father knew about the filters, his good friend–the man who had brought me to the Island–did not. He would have said something about them otherwise.

"Jacques doesn't know," I offered.

"Clearly not."

"But why wouldn't Dad tell him? They went through a lot together. They were close."

"I'd guess," said the carpenter, looking out his window, "that your father was ambivalent about the binoculars–about their value and about the wisdom of their very existence."

I was shaking my head, baffled–overwhelmed, really–by the ocean of facts I was being fed, first by Jacques and now by the carpenter. He caught the motion; turned back toward me.

"You are confused," he said.

"I guess so," I said. "That . . . and not yet convinced. There's . . . so much. And even if I were to buy into this, I'm not quite sure how I fit in."

"Oh, that is easy," the carpenter replied.

"It is?"

"Yes. I thought you must know by now. It is because you possess the binoculars."

"The binoculars," I repeated, and shook my head. "I don't understand."

"Well, to put it bluntly . . . I want them," he said. "They are too dangerous to be left out in the world."

"You want the binoculars."

"Yes. Although you don't make it easy. You thought to bring them with you to the Island only because I reminded you. Mental suggestion."

"Really," I said noncommittally, but then recalled that I had grabbed them off a shelf at my house on my way out the door–at the last second. I truly had almost neglected to bring them. So maybe what he said was true. "Well, I'm not sure I'd want to give them up. They're a family heirloom; worth something on a personal level."

"I would hope to dissuade you of that position," he said.

I shrugged in reply; didn't know what else to say. His simply wanting them wasn't enough.

"Of course," he said after several moments, "I realize you don't have them now. But do not dismiss my request out of hand."

I recalled the boy and the fishing line, and how the binoculars had dropped from my shoulder to the shore of the Twin Lake.

"Right," I said. "I dropped them back near the water."

"You were meant to," he said. "They have no place here. They must be dealt with in a secular setting. Not . . . in these woods."

I looked out the window.

"This isn't secular?" I asked. "It's still the Island, isn't it?"

"Yes and no," said the carpenter.

A shiver coursed through me.

"Just where are we?" I said. It came out a whisper.

He shrugged.

"We are here," he said. "That's all you need know."

I considered the answer, and decided not to pursue it further;

was, I think, afraid to. And so we stood, silent, awkward, at a seeming conversational dead-end.

"There is more," he said at last. "I didn't wish to alarm you, but apparently must . . . explain things more fully."

I laughed.

"What more could there be?" I said.

"There is," he said, "the matter of Beelzebub."

"Beelzebub?" I said. "You mean Satan?"

The carpenter shrugged.

"Satan. Lucifer. Beel. Or his favorite: Billy. Whatever you want to call him."

I took a deep breath. More religion. I wasn't sure I was ready for this.

"How does he fit in here?" I asked at last.

"Oh, he plays a key role," said the carpenter. "It is he who introduced Mussolini into the equation."

I was momentarily stunned at the simplicity of the statement; and together with the day's various revelations, suddenly felt tired–too tired to mount my usual degree of skepticism.

"Oh, hell," I said. "We're back to that; I'd almost forgotten. I gather that at some point here I'm simply supposed to accept the fact that Mussolini is really, truly inhabiting the old man. Oh, brother . . . Imagine that."

"Oh, it's far short of imaginary. It's quite based in fact."

"Uh huh," I said. "Okay. Let's assume it's possible. Are you quite sure Mussolini is in there? It couldn't just be an old man's senility? There's no room for mistake?"

"None," he said. "But Mussolini is more than inhabiting; violating, is more like it."

"And you're saying Beelzebub did that?"

"Arranged it. Yes. Billy," he said.

The mention of the devil triggered a memory.

"Wait . . . my father," I said, recalling something in Jacques' story. It was another piece that neatly fit this growing mosaic of mythological and religious assertions.

"What about him?"

"He told Jacques, when they were nearing the Ligurian Sea with Mussolini, that he felt like something bad might happen if they didn't keep moving. Kept looking over his shoulder. Well . . . Jacques decided that Dad had sensed the devil himself."

The carpenter was nodding.

"He was right," he said.

My mind was awhirl. All these facts, seemingly fitting together: Jacques' story, the carpenter's, this visit . . . Could it be that Mussolini . . . Il Duce . . . was actually on the Island? On the Island of my childhood? If so . . . if so . . . that just couldn't stand. A wave of skepticism washed over me, and again I doubted the possibility. But then the fatigue came again in equal force, weakening my resolve. I felt, actually felt for the first time, that what Jacques believed and Addie believed–the power they ascribed to the crystal–might actually be true. And with that growing acceptance came a touch of panic.

"But if he's in the old man, why don't you do something?" I said. "Get him out of there!"

The carpenter shook his head.

"It is not my job to directly combat evil," he said, and then, waving his hand as if dismissing the thought, added: "Besides, it is not of primary importance to me."

"Why not?" I said, a little too loudly, and then toned down my volume. "I mean . . . Mussolini. The guy was . . . still is . . . poison."

"Yes, indeed, he is that," said the carpenter. "Evidenced by the effect he's had on his surroundings; you have no doubt noticed the stench in the woods. But he is now in an old frame, one that limits his mobility and capacity for mischief. This, like all evil, will pass."

"Yeah, but Jacques doesn't want to wait," I said. "He wants Addie and me to perform an exorcism."

The carpenter scoffed.

"Foolishness," he said.

"Perhaps," I replied. "But Jacques wants his father to be able to die with dignity, rather than suffer possession. So . . . if Mussolini's actually in there . . . then I can't disagree with him."

"Foolishness," he said again. "An exorcism is generally futile. Beelzebub does not scare off at the drop of a religious ceremony. That would be a lark to him; his idea of recreation. He'd just fight you off with some of his mind games."

"Mind games? Like what?" I said.

"Oh, dreams are probably his favorite sport," the carpenter said.

"Dreams?" I said, suddenly suspicious, and approached the subject of my dreams obliquely. "I don't suppose he shows up as himself?"

"Oh, not usually. Unless it were to his advantage. He's usually in the guise of someone else. Whatever suits his purpose."

"Like Turk McGurk," I said softly to myself.

The carpenter studied me.

"You have seen him," he said.

"I had a couple of dreams out at Jacques' cabin," I said. "Each time, it was Turk McGurk appearing, trying to steer me away from doing anything about the old man; saying Jacques was crazy."

"Billy," said the carpenter, nodding. "Old Turk hasn't been around out there since shortly after his death. The place was vacant for a while, and he got bored and went on to . . . well, it doesn't matter where. No . . . you definitely have had contact with Billy. Interesting . . . you say he's been warning you away from Jacques' father?"

"Yes. But of course I haven't paid any attention. If anything, it's driven me toward the old man."

There was a silence then. I waited while the carpenter chewed his lip, obviously pondering something.

"And in what temper–mettle–did you find him . . . Jacques' father?" he asked. "Was he receptive to having visitors?"

"Not terribly," I said. "We were going to try again . . . just before you waylaid me out at the lake. In fact, that's why I was carrying the binoculars. Jacques thought that since they were from World War Two–and apparently hold some sort of evil aura, probably from all that bloodshed you've told me about–that Mussolini would be attracted to them. That it might help me get past this barrier he's thrown up. He doesn't much like me."

The carpenter snapped his fingers.

"Of course," he said.

"What?"

"Billy is after the binoculars, too," said the carpenter. "He's been playing a kind of chess game with me, and I didn't even realize it."

He turned and stared out the window again, clearly deep in thought. But I broke into his reverie.

"Excuse me," I said. "I'm having trouble with this. Old Billy, as you call him, is playing a game you didn't know was being played? I thought you knew everything."

The carpenter shook his head slightly, bringing his focus back to me.

"What?" he said. "Oh. 'Everything.' That's a human crutch. I know everything that matters, as a rule; but there are just too many things, and some far too meaningless to bother with. You folks should really get a grip on existence, you know. While you're in this world, you're pretty much on your own."

"Our own," I said.

"Your own," he repeated. "With exceptions, of course, where circumstance warrants an intrusion. Like now, I should guess. Listen, we're going to have to get back in this game. I really don't want those binoculars to fall into Billy's hands. Too much mischief there."

"Whoa," I said, holding up my right hand in a stopping gesture. "Let's back up. If the glasses are so important, why don't either of you just grab them?"

"Aren't you listening?" the carpenter said. "We don't get involved; can't directly. Everything's indirect: spiritual guidance, belief systems that lead people to actions, that sort of stuff. We can't physically obtain anything. And in the matter of the binoculars, Billy needs them to be given up willingly. Remember the Legend of the Crystal? That's the only way a crystal can maintain its power. So he's angling for that; you can bet on it. And he's doing it through Mussolini. That's why he set that bastard on the old man. It got Jacques involved, and got you here. Right near one of the windows."

"Windows?" I said. "I don't understand."

"Windows. Portals. Transfer sites. We can access something only if it's in one of the right spots."

"Right spots," I said. I was beginning to sound like a parrot.

"Exactly," he said. "There are certain specific locales . . . windows . . . through which we can act. The Red Sea is one. The Bermuda Triangle–well, a portion of it, anyway–is another. The Pacific Ocean has a spot, too, where Amelia Earhart disappeared from your sphere."

"Earhart?" I said. "You mean you grabbed her?"

"Well, not me personally," he said. "I think . . . this won't be as difficult as it would be in another locale; we have geography on our side. I have a plan in mind for the binoculars, Avery, a way to stop Billy from getting them."

I was standing there shaking my head, totally mystified.

"If the binoculars will only work for him if I give them willingly," I said, "why bother with a plan? I simply don't give them to him, that's all. As long as I know what he's up to, then he's out of luck."

The carpenter reached out and gently took hold of my shoulder.

"You have no idea," he said, "just how persuasive Billy can be–the subterfuges he might use to gain his end. No . . . believe me when I say this is necessary. If you proceed on the assumption that a simple refusal will suffice, then all is lost. We must proceed with my plan."

I tossed up my hands–half in surrender, I think, and half in frustration. It was clear that simple logic wouldn't win the day here; I was dealing with something beyond my experience and, I realized, maybe my control. Perhaps the matter was best left in the hands of someone who did understand. And that meant the carpenter. But still something–I think it was my inborn skepticism, for it hadn't totally vaporized–held me back.

"Maybe," I said. "Maybe . . . But I want to hear the plan first. Just what do you have in mind?"

"We are near one of those windows of which I spoke," he said. "We need to get the binoculars there, and at the same time take the old man with us."

"The old man? Why?" I said, aghast at the idea. "I don't know what this window's like, but if it's anything like the Bermuda Triangle or those other spots, it doesn't sound safe. I'm not going to put Jacques' father in danger just to suit your plan."

"But he might keep Billy off of us," the carpenter said. "Since Billy is behind Mussolini's intrusion, he'll want to protect his investment."

"No," I said. "That's crazy."

The carpenter held up his hand, palm toward me.

"Okay, tell you what. We'll combine our two needs here. You get the binoculars out there, and the old man . . . and I'll see that Mussolini is chased clear of him. I'll see that the old man is freed from that tyrant."

I was taken aback; hadn't expected the offer. But saw the opportunity.

"You mean like an exorcism?"

"Oh, much more efficient," he said. "We can sweep him up in the same window as the binoculars."

"You mean sweep up Mussolini; not the old man. Right?"

"Absolutely," said the carpenter.

"Okaaaaaay," I said slowly. I tried to muster some skepticism for the plan and, really, for the whole Mussolini-binocular-crystals saga, not to mention for the current conversation itself; but despite the effort, I found myself starting to buy into everything. This whole experience–the lake, the bear and the carpenter, in a strange wooded setting–could be an illusion, I told myself; but it all seemed quite real. It looked real, smelled real, felt real–not at all like a dream or hallucination or whatever. I even pinched myself to see if it would hurt, and it did.

So I was in an accepting mood. And in that mood, I decided the carpenter's plan sounded better than the exorcism proposed by Jacques and seconded by Addie. I couldn't help but note, either, that it would be orchestrated by someone more attuned to the supernatural than Addie was.

"You keep mentioning a window," I said. "I gather this is some specific locale?"

"Yes," he said. "Where do you think?"

"I haven't a clue. That's why I'm asking."

The carpenter smiled.

"You've been there," he said. "Think back."

I gave him a blank look.

"Think thunder and lightning," he said. "It's part and parcel of a window exchange."

"Oh, my," I said, suddenly realizing.

"Right," said the carpenter. "We have to get the binoculars and the old man out to Gull Island."

****

A surge of adrenalin at the thought of another Gull adventure made me momentarily giddy, and I found the scene in front of me fading. For a moment, I could see Addie and Jacques along the shore of the western of the Twin Lakes, frozen as they had been upon my departure from their company.

"Wait," I said, but not to them. I was speaking to the carpenter, trying to get back to his cabin, to his side, to his knowledge and counsel. And as that desire to return took hold, the giddiness retreated, and I found the carpenter and his home coming back into focus, first in shadow and then, gradually, into a three-dimensional stage in which I was once again a player.

He was standing there as he had been, a patient look on his face.

"Adrenalin," he said. "I know. It knocks things askew. But you are back, and I gather with more to address."

I felt a wave of nausea ripple across me, steadied myself and took a deep calming breath.

"Gull," I said after several moments. "It's a transfer site?"

"Yes."

My mind went back to that night four decades earlier.

"I don't suppose," I said, "that what happened out there in '56 was a window transfer?"

"What? No, of course not. Why do you ask?"

"Well, it's obvious," I said. "It's a transfer site, and Addie was–well, thinks she was–transferred out; died. And then brought back again. Why wouldn't I ask?"

The carpenter was smiling, gently shaking his head.

"Right, right," he said. "No . . . that's coincidence."

He stroked his beard and strolled past me, back to the window. From there, he looked across to the tree line, but not seeking something in the woods, I decided; he was looking inside himself and backward to that long-past event, formulating his reply.

"That was no transfer; it was natural forces at work. It was simply your friend's time. That's all." He said it so softly I almost didn't hear.

The carpenter turned from the window and considered me.

"Of course," he said, "old Billy could have had a hand in it. He's always trying to create problems . . . sadness . . . grief."

"What? Are you saying she really did die?"

"Of course," he said.

"Whoa," I whispered, trying to digest the validation. Surprisingly, my skepticism on that point, too, seemed to have disappeared. Acceptance took but a second.

"And Beelzebub killed her?" I asked, my mind working past the fact of her death to the cause. "I thought you guys didn't do things directly."

"No, no . . . he wouldn't have killed her," he said. "Directness is not permitted. But he may have caused her to be killed; I'm not sure how. Maybe he tossed a wave of confusion over you; forced you to turn the wrong way in the water at a key moment in your frantic search for the girl. Maybe he made *her* turn the wrong way. Maybe he delayed Eliot Ness's rescue efforts, even for a moment. Who knows?"

"When she died," I said, "how was it that she returned? Was it my grandfather's cries?"

He nodded.

"Then he really did die for her?"

"He was old," the carpenter said. "His time was coming anyway. But . . . we waited for him; didn't rush him. He was really very impressive that night. Earned a lot of respect."

"Are you the one who sent Addie back? That night, I mean."

"Me? No, I had little to do with it."

"But somebody . . . or something . . . sent her back."

"Well, yes. I suggested it. But it was . . . you know . . . Him."

The next words came out of my mouth a whisper.

"Oh, God," I said.

"Indeed," he responded. "Now, then . . . to change the subject. There is the matter of your father."

I looked at him in what I suppose was a fairly stupid way. With the sudden leap in topic, I had trouble following him.

"What?" I said. "What about my father?"

"There is something . . . about the binoculars."

The binoculars again; we were back to them. He seemed determined not to let the subject lie . . . continued to press his case–although, in truth, I was already sufficiently swayed by his Gull Island plan.

"What?" I said, rubbing my eyes; they suddenly felt strained, a little overworked in the dim light of the cabin.

"Well, I don't suppose there is harm in telling you this: I talked to him about the binoculars–right here, in fact–on one of his Island visits."

I was surprised, and must have shown it. He had only minutes before talked in mostly speculative tones about the extent of my father's knowledge–but here he was saying they had discussed the matter.

"Yes," he said. "In this very clearing; of course, I didn't have but a shanty here then. I related to your father what I've related to you: the history of the binoculars. I do not know for sure the extent of his knowledge to that point; but when I was finished, he understood as much as you do now. And I thought I convinced him of the wisdom of turning them over to me. But I don't think he believed after the fact that he had really seen me. Some react that way after a visit; they chalk it up to hallucinations or something. Or forget completely. Or remember but decline to consciously concede my reality. I cannot say for certain whether the information I imparted stayed with him. In any event, we didn't follow through; he kept the binoculars."

Something about his words triggered the memory bank I harbored on my father. I mentally pored over several images, and settled quickly on the one that will forever leave a part of me saddened: the scene at his deathbed. But beyond the sadness was a revelation.

"Oh, my," I said.

"What?"

"I'm pretty sure," I said, "that he recalled your meeting. He said a few words just before he passed away. He said . . . he said the words "carpenter" and "bear." He remembered you, all right; you and your large hairy friend. So I guess it's reasonable to assume that his response to your talk was intentional resistance; that he just didn't feel he could part with the glasses."

"Yes," said the carpenter. "That would fit. So it brings me back to this: Will the son part with what the father would not–take the high road for the greater good?"

Son. Father. The words again triggered the image of my Dad's deathbed. I could visualize it, and then feel it: the emotion of the scene, and even the antiseptic smell of it. I could sense my father near me, mumbling his final words, breathing his final breath.

"The binoculars," he had said. "You take . . . carpenter . . . moose . . . bear . . ."

"Oh my God," I said to myself.

"Pardon?" said the carpenter.

"My father," I said. "He wanted me to give you the glasses . . . said to take them to you. And . . . just before he died, he also said the word 'moose.' As in Mussolini. It had to be. What other moose was there? He must have known . . . even before Jacques . . . about the possession."

More of my father's final words flashed across my mind, adding another layer of certainty.

"And yes," I said. "He definitely did know about the filters."

"Oh?" said the carpenter. "What has convinced you?"

"His last words. Dad said, 'fill . . . terse . . . see . . . a . . . head.' It made no sense to me at the time. But he was telling me about their power."

"Well . . . good," said the carpenter, smiling gently. "Then it is settled. You will help me?"

I shrugged. I was, as I said, pretty well convinced of the plan's desirability, if only because it offered the chance to drive Mussolini from the old man. But now, beyond that, allegiance to my patriarch also seemed to dictate that I help. The discovery of the meaning in my father's message had left me feeling . . . I don't know . . . both pleased with myself and pleased with the carpenter. And in the grip of that pleasure, I found myself wanting to share the internal glow it created–a feeling of power that comes with knowledge.

The decision was easy.

"I guess so," I said, and smiled. "It's what Dad wanted. Right?"

"Right," the carpenter answered.

THIRTY-SEVEN

Into the Old Man's Lair

Our remaining discussion dealt only with the specifics of the plan for the binoculars.

Then, that completed, there was nothing more to be said, short of a thousand questions about religion and creation and the afterlife, but I couldn't quite ask any of them. I don't know if the reluctance was within me, or applied by the will of the carpenter, or simply a product of time and location. All I know is we finished and, in so doing, the carpenter shook my hand.

"Thank you for helping," he said softly, and nodded toward his front door. I turned, took the few steps to the door, and paused to look back.

"And don't forget the binoculars," he said.

"I won't," I said, and stepped through the door, expecting to be met by the large furry guide again. Instead, I instantly found myself back on the northern shore of the first of the Twin Lakes, with Addie and Jacques those several paces ahead of me, frozen in mid-step. I felt wobbly for a moment, as if my equilibrium had been compromised, but a deep breath seemed to correct the problem. Looking out on the lake for the boy and the old man in the fishing boat, I found a surface devoid of anything but gently rippling waves.

Scanning the shoreline around me, I spotted the binocular case just to my left, knelt to retrieve it and placed its strap back over my left shoulder.

Then, wheeling toward my companions, I saw them complete

the steps they had begun so long before–or what seemed like so long before.

"Hey, guys!" I called out.

As they planted their newly landed feet, they turned and asked in unison:

"What?"

"Wait up," I said. "You're going too fast for me."

****

We passed through the channel and hiked into the woods bordering the second lake, making our way through the thick growth until it gave way to the clearing surrounding the cabin. Before approaching the front door, Jacques turned to us.

"Now, are we agreed on the procedure? We feel him out, try to get him to submit to an exorcism. If my father holds any sway at all, we may be able to pull it off. If Mussolini has control, then I don't see that he would submit–except perhaps as a challenge. We might go for the manhood angle; make him feel like a coward for not taking up the gauntlet."

"Sounds okay," said Addie. "I just wish we weren't flying by the seat of our pants on this."

I didn't say anything, and they both looked at me.

"What?" I said.

"Are we agreed?" said Jacques.

"Oh, yeah, sure," I said, trying to sound nonchalant. "Whatever you guys want."

Jacques nodded, satisfied, but Addie looked at me closely through slitted eyes.

"What's going on?" she said.

I wanted to tell her, but I couldn't. I wasn't feeling the sense of denial feared by the carpenter, but was facing a simple fact: If I tried to describe what had happened, I'd sound crazy. After all, walking on water? A bear guide? The carpenter in the woods? Besides, even if I was so inclined, the old man's cabin was no place to get into it.

"Nothing," I said, trying to sound innocent. "Let's do it."

She studied me a couple of moments more.

"You heard him," said Jacques. "Let's go."

She shook her head slowly, almost imperceptibly. I don't think Jacques saw it, but I did.

"Sure," she said. "Why not?"

Jacques knocked, and the old voice carried through to the front stoop.

"Who the hell is it?" it shouted.

Jacques sighed.

"Sounds like we'll have to challenge the bastard," he said, before raising his voice and shouting back.

"It's Jacques, Papa, along with Addie and her friend Avery."

"You can come in, and she can!" the old man shouted. "But that young pup can stay outdoors!"

Jacques turned toward me, seeking help.

The carpenter and I had, in our final moments, anticipated the old man's possible responses upon my approach; this was the most likely. So I was ready.

I whispered instructions to Jacques.

"Tell him I've brought the binoculars, but add this–that I thought he might like to hear a story about . . . how they are part of the Legend of the Crystal of Death."

Jacques stared at me, no doubt wondering what game I was playing. How, I imagined his look to be saying, did the binoculars fit into the legend?

"What are you doing?" Addie hissed. "We didn't discuss any such story."

Jacques reached out and touched her shoulder.

"Wait," he said, and thought a moment before turning back to me. "You have such a story?"

I nodded once, quickly.

Jacques gave a little motion of his head, and turned back to Addie.

"It's all right," he said. "Let's go his way."

She appeared to want to say something, but held it in check, whatever it was. Jacques, satisfied, spoke through the door again.

"The young man has something to tell you, Papa. He knows what a World War Two buff you are, and has brought along some binoculars that once belonged to a Nazi. He thought you might like to see them, and hear how they are connected to Il Cristallo di Morte."

There was silence from within, and I think I heard a snort before the voice was raised again.

"The Crystal of Death?" the voice answered.

"Yes, Papa."

Another silence was followed by accord.

"Very well," he said. "He may come in, too. But I expect him to be on his best behavior."

"He will be, Papa," said Jacques, opening the door and leading us into the cabin.

****

The interior was without lamp or other artificial light. The only illumination was from the sunlight coming through the three windows adorning the living room, but the old man had minimized that too by almost completely closing the windows' curtains.

He was seated in his reading chair, but in the absence of light was not reading this time. I suspect he had been napping when we approached. Anyway, it took the better part of a half-minute for my eyes to adjust to this shadowed interior–before I could clearly see the expression on his face. But I could tell from the tone in his voice how pleased he was to once again have Addie in his midst.

"Ah, my dear," he said, extending his bony right hand toward her. She in turn placed her right hand in his and allowed him to bestow a gentle kiss upon her knuckles.

"Mr. Lafitte," she said softly. "How very good to see you again."

"The pleasure is all mine, my dear," he said. "Please sit down next to me. Jacques, pull that chair by the window over here."

Jacques went to the western wall, where a spindle-backed chair was set. He carried it across the dozen or so feet to the side of the old man, set it down and dusted it with his hand. A small cloud lifted from it. Once he was done, Jacques motioned to Addie to seat herself, and she complied.

Only then, after she was seated–and after giving her another kindly smile–did the old man turn toward me and acknowledge my presence. But it wasn't really my presence that he was interested in; it was what I had brought with me.

"So," he said, setting his eyes upon mine. "You have brought something? A memento from the war?"

"Yes," I said, lifting the binocular case from my shoulder and cradling it in my arms. From that position, I was able to disengage the clasp, open the top and pull out the glasses. I then held the binoculars by their strap in my right hand and let them dangle in midair in front of the old man, safely out of reach.

After staring at the glasses for a protracted period, he spoke.

"What do they have to do with the crystal?" the old man asked. "Is this story of yours fact or fiction?"

"Oh, I'll let you be the judge," I said, and looked at Addie and Jacques. It was for them, too, that the words would be spoken. I found it necessary–in light of the plan the carpenter and I had decided upon–to tell them some of the binoculars' history, without mentioning the carpenter. That particular aspect would remain confidential for a while, and perhaps forever: a private memory. But I needed my friends to understand the power of the binoculars; and I needed Mussolini to know too, but for a different reason. I needed him to know so that he would feel an overwhelming compulsion to obtain them, to possess them, to use them to his own evil ends.

And in so doing, I could set up the transfer, and get him out of the body of Jacques' father.

****

I reviewed the legend of the bear, with emphasis on the rare blue oval crystal, and related the history of Abraham Mann and his visions and his ocular creation. I went over the horrors inflicted on the Jews in Berlin and of the Nazi stranglehold that ultimately swept Abraham up and sent the binoculars on their way; recounted the glasses' path as they worked their way across Europe to my father's hands; and told of my father's final moments and how the binoculars had consequently been passed to my care-taking.

When I finished, I waited for a response, but none was immediately forthcoming. The old man had his eyes fastened on the binoculars as I continued to hold them and, periodically, swing them gently in front of him. Jacques was looking in turns introspective and curious, his eyes darting from the old man to the glasses, over to me and back to some point in front of him as he absorbed all of this new information. And Addie . . .

Addie was looking at me as though I had stepped out of an alien spacecraft, as though she didn't recognize me but wanted to discover, through dint of visual study, what made me tick. I gloried in her response, and gave her an enigmatic smile in return that probably came off a little smug. But then, I felt a little smug.

The old man was the first to speak.

"And the filters are . . . in the glasses?"

I patted the binoculars case.

"In here," I said. "Where they're normally kept–set in little protective sleeves."

"Can I see them?" he asked. "Try them?" The tone was almost polite, but a touch of greed was in there, too.

"Not here," I said. "They work best in sunlight, and where the vista is clear and distant."

That wasn't the case at all, as far as I knew, but it was essential that he think so.

"When then?" he asked. The words were practically spit out.

"Soon," I said. "I was thinking of maybe on the western shore, over at your son's cabin. They should work well there. What do you think, Jacques? Can we arrange a little get-together, say tomorrow?"

"Why not now?" the old man said.

"Too cloudy," I said, embroidering. "Tomorrow is supposed to be clear and bright. We can do it early–say around 10. What do you think, Jacques? All right with you?"

Jacques wasn't at all sure what was transpiring. I could sense that I had confused him with my story–where could I have come up with it, and to what end?–and with my sudden evident belief in the legend, not to mention my assertiveness in dealing with the old man. But he decided to play along.

"Yeah. Sure. Ten would be good," he said. "Papa, I can swing by and get you a little earlier, then take you out to my place."

"No need," I said. "I'll come in and pick him up; save you a trip. Then we'll meet you and Addie back at the cabin. I'd like a little time alone with him, anyway. Okay with you?"

Jacques studied me, glanced at the old man, and shrugged.

"Whatever," he said. "If that's what you want."

"Addie?" I asked.

She was still staring at me, gauging.

"Addie?" I said again. "Okay with you?"

Her eyes flickered, and she worked a smile onto her face.

"Fine with me," she said, almost convincingly. The old man didn't seem to notice her hesitation.

"And you, Mr. Lafitte?"

He pried his eyes from the binoculars and looked up, his eyes seeking mine in the dim light of the cabin's interior.

"Don't be late!" he said.

THIRTY-EIGHT

Visit to an Old Haunt

By the time we had finished with the old man and returned to the northwest shore, neither of my companions was talking to me.

Jacques and Addie were clearly thrown off by my sudden acquisition of the Abraham Mann saga and by my sudden change of spots, as it were, from skeptic to proponent of the ethereal.

Addie kept shooting me looks that suggested I was a turncoat, even though the turn had been in her direction. What bothered her most, I was certain, was my failure to confide in her before relating the saga in the presence of the old man–although where or when I might have accumulated such knowledge was no doubt gnawing at her, too.

Jacques was more difficult to read–part of his normal persona as a rule, but more pronounced now, as though he had pulled a shade down over his eyes that said "Do Not Enter." His thoughts I could perhaps surmise, but the effort seemed too daunting; I was having enough trouble dealing with my own.

Disapproval I could take, but the silence each was imposing on me was a bit much, so I opted for a walk in the woods.

"Going out," I said.

"Oh? Where to?" asked Jacques.

"Why bother asking?" asked Addie. "He won't tell us, anyway."

I gave her what I thought was a suitably wounded look before answering.

"Oh, back on the track, then maybe into the woods. I haven't really explored much in this area yet."

"Well . . . be back before dinner," Jacques said. "I've got plans for us."

"Oh?" I said. "What?"

"Plans," he said. "I'll tell you later. Now go . . . go."

He pushed his hands forward, as if shoving me away.

"Yes. By all means go," said Addie, her nose up.

I grabbed my coat and started to leave, but turned back to pick up the binocular case from the card table and hang it by its strap off my right shoulder. As I reached the door a second time, I stopped, looked back at Addie and gave her a smile. I meant it as a peace offering, but I guess she could have interpreted it otherwise. Anyway, she saw it but pretended not to, turning her head suddenly aside.

"Back by dinner," I said, swinging the door open and then closing it softly behind me.

****

The walk did not yield much of discovery at first–a couple of deer, some solitude and a windbreak–but provided me a chance to ponder all that had transpired that day: the trip to see the old man, complete with some half-baked notion of an exorcism; the boy and man on the lake, and my first-ever walk on water; the bear; the carpenter; the tale of Abraham.

As a trained observer, it all seemed real to me; and yet, as a trained observer, it all seemed a bit beyond reason.

I found a clearing in the woods and sat, my back against a tree stump, the day's weak and sporadic sunlight filtering lightly down around me. As I rested there, the light seemed to brighten, caressing me, urging me to continue my thought process.

Was it possible that all of that had really happened? I told myself that logically–by the laws of physics and everything earthly–it could not have. But then again, what had happened–if it happened–was not of the earth, and so why should physics and logic apply?

Could I have hallucinated something so detailed, remembered it so vividly, learned a history so layered and so tightly fitted to the one that Jacques had related?

Did not the words my father uttered on his deathbed make sense in view of what I had now seen and heard?

Or was my subconscious working overtime trying to make something of those very words–creating a scenario by which I could understand my father's dying message?

"Oh, my," I muttered, rubbing my eyes, closing out the sun's rays and the gently shadowed scene before me. Perhaps if I just kept my eyes closed, looked elsewhere, looked inward . . .

Looked elsewhere.

I uncovered my eyes, staring ahead at nothing in particular, weighing whether I really wanted to do it, or whether I should. "What if it doesn't work?" I mumbled to the woods, and when they failed to answer, I asked this: "What if it does?"

I hadn't really given direct thought before to the possibility of putting the carpenter's story to the test. And now that I was thinking about it, I could feel my heart accelerate as if I were running. My left hand worked its way across my chest and down my right side, to where the binocular case rested, angled on the ground and against me, its strap still dangling from my shoulder.

"Well, what the hell," I said. I slid the strap down and lifted the case up onto my stomach, unfastened the clasp and pulled free the binoculars. Then, gingerly, careful not to damage them–or perhaps a little wary of them–I pulled the two filters from their slots.

They were unremarkable, just blue bits of glass encased in circular black metal framing. Small, I thought. How could anything so small be the cause of so much mischief?

I held one up toward the soft light above, trying to see something, anything, on the other side, but all it yielded was a dark blue hue.

Holding the binoculars steady in my left hand, I placed the filter in the eyepiece on the right and snapped it in place.

"Easy enough," I said, marveling that I had never utilized them–whether my father had removed the filters from the case years ago or not. I had, after all, had them in my possession since his death.

I took hold of the second filter and placed it in the left eyepiece and felt it seat itself. Then I sat for several moments . . . perhaps more than several . . . screwing up the courage to take a look through the binoculars.

"Come on," I said to myself. "It's the only way you'll know for sure."

But as soon as I said it, I wondered whether even a vision of the future would thoroughly convince me–for if I somehow had hallucinated the bear and the carpenter, surely I could hallucinate a future that would never be.

"Oh, lord," I said. "Get a grip. You're here alone, on the Island, in the woods. This is all real, just as that was all real. Your butt is freezing, for heaven's sake, so get a move on."

And that was the clincher, really: my rear end was cold. I was sitting in a damp spot, and the cold of the forest floor had worked its way through my pants and was starting to numb my backside.

My eyes and ears might deceive me, I decided, but my rear end wouldn't . . . and wasn't. Whatever was about to transpire was grounded in reality.

And so, with barely a breath between that revelation and the subsequent motion, I lifted the binoculars to my eyes and peered through them into the forest.

****

I encountered Addie in front of Jacques' cabin upon my return. I had been gone longer than I expected–wandering the woods, thinking–and early evening had taken hold, bringing with it a dimming light and a hint of the chill of the coming night.

"What are you doing out here?" I asked. "Where's Jacques?"

"He said he wanted to rest," she answered. "Besides, I needed some fresh air."

She was seated on his small front porch, legs touching the patch of lawn that fronted the building. I sidled up next to her, but didn't sit, leaving one foot on the lawn and placing one on the porch. From there I could look down at her and, following her gaze, out across the Straits in the direction of Mackinac.

"Pretty," I said, for the scene was more than just an island a few miles away. The sun was off to the left of Mackinac, softening as it fell, leaving the Island shadowed from our perspective: a dark mass to the right of a reddish evening flame cast across the Straits, a flame reaching all the way to the shoreline a few feet in front of us. The water, rippling slightly in the gentle wind, gave the flame the illusion of motion, as though it were swaying slightly, dancing to the song of the handful of stars coming out in the sky overhead and to the east. Stars seemed to be dotting Mackinac, too, as a few of the shop lights on the island's main street popped on.

"Do you remember our visit to Mackinac?" Addie asked. "Our tandem bike ride around the island, our swim, our trip to the Grand Hotel?"

"Indeed. It's indelibly etched. Especially the swim." The image of Addie stripped to her underwear that long-ago day–and me to mine–brought a chortle from somewhere deep inside me.

Addie swung her arm into my leg; it was intended as rebuke, but came off as something much less.

She smiled.

"It was a grand day, a grand summer," she said.

"Yes," I agreed. "And it seems as though it doesn't want to let go."

Addie looked up at me, squinting in the dusk, trying to see what my face revealed, and–finding an answer there–nodded.

****

"Jacques?"

Addie and I had just walked in, but didn't see our host. I called out softly, so as not to wake him if sound sleep had claimed him.

"In here," he called from the bedroom, and stuck his head out. "Just getting up; be right out. You were gone a long time. Have a nice walk?"

"Yes," I said. "Quite interesting. The Island is a very . . . inspiring place. Good for clearing the cobwebs."

"Yes, it is," called Jacques. "But listen, I was thinking. How'd you guys like to see a different island tonight?"

Addie clapped her hands and looked at me with bright eyes. "Mackinac," she said. "Oh, let's."

Jacques came into the living room. The only interior light came from an overhead bulb in the kitchen. It was supplemented by the rapidly fading sunlight wafting through the various windows.

"I thought you'd like that," he said. "It will be a good change of pace; let us all clear our minds a little."

Mackinac. It had a certain appeal; might relax me. And relaxation was something I could use–for the uncertainty of the next day was weighing on me.

"Well, I don't know," I said. "There's not much to do over there. I'd definitely say no if you had a TV, Jacques . . ."

Addie hit me in the arm.

"Ouch," I said. "I mean, great idea. It's been too many years . . . Really. It sounds good."

"That's better," she said.

"There's still a handful of shops open, a couple of night spots, the Grand Hotel," said Jacques. "The island will be pretty much shut down for the winter in another week, except for a couple of restaurants and bars. Snowmobilers and cross-country skiers are about all it will soon be seeing."

"The Grand Hotel!" said Addie. "Oh, yes; it would be such fun to see it again."

I liked this Addie a lot better than the one who had been casting verbal aspersions and nasty looks my way earlier, and I hated to put a damper on her enthusiasm. But there was an obvious question that needed to be asked, and I just hoped Jacques had a good answer.

"But Jacques, how do we get over there?" I said. "There's no boat at your dock. We gonna have Johnny take us over?"

"No," said Jacques. "Remember the day of Gull Island, back in '56, before the storm, when you needed a ride back to Pointe aux Pins? You had gotten a lift out here to Turk's cabin with Freddy Vanderpool when you thought Eliot needed help, and Freddy left in a huff after discovering that Eliot was in no danger. Remember how you got back?"

"Sure," I said. "You had the *Sylmar* anchored up around the bend, in a little cove."

Jacques was smiling broadly.

"Oh, wow," I said, suddenly excited. "You don't still have the *Sylmar*, do you?"

He was nodding, almost giggling.

"But Jacques," said Addie, "you're not in competition with your own son, are you?"

"No, no," he said, "it's just something I've kept for private use. It's almost like a member of the family. Anyway, it's there, and we can be on it and under way in a matter of minutes. First, though . . ."

He walked over to the kitchen, lifted a crock-pot from the counter and carried it to the card table. I hadn't even noticed it there, despite the aroma of cooking food. Removing the lid, he smelled the contents.

"Ah, yes," he said, pleased. "First we have some chili con carne. That'll give us a little stick-to-the-ribs sustenance for the cold night air."

He retreated to the kitchen again for a minute, returned with bowls and spoons and drinks, and we all dug in.

****

Little detail of the *Sylmar* could be seen in the dark, but the short dinghy trip felt like a homecoming, anyway, for the *Sylmar* held a place in my memory as a vital and appealing link between mainland life and the magic of the Island. A *Sylmar* journey had been the first and last Island-related experience every summer in which my family had gone to Bois Blanc. My memory bank cherished the quality of those rides: the hum of the engine, the swaying motion, the spray kicked up as the ferry sliced through the waves, and the foghorn voice of the skipper–Jacques, Lightfoot Jack–as he casually piloted the craft while chatting with his passengers. And I remembered–embraced–the role the boat had played in saving me from the Gull Island storm, and in bringing Addie back from apparent death that violent night so long ago.

After we reached the *Sylmar* on this night and climbed up from the dinghy, the first thing I did–the moment I was on deck–was caress the boat's port railing, as though it was a long-ago lover.

"Beautiful," I muttered as I wandered the deck, examining the vehicle and passenger areas, touching a window here, a chain there, a seat cushion, and finally the pilot's wheel itself.

"Yes," said Addie, reacting in much the same way, joining me on my tour.

"Okay, time to go," Jacques said after securing the dinghy and checking out the engine compartment astern. He moved quickly across the length of the boat and claimed his seat, forcing Addie and me aside.

He started the engine quickly, and we were under way.

I couldn't see much through the windshield, other than some lights along the Mackinac shoreline–shops on the main street–and, up the hill to their left, the brightly lit portico of the Grand Hotel.

The trip was bearable despite the chill because of the presence of a heater to the side of Jacques' perch. After she had warmed herself, Addie wandered to the rear of the cabin–separated from the open ferry area by a canvas flap–and, lifting the flap's edge, ducked underneath it and went outside.

Jacques and I exchanged a look, and then I followed her, lifting the flap as she had and passing by into the night air. I was stunned at first by the cold–a product of the autumn temperature, the *Sylmar*'s motion and the spray that was flying by as the boat cut a swath to Mackinac. But a couple of deep breaths helped me adjust, and I continued toward the rear.

Addie was standing slightly to the starboard side, a bit more than halfway back, looking down at the spot where, so many years before, she had lain apparently dead while my grandfather had keened to the heavens above from a position farther astern.

She had come back that night, and lived, and served her God for most of her natural existence–and now, in this moment, had returned to the very spot, though not geographically, from which she had recovered and risen.

I tried to think of something fitting to say, but was at a loss. She broke the silence.

"Funny," she called out above the wind. "I don't feel any older; not really. It seems like it just now happened." Then she looked up at the sky–a starlit heaven with an occasional rapidly moving cloud–and then at me.

"Your grandfather," she yelled. "He's out there, you know."

She motioned skyward with her hand, and I scanned the stars.

"I suppose," I said. "But where?"

"The place where good souls go."

"Can you point it out?" I said, feeling a bit churlish. "Is it, like, near the Big Dipper, or what?"

She moved closer and reached up to touch my cheek.

"You'll see him someday," she said. "Because you are a good soul, too. I know . . . it's difficult to visualize such a thing, but believe me: souls exist, and leave the body, and the good ones go to a place of grace. I've seen them, and I feel their peace. I can't tell you where this place is . . . but I believe it is out there."

"And the bad ones?" I said.

"I've encountered a couple," she said. "They feel the antithesis of peace."

"Fear?"

"That, regret, resentment . . . many negatives rolled into one. They know that something unpleasant is ahead."

"But not what."

"Not at the point where I've seen them, no."

I looked into her eyes, thought of the closeness we once felt, the closeness we still felt, though of a different order. I reached out and touched her hair lightly.

"Let's go back in," I said.

"Not yet," she said. Instead, she strode to the stern, where she looked back across the water we had traversed, back to the south and Bois Blanc. It was darkly shadowed there save for one window–Jacques' kitchen window–giving off a pinprick of light.

I positioned myself next to her again, to her left, and leaned on the rear gate that for years had doubled as an entry and exit ramp for all those vehicles the *Sylmar* had ferried. It had probably been turned up in its locked position now for a decade or two; might even be rusted shut.

"What happened to you out there today, Avery?" she said softly, leaning in so I could hear her over the wind and the waves and the engine's whine.

I thought of several possible answers, some way around the truth that would not set her off on another of her fits of pique. Well, I thought, I would have to tell her the truth sometime, so why not now? But I couldn't–it was too complex, too bizarre for me to deal with right then–and so I decided instead on a simple, direct and misleading response that elicited exactly the kind of reaction I should have anticipated.

"I found Jesus," I said.

Her reaction was swift and well aimed. This time her punch had some speed and meaning to it, and caught me in the fleshy part of my right arm.

"Owww!" I howled. "Geez, Addie. Chill out."

"Damn you, Avery," she hissed. "I asked a perfectly reasonable question. I do not expect a smart-ass answer."

I was rubbing my arm, wondering what–if anything–to say next. What was safe?

"Sorry," I ventured, taking a step back just in case. "Let's just say I had . . . a revelation."

"A revelation," she echoed, a touch of sarcasm in her voice. But then she said it again, toyed with the word before continuing. "A revelation . . . what, like a vision or something? Or aren't we really talking theologically here? I mean, where did that binocular story come from?"

"The story . . ." I said, trying to figure out an acceptable response that wasn't a blatant lie, yet something that would satisfy Addie's evident view of me–religiously speaking–as a doubter, a skeptic, and a person whose beliefs lay somewhere in the muck.

And then I remembered my distant ties to old Abraham Mann. "Let's just say the story is an old family heirloom," I said, "passed down from one generation to another."

"Ah, hah," she said victoriously. "I thought so. It's like the myth . . . but not true. I mean . . . you can't see the future through those things. Right? No . . . of course you can't. What am I saying? Like you'd be in charge of a magic crystal."

I smiled. She was making this pretty easy. But I decided to string her along a little–to play hurt.

"What do you mean?" I said. "Why wouldn't I be?"

Addie looked at me to see if the tone–accompanied by a pained expression–was sincere. And decided it wasn't.

"Yeah, right," she said. "I'm sure that the powers-that-be would entrust something like that to Mr. Skeptical."

I looked at her and just gave a quick half-smile, as though to say, *"Okay. You win."* But she wasn't through; wasn't quite ready to let it go.

"In a pig's eye, they would," she muttered, and then another thought clearly struck her. "But then . . . what's all this about tomorrow, Avery? With the old man? Why get him over to Jacques' place?"

"Oh, that," I said airily. "Just to get him away from his little castle; his little throne. I thought we might have an advantage on our own turf."

"Yeah . . . okay," she said slowly. "But what about the binoculars? I mean, as soon as he looks through them, he'll know it's a con."

"Addie," I said, tiring of the questions, "trust me on this one, okay? I've got it covered. Let's just enjoy the evening; forget about the old man and try to enjoy ourselves. Any chance of that?"

The *Sylmar*'s horn sounded, startling us both. We turned in unison and looked around the starboard side of the cabin, to the approaching docks bordering downtown Mackinac. The shop lights shone brightly now, the darkness of night having long since settled in.

"Okay," she said, leaning back toward me. "A little fun would be fine. But Avery . . ."

"What?"

"Jacques is counting on us to help him with that old man. Whether you believe the Mussolini story or not, I need you on this one."

I was nodding my head, but wasn't sure she saw it.

"I know," I said.

****

Mackinac Island–home of fudge and leather and an historic old fort on a bluff overlooking the Straits–is a tourist mecca in the summer. But come autumn, it starts folding in on itself until only the hardiest of souls–winter-lovers–venture to its shores. Most of it essentially goes into hibernation.

Now, though, it still boasted fine dining, entertainment and–up at the hotel–a show of wealth. As soon as we docked and made our way to Main Street, we could see the effect of summer's end in the locked doors and "Closed for the Season" signs in more than a third of the shops. But that left two-thirds, and so we wandered into and out of them before deciding to visit a local tavern that was featuring a ragtime piano player.

The tavern, a second-story affair of worn wooden floors, polished brass fixtures and comfortable round tables bearing the scars of knives and forks, offered a basic menu of chicken wings, pasta and beer. Jacques and I opted for the beer and some beer nuts, but Addie asked for a soft drink.

"Never liked the taste," she said, grimacing at our frosty mugs.

The piano player was a middle-aged fellow in striped vest, baggy dark pants and bowler hat. He was taking requests, but fortunately had his own songs, too, to fill in the time. The tavern turnout–low–was yielding few people with a yen to hear personal favorites.

The three of us watched, mesmerized by the man's dancing hands, until he took a break nearly a half-hour after we'd arrived.

"He's good," said Jacques. "I'd forgotten that they get some pretty sizable talent over here. I come to Mackinac quite often, but it's been years since I did something like this."

With the break, and warmed by the food and drink, we left, wandered back down Main Street, took a left and climbed a gently sloping road toward the old fort, a structure overlooking the Straits that had been a key point of defense two hundred years earlier but was now but a curiosity and a visitor attraction.

When we reached the base of the fort's bluff, we looked up at the long walkway that would take us up to the fort's entrance if we so desired; at this point, though, it would be but a matter of exercise, the fort being a strictly daytime operation. It was locked tightly now.

"I think," I said, "that we've probably walked off our food; I don't fancy that climb."

"Nor I," said Jacques, looking up the walkway and then back down the hill we had just negotiated. "You know, it's very peaceful up here–at least at night; it's too busy during the day, really. This is my favorite time on this island; the quiet seems to help conjure up the glory of its past. It's quite a rich history, you know; the French, the British . . ."

He lapsed into a silence, and the three of us stood there, looking out over the roofs of the Mackinac shops and restaurants, out into the darkened Straits, the night cold slowly working its way back into our blood.

"Well," said Jacques at last, shaking himself from whatever reverie had overtaken him. "Shall we move on?"

"By all means," I said, eyeing that long walkway up to the fort again and giving silent thanks that Jacques wasn't in a climbing mood.

"Where to?" said Addie.

"Over a couple of blocks," said Jacques.

"The Grand Hotel?" she asked, a touch of excitement in her voice.

"The Grand Hotel," he answered.

****

We were stopped at the entrance to the opulent hotel by a male employee who wore a uniform that was the same rich red color as the carpeting we could see in the lobby beyond him.

"Registered guests?" he inquired.

"What? No, no, we just wanted to see the place," Jacques answered.

"I'm sorry," the doorman said, "but we can only let our registered guests into the hotel, unless one has placed you on a special visitors list. I take it you are not on our list?"

"No, I'm sure we're not," said Jacques.

"Then I'm afraid I must refuse you entrance," the doorman said. "Unless, of course, you are here to register."

"How much are rooms?" I asked, curious.

"They start at $250, sir," he said.

"A week?" said Addie. "That's not too bad."

"No, ma'am," the man said. "That's nightly."

"What!" she said. "Good lord. What's the high end?"

"Rooms can be booked for as much as $750 per night, ma'am."

Addie leaned over and whispered to me.

"They've gotten a little snooty," she said.

"I think they always were," I whispered back.

"Yeah, but they used to let us in."

Jacques spoke up again.

"My good man," he said. "Perhaps you would find it in your heart to make an exception in this case."

"I'm sorry, sir," the man said. "Rules are rules."

"Yes, so they are," said Jacques. "But . . ."

"Excuse me, but is there a problem?"

The voice came from within the lobby–a voice belonging to man I could not at first see, my vision obstructed as it was by the doorman.

"No, sir," said the doorman, straightening perceptibly and turning slightly toward the oncoming man. "I was just explaining . . ."

"Jacques!" said the newcomer, who now came into my view to the doorman's right. "What are doing out on such a cold night? I thought your joints were too old to stand such weather."

Jacques stepped forward, brushing past the doorman and clasping hands with the stranger–who obviously was no stranger, at all; at least to Jacques.

"Bernard," he said, smiling up at the man, for the fellow stood a good five inches taller than Jacques. "I was just about to ask for you through this gentleman. It's good to see you; it's been too long."

"Indeed," Bernard said, and then turned to the doorman. "Consider these people my guests, Cecil."

"Yes, sir," said the doorman, stepping to his right–our left–to clear the way for our entrance. Accordingly, we took several steps inside, stopping near Jacques and his friend.

"And who," said Bernard, peering down nearly a foot to Addie, "is this enchanting creature?"

"Ah, Bernard," said Jacques. "Allow me to introduce Miss Addie Winger and Mr. Avery Mann. They are friends of mine, visiting for a while and staying on the Island with me."

"Indeed," said Bernard, as he took Addie's hand. "It is an honor to have you here, Miss Winger. And you as well, Mr. Mann." But I doubted his sincerity in my case, since he barely looked in my direction.

"The place looks great, Bernard," said Jacques. "But I didn't realize you'd buttoned it up so tight. Don't like the public invading anymore?"

Bernard gave Addie a last smile, and let loose her hand. Then he straightened and turned to Jacques.

"Ah, it is not that exactly. We would love to accommodate everyone, but it is increasingly difficult–especially since that movie they filmed here . . . that "Somewhere in Time," with Christopher Reeve and the Seymour woman. It has gained a cult following, you know, and . . . well . . . has inspired some of its devotees to seek souvenirs beyond those available in the gift shop, if you get my drift."

Jacques nodded.

"I think I do," he said. "Short of nailing everything down, there's no real way to defend against sticky fingers, is there?"

"Indeed," said Bernard. "And so we reluctantly have become more exclusive."

"A shame," said Jacques, who then addressed Addie and me.

"Bernard is an old friend. He too has ancestors up in the graveyard. And as is clear here, he has a position of responsibility at the hotel. What's your title now? Night manager?"

"Yes," Bernard said. "Not bad, eh? I started as a bellhop, and now I'm in charge after dark."

"Indeed," said Jacques. "Well . . . what are the chances of a little tour? My friends here visited this place many years ago, and were looking forward to doing so again. I'm afraid I encouraged them, not knowing your visitor policy."

"Not a problem; not a problem," said Bernard.

"I would like in particular one thing," said Jacques.

"And what is that?" said Bernard.

Jacques motioned to their right, held his hand out for us to stay where we were, and adjourned to a point some twenty feet distant, where he whispered in his friend's ear for the better part of twenty seconds.

When Jacques was finished, Bernard thought a moment, and then nodded.

"Yes," he said. "That can be arranged."

Jacques returned to us, and nodded.

"He'll give us the tour now," he said. "Ready?"

"What was that all about?" I asked.

"Yes," said Addie, her words laced with suspicion. "What 'particular thing' is it you want, Jacques?"

"Oh . . . just a personal favor," said Jacques.

"Like what?" I said.

"Just personal," he repeated. "You'll see."

And he set off after Bernard, who was moving now toward the right rear of the lobby, heading–if I remembered correctly across forty years–in the direction of the dining room.

*****

My memory was sound.

We entered the dining room and crossed it briskly, heading toward what I gathered was the area of the kitchen. Along the way–through a front room and a larger rear dining hall, I noticed but a dozen tables in use by patrons, and decided the hotel was surely on its last pre-winter legs.

We exited the dining area through a swinging door, and indeed entered the kitchen–a stainless steel-dominated, L-shaped room that was likely akin to a beehive in the summer, but was now lethargic in pace and manned by a mere handful of employees: a dishwasher, a couple of chefs and what I assumed were two busboys–both leaning against an unused sink, chatting as we came in. When they saw Bernard, they jumped to attention.

Bernard paid them no heed, though; just marched past them, around a couple of counters, and took a right at the room's L–at which point we lost sight of him. Jacques followed him around the corner, and Addie and I–lagging behind–regained visual contact with the two men only after we too had reached the room's turn. They had by then stopped several yards distant, at the entrance to a large walk-in cooler. Bernard was opening its heavy door, and stepping inside.

Jacques turned as we approached.

"Stay here a moment," he said, and followed his friend into the cooler, closing the door behind them.

Addie and I looked at each other in the ensuing silence.

"What's going on?" she said.

"You tell me," I said.

We stood like that for perhaps three minutes, maybe four. During that time, we said nothing; conversation seemed somehow out of place in that sterile environment. Finally the door swung open, and Jacques came out.

"Ready?" he said.

"For what?" I answered.

"For this," he said, and stepped aside.

Bernard was coming through the door now, his arms outstretched and palms up in front of him, carrying a sizable chocolate-covered cake. Three candles stuck through the frosting were burning atop it.

"Voila," said Bernard, and bent over so he could hold the cake low, at an angle. In that way we could see the top–or more specifically the script written in white frosting across it. It said this:

"In 3 there is strength. Thank you, my friends."

I looked at Jacques. He was beaming.

I looked at Addie. She was crying.

"Oh, geez," I said. I never could deal with a woman's tears.

And in light of the sentiment expressed on the cake, I had to wonder if I was doing the right thing–if my plan the next day was the proper one . . . or perhaps a misguided venture that by its very independence marked it as a fool's errand. Perhaps the strength Jacques saw in our friendship was the key to solving his father's plight.

But then I recalled what I had seen that day in the binoculars, and renewed my resolve. I felt slightly traitorous about it, but saw no alternative. And so, as we retraced our steps to the dining hall, cut the cake, ate it and washed it down with champagne supplied by Bernard, I celebrated our trinity as I plotted my own separate course.

THIRTY-NINE

Gull Island

The morning broke as predicted in the forecast: bright and clear, with the promise of some warmth. I was the last one up, and entered the cabin's living room just as Jacques and Addie were sitting down to eat some pancakes that Jacques had prepared. The pancakes were stacked on a platter, and he was shoveling three of them off onto Addie's plate.

Jacques nodded to me as I entered, but Addie cast what I took to be a wary look. Her eyes seemed to say that she still didn't like my plans for the old man as she understood them, with this addendum: Don't let Jacques down.

But Jacques cast no such looks, maintaining his inherent civility.

"Plenty of flapjacks," he said. "You're welcome to dig in."

"Thanks. Don't mind if I do." I knew I would need fortification for the challenge that lay ahead, and pancakes seemed to offer a suitable energizer.

I sat down opposite Addie, and Jacques dropped three pancakes on my plate and two on his. I slopped on some butter and poured a liberal dose of maple syrup on top, and dug in. My companions seemed equally famished; the meal went on for several minutes without conversation. We were all intent on filling our bellies.

After finishing and wiping my mouth with a napkin, I watched Addie take the last couple of mouthfuls from her plate and then, together, we watched Jacques polish off his last bite.

Now done, we sat there, each casting glances at the others.

But nobody said anything, and after a few moments Addie rose, walked to the front door and quietly exited. I excused myself a short time later, went into the bedroom, gathered up the few items I would need for my morning's journey–a yellow rain poncho that compressed into a small pocket-sized pouch; a couple of candy bars for fast energy in case it got too enervating out there; and of course the binoculars–and bid Jacques goodbye.

"Be careful on the curves," he said. "The truck's kind of loose. Too fast and you might lose it into the trees."

"Right," I answered. "No problem."

I stepped outside the door and turned to my right, toward the truck parked at the side of the cabin. As I swung in that direction, my eyes caught sight of the figure of Addie out on the end of Jacques' dock, her legs dangling over the edge, swinging, her shoes not quite touching the water.

Stopping to watch, I couldn't help but be reminded of the young Addie, about the same size, who had seemed so easily dwarfed by the scope of the Straits and the sweep of the woods and the wide northern sky. From here, at this distance, I could almost believe I was looking at the girl who had so enchanted me in my formative years.

But of course I wasn't.

After a few seconds, she turned her head to look at me, squinting her eyes against the bright morning sunlight. We stared at each other for several seconds, but said nothing; and then I resumed my mission, heading for the truck and, once there, starting it and heading down the track away from Jacques' cabin–driving toward the Island's interior and an evil old man whose time should have long since passed.

****

The trek to the Twin Lakes was uneventful, and I drove closer to the cabin than on the two previous visits by continuing up the narrow tree-lined track and parking near the rough entrance drive that Jacques had told me about–that he hoped one day to repair enough to use. I could see as I got out of the truck that the drive was impassable–overgrown and full of huge holes and swales that would rip a vehicle's underbody to shrapnel in moments. I didn't like the idea of parking in the one-lane roadway, but saw no choice. I reasoned that the old man's condition wouldn't permit the lengthy walk along the two shores that Jacques, Addie and I had negotiated; that it was worth the risk of temporarily blocking an oncoming car or two. As it turned out, none happened to approach while I was parked there.

The old man slowed my progress after I arrived at the cabin; he kept me waiting while he put in his dentures and puttered around his bedroom. It was odd, I thought, considering his seeming impatience the day before to try out the glasses and filters; although I think, in retrospect, that perhaps he suspected something was amiss and part of him was forestalling whatever unpleasantness might await him. I could swear I heard him muttering in Italian in his bedroom, which struck me as fairly careless.

Then the walk to the pickup–despite the abbreviated distance–took longer than expected because of his deliberate gait, his joints and bones having rusted years before.

"Slow down," he said as we worked our way through the woods, even though I had already slowed more than I wished. "I can't possibly keep up this pace, short of having a heart attack."

I ignored him for several paces, but was brought up short when he grabbed my sleeve and yanked on it, digging in at the same moment with both heels.

"Or maybe you want me to have a heart attack," he spat, eyes narrowing.

"Nonsense," I said. "It's just that if we take too long, we may lose the good light. I've heard it'll cloud up this afternoon."

"Light, schmight," the old man muttered. "We go slower, or we turn back."

I reached toward the binocular case, hanging by its strap from my neck. Taking hold of the strap, I leaned forward so that the case was temporarily dangling away from my body, and swung it gently, tantalizing and taunting him at the same time.

"We turn back, you don't get to see these," I said.

He glared at me, and I in turn smirked at him until, after a standoff of some seconds, he grunted.

"Let's go," he said. "We're wasting time standing here. Just slow down."

I nodded.

"Right," I said. "Slower."

And we continued on to the pickup at the same pace.

****

When we turned left at the end of the side road, toward Pointe aux Pins instead of Jacques' cabin, the old man–who had seemed to weather the walk well–was quick to react.

"You turned the wrong way," he said.

"No," I answered. "Didn't I explain? We're on Plan B."

"You said nothing."

"Well, Addie figured that if we wanted a good clear view, we might as well go out on the water. That way, you look around in all directions without obstruction. From Jacques' shore, you basically only have the west and southwest to look toward, and part of that is obstructed by Round Island. You know . . . that little state-owned preserve off of Bois Blanc?"

"I know, I know," the old man muttered, though whether he did or not I couldn't be sure. If there was still some of Jacques' father in there, then of course he knew; any resident of Bois Blanc would be very familiar with Round Island. But if Mussolini had gained total control . . .

"So, anyway," I said, "the idea is to take Jacques' old boat, the *Sylmar*. But the water at Jacques' dock is too shallow for the *Sylmar* to get in there, so rather than have you try to board it on a wobbly dinghy, Jacques and Addie will swing around and get us on the main dock on the south shore. Sound all right?"

The old man didn't answer.

"Okay?" I said.

He lifted a bony hand and waved the question away.

"Whatever," he said.

****

The main dock wasn't particularly busy, it being a good hour or more, I figured, before Johnny and the *Sylmar III* came across from Cheboygan on its daily mail run.

There were a handful of mid-sized craft tethered to the dock, and a couple of them had activity aboard. Beyond that, a half-dozen or so people were spaced out along the length of the dock, a couple on the dirt causeway that jutted out from the main road to the dock's concrete and steel, and the rest on the dock proper. One man was fishing, while a trio was deep in conversation near him, seated on three of the hundreds of huge boulders that were piled along the dock's exterior to serve as a breakwater. The trio seemed to be doing exactly what they intended to do for most of the day: waste it.

As we parked in the dirt lot along the shore, the old man scanned the scene ahead.

"They're not here," he said. "I thought you said they'd meet us."

"Yeah. I guess they're running a little late," I said. "No problem. Let's just go out to the end of the dock and wait."

"What's wrong with here?" he asked. "I'm comfortable."

"No breeze," I said, and indeed it was easily the stillest I had seen the Island since arriving–and rapidly gaining warmth. "Too uncomfortable here. We can catch some wind out there. Come on."

"Oh, hell," he said, opening his door and struggling to the running board and then down to the ground. "Dragged all over just to get a look through some binoculars."

I smiled at his discomfort, and saw him eyeing the binocular case hanging from my neck and resting on my chest.

"Well, we can always take you back," I said. "I don't care if you look through them or not."

The old man grimaced at me.

"I've come this far," he mumbled. "Might as well go the rest of the way." And he pivoted and marched–if an aged limp can be called a march–to the beginning of the dock and out onto it.

****

We waited out there, seated at the end of the concrete walkway, our feet dangling over the pier's edge, for 10, then 15 minutes–long enough so the old man was getting impatient and starting to let me and anybody else within earshot know it.

"Plan B, eh?" he said. "And a mighty fine plan it is. What moron came up with this, anyway?"

"Addie," I reminded him.

"Oh, that's right," he said. "Well, shows not even she's perfect. Horrible idea. Damned boat probably wouldn't start; or sank. And I thought you said there'd be breeze out here; it's so dry it's practically suffocating me. I'm not gonna sit here much longer."

He went on for a couple more minutes in that vein, but eventually paused–just long enough for a voice to break in on us from behind.

"Excuse me," it said, and I turned to see a man standing not three feet to our rear. The old man didn't seem to notice, so the stranger repeated himself.

"Excuse me," he said again, and the old man turned and looked up. The stranger was backlit from our angle by the bright gray sky, and so his features were obscured.

"What?" the old man answered gruffly, squinting hard against the light.

"I'm sorry, but I couldn't help but overhear," the stranger said. "You seem to be waiting for a ride. I have a boat off the end of the dock here, and was wondering if I might be of assistance. I was just about to head out toward Cheboygan; I have business there that will take about an hour. Is there any chance you'd be going in that direction?"

The old man looked at me, and then leaned back to see around me to our left. I followed his gaze to a ramp running down from, and parallel to, the dock, and to the boat tethered there: a red-hulled inboard with seating for four. It looked powerful enough to get us across the Straits in short order, but of course that wasn't the intended goal.

"You say you'll be over there an hour? Then what?" the old man said, looking up at the backlit figure again.

"Then I'll be coming back here. Why? You planning on returning here today?"

"Yeah, you might say that," answered the old man, who clearly was going for the bait. He wanted to get out on the water and try the binoculars.

"No problem," said the figure. "I can bring you back, too."

The old man struggled to his feet, looked over the breakwater to the west, turned to check out the east, and then scanned the open water south. There was no sign of the *Sylmar*.

"We accept," he said.

"Now wait a minute," I said, figuring that good form mandated I at least try to put in a word on behalf of our tardy friends. But the old man cut me off.

"We accept," he said again, looking down at me. "It's better than nothing. No arguments."

I gave a slight shrug, pushed myself upright, and looked up at our benefactor. With the backlighting no longer in play, I could see the beard and the long hair and the military-style jacket. His face was serious; and I guess mine was, too.

"My name's King," he said, holding out his right hand. I extended mine to his, and taking hold, he pulled me in close, whispering in my ear.

"This part was easy," he said, and backed away, pivoting toward the old man, who was waiting now at the edge of the dock, where the ramp began. The carpenter took him by the arm and guided him down the ramp and onto the boat.

As he did, and as I followed them on board, I couldn't help but think ahead to the grim nature of our self-imposed assignment.

****

The storm materialized out of nowhere, its huge blackness and ferocious winds preceding a sheet of rain that we first saw racing toward us off the starboard bow and ahead of us–a hundred yards to the west and south.

"What the hell?" I yelled. "Where'd that come from?"

I was behind the carpenter, in a rear-facing seat but kneeling so that I faced forward. The carpenter was directly in front of me, the old man in the seat to his left. On the dashboard in between them hung a coil of rope on a hook. We had been out for but a couple of minutes, a ride that proved rougher than the old man had envisioned. Where the *Sylmar* or *Sylmar III* could ride small waves smoothly, this craft bounced over them with sharp slapping movements. The old man was gripping his seat, and had gone paler than usual; the thought of trying to use the binoculars had not been raised since the carpenter accelerated away from the main dock.

And now this: a sudden storm of frightening dimensions.

"Turn!" the old man yelled. "Turn it around! We can't go into that."

"No kidding!" the carpenter yelled, and veered left, away from the wall of falling water that quite literally had developed in a matter of seconds. This was completely contrary to most Straits storms, which you see and smell coming for miles. It was, however, reminiscent of the startling abruptness with which the storm had struck in 1956, stranding Addie and me on Gull Island–the storm in which she had died, in which she had lived.

I don't pretend to understand the powers that directed that storm of '56, nor do I possess any inside information on how this current one was being engineered. I only knew that it was in the hands of the carpenter, part of the grand plan he had outlined for me in the most general of terms before my departure from his cabin the preceding afternoon.

"Trust me on this," he had told me near the end of that session. "We'll start things, and let nature do most of the work. It will be a fury."

And so here it was, to our right and straight ahead and–I could see as we turned sharply east–also to the north, the direction from which we had just come. It was in the shape of a horseshoe, leaving us but one direction in which to travel ahead of its path, one safe passage to pursue as it narrowed at our sides and closed in behind us.

We sped along, throttle wide open, bouncing higher now as the waves ahead joined their compatriots around us in swelling and slapping at the hull of our craft. The wind, howling, may have been actually pushing us, adding to our forward progress; I don't know. I was too intimidated by the slashing sheet of rain and the lightning starting to dance in its midst to take stock of such fine detail.

I couldn't gauge for sure, but thought in the midst of this mayhem that the carpenter had surely worked it all out. Our path was on a direct line to the only body of land we had a chance of reaching before being absorbed into and tossed about by the elements. We would no doubt reach it in time, I told myself; gain some measure of safety by the very fact of footing underneath us.

Yes, that bit of land directly ahead was his intended destination; had been all along.

We were heading for Gull Island.

****

The next couple of minutes, as we bore down on Gull, were a whirlwind of fear and uncertainty and anticipation. I kept looking behind and to the sides, fearful of the lightning above all else, as I had been in that storm those many years before. In the midst of the wind and the fear, I somehow managed to pull out, and unfold, the yellow poncho I had grabbed before leaving Jacques' place; but that precautionary garb, born of the carpenter's weather warning, did me no good. A massive gust caught it and ripped it from my grasp, and carried it out into the Straits.

The carpenter, meanwhile, was steady at the helm, keeping the boat on course, skipping from wave to wave and ahead of the horseshoe-shaped curtain of rain. The old man was still gripping his seat, and I think whimpering, though it was difficult to hear in the wind and the thunder and with the boat's engine whining.

Landfall seemed one moment to be immeasurably distant, too far to outrun the oncoming storm, and in the next almost upon us. Being a small piece of land with probably no more than 500 square feet and but one defining characteristic–a tough, gnarled old tree that was top-heavy with thick leaves up high, and devoid of branches down low, a tree still thriving more than forty years after I'd first seen it–Gull didn't look large either at a distance or close up, accounting for the seeming suddenness with which we were on it.

The carpenter kept the engine going full bore until the final few feet, and then cut it and gripped the wheel with one hand and his seat with the other to brace for impact. I wrapped my arms around the sides of my seat, hugging in closely. The old man, I saw, had one arm braced over the back of his seat, and one extended out to the dashboard.

We hit the western edge of the island straight on, and the boat–slowed but still moving forward–careened up and, airborne, cleared half of the Island's width before landing hard and then sliding. It came to a stop about three yards short of the eastern edge, and the carpenter jumped right into action.

"Out!" he yelled, just as the forefront of the storm hit us from behind. I rolled out over the port gunwale and helped the old man do the same, thinking he looked pretty dazed by what had just happened, and noticing a trickle of blood on his forehead. I then turned instinctively to the carpenter for the next order.

"Turn it over!" he shouted, pointing to the starboard side at which he stood.

The old man and I hurried around the bow and over next to him. Then we all reached low on the hull, finding a grip in the fiberglass molding, and lifted, although I can't say just how much good the old man was doing. But the boat slowly rose upward at our urging, and we managed to get it high enough so that the wind did the last of the work, pushing the craft until it rolled over, hull up. As it landed, the windshield crumpled, and the boat settled lower, hugging the ground.

"Underneath!" was the next command, and the carpenter leaned down, grabbed the gunwale and lifted the boat up about a foot, providing space for the old man and me to scurry along the ground and into the relative shelter of the boat's interior, now a protective bubble.

As soon as the two of us were in there, I had a disquieting flashback to 1956, when Addie and I had tried a similar maneuver with a smaller boat and had had it blasted off of us by a bolt of lightning. I found myself doing two things in the moment of remembering that: I crossed myself and looked anxiously for the carpenter. But he was not there; had not followed us to shelter.

The old man discovered the same thing at the same moment.

"Where is he?" he had to yell, for while the sound of the wind and the waves and the thunder was muted, the torrent outside was drum-beating loudly on the hull.

"I don't know!" I answered.

"He shouldn't be out there!" the old man shouted. "We need him here!"

There was a wild edge to the old man's voice, and I suspect his eyes would have reflected it–if there was light in there to reflect anything. But it was dark enough so that I could barely discern his outline, even though he was but a couple of feet away.

I was debating what to do when I felt the old man's bony hand on my forearm; he was squeezing hard.

"We need him here!" he yelled, his voice high and panicky. The grip was quickly turning painful.

I had no idea why he was so desperate for the carpenter's

presence, for they had just met for the first time on the dock scant minutes before. Perhaps the carpenter comforted him; he could have that effect. But to allay the old man's fears–and more importantly my own–I announced a course of action as an alternative to staying put.

"Okay! I'll check!" I yelled, and pried his hand from my arm. But rather than relinquish me completely, he clutched at my shirt–and caught hold of the binocular case still hanging over my neck.

I realized only when he started pulling on it that he had gotten a firm grip; and as we struggled in opposite directions, I felt my neck being forced awkwardly to the left by the taut strap. I felt a muscle pull and ducked down to ease the pain, and in that moment he pulled harder and yanked the strap over my head and grabbed the case away from me.

"Go get him," he yelled, "and I'll give them back!"

I knew he wouldn't without a struggle, but considered the matter of little importance at that moment, in that circumstance. He was too scared and too feeble of hand–and it was too dark–for him to even try to find the filters and install them in the eyepieces. And even if he'd been able, I knew it would do him no good.

And so I left him the glasses, turned, lifted the edge of the boat and rolled out into the screaming wind and crashing surf and pounding raindrops attacking Gull Island.

****

The shock of the cold rain forced me to hunch down before I could get my bearings. Collecting myself and shielding my eyes from the onslaught, I managed to raise myself upright and peer around after a few moments, scanning quickly, keeping the rain slanting in from the west at my back. Then I started backing into the rain, looking right and left, swiveling my head, trying to find some sign of the carpenter.

I ran into something solid, and thought for a second that it was the gnarled tree. But then I saw the tree to my right–illuminated by a flash of lightning–and turned quickly.

"Nice night!" the carpenter yelled into my face, and I momentarily staggered with the surprise of the greeting. He caught me at the elbows and steadied me, looking me over as he did so.

"The binoculars!" he said, leaning in close to my left ear. "Where are they? Does he have them?"

I nodded vigorously.

"He grabbed them!" I shouted. "Almost broke my neck. I was gonna just leave them, like you said, but he really wanted them. The bastard's strong!"

The carpenter leaned in close again.

"Good!" he said over the storm. "Whether you left them, or he took them, it doesn't matter. We're all set for the next phase."

"You mean the transfer?"

"Yes," he said. "I think you'll appreciate it. I don't think I mentioned it, but you might want to hunker down by that tree. It's going to get nastier."

The tree again. Forty years before, Addie and I had lashed ourselves to that very tree to try and ride out the storm that had erupted around us so suddenly. Then Eliot and Grandpa had arrived with Jacques, and Addie had been taken from me by the Straits, only to be resurrected. But "hunkering down" would do little good without something with which to secure myself.

"Here," the carpenter said, holding something out to me. At first, with the storm's fury, I couldn't make out its shape, but a prolonged lightning flash revealed it to be the coil of rope I had seen in the boat.

I took it and stepped back, trying to read in his face the strategy here, but the rain obscured his features. In the process, I squared directly to the wind and now caught the full force of a blast of air and rain. I stumbled back another step before righting myself, only to find myself flinching at an especially bright bolt somewhere above. But in the light of the moment, I managed to see something that seemed out of sync with the fury of the storm and the nature of our task: the carpenter was wearing a broad smile. He was fully enjoying himself.

It was but a moment between that smile and the carpenter's gentle touch on my arm, a directional push accompanying a movement of his head in the direction of the tree. As soon as he took a step toward it, I followed, looking back over my shoulder at the boat, wondering what the old man underneath must be thinking, wondering if he had pulled the binoculars free and was frantically trying to find the filters, wondering whether he was feeling fear in the midst of the maelstrom, or indeed if he were even truly capable of fear; for he was, I had to remind myself, the remnant of a horrible dictator who had killed without compunction in Italy and aligned himself with an even greater beast across the Alps, in Germany.

As the carpenter and I reached the tree, we turned in tandem back toward the boat–some twenty-five yards distant–and, leaning into the wind, fought off the continuing deluge.

"What now?" I yelled.

He pointed to the rope in my hand.

"You'll want to wrap that around the tree and tie yourself in," he called back. "As soon as it starts."

Then, his message evidently complete, he cast his gaze skyward, into the dark, looking for something, though exactly what I could only imagine. All I could see, looking up, was the tree bending in the wind and, beyond that, sheets of rain.

And then it began.

FORTY

The Carpenter's Solution

I thought at first that the light was a bolt up high, directly overhead. But after it flashed brilliantly to announce its presence, it did not disappear; it diminished in intensity only slightly as it made its way down in a narrow cylindrical band through the clouds, through the rain, through the wind, illuminating the crashing surf and settling onto the red hull of the overturned boat on Gull Island.

I turned toward the carpenter.

"What's happening?" I shouted.

"The transfer!"

"Obviously!" I yelled. "But how is it happening? Where does that come from?"

The carpenter was shaking his head.

"Trade secret!" he yelled. "Just watch. You will learn all that you are capable of learning through your eyes. I can add no more."

I looked at him, thinking–with journalistic curiosity, I suppose–that there must be some way to pry more out of him, but he was not looking at me. He was looking up at the beam, and then looking at the boat where the beam had landed.

"It will get rough now," he said. "Time to lash you down." He took my arm and had me sit by the tree, facing west–away from the boat–shook the coil of rope free and wound it around me and the tree, securing me to the trunk for the second time in my life. The rope was loose enough, though, so that I could maneuver my body left and right–twist to see what was happening around me.

"What about you?" I yelled. "Shouldn't you be tied down, too?"

"No need!" he answered, and took a step back, focusing his attention on the light show and then turning at the sound of fury arriving from the east. I swiveled and, straining, looked east as well, and saw the funnel as it sprang up from the Straits not fifty yards from our tiny atoll, a dark foreboding shape that would have been obscured if not for the beam of light playing upon the overturned boat.

The distinction between the two phenomena was simple enough, as was the general role of each: positive and negative forces were at play, antitheses that I suspected would soon collide.

As I watched, the funnel kept climbing from the surface of the water, feeding from it, gaining in intensity until, a hundred yards high and perhaps ten across, it started moving away from its place of birth, moving south a few feet and then north, as though trying to find its balance. Then, settling, it started moving steadily in our direction, straight for Gull, its rushing sound competing successfully with that of the storm still breaking on all other sides of us.

Inexorably it came our way, my way, gaining speed as it approached, sweeping in quickly now, throwing mist ahead of it and then–as it churned closer to land–bits of sand and some small pebbles. They hit me like tiny razors, forcing me to stop watching, to snap my head back toward the west, away from the funnel, positioning my body so the trunk of the tree was shielding me.

When it reached the shoreline, the bite of debris on skin increased, though it was merely hitting me on my right shoulder, the part of my body exposed from that angle. And then–I could see this peripherally, without turning my head much–the dark funnel collided with the beam of light, and lifted up, clear of the sand, to a point some yards above Gull, and stopped sending the small stinging missiles.

With the cease-fire, I ventured a look to my right and up, and saw the beam and funnel bumping, the dark shape bouncing back a few feet and then crashing into the light one, and then repeating the maneuver, as if trying to break through a protective zone. On perhaps the tenth such collision, the two merged, and the light faded from intense to something less. The funnel maintained its shape and dark texture within the confines of its brighter partner as they started a slow rotation.

Wiping aside the water running down from my hair and into my eyes, I lowered my gaze to check the status of the boat that covered the old man. There, in the light still touching the boat, I saw a name stenciled or perhaps engraved on the rear of the hull–something I had not seen at the dock or, naturally enough, out on the water. It was upside down now, and so escaped my immediate understanding; but my subconscious played with the lettering for a few moments and fed me what my eyes could not decipher.

The name was this:

Ligurian C-2.

The first word I understood. But the meaning of the letter and number designation initially eluded me. I sought out the carpenter; he had disappeared from my sight, but I spotted him on the eastern side of the tree.

"Hey!" I yelled.

He edged over.

"What?"

"What's the C-2 mean?" I yelled.

"Just that!"

"What do you mean? I don't get it!"

"Just sound it out!"

And so I did. And then I grasped what it stood for–if not its complete meaning.

Sea Two. Ligurian Sea Two.

It was a reference to the locale of Mussolini's initial "death." I gathered it meant that this transfer was simply designed to finish the job.

"What's going on under there?" I yelled. "Under the boat?"

The carpenter didn't answer, and the beam of light changed

from its semi-bright cast to yellow-orange as the dark funnel lost its definition and merged completely with its host. Then the light turned red, and the boat started to vibrate. I thought for a few moments that it might splinter, much as the smaller boat had forty years before.

"What's going on?" I yelled again.

"Don't worry! It isn't going to blow up," the carpenter shouted back, as though reading my concern.

"Good," I said, as much to myself as to him, and then watched as the vibrations intensified. "But what's it gonna do?" I muttered.

The light turned a deeper and deeper red, reaching a richness that reminded me of velvet, before snapping into a bright multiple hue, a rainbow of colors that seemed to be dancing about but were, I decided, actually rotating; the beam was twisting about now, carrying its colors with it in a counterclockwise direction.

And then the rotation stopped, so abruptly that I thought the light show might be ending. But instead the beam lifted slowly off the ground, an inch and then a couple more, and with it arose the boat itself, the *Ligurian C-2*.

Maybe ten inches up, maybe a foot, the beam resumed its rotation, gradually at first but picking up speed, its colors dancing, reflecting off the sheen of the hull, piercing the darkness and enhanced by the raindrops, spinning faster and faster and starting to take the boat around with it, slowly at first, then picking up speed until beam and boat were a blur, an inverted T cutting a colorful path in the maelstrom, impervious to the violence of the storm around it, creating its own violence, its own physics.

I could not tell, in the brightness of the light show, what might have become of the old man. It was still shadowed underneath the central portion of the craft, at the axis of its wild spin, and the boat's rotating movement, combined with the storm's contributions, helped obscure visibility even more.

It didn't seem that the rotation could be any faster, but it increased in tempo almost as soon as I had dismissed the possibility, and continued to speed up for fully half a minute, the rainbow of lights and the red hull fusing into a beam that soon only hinted of the colors and then lost them entirely, becoming a mass of white that started lifting upward a foot, then two, then five, finally stopping about ten feet above Gull, spinning faster the whole time, kicking up not a bit of surf or sand but clearly–I could see now in a softer, trailing light–leaving nothing underneath the boat: no old man, no binoculars; nothing.

"Jesus," I said, and then glanced at the carpenter, wondering if he had heard the name.

"It's all right," he said. "I don't mind."

And together we watched as the spinning light show started crackling, little sparks popping out from its border. Then the light turned orange, segued to a deep red again, and shifted back to white before gradually changing from a constant brightness to something else–a brightness inhabited by some form, some shadowy substance or image; I couldn't tell what at first.

But then it came into focus, gaining in shape quickly, and bringing from me a gasp: I was looking at a face, the face of a bald-headed man, the face of a man being squeezed agonizingly, the face of a man I had seen in old newsreels and history books–the face of Il Duce, Benito Mussolini.

"Is that his spirit?" I yelled to the carpenter.

"Yes!"

I still could see no sign of the old man, and worried at that–but decided not to ask. It would do no good, I figured. And so I just watched.

And as I did, the shadowed face of Mussolini started screaming, an ear-splitting emanation cutting through the wind and the rain and the thunder, piercing the air of Gull Island, shaking the ground underneath us, sending a shiver from my head down through the nerve endings of my extremities. In the moments that followed, a parade of images appeared on the face, a flickering light on the dark contours of the eyes and nose and mouth; it was like viewing an old newsreel with the projector vibrating. I could make out scenes of Mussolini speaking to a crowd, ranting, waving his arms; and troops marching through the streets, passing in review in front of Il Duce; and him sitting, talking to Hitler; and an execution of some poor fellow by firing squad, and of another by hanging. And I saw images of Mussolini making love to a woman; and being hustled away by German paratroopers–no doubt his successful rescue; and being nearly killed in a roadside garden; and ducking down in the middle of a firefight with red-banded Nazis; and falling into an ocean and struggling underwater with someone–a young Jacques; and grabbing hold of the Crystal of Death in that struggle, and then . . . then sitting in an easy chair in a cabin, reading, and cackling.

And as suddenly as the images started, they stopped, and the face of Mussolini registered surprise, and was contorted, and was squeezed inward as the beam of light–still rotating rapidly–narrowed in diameter from feet to inches and started accelerating upward. Another scream, but this one low and mournful, signaled Mussolini's departure as the light continued upward, its tail its brightest spot, the mass growing smaller until it was dimmed by the storm clouds overhead and finally disappeared, leaving us with little light, no boat, no binoculars and . . .

I heard the moan before I saw the figure; thought at first it was the wind playing tricks. But no . . . there was a figure where the boat had been, where there had been no figure before, and it was lying on the ground, writhing about. I freed myself from the tree and–a little frantic, I realized–started scrambling on my hands and knees in that direction. As I neared the figure, I saw through the gloom that it was, as I had thought, the old man. He was lying there stark naked, his bony old frame hunched over like a newborn babe.

I glanced back at the carpenter. He was standing behind me, removing his military-style jacket, which he then handed me.

"Cover him with this," he said.

I took the jacket, at the same time casting a look about to see if there were any other clothes at hand, or the binoculars. But the area was picked clean; the old man's naked body was the only object there. As I placed the jacket over him, he looked up at me with questioning eyes; he was disoriented.

"Just lie still," I said. "We'll get you out of here as soon as things let up."

Still on my knees, I leaned back and pivoted in the direction of the carpenter, intending to ask him just how we were supposed to get off the island without a boat. Perhaps walk on water? But he was not there–not anywhere behind me. I looked to my left, but that section of the island was empty too. Pushing up and twisting, I took in the remainder of Gull in one fluid motion, keeping it slow so as not to miss anything. But he wasn't there.

"Oh," I said, the word escaping my lips as a hiss. "Now what does this mean?"

A groan from behind me brought my attention back to the old man, and I knelt by him again.

"Where are we?" he asked, and I realized as he did so that I could hear him clearly despite a weakness in his voice; the noise of the storm was no longer dominant. The wind was dying rapidly, and with it the howling, and the rain was reduced in an instant from deluge to trickle. The sky was turning quickly from near-black to gray, and the thunder and lightning were ceasing their dance with but a flickering afterthought.

"Gull Island," I answered him.

The old man tried to rise, but the strength wasn't there. He held his hand out to me, and asked:

"Could you help me sit up, please?"

I took hold and leaned back, and pulled. We were both now at the same level, and studying each other. I wanted to make sure he was okay, and that I wasn't still dealing with an old Italian bastard. I didn't think it possible, considering the light show I'd just witnessed; but confirmation seemed imperative. Before I could say anything, though, he spoke.

"We've met before?" he asked. "You look familiar, but . . . no, I don't think so."

"My name is Mann," I said.

"Mann?" he asked, and looked closer. "Ah . . . it's in the eyes. Amory's boy. You must be."

"Yes," I said, encouraged that this man was nothing like the one I had been experiencing in his stead.

"That's right. I'm Avery."

"Avery, yes," he said. "Your father . . . he was a good man. I was sorry to hear of his passing."

"Thank you," I said.

The old man was looking around now, taking in our situation.

"I'm afraid I don't remember how we got here," he said, and seemed embarrassed by it. "I've been a little . . . indisposed lately."

"I know," I said. "That's part of why I'm here."

"It is? I don't understand," he said. "My mind; it's been . . . unbalanced, I think. Like I wasn't in control; wasn't . . . myself. But I seem fine now. But . . ."

He paused, and looked confused.

"What?" I asked.

"What . . . has happened? Why am I not wearing clothes?"

I was about to answer when I heard the noise coming from the northwest, from the direction of the main dock on Bois Blanc. I smiled at the old man.

"I think your son can fill you in," I said.

"Jacques?" he said, and looked around the island again.

"He's coming," I said, and swung my left arm around, toward the sound I had picked up, a sound the old man with ancient ears had not yet heard.

He looked past me, squinting, in the direction I was pointing.

"Ah, yes," he said.

I smiled at his evident pleasure, and turned, too.

There, in the distance, cutting a swath through the Straits of Mackinac and heading directly for us, was the *Sylmar*–its familiar throbbing engines laboring against the still-churning surf.

FORTY-ONE

After Gull

Jacques decided to take his father back with him to the cabin on the northwest shore, rather than to the Twin Lakes. The old man was enfeebled by his exposure to the storm, and would be in need of some supervision until he got his strength back–assuming he did get it back; but he had sustained no injuries requiring medical attention despite the fury of the transfer. Jacques deemed himself the logical nurse, since he would have little else to do with his time now that the invader had been ousted.

It was readily obvious to both Jacques and Addie that Mussolini had been dispatched; the difference in the old man's temperament, speech and appearance was far softer than it had been before Gull and consistent with the personality Jacques had known his father to possess almost all of his life. But what they didn't understand was how the restoration of that personality had come to pass; they had seen the lights cast by the dancing funnel and beam from a distance through the storm, but nothing definitive. The transfer show had mainly served as a multi-colored beacon for them.

Little had been said upon their arrival at Gull. Their energies were focused first on getting from the *Sylmar* to the island in a dinghy, and once there helping me hoist the old man into the dinghy and then on board the *Sylmar* for the trip back home. The return route chosen was north around the eastern shore of Bois Blanc and then west.

We lay the old man on the deck in the *Sylmar* cabin, a bench cushion underneath him for comfort. I sat behind Jacques as he piloted the craft; Addie knelt by the old man, holding his hand and casting agitated looks in my direction.

We had reached the southeast corner and turned before anybody said anything beyond the instructions we had provided each other in transferring the old man from the island to the boat. Addie uttered the next words.

"Not very bright, Avery." It came out a hiss.

At first I wasn't sure she was speaking, what with the sound of the boat's engine. But when I looked at her–saw the anger in her eyes–I knew she had spoken and wasn't finished.

"You could have killed him," she added, this time at a level I could clearly hear.

"But I didn't," I said. "As you can see."

She left the old man's side, sliding over toward me on her knees, to within comfortable earshot.

"You had no right to do this alone," she said.

I looked to my left, toward Jacques. He was keeping his eyes forward, though I'm sure his ears were working past the whine of the engine and the sound of the surf, and homing in on our words.

"No right to do what?" I said. "To get rid of an Italian murderer? You're the one who wanted to do an exorcism. You don't think that might have killed him?"

"That's different," she said. "That would have been under controlled conditions; in a bedroom if we wanted to, for Christ's sake. But this . . . out in a storm. And alone!"

I rubbed my eyes. They, and I, were suddenly very tired. I looked past Addie, out past the stern, and marveled at how the overcast left in the wake of the storm had now broken up. Sunlight was playing off the Straits, becalmed now as the sun passed its zenith.

I turned back to Addie.

"You think I got us out there on Gull by myself?" I asked.

"Well . . . didn't you?"

I hesitated, pondering the best response . . . the best way to lead up to who had taken us out there–and decided to answer instead with a question.

"You two knew we were out on Gull," I said. "How?"

Addie started to speak–I assume, from the petulance still readable on her face, in an argumentative vein–but my question had clearly thrown her. She thought better of whatever she was going to say, and took a softer tack.

"Well . . . when it became clear you weren't coming back to the cabin," she said, "we decided to find out why. We didn't have any transportation except the *Sylmar*, so we boarded it and headed for the main dock. By the time we got there, the storm had hit out on the Straits. It was placid in by shore, but clearly dangerous farther out."

She paused, looked over at Jacques as if seeking his input, saw there was none forthcoming, and continued.

"A couple of fisherman said you'd gone out not long before in a powerboat. By then, Jacques had picked up your distress signal–your fear–like he did back in '56."

"Uh huh," I said. "And did these fishermen say how we came to take this particular craft?"

"Ummmm, no," she said. "Jacques picked up on your problem before we got any more information. We kind of left the dock in a hurry."

Addie was calm now; a little curious, I could tell, and confused by where I was going with these questions.

"So . . . you think I just happened to come up with a boat out of the blue, stole one in plain view of fishermen and whoever else might be lurking around at what amounts to the Island's midday social center?"

"Well . . ."

"We were invited, Addie. It's that simple. I was invited with the old man to go out on a boat, and we were taken to Gull Island."

"By whom?" she said. "No; wait a minute. There was no boat out there when we arrived . . ."

"Destroyed in the storm," I said.

"And nobody else but you two," she added. "There was nobody else."

"True enough," I said. "Not by the time you arrived."

"Meaning what?"

"Meaning he was gone by the time you and Jacques got there."

"Who was?"

I looked at her, at the old man, over at Jacques and out the starboard windows, and took a deep breath. How much could I tell? How much did I believe? How much would she believe? How crazy was I?

But before I could answer, Jacques interjected.

"*He* was," he said.

My old friend's voice jolted me, it was so unexpected. Addie looked taken aback, too.

"He?" she asked. "He who, Jacques?"

"I'm not sure," Jacques said. "But . . . I sensed a third person out there, when we started toward Gull from the main dock. He had . . . I don't know . . . an aura that precluded fear. There was excitement, and satisfaction, but no fear."

"I don't understand," said Addie.

Jacques swung sideways in his seat, so that he could see both ahead and back into the cabin. It was the same physical maneuver he had adopted long ago when ferrying customers from Cheboygan to the Island and back again. He could navigate and chat as though the two went hand-in-hand, although of course they didn't. It was an ease born of years of practice.

This time, his words were directed at me.

"It *was* him, wasn't it?" he asked.

"Him who?" Addie said. Her tone signaled a growing exasperation.

"I'm not sure I know who you mean," I answered.

"You saw someone on the road shortly after your arrival on Bois Blanc," he said. "In the woods, on the way to my place."

"Yes," I said.

"I saw no one," he said, "and you let it drop. But there was someone there; I know that. I picked up a faint emanation. Almost as if it was the vapor of a person. It was the same man, wasn't it? The same man who took you to Gull."

I thought of working around the question; denying it, saying I wasn't sure, anything but what I had perceived. But Jacques' eyes held a light–whether reflection of the afternoon sun or something burning from within, I wasn't sure–that demanded an honest response.

"Yes," I answered.

"Who?" Addie interjected. "Who are you two talking about?"

"Are you going to tell us?" asked Jacques.

I looked at Addie, now full of frustration and confusion and curiosity; and at Jacques, who I think believed I held the key to a secret door that needed unlocking.

"Yes," I said. "But where it's quiet. Let's get home first."

Jacques nodded in satisfaction, put his right index finger to his lips as he glanced at Addie, and swung back around for the last few miles of our trip to the northwest corner, to his cabin, to the cabin of Turk McGurk.

****

After the old man had been fed some warm soup and tucked into the lower bunk in the bedroom, Jacques motioned Addie and me outside.

"It's best to keep it quiet here for awhile," he said. "Let's walk."

We followed the path used by the pickup–which was still stranded over at the main dock–and hiked south, away from the cabin, toward the woods. Halfway there, Jacques spoke again.

"Okay, Avery. I think we'd like to hear what happened."

I was silent for several paces.

"Avery?" Jacques said.

"I'm thinking," I said.

"Tall order," said Addie.

I thought she might still be angry with me, but a look at her face told me otherwise. She was walking quietly, pensively, patiently, and flashed me a smile to reassure me. Mercurial, I thought.

"Yeah, well . . ." I said, trying to find a point at which to begin.

"Now that it's all over, I'm not exactly sure what happened. I mean, I think I know, but I might have been hallucinating . . ."

I thought back to my walk alone in the woods, and what I saw when I had looked through the binoculars; or more precisely through the filters and the binoculars.

"No," I said, taking back my hesitancy. "Scratch that; it definitely happened. Only . . . it wasn't what it would seem to be."

Jacques slowed, and Addie and I slowed with him. And then he stopped, bringing us all to a halt.

"I think," he said, "that you had better start from the top–begin from the beginning. Slowly. Then perhaps it will make better sense."

"I'm rambling," I said, realizing it.

"A bit," he said. "It helps me sometimes to think things through chronologically. So . . ."

"Okay," I said. "I'll start when we were on the road, when I first saw him. Fair enough?"

"Fine," he said. "And be as detailed as you can, okay? It will all be rather fresh to me, and completely new to Addie. We are a rapt audience."

I started walking again. The two of them hesitated until I turned and waved them forward.

"I think and talk better when I'm moving," I said.

I waited for them to catch up before I resumed walking. A few steps later, I started my account.

I told them about the man on the road, and about the boy and the old man on the lake, and about the bear, and about the cabin in the clearing, and about the carpenter and the light in his kitchen, and about his plan, and about my father's last words, and about Gull Island.

I talked slowly as the three of us meandered along the track, well into the woods, into the shade of the forest's overhanging trees. I related it roughly as I have related it on these pages, with one exception.

And they listened intently–didn't interrupt me; didn't speak until I was done.

FORTY-TWO

What About Father?

The one thing I didn't tell them, couldn't tell them, was what I had seen in the binoculars. I saw little need of that. Mussolini had, after all, been routed, and the old man was still alive. That was the crux of the original mission as planned by Jacques and joined by Addie.

The full truth could lie dormant; could wait.

Besides, I wasn't fully confident I was right in my assessment—at least then. I was still sorting out some of the particulars. And so I let it rest.

In the end, I stayed but one more day. That afternoon, Jacques and I went on the *Sylmar* over to the main dock to retrieve the pickup; I drove it back across the Island while Jacques returned home in the boat. We linked up again at the cabin with Addie, who had remained behind to keep an eye on the old man.

In the evening, I stayed with Addie while Jacques drove back to his father's cabin to retrieve some of the old man's clothing and personal possessions.

"He'll be living here awhile," Jacques explained. "Can't have him feeling like a stranger."

While Jacques was gone, the old man slept, and Addie and I found ourselves chatting about the day, and about Mussolini, and about the carpenter, and about the Island.

"Did you notice," she asked, "that on the way back from Gull, we passed the lighthouse?"

"Yeah," I said. "Something, huh?"

The route we had followed, westerly along the Island's northern shore, had taken us past an occasional isolated cottage and–we could not help but notice–past the Island lighthouse. Addie and I had visited it as kids on a 1956 daytrip with my grandfather and his friend Al Jones, the Island conservation officer. Addie and I had climbed the old lighthouse tower that long-ago day, a feat of bravado that had left me perilously close to vomiting in fear.

The place was vastly different now, though. Instead of rundown and vacant, as it had been in '56, it was shipshape and clearly occupied–by an individual, I surmised, instead of by the state. It had that loving touch that comes so often with private ownership, and so rarely with bureaucracy. The bricked residential portion of the structure, which had traditionally housed state-employed lighthouse-keepers before it became too costly and difficult a post to man, was sandblasted now, and its wooden trim-work was painted a dazzling red. And always telltale of residence: the windows were curtained. The old attached tower, a painted wooden structure that had been peeling badly and was in danger of rot forty years earlier, was now a bright white–a clear sign of maintenance.

"Someone's living in the house!" Addie had enthused as we passed by on this day. And then, softly, she had added what I was feeling at seeing an old signpost from my childhood turn out so well:

"That's grand," she said.

****

Addie and Jacques turned in early that evening, before 9 p.m. We moved Addie to the bunkroom where Jacques' father was now ensconced, while Jacques and I took over the living room. I drew use of the couch on Jacques' insistence; he said sleeping on the floor, while a bit unusual for him, might help a sore back he'd been nursing.

"I never go to bed this early," I said as we all exchanged goodnights in the living room. "So I think I'll do a little reading."

Addie had moved her suitcase into the bedroom, and then had come back out. She and I were stationed near the bedroom door, while Jacques was rolling a sleeping bag out onto the floor.

"With the kind of experience you've been through," said Jacques, "I'd think you'd be exhausted."

"No argument there," I said. "I feel tired; but oddly energized, too. Like my brain doesn't want to let go of the day; it's still replaying things."

Addie reached out and patted my shoulder.

"Good night," she said softly, and then, to our host, spoke louder: "I'll keep one ear open for your father, Jacques. You know . . . his breathing and so on."

"He should be all right, Addie, at least for now," said Jacques. "He just seems . . . tired. I've been thinking, though. Tomorrow, if he has the strength, I might take him over to Cheboygan for a checkup . . . though I doubt he'll cooperate. Never has."

"Yeah, about tomorrow," I said, and they both turned to me.

"Well, I'm planning to leave, you know . . . but not until the afternoon. I was just wondering if anybody had any ideas on what we might do before then."

Addie was smiling.

"What?" I said.

She shook her head.

"Nothing," she said. "You'll see."

****

We were up relatively early and ate a ham-and-eggs breakfast before Addie and I took a walk along the shoreline up toward the *Sylmar*. Upon our return, Jacques said his father had awakened, eaten a light meal and fallen back asleep.

"I think I'll stay with him; let him rest," he said. "Why don't the two of you go somewhere and enjoy the day? Then maybe we can all go later to the main dock when it's time for Avery to leave.

And if he's strong enough, I'll take Papa across the Straits then for that checkup."

And so Addie and I headed south in Jacques' truck, with me driving, toward the other side of the Island.

"Where to?" I yelled over the engine after we had passed the airfield and the dump and were approaching Pointe aux Pins.

"I don't know," Addie called back.

I glanced over at her. She had scrunched up her face, holding back a smile. But she couldn't, and it shone through.

"Down near the hotel," she said finally.

"It burned down. Remember?" I said.

"I don't mean go there," she said. "Just near there. Across the way, on that side street."

"Ah," I said, remembering a visit we had made there after our first Gull Island experience.

"Right," she said. "The church. A lovely little place."

"Yes, it was," I said.

"Still is," she said, and her smile brightened. "At least that's what Jacques tells me."

A few minutes later we reached the edge of the clearing that signaled the start of the village, and slowed for the left turn. Then, maneuvering slowly onto the street, it being narrow and tree-lined, I parked the truck alongside the road maybe thirty yards in–directly opposite The Pines' lone church, an Episcopalian structure called the Church of the Transfiguration.

There, sitting primly amid a host of pine and birch trees, was a building that seemed quite old but at the same time fresh, which of course meant someone had been tending to its physical needs.

It was, in fact, not exactly as I remembered it. Where I had recalled a stone and white-clapboard structure, it was mostly clapboard. There was a stone structure–an arch–but it fronted the church, giving entrance to a short walkway. A wooden peak topped the arch; it housed a small bell used to call the congregation to service. A sign out front listed Sunday services, but no minister.

"They have church without a minister?" I asked.

"Yeah," said Addie. "Without a regular one. They have guest and lay ministers. But just during the summer."

Before moving under the arch and up the short walkway to the church's green wooden steps, we paused while Addie knelt and said a short silent prayer. Then she rose and, looking up at the bell above the arch, smiled. As we approached the church, her attention shifted to the grounds on the church's east side, where a picket fence surrounded a plot lined by trees and perennial plants.

"We talked to the Reverend over there. Remember?" she asked me without taking her eyes off the grounds.

"I do," I said. There had been benches outside the fence back then, benches upon which we had been seated during one of the most unsettling discussions I believe I've ever had–at least in terms of permanence. It was there that the Reverend J.J. Stellingworth had assured us that Jacques was right about Addie's death, an endorsement that was still ringing down through the years.

Addie's focus swung back to the church building.

"Well," she said, "we might as well go in. I'd better get the lay of the land, so to speak."

"Why?" I asked. "Planning on buying it?"

"No, silly," she said. "Churches aren't generally for sale."

"Duh," I said. "I was just kidding."

"I know," she said. "Let's go in."

I reached out and took hold of her arm as she moved forward; held her back gently.

"Why?" I asked again, and this time I was pretty sure of the answer.

"Don't you think," she said, "that the new Bois Blanc minister should see the house in which she plans to worship?"

I found myself smiling with her.

"You," I said. "That's great. But I thought they only had summer services. How did you manage to get assigned here?"

"I haven't," she said. "But I will. This church–this Island–needs somebody who has a feeling for its history and its soul–and for more than just the summer. It isn't just summer folks here; there are several dozen year-round residents, too. My bishop's been talking about doing this; mentioned it a couple of times to me. I'm sure he was suggesting–without really saying–that he thought it should be me. So when I ask, I have absolute faith that they'll give it to me."

"How did this come about?" I asked. "You didn't mention it before."

"I'm not sure," she said. "I woke up yesterday thinking about it, and the idea just kind of grew. It was like someone had given me a jolt of inspiration while I was sleeping."

I nodded, satisfied. It felt like a good decision for her.

"You're set on this?" I said. "It's what you want?"

"Absolutely," she said.

****

Addie and I entered the church, and while she wandered about–gently touching statuettes, carvings and the small stained glass windows that ran along the building's two long sides–I examined a couple of ceremonial objects near the altar and then sat in one of the pews and waited. It was there, so long ago, that my grandfather and father had jointly undergone Confirmation under the tutelage of the Reverend, in the closing days of my grandfather's last summer with us–the summer of Gull and Eliot and Turk. The service had come after Addie had departed for home, for Ohio, and I had been left heartbroken in her wake.

But now, long past that first lost love, and here in the church with that very same girl turned woman, I felt as though I had come full circle. And if I hadn't, certainly Addie had, for she was intent on staying, on taking up the calling that began for her the moment she was revived on the *Sylmar* in 1956, the moment she was brought back from death. It had all started for her here–this fervent belief of hers–and so a return to the geographical source of her faith seemed fitting.

How it had come to pass was a mystery to her, of course, but not to me.

She had gone to bed without the idea, and had awakened with it–clutching it, wanting it, planning it.

That kind of thing does not materialize from nothing.

No. She had had some help.

Turk had paid her a visit: the Turk the carpenter told me was the devil in disguise. Turk had given her the idea, had sent her in the direction of this small church; had in so doing given the church new life, and the Island the possibility of renewed spirit.

Hardly devil-like, I mused.

But then, of course, Turk wasn't the devil at all.

****

When Addie was done with her inspection–"It's neat," she decided–I said it was my turn to pick a destination, and so chose Snow Beach, a white-sand oasis on the Island's southeast corner that we had visited as kids. The drive out seemed longer than I remembered, and extremely bumpy, especially after we passed the turnoff that would have taken us north toward the lighthouse; from that point eastward the Island seemed even wilder and more primitive than the western and northern sections, if that was possible. The journey proved a disappointment, in any event; after arriving, we found a bitter wind knifing through.

"Ugh!" Addie said. "Not exactly beach weather."

"You're right," I said. "Okay; let's go back. Your choice."

She opted this time for another spot in Pointe aux Pins: the southwest corner. After traversing the Island and parking near the old pump house, we walked along the beach that had once borne the auto graveyard, and on past some of the Island's more expensive cottages. Cutting back along a forest track, we eventually exited the woods and came to a corner lot across the street from the old main dock.

It was a route we had followed as children.

The lot had long ago housed a tennis court, but was now occupied by a ranch-style home. There was no sign of the blacktopped playing surface that had once existed, although the house bore a sign that said "Wimbledon."

"Hmmmph," I said.

"What?" said Addie.

I pointed to the sign on the house.

"A tennis fan bought it, but took out the court. Kind of a contradiction, don't you think?"

Addie shrugged.

"Dunno," she said. "A house seems a little more practical. Oh . . . look." She walked to the property's edge, reached down for some weeds growing there and, grabbing a handful, yanked on them.

"Remember these?" she said, holding them aloft. In her hand were a dozen or more pointed, and quite sharp, "stick-ems"–the name we had given years ago to Island weeds that became weapons when they were unsheathed from the base of the plant. Each one, when free of the base, had a nasty little tip that could stick to clothing and issue a wound like a pinprick.

"Sure do," I said.

"We used to throw these at each other. Remember?" she said.

"Sure," I answered, and then I saw the smile. "Addie, I don't think that's a good . . ."

Before I could finish the sentence, she drew her arm back and hurled the fistful of darts at my midsection. Her aim was true; most of the weeds stuck in my jacket, and a few went lower, piercing my pants and poking the skin of my left leg.

"Ouch!" I yelled, and it wasn't for effect; those little points truly smarted.

"Gotcha!" she yelled, just as I was reaching down to scoop up a handful of my own. She was laughing as I unsheathed the darts, and turning as I cut loose. They hit harmlessly on the back of her fairly thick pea coat, a few sticking but most tumbling to the ground.

She turned back, still laughing, and I joined in it. Gradually we subsided to giggling, and then to just smiling at each other.

Addie was happy, and I was happy for her.

She had found her niche, a home, a cause to carry into her future.

And I . . . I had found an old friend.

****

Another order of business: my father.

Jacques' long and detailed story of my dad's war exploits had gotten buried in the wave of events that followed the telling of the tale. But now, with time to ponder, I began to wonder just what kind of man Dad was. All my life I had known him as salesman, family man, tennis player and then, in his late years, golfer. He was a man who loved to tell a story or joke, to entertain whatever company he might bring home for dinner in his role as salesman. His sense of humor was spontaneous, his laughter ready to erupt.

I did not know the warrior, for in my realm of experience he was a man of peace, forbidding guns in the house and sidestepping confrontation whenever a kind and gentle word would assuage. Fighting among his three sons was discouraged, as were contact sports.

"Aggression breeds aggression," he would say, and I would nod sagely in my younger years while not understanding. Later, of course, it all made perfect sense.

What I couldn't make sense of now was the secrecy surrounding his wartime role. He had been in the Navy, I'd been told; had seen no battle action; and had found the binoculars on the desk of a Nazi after the Germans had cleared out of an industrial school in Bremerhaven at the war's end. Well . . . at least the two accounts dovetailed in Bremerhaven. That was somehow reassuring.

It is difficult, when you've been told one story all your life, to hear an alternate version so far-flung from the original. And so it was that Jacques' account had tested my belief system. Was I to believe my old friend, or my father's rendering? Clearly one was not true; and the wealth of detail provided by Jacques–and buttressed by the carpenter–told me logically that Dad had not been very forthcoming.

But even though relatively certain of the validity of Jacques' account, I felt compelled to verify it. Call it journalistic training; call it caution; call it a nagging skepticism.

It was time, I decided, to check in with the one person who knew my father best. It was time to call my mother down in Florida. I used the phone at the church.

****

"Hi, honey," she said. "How's my baby?"

"Fine, Mom," I said. "How you been?"

"Good," she said, "but it's been cold down here. Not great golf weather."

"Too bad," I said. "It's pretty cold where I am, too."

"Right. The Island," she said.

As related in the book that precedes this one, I had called her several days earlier seeking information about Jacques and his whereabouts before I had contacted the man himself and agreed to travel to Bois Blanc from my New York home. She had professed at that time not to know what had happened to him, but now that I thought about it, she might have known but been reluctant to part with the information; might have suspected what I'd learn.

"Yeah," I said, "but I don't remember telling you I was definitely coming here."

"You didn't," she said. "I called your home. Susan told me. Which you would have known if you'd been calling home yourself."

"Yeah, Mom, I will," I said. "Just as soon as I'm done talking to you. Listen, Mom, I've been talking to Jacques a lot and he's been telling me about his experiences in World War Two, and . . . he's raised some interesting questions in my mind."

There was no response, and I thought for a moment I'd lost my connection.

"Mom?" I said after several seconds had passed.

"I'm here," she said.

"Well, about Jacques . . . he was telling me some things about the war that I had never heard before."

I was hoping for some sort of reaction, but wasn't getting one.

"They were things," I went on, "about how he actually knew Dad in the war, in Italy."

There was still silence, and it struck me as a little on the chilly side.

"Did you know they'd met in the war, Mom?"

More silence.

"Mom?"

She cleared her throat.

"Of course," she said. "There wasn't anything that your father and I didn't share."

"Uh huh," I said, going carefully. "Well, I found it kind of fascinating, since it was something I'd never heard before. In fact, I was under the impression somehow that Dad had never seen any action in the war. But Jacques says otherwise . . ."

"That old man's crazy, you know," she said.

"So I've been told," I said. "But that doesn't really answer the question. Crazy or not, is he telling me the truth?"

I heard her sigh.

"It's nothing I wish to discuss," she said. "It was an unhappy time in the world, and an unhappy time for your father and me. Accept what your father told you of it, and let it go at that. It's all you need to know."

"Well," I said, recognizing dangerous ground when I was on it, "Jacques was very detailed, Mom. He told me an interesting story about Mussolini . . ."

"A horrible person," Mom hissed.

"Who? Jacques"?"

"Mussolini," she said. "A brute. He should have gotten worse than the Ligurian Sea."

There was another silence, and in it I could hear her realize her mistake: her indirect concession that Dad had hooked up with Jacques, had spirited Il Duce away, and had lost him at sea.

And in the mistake was something else–a clear indication that she was unaware of Il Duce's re-emergence on Bois Blanc. He had, to her knowledge, sunk for good in the waters off Italy. But Dad had said "Moose" in his closing words; he had known what Mom clearly did not, that Mussolini had resurfaced, so to speak.

So Mom was wrong in one regard: she and Dad hadn't shared *everything*.

"Mom," I said softly. "History tells us the partisans shot Mussolini. Strung him upside down like a slab of meat in a Milan plaza. Nothing about the Ligurian Sea."

"Oh," she said, even softer. "I must have been mistaken."

"Yes, I guess so," I said, and decided to try one more subject. "There was another thing, Mom. It was about the binoculars . . ."

"I'm tired, son. Finish up there and go home. Your family needs you, just like you needed your father. Remember that."

I didn't know what else to say, and so opted to end the conversation. Something in Mom's voice warned me that it was time.

"I will, Mom. Be good; be healthy."

"And call your wife," she said. Then the line went dead.

****

I did as she bid, called home, and told Susan I'd be leaving later that day, arriving home the next.

"How's the Island?" she asked me. "Much changed?"

"Oh, yes," I said. "Quite a bit. Not the fun it was."

"You were a child back then," she said. "A child can find fun in the unlikeliest of places."

"No, it's more than that," I said. "It's lost some of its spunk. But Addie should help cure that. She's staying on as minister here."

"Addie's there?" she said. "You didn't say anything about Addie being there."

Whoops, I thought. Susan had read my account of that long-ago summer, and so was acutely aware of the role Addie had played in my youth. After reading *Island Nights,* in fact, she had urged me to visit Jacques–to learn the truth about Addie's apparent resurrection. But she hadn't figured on Addie showing up. In fact, the possibility had likely never entered her mind.

I had been wondering how to broach the subject, and then stumbled blindly into it. Stupid . . .

"Yeah," I said. "Well . . . Jacques invited her."

"I see," she said, and there was silence on her end.

"Susan?" I said. "Still there?"

"Yes," she said. "Did you . . . um . . . say she was a minister?"

"Yeah. Episcopalian. Very religious," I said.

"No kidding. Well . . . that's good."

"Yeah," I said. "I thought so."

There was another pause before Susan spoke again.

"How is she?" she said. "Changed much?"

"Well . . . she looks the same," I said. "But she's a whole lot different."

"Different."

"Well . . . yeah."

"Different how? Like . . . better?"

This was not going well. I had to try harder.

"Yes, I guess; but not in any particularly feminine way. She's . . . close to God."

"Religious," Susan said.

"Oh, yeah. A hell of a lot more religious than I'll ever get. She's really into that stuff."

"Married?"

"No," I said. "I can't imagine she ever would be."

There was another pause before she responded.

"Oh? Why?"

"She's married to her work. It's like her life. You know?"

"Ah," said Susan, and in that simple word I could hear her relief. "That's very good."

FORTY-THREE

Leaving the Woods Behind

"You'll come back and visit, won't you?" Addie said.

We were on the main dock, near the *Sylmar III*; its engines were warming for the trip to Cheboygan. I would be picking up my car over there and, with any luck, make Sarnia, Ontario, by bedtime, cross Canada the next morning, re-enter the U.S. at Niagara Falls and be home four hours after that.

"Without a doubt," I said. "How could I not with such magnets as yourself and our old friend here?" I glanced to her side, where Jacques stood watching his son readying the boat. "Well . . . it's certainly been an educational experience, and I hope one with closure."

"Oh, I think it was that," said Addie. "Closure, but a new chapter as well. I've never felt so right about anything since I entered the ministry."

"You'll do great here," I said. "I'm just sorry I'll miss the first service."

Addie had contacted her bishop an hour earlier and gained tentative approval of her plan, along with the go-ahead to preach at the next Sunday service.

"Stay three days and you won't," said Jacques. It was late Thursday afternoon, and the sun, shielded by gray clouds, was going low in the west, out past Pointe aux Pins.

"Can't," I said. "The family and responsibility beckon."

"Too bad," said Addie, a touch of a smile on her face. "It would have been nice to see more than just Jacques at the service."

"Oh, I'm sure they'll turn out in droves," I said. "Well, if they had droves around here, they would. What's the population this time of year, anyway, Jacques?"

"About fifty, I guess," he said. "It'll shoot up for awhile with deer season, but won't crest until summer. There'll be a few there Sunday, though. I'll see to that."

"Yeah, I bet you will," I said.

"Time to go," Jacques said, motioning past me to the boat. I turned, and Johnny was waving to us. Jacques' father, en route to a checkup in Cheboygan, was already on board, as were several other passengers–including, as luck would have it, Claude and Willi Smythe again. Johnny was on the dock, at the bow, ready to free the line. Another Islander–one I didn't recognize–was holding the aft line.

I turned to Jacques.

"Just a sec," I said.

"Certainly," he answered. "I'll see you on board. But do not tarry. Johnny gets impatient. And I'll see you later, Addie."

Jacques strode the two dozen paces to the boat, stepped on deck, and headed for the passenger area where his father sat waiting.

Addie and I stood, watching, then faced each other, both a little shy at this second Bois Blanc farewell. Our first, forty years earlier, was playing on my mind, and probably on hers–a farewell that had ended in a heartfelt hug and romantic kiss. But of course, there would be no romantic kisses now.

"Let's keep in touch," I said at last. "Maybe better than we did as kids."

She laughed.

"Yeah, our letters kind of petered out fast, didn't they?"

"Puppy love," I said. "It sort of gets trampled by time."

"You have my number," she said. She meant the church rectory's phone I'd used to call Mom and Susan earlier in the day.

"And you have mine," I said.

We came together then in a hug. But this was without the emotion of the one in 1956; this was a hug of kindred spirits who have worked their way back to each other, and are on call for the future.

Pushing apart, we held each other at arm's length, and studied one another's eyes. Then I turned, crossed over to the *Sylmar III* and boarded. Johnny and the other man cast off the two lines, and Johnny hopped aboard and raced up the ladder to the pilot's house. Once there, he slowly opened the throttle and edged the boat away from the dock, toward the end of the concrete walkway and the breakwater. Then, slowly gaining speed, he swung to the right around the breakwater and accelerated away from the Island, out toward the Straits, toward the mainland.

I watched this from a perch aft, out in the open air. Then, after checking to see that Jacques and his father were comfortably ensconced in the passenger cabin, I nodded in satisfaction, gave a little wave of greeting to the Smythes–who were at the port side just outside the cabin–and returned to the aft railing. From there I could still see the dock, and on it Addie. She was watching our departure from the concrete walkway–short hair barely moving in the breeze, hands tucked down inside the big pockets of her coat, a determined look on her face.

"She's tough, isn't she?" someone said at my elbow.

I glanced to my right, but didn't really need to; I recognized the voice of the carpenter.

"That she is," I said. "She'll do fine here."

"It's not without challenges," he said.

"I suspect she'd have it no other way."

As the boat sped on, carrying us southward, we watched the outline of Addie diminish to little more than a dot.

"Well," the carpenter said at last, "the reason I'm here is this."

He was holding something in front of him, out toward me. For a moment I didn't realize what it was; my mind was still back on the Island, on the dock with my friend. But then I saw: it was the binocular case, dangling from his hand by its strap.

"Hey!" I said, delighted. "The binoculars! I thought I'd seen the last of those." I reached out, but was stopped by a sudden thought. "Wait. If you could only get these through the transfer, how can you just hand them back to me?"

"One way is hard, but the other is easy," he said.

I was about to ask why, but he waved me off.

"Don't bother," he said. "I've never understood it either. Just one of those things."

"So . . ." I said, taking hold of the case. "They didn't do you much good, did they?"

"You could say that," he muttered. "Kind of worthless without the filters. You realize, of course, that you proved to be a great disappointment."

"I imagine," I said. I could, in fact, clearly envision his consternation when he had discovered the filters were missing; and the anger he must have felt–if his kind feels anger.

"When did you find out?" he asked.

"Oh, I think part of me might have known all along," I said.

"Uh huh," he said. "But there must have been something specific. I thought it was a pretty good setup."

"Well," I said, and peered back over my shoulder to see if anyone was looking our way. I wondered–in light of Jacques' inability to see him on the road that first day–if the carpenter was visible now to anyone else. Since the old man had seen him on the dock before the Gull Island trip, I figured the carpenter could pretty much cloak or reveal his presence at will; I had no idea whether he was cloaked now or not.

Scanning the deck and the half-dozen cars on it, I saw only one person–Claude Smythe–and he was facing away from us. So I figured the matter was of little importance.

"Well," I said again, "first I'd like to know what to call you. Is it like you said earlier: Billy?"

"Right," he said.

"Okay, Billy," I said. "Here's the deal. I took a little walk in the woods after I talked to you at your cabin, and decided to try out the filters for myself. See what all the hoopla was, you know?"

I waited for a reaction, but none was forthcoming.

"I was sitting there," I went on, "all alone in this wooded glade, and I popped the filters in and looked through, and you'll never guess what I saw."

I waited longer this time, and finally he responded.

"Pray tell," he said. "I'm all ears."

"Hmmmm. Yes, I thought as much."

I paused, glancing once more over my shoulder. Again, no one seemed to be watching.

"The fact is," I said, "I was looking south, in the general direction of the Twin Lakes. I don't know how it worked–what with miles of woods between me and there–but there they were in the glasses: the lakes, and then the shoreline beyond, and then the cabin you were building in the woods. I gathered–since that is what the filters offer–that I was looking into the future. I saw you there, outside your building, looking like you do now with your beard and your long hair and your military jacket–and dangling from your neck were these."

I tapped the binocular case in my hands. "You walked inside, and then I could see indoors, and the place was dimly lit, as it was on my visit. But it was light enough so that I could see you walk to the fireplace and set the binocular case down on the mantel. And then I could see you standing there, transforming, suddenly evaporating. You became a kind of wobbly transparent image, like the heat that rises from blacktop. Then you were a flash of flame, and then . . . I don't know . . . you went through all sorts of human shapes, like a snake trying on different skins, until you settled on one that seemed to suit you."

I looked at him again, expecting some reaction, but there was none. And so I continued.

"And you sighed, as though contented, and pulled the binoculars from the case and inserted the filters and looked through them . . . and started cackling. And I knew I had to do something to see that this scene didn't really happen; that the filters were beyond your reach.

"I remembered your tale of Abraham Mann, and how the

future he foresaw seemed immutable; seemed destined to happen the way it appeared through the filters. But then I remembered the Legend of the Crystal and how the bear warned the old gypsy that the blue crystals were dangerous in the wrong hands; that the future could be altered. And so I decided–saw no other choice, really–that I could in fact do the altering, though not for harm as the bear warned.

"The thing was, the shape you had chosen was very familiar to me. Hell, it would be familiar to anybody who knows anything."

I hesitated, looked to my companion, and continued.

"You were Hitler," I said, and paused again. The sound of the boat and the water churning behind it filled the void in the silence that followed.

After a few seconds, maybe longer, he answered.

"So?" he said. "I looked like Hitler. So what?"

"That's not what I mean," I said. "I mean you were Hitler . . . back in the war. You were Hitler. You went through all these shapes in the cabin and came up with a comfortable one . . . one you were used to, had worn before. And it was Hitler."

Billy laughed.

"Nonsense," he said.

"Not nonsense," I said. "Everybody's always saying that Adolf Hitler was the personification of evil. It makes perfect sense. Besides, I've been fooling around with the letters of his name. Pretty interesting. And pretty alarming.

"You can rearrange the letters in 'Adolf Hitler' to read DEATH FILLOR . . . death filler. He was . . . you were . . . filling some sort of need, or quota, in which people were required to die frightening, cruel, violent deaths."

Billy was grinning at me, but not in mirth. It was a grin that bared his teeth; signaled opposition.

"So?" he said. "You have some point?"

"Yeah," I said. "A question, really. One word: Why?"

"Why?" he echoed, and cut loose with a short bark. "Hah! Why indeed. Why not, is more the point. Everybody dies, Mr.

Mann. And everybody is sinful. And everybody is virtually nothing. You are all experiments in the scheme of existence–nothing more. So why should I not experiment?"

"What, like with lab rats?" I asked.

"What makes you any better than a lab rat?" he said. "Your kind kills them without compunction; I see that your kind is killed. It's no different."

"Christ," I said, and felt a chill sweep through me. It occurred to me, not for the first time, that he could probably do something violent to me, too, if he was of the mind. But then . . . so could just about any human. Somehow I found that fact reassuring: sort of a perversion of the safety-in-numbers dictum.

Another thought struck me, and I found myself smiling through the fear.

"What?" said Billy. "You are finding humor in other people's suffering?"

I shook my head.

"No," I said. "It's just that you ended up doing a good deed out there on Gull–sending Mussolini packing. What was that all about?"

"Maybe I'm not such a bad guy?" he answered.

"Yeah, right," I said sarcastically. "A real prince. Remember: I saw the agony Il Duce was going through in that funnel. Not a pretty sight. So what happened with you guys: a falling out?"

Billy was looking down into the water at the rear of the boat, watching the wake. Just as I thought he was going to ignore the question, he surprised me with a response.

"I . . . had asked him to leave; he was complicating the equation. As you got closer to him, I figured he would talk; try to gain his own ends by blabbing about who I really was. He never was very close-mouthed; got him in all sorts of trouble in Italy."

He stopped, and I waited.

"But he laughed at me," Billy said. "Told me he was going nowhere. And so, when you were balking at handing over the binoculars, I figured that was an opportune time to offer up his ouster.

But . . . well . . . he had it coming anyway, the fat bastard. He was becoming tiresome."

He paused.

"So . . . if you hadn't looked through those filters, I'd have had them?" he asked. "You wouldn't have removed them?"

"I don't know," I said. "I was already a little suspicious on some subconscious level. There just seemed to be so much . . . I don't know . . . death and violence and evil involved with the glasses, that I had to ask myself if the real carpenter, if he exists, would be a part of it all–all those wartime fatalities.

"And I also had to think he–you–was a pretty heartless deity if he didn't really care that an old man had been invaded by a thug like Mussolini. Which you just sort of pooh-poohed at first . . ."

"I have to take exception to that line of thought," Billy said. "I think the carpenter gets more credit than he's due. He's not really all that nice a guy. Has a real strain of arrogance. Quite frankly, I think this whole faith thing is overrated.

"Besides," he added, "just who's calling whom heartless? If you knew what I was up to, how could you possibly trust that old man to my caretaking? I could have just let him die in the Gull transfer, you know."

I was nodding my head before he finished.

"You're right," I said. "I was heartless. If you had let him die, there would have been hell to pay from Addie–but Jacques would have accepted it as an improvement over Mussolini's presence. Call it a calculated risk; when I saw you through the filters–when you were changing shape–it occurred to me that since the binoculars were in your possession in that particular future, that I had willingly given them up. And the logical assumption beyond that was that in the giving, I had received in return something of value to me–in this case the return of Jacques' father. The myth–and your own description of the rules involved in transfers–seemed to indicate you wouldn't cheat. That you needed to play fair in order to attain your goal."

"Hmmmph," said Billy. "You know what they say about assumptions."

"Yes, I do," I said. "But I was willing to risk being an ass."

"You were that sure I'd leave the old man alive."

"Yes," I said.

"And then you went and double-crossed me."

"Yes," I said again.

He shook his head.

"You give the concept of 'good' a bad name," he said.

"My pleasure," I answered. "Oh, by the way . . . I think you should know that your act needs working on. Nice touch, with the bear and all: resonant of the legend, and somehow warming. But telling me that Turk was actually Billy–was you–didn't wash."

"Why not?"

"Why would you warn me away from Jacques and Addie? If I'd listened to those warnings, odds are I would have simply fled the Island. And that wouldn't have helped you at all. Besides, I'd seen Turk years ago, knew his general aura. It just seemed like him . . ."

"Seemed like him," Billy said. "In other words . . . intuition."

"Yeah . . . maybe," I said.

"How annoying," he answered softly.

"Yeah, well," I said. "One thing I don't get, though: If Turk really wanted to warn me away, why didn't he just tell me your game plan? Let me know who I was dealing with out at your cabin?"

"Ah, how little you understand," said Billy. "There are rules of warfare, Mr. Mann. Rules of warfare. Turk was merely abiding by them."

I was shaking my head.

"No, I don't understand," I said.

"Anything else?" he was asking. "Any other mistakes I should work on?"

"Oh . . . yeah," I said. "That light show out on Gull. Very impressive, and maybe that's how you normally do a transfer. But it's not how the carpenter would."

"And just how do you come by that?" he asked.

"I was out there forty years ago, remember? Addie was taken without any of those theatrics. That was the real deal: low-keyed . . . at least compared to your show."

"Whoa," he said. "I told you that was no transfer in '56; that was a natural crossover–a natural death. I wasn't lying about that. And just to clear up the record . . . I didn't have a hand in that little matter."

"Then tell me I'm wrong," I said. "Would the carpenter put on as big a show as you did?"

Billy was smiling.

"No . . . not usually," he said.

"One other thing."

He sighed.

"What?"

"How much of the history you fed me about the binoculars was on the level? Were they really created by a relative?"

"Oh, that. Yes. That was all on the up and up."

"But how did they find their way from Abraham Mann–a relative in one branch of our family–to a relative in another branch. You didn't by any chance have a hand in that, did you?"

Billy shrugged, a sheepish look on his face.

"Naturally," he said. "While the course of the glasses was random at first, it was ultimately directed."

"By you," I prompted.

"Yes . . . by me. Their desirability was clear from the outset, and so your father–kin of the late Abraham–was selected. It was apparent that such a relationship could be utilized to my advantage; that your father might respond to the kinship and–informed of the inherent danger in the power of the glasses–deliver them to me. Bremerhaven happened to be the most convenient spot to give them to him."

"So simple," I said.

"Yes," he said. "It didn't hurt that your father received an invitation from Jacques and was headed, ultimately, for this island. With Gull so close, the loose ends seemed to fall into place."

"But what about the crystals?" I asked, touching on a subject that had bothered me from the moment I'd embraced the truth behind the myth. "Where did they really come from? How do they work?"

Billy smiled.

"You really don't understand much, do you?"

"Not about the crystals."

"And you never shall. They are beyond human ken, Mr. Mann."

"But they have to come from somewhere," I said. "Certainly I can understand that . . ."

Billy was shaking his head.

"They come from no place physical, no place mental, no place of dimension. They just are–although I must say they are exceptionally rare; especially the blue ones. I've yet to find another, though you can bet I'll keep looking."

"The legend, then," I said, refusing to let go of the subject. "It wasn't real? It didn't happen? Then how did the gypsies get the crystals?"

Billy laughed.

"Such persistence," he said. "Really. Some things will just have to remain unknowable. Now then . . . I don't suppose I could invite you to drop the filters off somewhere convenient, like at Gull Island, or perhaps in the Bermuda Triangle."

"No, I don't think so," I said.

"I thought not. But just to satisfy my curiosity, what did you do with them?"

"Oh, they're in a safe place," I said. "Quite safe."

"Mmmmmm," he said. "I was afraid of that."

I patted the binocular case.

"I'm glad, of course, to have these back. But why did you return them? I imagine you plan on gaining something from it."

"Perhaps," he said.

"Perhaps," I echoed.

"Yes. Well . . . I'm betting that with them in hand, you're going to be very tempted to misuse them. Employ the filters yourself. And you can't without the glasses."

"Misuse them?" I said. "You mean as you would have?"

"Oh, I doubt you're as imaginative as I would have been. But . . . in essence, yes. And quite frankly, a little mayhem is better than nothing."

"Uh huh," I responded. "And you figure that as long as I'm tempted–as long as I have the means at hand to wield this power; to use the knowledge the glasses and filters together impart–I'm not likely to harm the prize."

Billy smiled.

"You said it; not me," he answered. "Well . . . until next time."

"One more thing," I said, this time with a slight edge to my voice. He had started to fade from my sight, but rematerialized.

"What?" he asked, a trace of annoyance in his voice.

"Don't give Addie trouble. Give her a hard time, and I *will* smash them."

He smiled back.

"That leaves me little choice," he said. "Ciao."

"Ciao," I echoed.

And he disappeared.

*****

I popped loose the snap on the case. Pulling the binoculars out, I put my eyes to them and looked in the direction of the Island. I could barely see the main dock, and Addie was but a memory. I was too far away. But I could imagine her walking along the dock, toward shore; reaching the parking lot and Jacques' pickup; climbing in, starting the engine and grimacing at its roar; and pulling out of the lot, kicking up a dust cloud as she headed west, back toward Pointe aux Pins.

"Hell," I said to myself, her image clear in my mind. "Who needs binoculars, anyway?"

And then, tucking them back in their case and looping it over my neck, I answered myself.

"I do," I said.

*****

In Cheboygan, at my car, I said goodbye to Jacques. He had left his father momentarily in Johnny's care while he saw me off.

"Listen, Jacques," I said. "I want to thank you."

"For what?" he said. "It is I who should be thanking you. You gave me back my father."

"No, really," I said, "I want to thank you for, you know . . . for the 'call,' the hospitality, the family history . . . This whole experience should make for interesting reading–that is, if you don't have a problem with me writing about this . . ."

He shook his head.

"None," he answered. "As I said, I am obliged. It would be rather petty of me to object to you practicing your craft."

I held out my hand, and he took it, grasping firmly. When I moved to let go, he held firm.

"There is one last thing," he said. "About your father."

"My father?" I said. "What?"

"His last visit here, the summer before he died, he expressed certain . . . misgivings."

"About what?"

"About . . . being less than truthful with his family regarding his role in the war. He was able to raise you boys easier that way–it made the maintenance of a peaceful environment more easily attainable. He didn't want you growing up thinking violence was an answer. But while the ends were attained, the means bothered him."

"Oh, I think I would have figured that out," I said. "It's not a problem."

"Good," said Jacques. "Remember, we all have secrets, and most of them for very good reasons."

"Not me," I said, straight-faced.

"Everyone," said Jacques. "Anyway, he wanted to tell you the truth, after you had matured, but could not bring himself to broach it . . . until it was too late. And there was your mother . . . she was disinclined to discuss those years or have them discussed. So that was an inhibiting influence."

"I understand, Jacques . . . really," I said. "It's not an issue with me. It just makes him a little more . . . complex in my mind. I'm fine with it. We all have skeletons, and we all have fictions."

"Good," said Jacques. "Then I can bid you farewell now."

I wanted to smile, but found myself mirroring the serious expression on Jacques' face.

"'Bye, old friend," I said. "I'll be back this way."

"Not so long this next time," he said. "I cannot guarantee I will be here another forty years."

"Maybe in the summer," I said.

"Good," he answered. "I will look for you."

And with that, he turned quickly and strode away, his hair blowing in the wind that was whistling through the Straits.

FORTY-FOUR

A Safe Place

The traffic south toward Flint was sparse, and so I put on the cruise control and the radio and coasted along comfortably, just under the speed limit.

I thought, with so much that had happened, that my mind would start replaying the past few days, but it didn't. I found myself, instead, humming and singing along with the tunes on the radio.

Part of that clear-headedness, I suppose, was a reaction to the sheer volume of events on my visit; it would take a long time to digest them all. And having accomplished that, it would take still more time to assess them and maybe get them on paper. But part of my reaction came from a sense of satisfaction, too; I had reached a place in my mind and my heart where I felt good about my father, and about the Island, and about a couple of old friends, and about the prospects of an afterlife.

I hadn't met the real carpenter, and still harbored nagging doubts about his very existence; though having met what amounted to his counterpart was certainly testament to the possibility that he was around. I contented myself on that point with the thought that the carpenter and I–should he exist–might yet cross paths before I left this curious orb.

But none of that was on my mind as I headed home. Mental calm prevailed. I was going back to my loved ones a slightly changed man, with the hope that the change was for the better. I was leaving behind a land that I had known as a boy and now, finally, knew as a man; and friends with whom I had lost touch but had now reconnected. I had attained a sense of fullness, a sense of direction in an otherwise meandering life.

I was also bolstered by the prospect of returning to the Island–to see those friends, to attend a service in Addie's church, maybe to revisit the lighthouse.

And, of course, to retrieve the filters.

I hadn't been kidding when I told Billy that I had put them in a safe place. I left them in a place I figured he'd never go, where the rules of warfare he espoused hopefully barred his entrance at the door, where I believed–I think correctly–that he literally couldn't find them. Not that he'd want to, now; they would do him no good without my acquiescence–at least as long as the rules he outlined were not altered.

I left the filters in the church. Addie's church. I put them there when we visited the building that final morning. I hid them while Addie was wandering about, getting familiar with what was to become her business establishment, so to speak.

I put them in the holiest place I could think of–a place that even I must concede was clever in its simplicity. I hid them in . . . no. No, no, no. I just can't. Won't. Better not.

It had best remain a secret. I don't want anyone who reads this going in there to check out my veracity, or claim the filters as a souvenir. And I don't want to tempt fate by letting Billy know.

Anyway . . . about my return to the Island. I told Jacques I might be back the next summer. That would give me time to sort everything out, I figured, give me a chance to decide if I would dare use the filters or should destroy them–smash them to dust.

In the meantime, I would have plenty to think about: Jacques, the war, Mussolini, the carpenter, the bear, the legend, Abraham Mann, Gull Island, Turk McGurk, and a Crystal of Death that carried the knowledge of eternal life.

And there was Dad to think about, too, and that deathbed message. I finally understood the first part, though comprehension hadn't come until near the end of the trip–with verification that the carpenter was not what he had seemed to be.

"Take . . . the carpenter," Dad had said. I had believed that he meant "Take the binoculars to the carpenter." That interpretation had temporarily misled me there in the carpenter's–in Billy's–cabin. I had thought that by handing the glasses over, I would be doing my father's bidding.

But that's not what he meant at all. Knowing now what I know of my father, I believe he meant quite the opposite.

The way I see it–the way I prefer to see it–is he meant "Take the carpenter." As in the fight manager's rallying cry to his boxer: "You can take him. Just watch out for that left hook."

Well, I don't think that I "took" him, but I did manage to avoid the hook–and to regain the binoculars in the bargain.

Yes, I succeeded, after a fashion. And in light of that, I knew there would be satisfaction in my future ruminations, a kind of congratulatory self-hug whenever I thought of Billy's chagrin at coming up empty.

And there would be a concurrent warmth as I thought about Bois Blanc and its many charms–its white woods, its twisting dirt roads, its thick forests, its scenic shoreline, its isolation . . . and its church in Pointe aux Pins.

And with the advent of a new minister, I figured the Island had more than a fighting chance against the encroachments of civilization and the whims of a willful force such as Billy.

If I was a betting man, I told myself on that drive home, I wouldn't bet on Billy. Not while he's on that Island. Not against that minister. If I were him, I wouldn't even let her know I was around.

The last thing he'd want to feel would be the wrath of Addie.

Printed in the United States
1775